Family Tree

Susan Wiggs is the Number One *New York Times* bestselling author of more than fifty novels, including the beloved Lakeshore Chronicles series. Her books have been translated into two dozen languages. A Harvard graduate, Susan lives with her husband on an island in Puget Sound.

Also by Susan Wiggs

CONTEMPORARY NOVELS

Home Before Dark
The Ocean Between Us
Summer by the Sea
Table for Five
Lakeside Cottage
Just Breathe
The Goodbye Quilt

THE BELLA VISTA CHRONICLES

The Apple Orchard
The Beekeeper's Ball

THE LAKESHORE CHRONICLES

Summer at Willow Lake
The Winter Lodge
Dockside
Snowfall at Willow Lake
Fireside
Lakeshore Christmas
The Summer Hideaway
Marrying Daisy Bellamy
Return to Willow Lake
Candlelight Christmas
Starlight on Willow Lake

HISTORICAL ROMANCES

The Lightkeeper
The Drifter
The Mistress of Normandy
The Maiden of Ireland

THE TUDOR ROSE TRILOGY

At the King's Command
The Maiden's Hand
At the Queen's Summons

CHICAGO FIRE TRILOGY

The Hostage
The Mistress
The Firebrand

CALHOUN CHRONICLES

The Charm School
The Horsemaster's Daughter
Halfway to Heaven
Enchanted Afternoon
A Summer Affair

Susan Wiggs

Family Tree

HARPER

This novel is entirely a work of fiction.
The names, characters and incidents portrayed in it are the work of the author's imagination. Any resemblance to actual persons, living or dead, events or localities is entirely coincidental.

Harper
An imprint of HarperCollins*Publishers* Ltd
The News Building
1 London Bridge Street
London SE1 9GF

www.harpercollins.co.uk

A Paperback Original 2016
1

A catalogue record for this book is available from the British Library

ISBN: 978-0-00-815129-4

www.fsc.org FSC™ C007454

FSC™ is a non-profit international organisation established to promote the responsible management of the world's forests. Products carrying the FSC label are independently certified to assure consumers that they come from forests that are managed to meet the social, economic and ecological needs of present and future generations, and other controlled sources.

Find out more about HarperCollins and the environment at
www.harpercollins.co.uk/green

In memory of my dad,

Nick Klist

—with deepest gratitude for all the love, the courage, the laughter, and the wisdom of a lifetime. He lives in the hearts of those who loved him.

1

Now

"I can't believe we're arguing about a water buffalo." Annie Rush reached for her husband's shirt collar, turning it neatly down.

"Then let's quit arguing," he said. "It's a done deal." He sat down and shoved first one foot, then the other, into his cowboy boots—the ridiculously expensive ones she had given him last Christmas. She'd never regretted the purchase, though, because they looked so good on him.

"It's not a done deal. We can still cancel. The budget for the show is already stretched to the limit. And a water buffalo? It's going to be fifteen hundred pounds of stubborn."

"C'mon, babe." Martin stood, his blue eyes twinkling like the sun on a swimming pool. "Working with a live animal on the show will be an adventure. The viewers will love it."

She blew out a breath in exasperation. Married couples fought about the dumbest things. Who left the cap off the toothpaste? Whether it was quicker to take the Ventura Freeway or the Golden State. The number of syllables in broccoli. The optimum thermostat setting. Why he couldn't clean his whiskers out of the sink.

And now this. The water buffalo.

"Where in my job description does it say water-buffalo wrangler?" she asked.

"The buffalo's an integral part of the show." He gathered up his keys and briefcase and went downstairs, boots ringing on the hardwood.

"It's a crazy misuse of the production budget," she stated, following him. "This is a cooking show, not *Wild Kingdom*."

"It's *The Key Ingredient*," he countered. "And when the ingredient of the week is mozzarella, we need a buffalo."

Annie gritted her teeth to keep from prolonging the fight. She reminded herself that underneath the fight was their marriage. Even at fifteen hundred pounds, the buffalo was a small thing. It was the big things that mattered—his effortless way of chopping garlic and chives as he cooked for her. His dedication to the show they had created together. The steamy shower sex they'd had the night before.

"It's gonna be great," he said. "Trust me." Slipping one arm around her waist, he claimed a brief kiss.

Annie reached up and touched his freshly shaven cheek. The last thing she needed was a dispute with Martin. He had no sense of the oddity of his idea. He had always believed the show owed its appeal to the outlandish. She was equally convinced that the success of their show stemmed from its authenticity. That, and a talented chef whose looks and charisma held an audience spellbound for an hour each week.

"I trust," she whispered, rising on tiptoe for another kiss. He was the star of the show, after all. He had the ear of the executive producer, and was used to getting his way. The details, he left to Annie—his wife, his partner, his producer. It was up to her to make things happen.

With the argument still ringing through her head, she braced her hands on the sill of the window overlooking the garden of their town house. She had a million things to do today, starting with the *People* magazine interview—a behind-the-scenes piece about the show.

A window washer was preparing to climb a scaffold and get to work. Martin passed by on his way to the garage, pausing to say something to the worker, who grinned and nodded. Charming Martin.

A moment later, his silver BMW roadster shot out of the parking garage. She didn't know why he was in such a hurry. The Monday run-through was hours away.

She sighed and turned away, trying to shake off the emotional residue of the argument. Gran was fond of saying that a fight was never about the thing being fought over. The water buffalo wasn't the point. All arguments, at their core, were about power. Who had it. Who wanted it. Who would surrender. Who would prevail.

No mystery there. Annie surrendered, Martin prevailed. That was how it worked. Because she let it? Or because she was a team player? Yes, they were a team. A successful team with their own show on an emerging network. The compromises she made were good for them both. Good for their marriage.

Another thing Gran would say was imprinted on Annie's heart—remember the love. When times get hard and you start wondering why you got married in the first place, remember the love.

Fortunately for Annie, this was not hard to do. Martin was a catch. He was the kind of handsome that made women stop and stare. His aw-shucks charm wasn't confined to the show. He knew how to make her laugh. When they came up with an idea together, he would sweep her into his arms and dance her around the kitchen. When he talked about the family they'd have one day, the babies, she would melt with yearning. He was her husband, her partner, an irreplaceable element in her life's work. Okay, she thought. Okay, then. Whatever.

Annie checked the time and looked at her work e-mail—all her e-mail was work—to discover that the scissor lift they'd rented to install new on-set lighting at the studio was having mechanical problems.

Great. One more thing to worry about.

The phone rang, and the screen lit up with a picture of a cat. "Melissa," said Annie, putting her phone on speaker. "What's up?"

"Just checking in," said Melissa. She seemed to check in a lot, especially lately. "Did you see that e-mail about the cow?"

"Buffalo," Annie corrected her. "And yes. Also, I have a note about a lift that's not working. And I've got CJ from *People* coming. So I guess I'll be in late. Like, really late. Tell everyone to sit tight until after lunch." She paused, bit her lip. "Sorry. I'm cranky this morning. Forgot to eat breakfast."

"Go eat something. Okay, gorgeous," Melissa said brightly. "Gotta bounce."

Annie turned back to her computer to double-check the meeting time with the reporter. CJ Morris was doing an in-depth piece on the show—not just its stars, Martin Harlow and Melissa Judd—but the entire production, from its debut as a minor cable program to the hit it had become. CJ had already interviewed Martin and Melissa. She was coming over this morning to visit with Annie, the show's creator. It was an unusual slant for a magazine article; casual readers craved gossip and photos of the stars. Annie hoped to make the most of the opportunity.

While waiting for the reporter, she did what a producer did—she used every spare minute to handle things. She studied the rental agreement for the lift to find a phone number. She and Martin had quarreled about that piece of equipment, too. The cost of the lift with the best safety rating had been much higher than the hydraulic one. Martin insisted on going with the cheaper one—over Annie's objections. As usual, she'd surrendered and he'd prevailed. Since they'd blown the budget on the water buffalo, she had to skimp on something else. Now the hydraulic lift was malfunctioning and it was up to Annie to deal with the issue.

Enough, she told herself. She thought again of breakfast and opened the fridge. Bulgarian yogurt with maple granola? No, her empty stomach rejected the idea of yogurt. Also those French breakfast radishes that had looked so enticing at the farmers' market were past their prime. Even a piece of toast didn't appeal. Okay, so no breakfast. One thing at a time.

She went to the powder room and ran a comb through her long, dark hair, which had been flat-ironed into submission yesterday. Then she checked her lipstick and manicure. Both cherry red, perfectly matched. The black pencil skirt, platform sandals, and flowy white top were cool and casual, a good choice in the current heat wave. She wanted to look pulled together for the interview, even though there wouldn't be a photographer today.

The buzzer sounded, and she hurried to the intercom. Yikes, the reporter was early.

"Delivery for Annie Rush," said the voice on the other end.

Delivery? "Oh . . . sure, come on up." She buzzed the caller in.

An enormous bouquet of lush, tropical blooms came teetering up the steps. "Please, watch your step," Annie said, holding open the door. "Just . . . on the counter there is fine."

Stargazer lilies and white tuberoses trumpeted their spicy scent into the room. Baby's breath added a lacy touch to the arrangement. The delivery woman set down the vase and brushed a wisp of black hair off her forehead. "Enjoy, ma'am," she said. She was young, with tattoos and piercings in unfortunate places. The circles under her eyes hinted at a sleepless night, and a fading yellowish bruise shadowed her cheekbone. Annie tended to notice things like that.

"Everything all right?" she asked.

"Um, sure." The girl nodded at the bouquet. "Looks like someone's really happy with you."

Annie handed her a bottle of water from the fridge along with a twenty-dollar bill. "Take care, now," she said.

"Will do." The girl slipped out and hurried down the stairs.

Annie plucked the small florist's envelope from the forest of blooms—Rosita's Express Flowers. The card had a simple message: *I'm sorry. Babe, let's talk about this.*

Ah, Martin. The gesture was typical of him—lavish, over-the-top . . . irresistible. He'd probably called in the order on the way to work. She felt a wave of affection, and her irritation flowed away. The message was exactly what she needed. And then she felt a troubling flicker of guilt. Sometimes she worried that she didn't believe in him enough, didn't trust the decisions he made. Could be that he was right about the water buffalo after all. It might end up being one of their most popular episodes.

The gate security buzzer sounded again, signaling CJ's arrival.

Annie opened the door and was hit by a wall of intense heat. "Come on in before you melt," she said.

"Thanks. This weather is insane. I heard on the radio we're going to break a hundred again today. And so early in the year."

Annie stepped aside and ushered her into the town house. She'd fussed over the housekeeping, and now she was grateful for Martin's fresh flowers, adding a touch of elegance. "Make yourself at home. Can I get you something to drink? I have a pitcher of iced tea in the fridge."

"Oh, that sounds good. Caffeine-free? I'm off caffeine. And the tannin bothers me, too. Is it tannin-free?"

"Sorry, no." No matter how long she lived here, Annie would never get used to the myriad dietary quirks of Southern Californians.

"Maybe just some water, then. If it's bottled. I'm early," CJ said apologetically. "Traffic is so unpredictable, I gave myself plenty of time."

"No problem," Annie assured her. "My grandmother used to always say, if you can't be on time, be early." She went to the fridge while the reporter put down her things and took a seat on the sofa.

At least Annie could impress with the water. A sponsor had sent samples of their fourteen-dollar-a-bottle mineral water, sourced from an aquifer fifteen hundred feet underground in the Andes, and bottled before the air touched it.

"What a great kitchen," CJ remarked, looking around.

"Thanks. It's where all the delicious things happen," Annie said, handing CJ the chilled bottle.

"I can imagine. So, your grandmother," CJ said, studying a vintage cookbook on the coffee table. "The same one who wrote this book, right?" She put her phone in record mode and set it on the coffee table. "Let's talk about her."

Annie loved talking about Gran. She missed her every day, but the remembrances kept her alive in Annie's heart. "Gran published it back in the sixties. Her name was Anastasia Carnaby Rush. My grandfather called her Sugar, in honor of the family maple syrup brand, Sugar Rush."

"Love it." CJ paged through the book.

"It was a regional bestseller in Vermont and New England for years. It's out of print now, but I can send you a digital copy."

"Great. Was she trained as a chef?"

"Self-taught," Annie said. "She had a degree in English, but cooking was her greatest love." Even now, long after her grandmother had died, Annie could picture her in the sunny farmhouse kitchen, happily turning out meals for the family every day of the year. "Gran had a special way with food," Annie continued. "She used to say that every recipe had a key ingredient. That's the ingredient that defines the dish."

"Got it. So that's why each episode of the show focuses on one ingredient. Was it hard to pitch the idea to the network?"

Annie chuckled. "The pitch wasn't hard. I mean, come on, Martin Harlow." She showed off another cookbook—Martin's latest. The cover featured a photo of him looking even more delicious than the melty, golden-crusted marionberry pie he was making.

"Exactly. He's the perfect combination of Wild West cowboy and Cordon Bleu chef." CJ beamed, making no secret of her admiration. She perused the magazines on the coffee table. *Us Weekly. TV Guide. Variety.* All had featured the show in the past six months. "Are these the latest articles?"

"Yes. Help yourself to anything that catches your eye." Annie's other prized book lay nearby—a copy of *Lord of the Flies,* a vintage clothbound volume in a sturdy slipcase, one of three copies she possessed. She hoped the reporter wouldn't ask about that.

CJ focused on other things—a multipage spread in *Entertainment Weekly,* featuring Martin cooking in his signature faded jeans and butcher's apron over a snug white T-shirt, offering a glimpse of his toned and sculpted bod. His cohost, Melissa, hovered at his side, her pulled-together persona a perfect foil for his casual élan. The caption asked, *Have we found the next Jamie Oliver?*

Food as entertainment. It was a direction Annie hadn't contemplated for *The Key Ingredient.* But who was she to argue with ratings success?

"He has definitely come into his own on the show," CJ remarked. "But today's about you. You're in the limelight."

Annie talked briefly about her background—film school and broadcasting, with a focus on culinary arts—which she'd studied under a special program at NYU's Tisch School of the Arts. What she didn't mention was the sacrifice she'd made to move from the East Coast to L.A. That was part of Annie's story, not the show's story.

"When did you make the move to the West Coast?"

"Seems like forever ago. It's been about ten years."

"Straight out of college, then?"

"That's right. I didn't expect to wind up in L.A. before the ink on my diploma was dry, but that's pretty much how it went," Annie said. "It seems sudden, but not to me. By the time I was six, I knew I wanted to have a show about the culinary arts. My earliest memories are of my grandmother in the kitchen with *Ciao Italia* on the local PBS station. I used to picture Gran as Mary Ann Esposito, teaching the world to cook. I loved the way she spoke about food, handled it, expressed herself through it, talked and wrote about it, and shared it. Then I'd do cooking demos for Gran, and later for anyone who would sit through one of my presentations. I even filmed myself doing a cooking show. I had those old VHS tapes turned into digital files to preserve the memories. Martin and I keep meaning to sit down and watch them one of these days."

"What a great story. You found your passion early."

Her passion had been born in her grandmother's kitchen when Annie was too young to read or write. But she'd never been too young to dream. "I assumed everyone was passionate about food. Still do, and it's always a surprise when I find out otherwise."

"So you were into food even before you met Martin."

Martin again. The world assumed he was the most interesting thing about Annie. How had she let that happen? And why? "Actually," she said, "everything started with a short documentary I made about Martin, back when he had a food cart in Manhattan."

"That very first short went viral, didn't it? And yet you're still behind the scenes. Do you ever want to be in front of the camera?"

Annie kept a neutral expression on her face. Of course she did, every day. That had been her dream, but the world of commercial broadcasting had other ideas. "I'm too busy with the production to think about it," she said.

"You never considered being a cohost? I'm just thinking of what you said earlier about those cooking demos . . ."

Annie knew what CJ was getting at. Reporters had a way of sneaking into private places and extracting information. CJ wouldn't find any dirt here, though. "Leon Mackey, the executive producer and owner of the show, wanted a cohost to keep Martin from turning into a talking head. Martin and I actually did make a few test reels together," she said. "Even before we married, we wanted to be a team both on camera and off. It seemed romantic and unique, a way to set us apart from other shows."

"Exactly," CJ said. "So it didn't work out?"

Annie's hopes had soared when she and Martin had made those early reels; she thought they might choose her. But no. The show needed someone more relatable, they said. More polished, they said. What they didn't say was that Annie's look was too ethnic. Her olive-toned skin and dark corkscrew curls didn't jibe with the girl-next-door vision the

EP was going for. "Not the right fit for this show," Leon had said. "You look like Jasmine Lockwood's kid sister. Could confuse viewers."

Jasmine Lockwood hosted a wildly popular show about comfort food on the same network. Annie didn't see the resemblance, but she surrendered, putting the show ahead of her ego.

"Anyway," she said with a bright smile, "judging by the ratings, we found the right combination for the show."

CJ sipped the water, holding the straight-sided glass bottle up to admire it. "When did Melissa Judd enter the picture?"

Annie paused. She couldn't very well say it was when Martin met her in his yoga class, even though that had been the case. At the time, Melissa had a gig as a late-night shopping network host. Her looks, she claimed in the pretaping interview with a straight face, had always gotten in the way, because people failed to see past her beauty to recognize her talent.

"She and Martin had that elusive chemistry that's impossible to manufacture," Annie told the reporter, "so we knew we had to have her." Annie didn't mention the prep work it had taken to get the new cohost ready for the role. Melissa's delivery was shrill and rough, her late-night-huckster voice designed to keep people awake. Annie was tasked with bringing out Melissa's more hidden gifts. She had worked long and hard to cultivate the perky, all-American girl persona. To her credit, Melissa caught on quickly. She and Martin became a dynamic on-air team.

"Well, you certainly put together a winning combination," CJ observed.

"Um . . . thanks." Sometimes, when she watched the easy banter between the two hosts—more often than not, banter she had painstakingly scripted—Annie still caught herself wishing she could be in front of the camera, not just behind the scenes. But the formula was working. Besides, Melissa had an ironclad contract.

Annie knew she should bring the conversation back around to her role on the show, but she was thinking about breakfast again. Scones, she thought. With a sea-salt crust and maple butter.

"Tell me about the first episode," CJ suggested. "I just streamed it again last night. The key ingredient was maple syrup, which is kind of perfect, considering your background."

"If by 'perfect,' you mean 'borderline disaster,' then yes," Annie said with a grin. "Maple syrup has been my family's business for generations." She gestured at a painting on the wall, a landscape her mother had done of Rush Mountain in Vermont. "It seemed like the ideal way to launch the show. The production set up, literally, in my own backyard—the Rush family sugarbush in Switchback, Vermont."

She took a breath, feeling a wave of nausea. She couldn't tell whether the discomfort was caused by the memory, or by the empty stomach. Could be she was worried about riling up something from her past. She still remembered that feeling of unease, returning to the small town where she'd grown up, surrounded by everyone who had known her for years.

Fortunately, the budget had only permitted them to spend seventy-two hours on set there, and each hour was crammed with activity. Every possible thing had gone wrong. The snow had melted prematurely, turning the pristine winter woods into a brown swamp of denuded trees, strung together with plastic tubing for the running sap, like IV meds reaching from tree to tree. The sugarhouse, where the magic was supposed to happen, had been too noisy and steamy for the camera crew to film. Her brother, Kyle, had been so uncomfortable on camera that one of the editors had actually asked if he was "simple." Melissa had come down with a cold, and Martin had spoken the dreaded *I told you so.*

Annie had been certain right then and there that her career—her dreamed-about, sought-after, can't-miss show—would end with a whimper, becoming a footnote on a list of failed broadcasts. She'd been devastated.

And that was when Martin had rescued her. Back at the Century City studio, the postproduction team had worked overtime, cutting and splicing images, using stock footage, reshooting with computer-generated material, focusing on the impossibly sexy, smart host—Martin Harlow—and his well-trained, preternaturally chipper sidekick, Melissa Judd.

When the final cut aired, Annie had sat in the editing suite in a rolling chair, not daring to move. On the verge of panic, she'd held her breath… until an assistant had arrived with her smartphone, showing a long list of social media feedback. Viewers were loving it.

The critics had adored the show, too, praising Martin's infectious love of food as he leaned against the sugarhouse wall, sampling a fried doughboy dipped in freshly rendered syrup. They applauded Melissa's charming relish in preparing a dish and the seductive way she invited viewers to sample it.

The ratings were respectable, and online views of the trailer piled up, hour by hour. People were watching. More importantly, they were sharing. The link traveled through the digital ether, reaching around the world. The network ordered another thirteen episodes to follow the original eight. Annie had looked at Martin with tears of relief streaming down her face. "You did it," she'd told him. "You saved my dream."

"Judging by the expression on your face," CJ said, "it was an emotional moment."

Annie blinked, surprised at herself. Work was work. She didn't often get teary-eyed over it. "Just remembering how relieved I felt that it all turned out," she said.

"So was a celebration in order?"

"Sure." Annie smiled at the memory. "Martin celebrated with a candlelight dinner… and a marriage proposal."

"Whoa. Oh my gosh. You're Cinderella."

They had married eight years ago. Eight busy, productive, successful years. Sometimes, when they went over-the-top with expensive stunts, like diving for oysters, foraging for truffles, or milking a Nubian goat, Annie would catch herself wondering what happened to *her* key ingredient, the original concept for the show. The humble idea was buried in the lavish episodes she produced these days. There were moments when she worried that the program had strayed from her core dream, smothered by theatrics and attention-grabbing segments that had nothing to do with her initial vision.

The show had taken on a life of its own, she reminded herself, and that might be a good thing. With her well-honed food savvy and some nimble bookkeeping, she made it all work, week in and week out.

"*You're* the key ingredient," Martin would tell her. "Everything came together because of you. Next time we're in contract talks, we're going to negotiate an on-camera role for you. Maybe even another show."

She didn't want another show. She wanted *The Key Ingredient*. But she'd been in L.A. long enough to know how to play the game, and a lot of the game involved patience and vigilance over costs. The challenge was staying exciting and relevant—and on budget.

CJ made some swift notes on her tablet. Annie tried to be subtle about checking the time and thinking about the day ahead, with errands stacking up like air traffic over LAX.

She had to pee. She excused herself and headed to the upstairs bathroom.

And that was when it hit her. She was late. Not late to work—it was already established that she was going to be late to the studio. But *late* late.

Her breath caught, and she stood at the counter, pressing the palms of her hands down on the cool tile.

She exhaled very slowly and reminded herself that it had been only a few weeks since they'd started trying. No one got pregnant that quickly, did they? She'd assumed there would be time to adjust to the idea of starting a family. Time to think about finding a bigger place, to get their schedule under control. To stop quarreling so much.

She hadn't even set up an ovulation calendar. Hadn't read the what-to-expect books. Hadn't seen a doctor. It was way too soon for that.

But maybe . . . She grabbed the kit from under the sink—a leftover from a time when she had *not* wanted to be pregnant. If she didn't rule out the possibility, it would nag at her all day. The directions were dead simple, and she followed them to the letter. And then, oh so carefully, she set the test strip on the counter. Her hand shook as she looked at the little results window. One pink line meant not pregnant. Two lines meant pregnant.

She blinked, making sure she was seeing this correctly. *Two pink lines.*

Just for a moment, everything froze in place, crystallized by wonder. The world fell away.

She held her breath. Leaned forward and stared into the mirror, wearing a look she'd never seen on her own face before. It was one of those moments Gran used to call a key moment. Time didn't simply tick past, unremarked, unnoticed. No, this was the kind of moment that made everything stop. You separated it from every other one, pressing the feeling to your heart, like a dried flower slipped between the pages of a beloved book. The moment was made of something fragile and delicate, yet it possessed the power to last forever.

That, Gran would affirm, was a key moment. Annie felt a lump in her throat—and a sense of elation so pure that she forgot to breathe.

This is how it begins, she thought.

All the myriad things on her to-do list melted into nothingness. Now she had only one purpose in the world—to tell Martin.

She washed up and went to the bedroom, reaching for the phone. No, she didn't want to phone him. He never picked up, rarely checked his voice mail. It was just as well, because it struck Annie that this news was too big to deliver by voice mail or text message. She had to give her husband the news in person, a gift proffered from the heart, a surprise as sweet as the one she was feeling now. He deserved a key moment of his own. She wanted to see him. To watch his face when she spoke the magic words: *I'm pregnant.*

Hurrying down the stairs, she joined the reporter in the living room. "CJ, I'm so sorry. Something's come up. I have to get to the studio right away. Can we finish another time?"

The writer's face closed a little. "I just had a few more—"

Bad form to tick off a reporter from a major magazine. Annie couldn't let herself care about that, not now. She was sparkling with wonder, unable to focus on anything but her news. She couldn't stand the idea of keeping it in even a moment longer. "Could you e-mail the follow-up questions? I swear, I wouldn't ask if it wasn't urgent."

"Are you all right?"

Annie fanned herself, suddenly feeling flushed and breathless. Did she look different? Did she have the glow of pregnancy already? That was silly; she'd only known for a couple of minutes. "I . . . something unexpected came up. I have to get to the studio right away."

"How can I help? Can I come along? Lend a hand?"

"That's really nice of you." Annie usually wasn't so reckless with the press. Part of the reason the show was so successful was that she and her PR team had cultivated them with lavish attention. She paused to think, then said, "I have a great idea. Let's meet at Lucque for dinner—you, Martin, and me. He knows the chef there. We can finish talking over an incredible meal."

CJ put together her bag. "Bribery will get you everywhere. I heard there was a six-week wait for a table there."

"Unless you're with Martin Harlow. I'll have my assistant book it and give you a call." Annie bade the reporter a hasty farewell.

Then she grabbed her things—keys, phone, laptop, tablet, wallet, water bottle, production notes—and stuffed them into her already overstuffed business bag. For a second, she pictured the bag she'd carry as a busy young mom—diapers and pacifiers... what else?

"Oh my God," she whispered. "Oh my God. I don't know a thing about babies."

She bolted for the door, then clattered down the steps of the Laurel Canyon town house complex. Their home was fashionable, modern, a place they could barely afford. The show was gaining momentum, and Martin would be up for a new contract again soon. They'd need a bigger place. With a baby's room. A *baby's* room.

The heat wave hit her like a furnace blast. Even for springtime in SoCal, this was extreme. People were being urged to stay inside, drink plenty of water, keep out of the sun.

Above the walkway to the garage, the guy on a scaffold was still washing windows. Annie heard a shout, but didn't see the falling squeegee until it was too late. The thing hit the sidewalk just inches from her.

"Hey," she called. "You dropped something."

"Sorry, ma'am," the workman called back. Then he turned sheepish. "Really. The thing just slipped out of my hands."

She felt a swift chill despite the muggy air. She had to be careful now. She was pregnant. The idea filled her with wonder and joy. And the tiniest frisson of fear.

She unlocked the car with her key fob, and it gave a little *yip* of greeting. Seat belt, check. Adjust the mirror. She turned for a few seconds, gazing at the backseat. It was cluttered with recycled grocery bags, empty serving trays and bowls from the last taping, when the key ingredient had been saffron. One day there would be a car seat back there. For a baby. Maybe they'd name her Saffron.

Annie forced herself to be still for a moment, to take everything in. She shut off the radio. Flexed and unflexed her hands on the steering wheel. Then she laughed aloud, and her voice crescendoed to a shout of pure joy. She pictured Martin's face when she told him, and smiled all the way up the on-ramp. She drove with hypervigilance, already feeling protective of the tiny invisible stranger she carried. Shimmering with heat, the freeway was clogged with traffic lined up in a sluggish queue. The crumbly brown hills of the canyon flowed past. Smog hovered overhead like the dawn of the nuclear winter.

L.A. was so charmless and overbuilt. Maybe that was the reason so much imaginative work was produced here. The dry hills, concrete desert, and dull skies were a neutral backdrop for creating illusion. Through the studios and sound stages, people could be taken away to places of the heart—lakeshore cottages, seaside retreats, days gone by, autumn in New England, cozy winter lodges...

We're going to have to move, thought Annie. No way we're raising a child in this filthy air.

She wondered if they could spend summers in Vermont. Her idyllic childhood shone with the sparkle of nostalgia. A Switchback traffic jam might consist of the neighbor's tractor waiting for a cow that had wandered outside the fence. There was no such thing as smog, just fresh, cool air, sweet with the scent of the mountains and trout streams. It was an unspoiled paradise, one she had never fully appreciated until she'd left it behind.

She'd known about the pregnancy all of five minutes and she was already planning the baby's life. Because she was so ready. At last, they were going to have a family. A *family.* It was the most important thing in the world to her. It always had been.

She thought about the fight this morning, and then remembered the flower delivery. This moment was going to change everything for them, in the best possible way. The stupid quarrels that blazed like steam vents from a geyser suddenly evaporated. Had they really argued about a water buffalo? A scissor lift? The missing cap on the toothpaste tube?

Her phone vibrated, signaling a text message from Tiger, her assistant. Major mechanical trouble with the scaffold. Need u now.

Sorry, Tiger, Annie thought. Later.

After she told Martin about the baby. A *baby.* It eclipsed any work emergency at the studio. Everything else—the water buffalo, the scissor lift—seemed petty in comparison. Everything else could wait.

She turned onto the Century City studio lot. The gate guard waved her through with a laconic gesture. She made her way around the blinding pale gray concrete labyrinth dotted with the occasional green oasis of palm-tree-studded gardens. Turning down a service alley, she parked in her designated spot next to Martin's BMW. She'd never cared for the sports car. It was totally impractical, given the kind of gear they often toted around for the show. Now that he was about to become a father, he might get rid of the two-seater.

Heading for Martin's trailer on foot, she passed a group of tourists on Segways, trolling for a glimpse of their favorite star. One eager woman paused her scooter and took Annie's picture.

"Hey there," the woman said, "aren't you Jasmine Lockwood?"

"No," said Annie with an almost apologetic smile.

"Oh, sorry. You look like her. I bet you get that a lot."

Annie offered another slight smile and veered around the tour group. This wasn't the first time someone pointed out her resemblance to the cooking diva. It was confusing to Annie. She didn't look like anyone but herself.

Martin, the golden boy, liked to say she was his exotic lover, which always made Annie laugh. "I'm an all-American mutt from Vermont," she'd say. "We can't all have a pedigree."

Would the baby look like her? Brown eyes and riotous black curls? Or like Martin, blond and regal?

Oh my God, she thought with a fresh surge of joy. A baby.

Power cords snaked across the alleyway leading to the studio. The trailers were lined up, workers with headsets and clipboards scurrying around. She could see the scissor lift looming above the work site. Fully extended, its orange steel folding supports formed a crisscross pattern, topped by the platform high overhead. Workmen in hard hats and electricians draped in coiled wire swarmed around it. Some guy was banging on the manual release valve with a black iron wrench.

She spotted Tiger, who hurried over to greet her. "It's stuck in the up position." Tiger looked like an anime character, with rainbow hair and a candy-colored romper. She also had a rare gift for doing several things simultaneously and well. Martin thought she was manic, but Annie appreciated her laser focus.

"Tell them to unstick it." Annie kept walking. She could sense Tiger's surprise; it wasn't like Annie to breeze past a problem without attempting to solve it.

Martin's cast trailer was the biggest on the lot. It was also the most tricked out, with a makeup station, dressing area, full bath and kitchen, and a work and lounge area. When they first fell in love, they'd often worked late together there, and ended up making love on the curved lounge and falling asleep in each other's arms. The trailer was closed now, the blinds drawn against the burning heat. The AC unit chugged away.

Annie was eager to get inside where it was cool. She paused, straightening her skirt, adjusting her bag on her shoulder. There was a fleeting thought of lipstick. Shoot. She wanted to look nice when she told him she was going to be the mother of his child. Never mind, she told herself. Martin didn't care about lipstick.

She quickly entered the code on the keypad and let herself in.

The first thing she noticed was the smell. Something soapy, floral. There was music playing, cheesy music. "Hanging by a Thread," a song she used to sing at the top of her lungs when no one was around, because the right cheesy love song only made a person feel more in love.

A narrow thread of light came from a gap under the window shades. She pushed her sunglasses up on her head and let her eyes adjust. She started to call out to Martin, but her gaze was caught by something out of place.

A cell phone lay on the makeup station shelf. It wasn't Martin's phone, but Melissa's. Annie recognized the blingy pink casing.

And then there was that moment. That sucker-punch feeling of knowing, but not really knowing. Not wanting to know.

Annie stopped breathing. She felt as if her heart had stopped beating, impossible though that was. Her mind whirled through options, thoughts darting like a mouse in a maze. She could back away right now, slip outside, rewind the moment, and . . .

And do what? *What?* Give them fair warning, so they could all go back to pretending this wasn't happening?

An icy stab of anger propelled her forward. She went to the workstation area, separated from the entryway by a folding pocket wall. With a swipe of her arm, she shoved aside the screen.

He was straddling her, wearing nothing but the five-hundred-dollar cowboy boots.

"Hey!" he yelped, rearing back, a cowboy on a bucking bronc. "Oh, shit, Jesus Christ." He scrambled to his feet, grabbing a fringed throw to cover his crotch.

Melissa gasped and clutched a couch cushion against her. "Annie! Oh my God—"

"Really?" Annie scarcely recognized the sound of her own voice. "I mean, *really*?"

"It's not—"

"What it seems, Martin?" she bit out. "No. It's *exactly* what it seems." She backed away, her heart pounding, eager to get as far from him as possible.

"Annie, wait. Babe, let's talk about this."

She turned into a ghost right then and there. She could feel it. Every drop of color drained away until she was transparent.

Could he see that? Could he see through her, straight into her heart? Maybe she had been a ghost for a long time but hadn't realized it until this moment.

The feeling of betrayal swept through her. She was bombarded by everything. Disbelief. Disappointment. Horror. Revulsion. It was like having an out-of-body experience. Her skin tingled. Literally, tingled with some kind of electrical static.

"I'm leaving," she said. She needed to go throw up somewhere.

"Can we please just talk about this?" Martin persisted.

"Do you actually think there's something to talk about?"

She stared at the two of them a moment longer, perversely needing to imprint the scene on her brain. That was when the moment shifted.

This is how it ends, she thought.

Because it was one of those moments. A key moment. One that spins you around and points you in a new direction.

This is how it ends.

Martin and Melissa both began speaking at once. To Annie's ears, it sounded like inarticulate babble. A strange blur pulsated at the edges of her vision. The blur was reddish in tone. The color of rage.

She backed away, needing to escape. Plunged her hand into her bag and grabbed her keys. They were on a Sugar Rush key chain in the shape of a maple leaf.

Then she made a one-eighty turn toward the door and walked out into the alley. Her stride was purposeful. Gaze straight ahead. Chin held high.

That was probably the reason she tripped over the cable. The fall brought her to her knees, keys hitting the pavement with a jingle. And the humiliation just kept coming. She picked up the keys and whipped a glance around, praying no one had seen.

Three people hurried over—*Are you all right? Did you hurt yourself?*

"I'm fine," she said, dusting off the palms of her hands and her scraped knees. "Really, don't worry."

The phone in her shoulder bag went off like a buzz saw, even though it was set on silent mode. She marched past the construction area. Workers were still struggling with the lift, trying to open the hydraulic valve. She shouldn't have let Martin talk her into the cheaper model.

"You have to turn it the other way," she called out to the workers.

"Ma'am, this is a hard-hat area," a guy said, waving her off.

"Leaving," she said. "I'm just saying, you're trying to crank the release valve the wrong way."

"What's that?"

"The valve. You're turning it the wrong way." What a strange conversation. When you discover your husband banging some other woman, weren't you supposed to call your mom, sobbing? Or your best friend?

"You know," she said to the guy. "Lefty loosey, righty tighty."

"Ma'am?"

"Counterclockwise," she said, tracing her key chain in the air to show him the direction.

"Annie." Martin burst out of his trailer and sprinted toward her. Boxer shorts, bare chest, cowboy boots. "Come back."

Her hand tightened around the key chain, the edges of the maple leaf biting into her flesh.

The Segway tour group trolled past the end of the alley.

"It's Martin Harlow," someone called.

"We love your show, Martin," called another girl in the Segway group. "We love you!"

"Ma'am, you mean like this?" The workman gave the valve a hard turn.

A metallic groan sounded from somewhere on high. And the entire structure came crashing down.

2

So, Dad," said Teddy, swiveling around on the kitchen barstool, "if the water buffalo weighs two thousand pounds, how come it doesn't sink in the mud?"

Fletcher Wyndham glanced at the show his son was watching, an unlikely choice for a ten-year-old kid, but Teddy had taken a shine to *The Key Ingredient.* Most people in Switchback, Vermont, tuned in to the cooking show, not because of the chef or the hot blond cohost. No, the reason was behind the scenes—a quick blip in the credits that rolled while the slightly annoying theme song played.

Her name was Annie Rush—the producer.

The most popular cooking show on TV was her brainchild, and she'd been born and raised in Switchback. Teddy's fourth-grade teacher had gone to school with Annie. A while back, the show had filmed an episode right here in town, though Fletcher had kept his distance from the production. Since then, Annie held celebrity status, even though she didn't appear on camera.

That was just as well, Fletcher decided. Seeing her on TV every week would drive him nuts. "Good question, buddy," he said to his son. "That one looks like he's walking on water."

Teddy rolled his eyes. "It's not a guy buffalo. It's a girl buffalo. They make mozzarella cheese from the milk."

"Then why not call it a milk buffalo?"

"'Cause it lives in the water. Duh."

"Amazing what you can learn from watching TV."

"Yeah, you should let me watch more."

"Dream on," said Fletcher.

"Mom lets me watch as much as I want."

And there it was. Evidence that Teddy had officially joined a club no kid wanted to belong to—confused kids of divorced parents.

Looking around the chaos of the house they'd just moved into, Fletcher pondered an oft-asked question: What the hell happened to my life?

He was able to precisely locate the turning point. A single night of too much beer and too little judgment had set him on a path that had changed every plan he'd ever made.

Yet when he looked into his son's face, he did not have a single regret. Teddy had come into the world a squalling, red-faced, needy bundle of noise, and Fletcher's reaction had not been love at first sight. It had been fear at first sight. He wasn't afraid of the baby. He was afraid of *failing* him. Afraid to do something that would screw up this tiny, perfect, helpless human.

There was only one choice he could make. He had shoved aside the fear. He had given his entire self to Teddy, driven by a powerful sense of mission and a love like nothing he'd ever felt before. Now Teddy was in fifth grade, ridiculously cute, athletic, goofy, and sweet. Sometimes, he was a total pain in the ass. Yet every moment of every day, he was the center of Fletcher's universe.

Teddy had always been a happy kid. The kind of happy that made Fletcher want to enclose him in a protective bubble. Now Fletcher realized that, despite his intentions, the bubble had been pierced. The end of his marriage had been a long time coming, and he knew the transition was hard on Teddy. Fletcher wished he could have spared his son the pain and confusion, but he needed to end it in order to breathe again. He only hoped that one day Teddy would understand.

"The water buffalo is a remarkable feat of nature's engineering," said the cohost of *The Key Ingredient,* who served as the sidekick of the life-support system for an ego, aka Martin Harlow.

"Why is that, Melissa?" asked the host in a phony voice.

She gestured at the sad-looking buffalo, standing in a small pen against a none-too-subtle computer-generated swamp. "Well, the animal's wide hooves allow her to walk on extremely soft surfaces without sinking."

The host stroked his chin. "Good point. You know, when I was a kid, I thought I had a fifty percent chance of drowning in quicksand, because it happened so much in the movies."

The blonde laughed and shook back her hair. "We're glad you didn't!"

Fletcher winced. "Hey, buddy, give me a hand with the unpacking, will you?"

The big items had all been delivered, but there were several loads of unopened boxes.

"The show's almost over. I want to see how the cheese turns out."

"The suspense must be killing you," said Fletcher. "Hey, you know what they make with the mozzarella cheese?"

"Pizza! Can we order pizza tonight?"

"Sure. Or we could just eat the leftover pizza from last night."

"It's better fresh."

"Good point. I'll call after we unpack two more boxes. Deal?"

"Yeah," Teddy said with a quick fist pump.

The new house had everything Fletcher had once envisioned, back when he'd had someone to dream with—a big kitchen open to the rest of the house. If he knew how to cook, delicious things would happen here. But the person who made the delicious things was long gone from his life. Still the old dream lingered, leading Fletcher to this particular house, a New England classic a century old. It had a fireplace and a room with enough bookshelves to be called a library. There was a back porch with a swing he'd spent the afternoon putting together, and it was not just any swing, but a big, comfortable one with cushions large enough for a fine nap—a swing he'd been picturing for more than a decade.

They tackled a couple of boxes of books. Teddy was quiet for a while as he shelved them. Then he held up one of the books. "Why's it called *Lord of the Flies*?"

"Because it's awesome," Fletcher said.

"Okay, but why is it called that?"

"You'll find out when you're older."

"Is it something dirty I'm not supposed to know about?"

"It's filthy dirty."

"Mom would have a cow if I told her you had a dirty book."

"Great. Here's a thought. Don't tell her."

Teddy put the book on the shelf, then added a few more to the collection. "So, Dad?"

"Yeah, buddy?"

"Is this really where we live now?" He looked around the room, his eyes two saucers of hurt.

Fletcher nodded. "This is where we live."

"Forever and ever?"

"Yep."

"That's a long time."

"It is."

"So when I tell my friends to come over to my house, will they come to this one or our other house?"

There was no *our* anymore. Celia had taken possession of the custom-built place west of town.

He stopped shelving books and turned to Teddy. "Wherever you are, that's home."

They worked together, putting up the last of the books. Fletcher stepped back, liking the balance of the bookcases flanking the fireplace, the breeze from the back porch stirring the chains of the swing.

The only thing missing was the one person who had shared the dream with him.

3

Open your eyes."

An unfamiliar voice drifted overhead. She couldn't tell if the spoken words were in her mind or in the room. The sound floated away into silence, punctuated by hissing and a low hum. Despite the request, she couldn't open her eyes. The room didn't exist. Only blackness. She was swimming in dark water, yet for some reason, she could breathe in and out as though the water nourished her lungs.

Other sounds filled the space around her, but she couldn't identify them—the rhythmic suck and sigh of a machine, maybe a dishwasher or a mechanical pump of some kind. A hydraulic pump?

She smelled . . . something. Flowers in bloom. Maybe bug spray. No, flowers. Lilies. Stargazer lilies.

Lilies of the field. Wasn't that from the Sermon on the Mount? It was the name of a high school play. Yes, her friend Gordy had won the Sidney Poitier role in the production.

" . . . more activity by the hour. She's progressed to minimal consciousness. The night aide caught it. Dr. King ordered another EEG and a new series of scans."

A stranger's voice. That accent. "Caught" sounded like "cot." Losing the *r* in "ordered" and "another." That was known as non-rhotic pronunciation. She remembered this from broadcast journalism training. Lose the caught-cot merger. Speak the rhotic *r.* Never let anyone guess where you come from.

The mystery speaker's accent was straight out of northern Vermont.

"Help me with this EEG, will you?" Something jarred her head.

Knock it off.

Ma'am, this is a hard-hat area. Were they putting a hard hat on her? No, a hairnet. No, a swim cap.

Swimmers, take your marks.

She could see herself bending, coiled like a spring, toes curled over the edge of the starting block. She was one of the fastest swimmers on the high school team, the Switchback Wildcats. Senior year, she'd broken the state record for the one-hundred-meter breast. Senior year, she'd seen her life roll out like an endless, shimmering river, with everything in front of her. Senior year, she'd fallen in love for the first time.

" . . . always wondered how I'd look with short hair like this," said one of the voices. *Shawt hay-ah.* The non-rhotic *r.*

Beep. The starting tone buzzed through the aquatic center. Annie plunged.

Dry. Why was her throat dry even though she wasn't thirsty? Why couldn't she swallow? Something stiff confined her neck. *Take it off. Need to breathe.*

She floated some more. Water the same temperature as her body. She had to pee. And then she didn't have to pee. After a while, there were no more physical sensations, only feelings pulsating through her head and neck and chest. Panic and grief. Rage. Why?

She was known for her calm demeanor. Annie will fix it. She fixed people's accents. Lighting problems. Set design. Stuck valves.

Lefty loosey, righty tighty. With the maple leaf key chain in her hand, she demonstrated.

"See? That movement—it's not random."

A voice again.

"She's left-handed."

Another voice.

"I know she's left-handed. So am I."

Mom. Mom?

"She looks the same," said the mom voice. Yes, it was unmistakable. "I don't see any change at all. How can you tell me she's waking up?"

"It's not exactly waking up. It's a transition into a more conscious state. The EEG shows increased activity. It's a hopeful sign."

A different voice. "People don't suddenly wake up from something like this; they come around gradually, drifting in and out. Annie. Annie, can you open your eyes?"

No. Can't.

"Squeeze my finger."

No. Can't.

"Can you wiggle your toes?"

No. *Jesus.*

"It can be a lengthy process," the voice said. "And unpredictable, but we're optimistic. The scans show no permanent damage. Her respiration has been excellent since we removed the tracheostomy tube."

Trache . . . *what?* Wasn't that like a hole in her windpipe? *Gross.* Was that why it hurt to swallow, to breathe?

"I'm sorry." The mom voice was thick with tears. "It's just so hard to see . . ."

"I understand. But this is a time to feel encouraged. She's avoided so many of the common complications—pulmonary infection, contractures, joint changes, thrombosis . . . so much that could have gone wrong simply didn't. And that's a good thing."

"How do I see something good here?" Mom whispered.

"I know it's been difficult for you, but believe me, she's one of the lucky ones. With this new activity, the care team thinks she's turned the corner. We're staying positive."

"All right. Then so am I." Mom's voice, soft with desperate hope. "But if… when she wakes up, what if she's different? Will she remember what happened? Will she still be our Annie?"

"It's too soon to know if there will be deficits."

"What do you mean, *deficits*?" The voice sounded thin and strained. Panicky.

"We have to take this process one step at a time. There'll be lots of testing in the days and weeks to come—cognitive, physical, neurological. Psychological. The results will give us a better idea of the best way to help her."

"Okay," the mom voice said, "how will we tell her everything? What if she asks for him? What do I say?"

Him. Who was he? Someone who felt like a heavy sadness, pressing her down.

"We're going to take each moment as it comes. And of course, we'll continue to monitor her constantly."

"Oh God. What if—"

"Listen. And, Annie, if you can hear us, you listen, too. You're young and strong and you survived the worst of it. We're expecting you to make a good recovery."

I'm young, thought Annie. Well, duh.

Then she wondered how old she was. Weird how she couldn't remember… She could easily recall being just four or five, in the sugarhouse with Gran. *See how it coats the spatula so perfectly? That means the sap has turned into syrup. We can use the thermometer, but we must use our eyes, too.*

Then she was ten, standing on the front porch of the farmhouse, watching her father leave in a storm of pink petals from the apple trees. The truck was crammed with moving boxes, and Dad walked with a stiff, resolute gait. Behind her, sobs drifted from the parlor, where Mom was curled up on the couch while Gran tried to soothe her.

Annie's world had cracked in two that day. She couldn't put it back together because she didn't understand how it had broken apart. There was a crack in her heart, too.

"You should go, Caroline," someone said. "Get some rest. This process—it can take days, maybe weeks. She'll be monitored round the clock, and we'll call you at the first sign of any change."

Hesitation. A soft sigh. "I see. So then, I'll be back tomorrow," said Mom. "In the meantime, call me if there's any change at all. It doesn't matter if it's the middle of the night."

"Of course. Drive safely."

Footsteps fading away. *Come back.* The voice in her head was a man's voice. She didn't want to hear it. She tried to listen to the other people in the room.

"... knew her in high school. She's from that big family farm on Rush Mountain over in Switchback." The voice was a gossipy chirp.

"Wow, you're right. I swam against her at State one year. Small world."

"Ay-up. She used to go around with Fletcher Wyndham. Remember him?"

"Oh my gosh. Who doesn't? She should have kept going."

Fletcher. Fletcher Wyndham. Annie's mind kept circling back to the name until it matched an image she held in her heart. She remembered the sensation of love that filled every cell of her body, nourishing her like oxygen, warmed her through and through. Did she still love him? The voice had said she used to go around with him, so maybe the love was gone. How had she lost it? Why? What had happened? *We're not finished.* She remembered him saying that to her. *We're not finished.* But of course, they were.

She remembered high school, and swimming and boys, and the most important person in her life—Fletcher Wyndham. There was college, and Fletcher again, and then there was a great cracking sound and he was gone.

She felt herself sinking as sleep closed over her. A phantom warmth lay across her legs and turned the darkness to a dense orange color, as though a light shone from above. Trying to stay with her thoughts, she wandered in the wilderness, a dreamscape of disjointed images—laughter turning to sadness, a journey to a destination she didn't recognize. After that, she sensed a long blank page with unrecognizable flickers around the edges.

No, she didn't know her age.

She didn't know anything. Only confusion, pain, breathing through water.

Swimmers, take your marks.

And Annie raced away.

Music. Soundgarden? "The Day I Tried to Live." And then Aerosmith. "Dream On." Why? Mom and Dad used to dance to the oldies when they played on the radio. At sugar parties during the tapping and boiling, they'd boogie down while the boom box shook in the sugarhouse. Gran would make fried doughboys sprinkled with maple crystals, and people would come from all over to sample the wares.

During the sugar season, there were parties every weekend on Rush Mountain. It was a time of hopeful transition, a sign that winter was finally yielding to sunny spring. The frozen nights, followed by warming days, caused a thaw, triggering a rush of sap during the daylight hours. The shifting season also brought on a rush of music, food, laughter, as the family hosted gatherings around the big steamy evaporator in the sugarhouse.

Dad used to put a tent board sign out by the road: *Sugar Rush—Warmest Place on the Mountain.*

More music drifted through the air—the Police. Hunters & Collectors. The B-52's. Song after song took Annie back to her childhood. "Love Shack" was the most popular dance tune of them all. Only a few people knew that the nickname for the Rush sugarhouse was "the Love Shack." Even fewer knew the reason for that.

In the winter of her senior year of high school, Annie had lost her virginity in the sugarhouse, surrounded by maple-scented steam as she sweetly yielded to the soft kisses of a boy she thought would be hers forever.

She'd never understood why people said "lost" her virginity. Annie had not lost a thing that night. She had given herself away—virginity, heart, self, soul. To the town bad boy, Fletcher Wyndham. So no, she hadn't lost anything. She'd gained . . . something new and unexpected and achingly beautiful. The world had changed color for her that night, like the crowns of the maples at the first touch of autumn frost.

He's bad for you. Mom had been adamant about that.

As if Annie's mother had become some kind of relationship expert after Dad left.

The space behind Annie's eyes hurt. She squeezed her eyelids together. Blinked. Big mistake. She felt a sharp flash of light, straight to the brain. *Ouch.*

The flashing made her curious, so she blinked some more despite the pain. Tried to rub her eyes, but her hands wouldn't work. Then something brushed her face. Cold drops touched her eyes. She held them shut until the cold was gone. Her hands wanted to work, but something kept holding them back. Tied. Her hands were tied. Not figuratively, but literally. Some kind of padding prevented her from making a fist.

More blinking, more shards of light. *Ouch.* She managed to keep her eyes open at a squint for a moment or two. She could move her eyes but not her head. Unfamiliar room. Plain beige walls. A grid of metal rails on the ceiling. For the camera mounts, right? She remembered an argument about the expense of the camera rails. Many arguments. Pain again. Not behind her eyes. Somewhere else. *Run.* Run away from the pain.

She had to pee again.

More looking. Blurry light from the rectangular opening overhead, the one that brought her to life when the warm glow passed over her. A skylight?

She missed the sky.

Eyes slitting open again in a squint. Yes, there was a skylight. Shifting her gaze, she saw a row of windows, too. Light from outside, filtered by gauzy drapes, streamed across the floor. Heat from an old-fashioned steam radiator created invisible eddies, wafting upward. Then her eyelids fell down, and she couldn't lift them.

Footsteps. Someone came in. Did . . . something. Moved a pillow. Did something lower down and she suddenly didn't have to pee anymore.

She tried to open her eyes, but they didn't work. She had turned into a ghost again.

The footsteps faded away.

Come back.

She concentrated on dragging her eyelids up, and this time her eyes stayed open. Confusion and sadness. Grief. Is this what grief was, this weight on her chest?

She remembered the feeling from the day a member of the tree-tapping crew came into the farmhouse and told them about Gramps. He had gone out on a four-wheeler one afternoon to cut a tree, and was crushed when a tractor overturned on him. Years later, there was that bright sunshiny morning when Gran wouldn't wake up.

Yes, Annie knew grief. Closed her eyes, but the pain didn't go away.

She struggled again to lift her eyelids. Images pulsated before her eyes and then slowly resolved into focus. There was a generic quality to the surroundings. Impersonal art prints on the wall. A budget hotel, maybe?

Her gaze moved from skylight to windowsill. Something new

there—a display of knickknacks. And these were not impersonal at all. She was certain she recognized the items from long ago. Forever ago.

Her tallest swim trophy, and a blue ribbon from the state-fair culinary-arts competition, 1998 Junior Chef Division. A copy of Gran's cookbook, its worn and homey cover evoking waves of remembrance. She tried to grab on to the memories, but each one drifted off before it was fully formed, borne away on a wave of liquid pain.

A boxy metallic container caught her eye. It was a half-gallon jug of Sugar Rush—the family's maple syrup, produced on Rush Mountain since 1847. It said so right on the container, although she couldn't make out the letters.

Like all traditional syrup tins, Sugar Rush depicted a typical scene in the winter woods—a barn-red sugarhouse and a team of horses hauling the barrels of sap to be boiled. In the foreground were two fresh-faced kids in hand-knit hats and mittens, riding a toboggan down a snow-covered slope.

What most people didn't know was that the quaint building was the actual one on Rush Mountain. The kids were Annie and her brother, Kyle. Their mom, with her singular artistic talent, had rendered the drawing from old photographs.

Kyle had hired a brand consultant to offer ways to increase sales, and one suggestion had been to redesign the old-fashioned package. Kyle had refused to consider it. "People don't want the things they love to change," he said.

Remembering her brother's words, Annie felt something even more powerful than the watery pain in her head. Yet she couldn't name the feeling. It caused an ache in her throat.

She listened to the soft hiss and thump some more. A percussion section warming up. Every once in a while, a quiet tone sounded. Not a beep but a tone. A tuning fork?

The sky within the skylight was impossibly blue, the kind of blue that made a person's eyes smart. What was this place? Where in the world was she?

"Hey," she said. Her voice was a broken noise, like an old-fashioned scratched vinyl record. Dad had taken the record collection when he left. "Hey."

The thing around her neck confined her, and she couldn't lift or turn her head. Her ankles and wrists felt bound by fleecy cuffs like unwanted sex toys. *No, thank you.*

She managed to move her left hand a little, angling it into view. The stiff thing holding her fingers straight was gone now. Was this her hand? It was a stranger's hand. The nails were cut short and unpolished. Which made no sense, because she'd just had a manicure the day before. She'd wanted to look professional for the *People* interview.

She touched her thumb to her ring finger. There was no ring.

A memory flickered. A home. A job. A life.

The grief came rolling back. *Whoosh,* like runoff in the springtime flumes through the maple groves. And just like that, the memories were swept away once again, no more real than a dream.

Footsteps again. More rushing around. Squishy rubber soles squeaked on linoleum as people came and went. Annie blinked, glimpsing a woman in cotton scrubs printed with kittens and stars. She bent forward, her breath warm and smelling of spearmint. "Annie. Hey, Annie? Can you hear me?"

"Uh." Broken voice again, noise coming in a toneless rasp. "Huh."

The woman's face blazed with a smile. "Welcome back," she said.

The sound of paper tearing, as if ripped off a roll of gift wrap. Footsteps again, hurrying off on a mission, then fading. Running. Running away.

Come back.

The woman spoke again, but not to Annie, to someone over her shoulder.

"Call the family—stat."

4

Caroline Rush removed the two coordinated art prints from the wall of Annie's room at the rehab center, and replaced the discount-store artwork with a pair of original paintings of her own. If—no, *when*—her daughter woke up again, Caroline wanted her to see something familiar on the wall. She still couldn't get over the feeling of wonder and gratitude she'd felt when they'd called. Annie woke up. She spoke.

But by the time Caroline had sped down the mountain and along the state highway to Burlington, Annie was asleep again.

"You picked two of my favorites," said a voice Caroline hadn't heard in years.

She froze. Stopped breathing. Closed her eyes. And then she rallied, inhaling deeply. She would not let this man take her breath away. She would not let him render her at a loss for words. Very slowly, she turned.

Her ex-husband walked through the door. Ethan was as lean and fit as the day she'd met him—a young man driving a truckload of fresh produce. "Hey, Caro. I got here as quickly as I could." He brushed past her and went straight to Annie's bedside. "What's happening?"

"They say she's in transition."

Ethan gazed down at their daughter, and his face went soft with sadness. He touched her bony shoulder through the faded hospital drape. "What's that supposed to mean—in transition?"

"That's a question for the doctor. All I know is what I e-mailed Kyle. I assume he forwarded it to you."

"Yeah. So she's finally waking up? Coming around?"

Caroline's stomach pounded with dread for her daughter, a feeling with which she was intimately familiar these days. "There've been signs . . ."

He pinched the bridge of his nose, his face taut with emotion.

Years after the divorce, Caroline still had no idea how to act around her ex-husband. Since he had left on that glorious pink-and-blue spring day, she'd only seen him a few times. Ethan had attended Kyle's wedding to Beth, a small and intimate celebration at the Grange Hall in Switchback. It had been awful, because Ethan had brought Imelda with him.

Caroline had actively hated him in that moment, and then she'd hated herself for letting her ex steal her joy on their son's wedding day. She did better at Annie's wedding, several years later. By then, she'd learned to put up an impermeable wall between herself and Ethan. She pretended her ex-husband was just someone she used to know, like the guy who came to root out the septic system once a year.

"I didn't realize you had a favorite," she said now, stepping back to make sure the paintings were level.

"There's a lot you didn't know about me," he said.

She swung around to face him. "What's that supposed to mean?"

"The right corner needs to come up a tad," he said, indicating toward one of the pictures.

"No, it's perfect." She took another step back, and saw that he was right. She reached forward and nudged the corner up.

She wondered why he'd said this particular painting was one of his favorites. It was a landscape of Rush Mountain, the view looking westward at sunset in early autumn. The sky had a special radiance at that time of year, touching the meadows and treetops with fire and lengthening the shadows in the valley leading downward to the town of Switchback. She had caught the light just so, managing to convey its fleeting nature.

Ethan had never liked the place, even though it had been their home for eighteen years. After they married and she got pregnant so quickly with Kyle, Ethan had stayed out of obligation. He'd left as soon as their son was old enough to take over the farm.

"Why is it your favorite?" she asked without looking at him.

"Because your heart's in it," he said, simply and unexpectedly. "And because Annie always loved the view from your studio."

Caroline couldn't argue with that. She had done a similar canvas for Annie as a wedding gift.

Their daughter had been breathtaking on her wedding day. All brides were. But Annie was the kind of beautiful that cut like a knife, imparting a sweet pain that made Caroline clasp her hands together in a stranglehold. She hadn't bothered to hold back her tears as Annie appeared on the secluded, rock-bound California beach at sunset. The setting was so different from Vermont, like another country. Another planet. Yet Annie's expression, so full of hope, had been the same expression she'd worn every Christmas morning when she was little.

Why did joy bring the same tears as sadness? Why did the throat and chest ache with fire, regardless? Was it because, deep down, everyone knew it was fragile and ephemeral? Did the tears come from the knowledge that everything could turn in the blink of an eye?

Caroline knew that happiness could be destroyed in the time it took a tractor to overturn in a ditch. The time it took for a husband to say, "I'm leaving."

The time it took for a piece of equipment to drop on a young woman's head.

She looked over at the bed. Ethan sat quietly beside Annie, gazing into her unmoving face the way Caroline had done for so many hours.

As if he felt Caroline watching him, he turned on the rolling stool. "What time will the doctor come?"

"They never give you a specific time," she said. The silence between them felt awkward, so she switched on the music, a playlist she'd made of songs she thought Annie would like. "How Do You Talk to an Angel" came through the speaker—an unfortunate selection, because it triggered a memory of Ethan, lip-synching the song as he acted it out with exaggerated gestures to make his little daughter laugh.

Did Ethan remember those moments? Did certain songs give rise to indelible memories within him? Did he ever think about the lost sweetness of their family life? Or did he only recall the stale discontent, the yearning for something different?

"Where are you staying?" she asked him, deciding it was best to stick with neutral topics. She didn't want to know anything personal about him. She didn't want him to know anything about her life. Yet when he looked at her even now, he seemed to know everything about her.

"Hotel across the way—it's a Best Western, I think. Next week, I'll move to my folks' place up in Milton."

"Kyle said your dad has finally decided to retire," she said.

"That's right. He's looking for a buyer for the business."

Ethan's father was an independent grocery distributor. That was how Caroline had met him, when he was driving a truck for his father's outfit and came to Rush Mountain for a shipment of maple syrup. The logo on the side of the truck—*Lickenfelt Fine Foods*—had made her smile, because it was such a funny name.

She pushed aside the memory. "Oh. I hope he finds someone to take over. Kyle brought him and Wilma to see Annie a couple of times."

They ran out of things to say. How odd that this man was a stranger to her. There had been a time when she knew everything about him—the smell of his skin and the taste of his breath. What his laughter sounded like, what his anger looked like. The shape of his hands. The things he dreamed about. His passion and his frustration.

They'd made two beautiful children. They had grandchildren together. Yet these days, she had no idea what he was thinking. She didn't know who he was, or how he'd gotten that whitish scar on the back of his hand, or if he needed reading glasses now that he was in his fifties.

The old songs kept coming. Most were from Annie's growing-up years. She gazed helplessly at the figure on the bed, that colorless face like a marble icon, smooth and unmoving.

"Sleeping beauty," Ethan said.

Caroline nodded. "I've been so scared. I hope the doctors are right about her coming around."

He pressed his forefinger and thumb against his closed eyes in a gesture she recognized—his way of containing his tears. "I hope so, too," he whispered.

"Ethan, they did warn me not to expect her to be exactly the way she was before the accident. There could be . . ." She didn't want to say it. "Some impairment. Deficiencies, I think someone called them. And no one will know the extent of it until she's fully awake. Even if there's no permanent deficit, she'll need intensive rehab."

"We'll do whatever it takes," he said.

"It's likely to go on for weeks. Or months."

"Whatever it takes," he repeated.

Oh. Well, that was something. In previous years, Ethan had come to Vermont only twice a year to see Annie and Kyle—two weeks during the holidays and another two in the summer, spending his short stay at his parents' place in Milton.

When he said "whatever it takes," did that mean he planned to stay? She bit her lip to keep from asking.

"Brand New Day" was playing now. The part of the song about turning the clock back hit Caroline hard. "I wish I could," she said softly, gazing at her daughter.

"Could what? Turn back the clock?"

She nodded. "Did I push her into that life, or is it what she really wanted?"

"What, producing a hit TV show? It seemed like exactly what she always dreamed of."

All Caroline could remember were the arguments. "Maybe I should have been more supportive of her and Fletcher," she said now. "You never met him, did you?"

"No. Annie told me about him. Hometown sweethearts." He shot Caroline a look. "It happens."

"But they were so young. How could I have known?"

"Cut it out, Caro." Ethan was the only one who ever called her Caro. "You don't get to take responsibility for your grown daughter's decisions."

"One of us had to take responsibility for everything," she fired back, falling into their old pattern as if no time at all had passed.

"Right," he said, his voice taut with anger. "And how's that working out for you?"

Annie heard voices, quietly arguing in the way people fought when they didn't want anyone to know they were fighting. They ought to realize that the technique never worked. Just because a quarrel was quiet didn't mask the fact that it was a quarrel. Even if the words were inaudible, the fight infested the air like a fog.

There was a haunting familiarity in the tense, sibilant whispers hovering over Annie's eyelids. She was ten years old, lying in the dark long after bedtime, straining to hear what her parents were saying to one another. She couldn't hear their words, but some part of her already knew they were on the brink of stripping away the safe cocoon of her family. She had caught Mom crying and hugging Gran, and she'd seen her grandfather's icy glare when he looked at Dad. The bad feeling sloshed through her head.

Open your eyes. Remembering the command, she tried very hard, but couldn't quite manage. She thought about speaking up, but didn't know what to say. She'd never been able to stop the arguments.

When she was little and a bad dream woke her, Gran would advise her to change the channel by turning her pillow over. It worked every time.

Yet she couldn't move. Couldn't feel the pillow beneath her head. Was forced to lie still as the argument went on.

She tried to think of something that would make the whispers go away. Something that would calm the churning in her gut. Her mind went to a place she knew with crystal clarity. She didn't know if that place was now or forever ago. Maybe it was just *away.*

5

Then

Annie wasn't expecting to fall in love that midwinter day in the middle of the sugar season. The dead cold of northern Vermont was just losing its grip on the mountain. The frozen nights gave way to daytime thaw, perfect for sugaring. It was late afternoon, and a rare glimmer of sunlight slanted across the mountain, touching the landscape with gold. Plenty of snow still lay on the ground, though it was melting as rapidly as the sap was running. The quality of the light through the clear, cold air created a stark beauty in the sugarbush. The bare maple branches resembled an intricate etching against the deep blue of the sky. The snow was silvery blue, sparkling in the sunshine and darkening in the deeply shadowed gullies that threaded through the landscape.

Annie was a senior in high school, dizzy with the possibilities her future held, her heart opening like a bud in springtime. She wasn't looking to fall in love with a boy, but with life itself. Poised to leave home and make her own way in the world, she wanted her life to be amazing, spectacular, singular, exciting... everything it was not on Rush Mountain in Switchback, Vermont.

But life had a way of interfering with one's plans. Things popped up unexpectedly, and suddenly a carefully plotted route had to be recalculated.

Sugarmakers who weren't ready with their operations risked missing out on the sap run. At the Rush sugarbush—two hundred acres of thriving sugar maples—it was the peak of the year. It was the same at all the other operations in the area—a swift frenzy of productivity, a race against the coming warmth, to capture the sap run before the maples budded out. The high school allowed early release time during the sugar season so students could help their families, or earn money on a tapping crew.

It occurred to Annie that this would be her last sugar season at home, maybe ever. In the fall, she would be going away to college. She'd won a scholarship to New York University, and she meant to make the most of it. She planned to study film and media, and had been accepted to a special interdisciplinary program focused on broadcasting in the field of culinary arts. Next year at this time, she would be away at college. She might be in France studying mirepoix techniques, or in a lecture hall discussing the First Amendment. The important thing was, she would be somewhere new, at last.

But at the moment, college seemed light-years away. The sap run was epic. Kyle had to hire extra help, a group of high school guys, to haul sap, move firewood, man the pumps, and keep a steady stream of fresh sap flowing toward the evaporator.

Kyle had used the tractor and stone boat to break road through the maple woods to the sugarhouse. Annie, her mother and grandmother, had all pitched in to wash and sterilize the sugaring equipment. The tapping crew drove spiles into the trees and ran miles of tubing through the groves, downhill to the collection tanks. The trees immediately surrounding the sugarhouse were equipped with old-fashioned covered galvanized buckets, a nod to the old way of collecting sap, but that was mostly for visitors who came by to see the operation.

Once the taps were in place, the sap run commenced, and the quiet winter woods turned into a hive of activity as the crews collected the sap at its peak of freshness. The elevated storage tank was connected to the reverse osmosis machine, which removed most of the water before boiling. The men would work until they lost the light, and the nighttime freeze turned their breath to clouds.

When the long days of boiling began in the sugarhouse, Annie's mother took the early-morning shift to get it over with. Gran stepped in at midday. She always brought along something fresh from her kitchen—donuts, hot coffee, warm biscuits. People would come around for a sample and a chat, and they would leave with fresh maple syrup, still warm in the tin.

Annie was in charge of the late-shift boiling, heading into the sugarhouse after school each day. By the time she took up her duties at the evaporator, the crew had usually decimated Gran's goodies, although Gran always set aside a little something for her in a wooden pie safe alongside her mom's sketchbook and pencils. A few years ago, Kyle had put an old Naugahyde sofa in the house so Gran could prop her feet up and keep notes in her journal while she tended the syrup. Sometimes the sap ran so fast that they boiled around the clock, and the sofa was a great place to take a catnap.

The sugarhouse was warm and steamy and fragrant. Two of the dogs, Squiggy and Clark, were curled up on blankets. The radio was set to Gran's favorite station—NPR mixed with classical music. Annie twirled the dial to the Top 40 station. The sound of Destiny's Child drifted and mingled with the crackle of the fire while she monitored the syrup in the evaporator, keeping the fire stoked with wood, checking the temperature, and skimming the foam. She liked to boil fast—it yielded a higher-quality syrup—and she was good at it. The fresh sap flowed into the evaporator's flu pan, the syrup pan, and finally the finishing pan. That was when the magic happened.

It was so elemental—the water, the fire, the billows of fragrant steam shooting up through the roof vents. When Annie was in grade school, her display of the process had won her a blue ribbon at the science fair. In her high school photography class, she'd done a photo essay, and a haunting shot of Gran, half hidden in the steam as she worked at the evaporator, was chosen for the permanent collection of the state museum of agriculture and industry.

As Annie watched out the window, the gathering crew came over the crest of a hill, the same sledding hill she had climbed a hundred times every winter, dragging her toboggan behind her. Degan Kerry, a kid from her school, drove the four-wheeler, which was hitched to a boxy red trailer loaded with twin gathering tanks. She recognized Degan by his red hair, catching the last of the sunlight. The four other guys seemed to have enough sense to wear warm hats.

Degan was captain of the hockey team. He was also the school bully, the textbook kind, hulking and unaccountably angry, surrounded by lesser minions who seemed to exist solely to egg him on. But Kyle claimed they were a good crew—strong, fast, and reliable—so when he needed sweat labor, he brought on Degan and his two friends, Carl Berg and Ivan Karev.

Because the sap run was a big one, there were two other hires on the crew this year—Gordy Jessop and Fletcher Wyndham. They were definitely not part of Degan's squad. Gordy was an unapologetic and clueless devotee of *Doctor Who* and of percussive electronic music. He had an unfortunate case of acne and was overweight, all of which had the effect of putting a big, round target on his back.

The final crew member seemed to be nobody's target—Fletcher Wyndham.

Quiet, aloof, and mysterious, he was new in town, which automatically made him an anomaly, not to mention an object of intense speculation. No one moved to Switchback in the middle of winter unless they had to. Enrolling in school so late in senior year made Fletcher a particular enigma. He was shaggy-haired, with a long, lanky frame and a slow, easy smile.

Annie had been secretly fascinated with the newcomer ever since she'd spotted him in Mr. Dow's homeroom. When he'd shown up at Kyle's office last week, looking for work, the sugar season suddenly turned more interesting.

No one knew much about him. He had come to town with his father. The two of them lived in an old shotgun house by the train trestle. In a place the size of Switchback, the absence of a woman in the family fueled plenty of conjecture. By appearances, he seemed to be the kind of kid mothers—including Annie's mother—told her to stay away from. *He's trouble. He's going to wind up in jail one day. He'll drag you down.*

No one could quite explain how such a troublesome kid didn't really seem to get into trouble. Since his arrival a few weeks back, he showed up for school on time, minded his own business, owned the court when PE was basketball, and was rumored to play guitar. Her mom would say it's early days, he's new in town, he'll be in trouble soon enough.

Annie thought he might be the coolest guy in school, but she kept her distance, certain he wouldn't have any interest in a girl whose life consisted of 4-H Club meetings, taking part in the statewide local foods cooking challenge twice a year, getting good grades, and working on the family farm.

After checking the temperature in the evaporator, Annie returned to the window. There were days during the sugar season when the weather was miserable, with snow piled so high that snowshoes were required, or so rainy and muddy it made sane people want to choke something. This was not one of those days. This was a day that made the mountain look like a dreamer's private fantasy of the perfect Vermont day—crisp air, blue sky, crunchy snow, brilliant sunshine. Her final season.

As she watched the guys hard at their chores, Annie was reminded that she was full to the brim with secret desires. She wanted to have sex. She'd never gone all the way with a guy. She had totally planned on doing it with Manny, her boyfriend, but they broke up and the opportunity was gone. She didn't regret it too much, though, because Manny hadn't been a great kisser, and he seemed way more into himself than into her.

She got rid of the boyfriend but not the wild inner yearning. What would it feel like, naked flesh pressed to naked flesh, someone's hand stroking her, endless kisses, bodies joined and building toward a pleasure she'd been dreaming of for a very long time? The questions filled her imagination.

Some of her girlfriends said sex was overrated, so she shouldn't expect too much. Celia Swank, by far the most beautiful and knowledgeable friend on the topic, said a girl had to learn to enjoy it, because sex was the only language guys truly understood. But Annie's very best friend—Pam Mitchell, who always threw her whole heart into everything—said if it was the right guy and the right moment, it was magic.

Annie had always been a big believer in magic.

The crew brought the loaded trailer over to the big holding and filtration tanks and hooked up the hoses to transfer the fresh sap. Fletcher went to collect the sap from the old-style buckets, which hung from the spiles that were tapped into the tree trunks.

Degan, Carl, and Ivan started teasing Gordy. Annie couldn't hear what was being said, but she could tell they were teasing just by watching. They circled the poor guy like a pack of coyotes, their faces taut with mean grins. Gordy kept his eyes averted and his shoulders hunched up, as though hoping to make himself smaller. Didn't he know that never worked?

As if to prove her theory, Degan cuffed Gordy on the back of the head, causing his hat with the earflaps to topple. Then he made an obscene gesture while Carl and Ivan guffawed.

What a bunch of jerks.

Gordy sidled away and tried to shrug it off, pulling his lips into an uncomfortable smile. Annie already knew that wasn't going to work either.

She heaved a sigh and put on her parka. "Come on, dogs," she said to Clark and Squiggy. "Let's see if we can get things back on track." Stepping out into the cold afternoon, she said, "Hey, could somebody give me a hand?"

The dogs trotted out and sniffed around, lifting legs and shaking off.

"Sure," Degan said, "I'll give you a hand." He slapped his gloves together in an exaggerated round of applause. "How's that?"

"Hilarious," she said. "Seriously, I need some help with the evaporator pans. Gordy, can you come?"

"Hell, no, he can't come." Degan grabbed the back of Gordy's collar. "I'm gonna give dipshit here a swirly in the sap tank."

"Do that and my brother will fire your ass," she promised, though she had no idea whether that it was true.

"Only if you tell him," Degan said, yanking Gordy toward a collection tank full of ice-cold sap. Poor Gordy looked ill.

"Which I'm about to do," she retorted.

"Yeah, sure." Degan let go of Gordy, shoving hard enough to send him to his knees.

Before Annie could breathe a sigh of relief, Degan grabbed her by the arm and pulled her inside the sugarhouse. His fingers dug deep through the down pile of her parka. She gave her arm a twist and tried to pull away, but succeeded only in shedding half her coat. "Cut it out, Degan."

"I'm here to help, remember?" he said, dropping the jacket on the floor. "You just wanted to get me alone. So here I am."

Annie ignored the insinuation. "Oh, good. Then you can haul these barrels outside and load them into the green trailer."

"What's in it for me?" Before she could reply, he pushed her back against the rough wooden side of the sugarhouse. "Manny told me you never put out for him, but there's a first time for everything."

Really? she thought. *Really?* She brought her knee up sharply. It was too much to hope she'd nail him in the groin, but he staggered back with the wind knocked out of him. He doubled over, and when he straightened up, he picked up a bucket of cold, raw sap. "You are so screwed," he said, and sloshed the contents at Annie. "Maybe that'll make you sweeter."

She tried to jump out of the way. The cold sap soaked her jeans and trickled down into her boots. "Hey," she said. "That's about enough, Degan Kerry."

"I'm just getting started," he said, taking a stride toward her.

When she saw the feral glint in his eye, Annie felt fear for the first time. Then the door slammed open, bringing in a gust of cold air.

"Is there a problem here?" Fletcher Wyndham's voice was not loud, but it seemed to cut a swath through everything. And although it was a question, he didn't wait for an answer. Fletcher was not bigger than Degan. But he made himself bigger by the way he carried himself. There was something piercing and intimidating in his eyes. "There's work to be done," he said.

"Yeah? Are you the boss all of a sudden?" Degan tossed his head and brushed past Fletcher, stepping outside. Instead of getting to work, he shoved Gordy toward an open tank beside a tree. "Didn't I promise you a swirly?"

Moving with startling quickness, Fletcher crossed to Degan and grabbed him by the back of the pants and the back of the collar. He lifted Degan up and slammed him against the trunk of a tree, looping his belt over a bucket hook.

"You're not so hot at listening," he said.

"What the hell?" Degan's toes dangled above the muddy ground. "Son of a bitch—"

His two minions snickered as he twisted this way and that, trying to get down.

Loyal to the end, thought Annie, beginning to shiver from the cold.

Degan heaved himself away from the tree. There was a ripping sound, and then he landed on his hands and knees in the mud. The dogs pranced around, thinking it was a game. When Degan stood up, his pants slid down, revealing jockey shorts and thick, hairy legs. He yanked up his pants and sent Fletcher a glare of fury. But the effect was lost because he had to keep a grip on his pants. "You are so dead," he snarled.

Fletcher shaded his eyes and looked up at the sky. "You guys can call it a day," he said, then turned to Annie. "Gordy and I will finish up with the filtering."

He turned his back on Degan and walked away. Degan made a growling sound and lunged, but his pants dropped again and he stumbled into the mud a second time. Fletcher didn't spare him a glance.

Degan picked himself up, his expression aflame with pure rage. But Annie saw something else in the bully's face—uncertainty. She planted herself in front of him and addressed Degan and his pals. "It's time for you guys to head home. Don't bother coming back. I'll bring your final checks tomorrow." Then she held her breath, praying they would cooperate.

Degan's uncertainty hardened into belligerence. Annie held her ground, although her stomach was churning. Go, she thought. Just go.

"You heard her," Fletcher said, standing behind her. "Take a hike."

Degan let loose with a string of sputtering invectives as he clutched his pants and marched away, heading down the mountain through the woods, toward the parking area by Kyle's office. Ivan and Carl looked at each other, then at Annie. She folded her arms across her chest and stared at them until they followed Degan.

"Good riddance," she muttered as they disappeared into the woods. Her heart was beating fast. She'd never been comfortable with drama and conflict.

She and Gordy followed Fletcher into the sugarhouse. Inside, she stood near the fire burning under the evaporator, trying to warm up.

"Hey, thanks, man," Gordy said, his gaze worshipful as he regarded Fletcher. "That was really cool of you."

The taller boy gave a shrug. "Don't thank me. Do yourself a favor and figure out how to quit being a target."

"I didn't know I was being a target," Gordy muttered, staring at the floor. "How am I supposed to know when Degan's going to go all *Lord of the Flies* on me?"

"It's not rocket science," Fletcher said, an edge of annoyance in his voice. "Look people in the eye and tell them to knock it off."

The dogs curled up together on their blankets.

Fletcher looked Annie up and down. "You're soaking wet."

"Looking him in the eye didn't really work for me," she said.

"Do you need to find some dry clothes?"

"It's warm here by the fire." She felt a flush rise in her cheeks. Despite her discomfort, she liked the way he was looking at her. Interested but not rude. At least, she hoped he was interested. Most guys gave her a pass, because she didn't have long, shiny hair or big boobs. She was small in stature, with curly hair that bordered on kinky, and olive-toned skin that didn't look quite right in Vermont in the winter.

"Wow, it's awesome in here," said Gordy. "I've never been inside a sugarhouse before."

Annie raised her eyebrows. "I thought everybody had." She turned to Fletcher. "What about you? Are you new to sugaring, too?"

He offered a quick flash of a grin. "My idea of syrup comes in a plastic squeeze bottle in the shape of an old lady."

Annie winced. "That imitation stuff will kill you," she said. "I don't even think it's legal in the state of Vermont. Real maple syrup is pure. There is nothing added and nothing removed, except water." Her legs felt clammy from the spilled sap, but she ignored the discomfort. There was work to be done and she loved having an audience. Besides, it was a way to shift gears away from the altercation with Degan. "This is where the real stuff is made," she told them. "We boil down forty gallons of sap to get a gallon of maple syrup." She showed them how the liquid flowed through the pans. "That's how it gets sweeter by the minute," she said.

"Too bad you can't use that technique on sisters," said Gordy. "I have gnarly sisters."

Annie checked the clock on the wall. Nearly dinnertime already, and she'd probably miss out, because the work wasn't done. "The sap has to be boiled while it's fresh," she told them. "That's why we boil as fast as we can during the season. And that's why my brother's going to be ticked off when I tell him I fired three of his guys."

"He won't be ticked off when you tell him why," Gordy pointed out.

She shrugged off the comment. Kyle had a family now; he'd married a woman with two kids. He was definitely more concerned with the bottom line than he was with high school bullies. "We'll see."

She showed them how to check the rendered syrup, knowing when it coated the spatula in a certain way that the temperature had reached 219 degrees, ready to be drawn from the finishing pan into barrels. Holding up the grading rack with its four clear bottles, she showed them the four grades of syrup—golden, amber, dark, and very dark.

"They all look good to me," Fletcher said, but his attention was not on the rack.

"Hey, how's it going?" Kyle showed up, stomping the snow and mud from his boots on the front step of the sugarhouse. He nodded a greeting at Gordy and Fletcher.

Kyle was eight years older than Annie, a guy's guy, strong and big-shouldered, dark-haired and dark-eyed like Annie. He was quick to laugh, but sometimes quick to anger. His full-time job was with the Forest Service, but in addition to that, all the operations on Rush Mountain—the sugaring, the orchards and lumber operation—had been his responsibility since he'd turned eighteen and their father had left.

"Things are going fine," Annie told him. "I should be finished in an hour or so."

He craned his neck to look out the window. "Where's the rest of the crew?"

Annie shot a glance at Fletcher, then looked back at her brother. "I sent them packing. They were slackers."

"Damn it, Annie," said Kyle, surveying the idle equipment outside. "We're only halfway through the season. I need all hands on deck."

"You don't need slackers," she said with a sniff. "Hire a different crew."

"Every sugarbush in the area is shorthanded this year. Where am I going to find more help?" He ripped off his hat and threw it down. "You know what it costs to lose even a day of sugaring."

"Um, can I make a suggestion?" Gordy said.

"What?" Kyle sounded exasperated.

"My sisters could help out."

"Your sisters. You're volunteering your sisters."

"Well, you'd have to pay them."

"You know what this work is like," Kyle said. "Cold, dirty, and back-breaking. Not exactly women's work."

Gordy rocked back on his heels. "You haven't met my sisters."

Kyle looked skeptical, but he jerked his head toward the door. "Let's go call them."

As they hiked up the hill to find a cell-phone signal, Annie went back to work. "Sorry about him," she said to Fletcher. "He gets stressed out during the sugar season."

"Why didn't you just tell him Degan was being a douche to you?"

"I didn't want—" She cut herself off. "Good question. I don't know why. And speaking of those douche bags, aren't you worried they're going to retaliate?"

He gave a short laugh. "It won't keep me up at night."

"Well, thank you for stepping in." She liked talking to him. He was… different. Not like the guys she'd come through school with.

"Want a hand with anything else?"

Yes. She tried to act cool. "Sure, that would be great." She checked the density of the syrup with a hydrometer. Then she showed him how the sugar sand was removed by pushing it through a filter press. The clear, golden syrup was ready, flowing into the barrels. She caught a sample in a coffee cup and handed it to Fletcher. "Let that cool a bit and take a taste. You'll never give that squeeze bottle another look."

He blew on the cup, his lips pursing as if in readiness for a kiss. She felt mesmerized, watching him. He took a taste, and a smile spread slowly across his face. "That flavor is amazing," he said.

They finished the chores together, working side by side as they talked. "You just moved to Switchback, right?" she asked. As if she didn't know. When he'd enrolled in school a couple of weeks ago, a tidal wave had spread through the girls of the senior class. New guys were rare in this small town. New guys who were cool and good-looking and interesting created a major stir.

"Yep."

"And?" she prompted.

He gave her a slantwise grin, full of charm. "And what? Where'd I come from, what's my family like, how'd I wind up in Switchback?"

"At the risk of being nosy, yes."

"I can handle a nosy girl." He helped her scrub out the equipment. "My dad's a mechanic, specializes in foreign imports, but he can fix anything."

"I saw where he bought Crestfield's garage in town."

Fletcher nodded. "He imports scooters from Italy, too. Fixes them up and sells them, mostly online."

"And your mom?"

"It's just my dad and me."

"Oh. So where's your mom?"

He shot her a look.

"You said you could handle a nosy girl," she pointed out.

"I'll tell you about her," he said. "Just not today."

"Fair enough." She felt bad for prying, and changed the subject. "My mother's an artist. She draws and paints. Never studied it formally, but she's really good. See the illustration on the maple syrup tin? And on our label?" She gestured at a storage shelf crammed with containers. "It's from a painting by my mom. The kids in the picture are Kyle and me."

"Hey, that's cool. What about your dad?"

"Hmm. I'll have to think about whether or not I want to tell you," she said, lightly teasing.

"It's cool," he said. "That way, we'll have something to talk about next time."

Next time.

"It's no big secret. My father took off when I was ten," Annie said. She wondered if the old fear and confusion and hurt still echoed in her voice. "I didn't see it coming. Which is weird, because they fought a lot."

"You were just a kid."

"Mom says he was always dreaming of adventure somewhere else. Then, right after Kyle turned eighteen, Dad said he'd bought acreage on a beach in Costa Rica, and he was going to build a surf camp there."

"Costa Rica sounds amazing."

"I thought so, too. My mom and grandparents, not so much. Mom was so mad she divorced him and took back her maiden name and changed mine and Kyle's to Rush, too. She wanted it to seem as if my dad had never existed." Annie paused, surprised at how easily the words came when she talked to him, a virtual stranger. "I guess for me and Kyle, it's a good thing he did exist. The name change was a good thing, too. My dad's last name is ridiculous—Lickenfelt."

He slapped his knee. "So you were Annie Lickenfelt? I guess you don't miss that."

"God, no."

"So how often do you see him? Do you get to go to Costa Rica?"

"I only went down there once. The beaches are just like you see in postcards, and I learned to surf."

"That's cool."

She nodded. "It's harder than it looks, but once you get up on a wave, you never want to stop. There was tropical fruit growing wild everywhere, and I thought the seafood tasted like candy. The local fishermen would bring it right in from the surf. And there were birds and monkeys like you wouldn't believe. And one day, we went zip-lining in a chocolate forest. Cacao, technically."

"Why'd you only go once?"

"My dad comes back to Vermont twice a year to see his parents over in Milton, so I visit him then. The airfare and travel time to get from here to Dominical are insane. Four flights from Burlington. Plus, I'm not a big fan of Dad's girlfriend, Imelda. She's mean as a snake."

"Yeah, but I'd put up with snakes if it meant surfing in Costa Rica."

"There are alligators, too. Big ones. They hang out at the river estuaries, so surfers have to watch out for them."

"I bet I'd still like surfing."

"You don't talk like you're from around here," she said.

"I've lived in a lot of places."

She waited for him to specify, but he didn't. Next time, she thought again, hoping this year's sugar season was a long one.

"You don't sound like you're from around here either," he said.

"Oh, I sure as tootin' can if I've a mind to," she said in her broadest Vermonter's accent.

He laughed. "Why don't you want to?"

"I'm going into broadcasting. One of the first rules is that you can't sound like you're from any particular place. Regional accents limit you."

"What do you want to broadcast?"

Annie tended to guard her dream from people, not wanting to hear it was going to be hard or it couldn't be done, or you had to know the right people or you'd never break in. Yet she instinctively trusted that Fletcher wouldn't say any of those things.

"A cooking show," she said.

"Cooking? For real?" He didn't seem to think it was funny or weird.

"For real," she said.

"Cool."

She went to the pie safe and offered him an iced maple pecan cookie. "We made these last night."

He took a bite and clutched his chest. "Man, that's good. You're gonna do great with your show. If everybody knew how to make something like this, it would probably bring about world peace."

She laughed. "See, this is what I love. Making food that makes someone happy."

"Oh." He crammed the rest of the cookie into his mouth. "This is me being more than happy. This is me being . . . oh, man."

She laughed again. "Maple is everyone's favorite. It's one of those things most people never get tired of. Ever try sugar on snow?"

"Nope."

She scooped up a ladle of hot syrup from the finishing pan, stepped outside and poured a thin stream over a mound of clean snow. "See? It hardens into the world's purest candy."

He broke off a piece and sampled it. "It's really good."

"When I'm feeling fancy, I make snowflakes and spiderwebs with it."

"Artistic, like your mom."

She couldn't stop smiling. How was it that everyone thought this guy was bad, just because he had long hair and came from nowhere? He was totally nice.

"How are you not the size of a linebacker from eating maple sugar all day, every day?" he asked.

She wondered if that was a compliment or merely an observation. "I've been on swim team since the third grade. Plus, I work like a rented mule around here. It's not just making sugar a few weeks out of the year. We have to take care of the trees so they'll be good producers. Then there's the firewood. I'm not much for cutting, but I've done my share. I usually drive the tractor with the stone boat behind it. In the summer, there's the garden and the critters. In the fall, the orchard keeps us busy. Apple cider."

"And you want to leave all this for the big city and a broadcasting career."

"Oh, hell, yes. Please. Why does that surprise you?"

He studied her in a way she wasn't used to—as if he was really seeing her. Not just her long dark hair and her boobs, but seeing who she was.

"Because just now when you were talking about this place, you looked like the happiest person in the world," he said.

"I did?"

"You did."

"Well. I suppose that's because I *am* happy. But I want to be happy trying something else, something I've always dreamed of doing."

"Fair enough."

"What about you? What are your plans after graduation?"

"I'll probably work with my dad. He needs the extra help getting his business off the ground."

Her spirits dampened just a bit. Her mother was constantly warning her about hometown boys with no ambition. "They'll hold you back," Mom would say. "They never amount to anything. They want to settle down and raise a family, same as their parents and grandparents."

Annie didn't necessarily see that as a bad thing. But doing exactly that hadn't worked out for her parents. No wonder her mother was so skeptical.

"So you're interested in being a mechanic," she ventured.

He grinned. "I'm interested in girls and beer. And maple syrup. I just added that to the list."

6

Fletcher Wyndham stuck around through the rest of the sugar season, coming up the mountain each day at the end of school, and all day Saturday and Sunday. True to his word, Gordy brought on his two older sisters. Paula and Roberta were large, like Gordy, but a lot more outgoing, and they seemed to love the outdoors. They gathered and hauled and worked as hard as any man.

Every day as Annie finished up the boiling, Fletcher would come into the sugar shack and they would talk—about school, life, family, the future, everything. She could listen to him talk all day. She liked the cadence of his voice and the light in his eyes when he looked at her. She liked his large hands and the easy, athletic grace with which he moved. She liked him in ways she'd never felt for a boy before.

She wondered what it would be like to go all the way with him. Sex was still this big unknown thing to her, even though she thought about it all the time. It was like Europe—a place she studied and yearned to visit, but hadn't had the opportunity yet. She was just waiting for her moment.

All her instincts and urges told her that Fletcher Wyndham was her moment. Yet even though he was totally easy to talk to, she couldn't figure out how to bring up the topic with him. Based on her past boyfriends, she figured all she had to do was offer, and he'd jump at the chance. She didn't want to do that, though. Fletcher mattered to her. His opinion mattered. She didn't want him to think she was easy, or worse, using him.

He might not like her at all in that way. How could a girl tell? They needed to get to know each other better. Maybe then it would happen naturally.

"There's a cooking competition at the Culinary Institute down in Montpelier on Saturday," she said one day as she was finishing the boiling. "Want to come?"

"And do what?" He peered at her through the steam rising from the evaporator. "I know how to make a few things, but competitively? Probably not."

"No, you'd watch *me* cook," she said. Then she blushed. "I realize it doesn't sound like a barrel of laughs, but—"

"Sure," he said. "Sounds great."

On Saturday morning. Gran helped her load her ingredients into an ice chest and wished her luck. "Are you taking the pickup?" Gran asked.

"I'm getting a ride with a friend," Annie said.

"Oh?" This was code for "You'd better explain yourself."

"Fletcher, one of the guys who's been working for Kyle." Annie noted her grandmother's furrowed brow. "He's fine. He's in my grade at school, and we're friends."

"I see." More code, this time meaning "Don't get in trouble." Gran studied Annie's face in that way she had, her dark eyes calm with wisdom. "So your friend, he's interested in cooking?"

"I think he's interested in me," Annie admitted. "At least, I hope he is." She slipped out the back door before anyone else was up, which was good, because her mom would probably give her a hard time. By the time Fletcher pulled into the driveway, she felt totally energized about the whole day.

"I love these competitions," she told him as they headed downstate to Montpelier. "Does that make me a show-off?"

"Maybe," he said.

"Nobody likes a show-off."

"Somebody likes you." He kept his eyes on the road. She could see a slight smile playing about his lips, and a warm, melty feeling spread all through her. After a couple of minutes, he turned on the radio, and they talked about the music they liked. She was a fan of new alternative, like Nelly Furtado and Cake. He liked his dad's old tunes—the Smiths, Led Zeppelin, David Bowie. She promised to put some of his favorites on her iPod.

By the time she entered the teaching kitchen at the New England Culinary Institute, Annie was feeling cocky about her entry. The theme of the competition was locally sourced cheddar cheese, and she had perfected her recipe for a cheddar, apple, and beer soup that used apples and cider from Rush Mountain.

"I'm sorry if this is weird for you," she told Fletcher as he took a seat in the gallery behind the adjudicators. "Usually, my grandmother or my friend Pam comes along, but they couldn't get away from the sugaring."

"It's not weird," he said. Then he looked around at the eclectic group of foodies and added, "Well, it is, but in a good way. Go knock 'em dead."

Maybe being too cocky was going to jinx her, she thought as she set out her ingredients and got to work. The student chefs were no slouches. There were dishes in flaky puff pastry, creations with truffle oil and gourmet foam, concoctions featuring foraged ingredients, fancy cuts of meat, homemade pasta. By comparison, her rustic soup seemed humble. She kept her game face on as she expertly put together apples, carrots, celery, and potatoes with beer made by Pam's dad, and stock she had simmered to perfection the night before. Every single ingredient down to the sprig of thyme came from within a few miles of home. Whirled in a blender with local cheddar and cream, the soup was smooth and comforting. The only fancy touch was a swirl of crème fraîche on top.

The judges—a celebrity chef from Boston and two instructors—sampled each dish, then invited the spectators to do the same. Annie's hopes rose as the pot of rich, cheddary soup disappeared, clearly an audience favorite. Fletcher gave her a thumbs-up sign. And the celebrity chef—Tyrone Tippet of Soul, a Boston institution—took her aside and said, "You got something there, girl. I love watching you cook."

"Really?" Annie nearly burst with pride.

"Uh-huh. The knife skills, the connection with the food. And you were looking at the audience like you wanted to give them all a hug. Even better was the way they were looking at you."

She flushed, knowing that Fletcher was the reason for that. "And how was the soup?"

"Tasty and perfectly seasoned," he assured her. "You know that, right?" He gave her his card. "I'm not the only judge, but if you're ever down in Boston, get in touch."

She knew then that she hadn't won. This was confirmed when the rankings were announced. Sticking the gold-and-white honorable mention ribbon into her backpack, she joined Fletcher in the foyer of the auditorium. "Well," she said. "That sucked. Sorry you had to come all this way to watch me lose."

"You're no loser," he said as they walked out together. "Yours was the best by far."

The more time Annie spent with him, the more she liked him. And the more she thought about sex.

"I can't believe the winner was mac and cheese," she grumbled. "How could they pick mac and cheese, of all things?"

"Bacon," Fletcher said. "Duh."

"Hey." She fake-punched him on the shoulder. "There was white truffle oil involved, too. Damn you, white truffle oil. And how is that a local product?"

On the drive home, she told him what the celebrity chef had said about her cooking, and the way people watched her, the connection she felt to the food and the audience. "Do you think it's strange," she asked Fletcher, "me being so into cooking, the way other people are into sports or music?"

"It's not weird," he said. "It's cool that you like something that much."

"I do," she said, tracing a foggy spot on the window with her finger. A heart. A flower. A bud about to burst. Sometimes she felt so full of dreams that she nearly exploded, like a kernel of popcorn in hot oil. *Pow.* "It's not just the food. I feel really greedy admitting this, but I want everything," she confessed to him.

"Everything? You might need to be more specific."

"I want everything in the world to happen to me," she said.

"Tsunamis? Avalanches?"

"Oh, come on. I mean like ocean waves and bullet trains and hunting for truffles and getting lost in a foreign city. I just want to see it all and try everything."

He glanced over at her, then turned his eyes to the road. "I have no doubt that you will."

He reached over and found a radio station playing nineties music. By the time they got to Switchback, it was getting dark. In the in-between season—not deep winter, but not spring either—the town had a bleak, exhausted look. Fletcher tapped the horn as they passed his father's place, renamed GreenTree Garage. She could see his father inside, working under a car that had been hoisted up on a lift. The garage itself looked bleak, with faded signs and rubber belts hanging from the walls, stacks of tires and oily-looking tools everywhere.

She wondered if Fletcher had other dreams besides working alongside his father, but couldn't think of a way to ask him without sounding insulting.

He drove up the mountain to her house and walked her to the door. The sounds of dinner in progress clattered from the kitchen.

"Want to come in?" she asked. "You could stay for supper."

He smiled and touched his stomach. "I filled up on samples at the contest."

"Me, too." She felt a mixture of disappointment and relief. She wanted to spend more time with him, but knew that bringing him to meet her family would be awkward. They would be totally nice, of course. They were always nice. However, there would be nosy questions and weird silences and forced conversation. She didn't want to subject him to that.

He stood for a moment, looking down at her. Then, with unhurried deliberation, he cupped one hand around her head and the other at her waist. With a gentle tug, he pulled her against him, leaned down, and kissed her.

She knew instantly that it was *that* kind of kiss, the kind that had the power to stop time. She would lie awake thinking about it half the night, and wake up in the morning still dreaming of this moment. It was the best feeling in the world. She had never felt this way about anyone. Ever. It was intense and euphoric and wholly exciting. Now she couldn't imagine how she'd lived for eighteen years without this blissful sensation.

"See you around," he whispered.

"Bye, Fletcher."

After he drove away, she walked into the house without even feeling the floor beneath her feet. Her family sat around the long table—her mother; Kyle and his wife, Beth; and the kids.

"Looks like a winner's smile on your face," Beth said, setting some cut up green beans on Lucas's high-chair tray. "Did you bring home first prize?"

"Not even close," Annie said, still floating in a cloud of bliss. Kissing Fletcher Wyndham was so much bigger than a dumb award. She couldn't even remember what disappointment felt like. She drifted over to the sink and washed her hands.

"The competition must have been rigged, then," her mother said loyally. "No way something could taste better than your beer cheddar soup. I'm sorry, sweetheart."

"It's fine."

"Did your friend like the competition?" asked Gran with a knowing look.

Annie couldn't stop smiling. "Fletcher liked it," she said softly. "He likes *me*."

"Fletcher Wyndham? That new boy?" Mom asked.

"He's not new anymore. He's been working the whole sugar season, right, Kyle?"

Kyle merely nodded, leaning over to cut up Dana's chicken.

"I don't think he should be hanging around so much," her mother said, passing the breadbasket. "You seem distracted by him."

Annie flashed a smile. "Uh-huh."

"You need to focus on your future."

"I just spent the day at a competition."

"True, but you said you didn't do as well as you usually do. Could that be because you were distracted?"

"Yes, exactly," Annie said. "I was making googly eyes at Fletcher and I didn't cook well."

"Oh, sweetie. You know that's not what I'm saying. I just want to see you going for your dreams."

"That's what Dad did, and you're still mad about it."

Beth and Gran watched Annie and her mom like spectators at a tennis match. Kyle and the kids dug into their dinner, oblivious.

"Your father left his family behind. It's completely different. Annie, this is your special time to create the life you want, all by yourself. You're at the beginning, when anything is possible. Don't let your choices be influenced by this boy."

"Mom." Annie bristled. "You don't even know him."

Her mother pursed her lips. "I know more than you think. You mark my words, Fletcher Wyndham will never give you anything but trouble."

7

Now

"All rise. The court is now in session," the bailiff announced, "the Honorable Fletcher Wyndham presiding."

"Please be seated," Fletcher told the room as he took his place at the bench. The courthouse was a venerable old building, its chambers drafty with echoes that seemed to whisper a sense of gravitas to the setting. Not so long ago, Fletcher used to walk past the place on his way to school or to his dad's garage, never imagining this would one day be his domain.

There was a general shuffling and scraping of chairs, a thumping of briefcases, and murmured conversation as people settled in. As he arranged his papers and gavel, Fletcher scanned the courtroom—clerks and lawyers, a few nervous-looking clients, Natty Gilmore from the *Gazette,* the court reporter and deputy, an observer or two. All eyes were trained on him.

When he'd first taken the bench, Fletcher used to feel massively self-conscious, entering the courtroom in his robe, knowing he was the center of everyone's attention. Knowing he sometimes had the responsibility of changing the direction of someone's life. Who would he help today? Who was hurting, angry, frustrated? Who had done something completely stupid and needed a way out? What fine shadings of the law would he interpret?

He felt his mobile phone vibrate in his pocket, but ignored it. His rules for mobile devices in the courtroom were strict, and he adhered to them, too. Friday-morning court was a grab bag. He and his secretary had already reviewed the day's administrative matters and routine proceedings. Today's schedule yielded the typical variety of business—a status conference, hearings, requests—with one possibly interesting twist. Earl Mahoney was suing some guy from Texas for selling him a breeding bull that had turned out to be sterile. The seller allegedly knew the bull couldn't perform, but sold it anyway. Trouble was, Vermont had no jurisdiction over Jimbo Childress, the Texan, because Jimbo had never been to Vermont or done business there. Earl, never one to give up, had arranged it so Childress "won" a free leaf-looking trip to Vermont last fall to view the glorious colors of autumn. As the unsuspecting Texan settled into his cozy B&B in the charming town of Putnam, a process server had delivered the summons to him.

Tag, Jimbo, thought Fletcher. You're it. He allowed the suit to go forward. And then he thought, Damn. I love my job.

Although he worked methodically through morning court, Fletcher never allowed himself to get bored or impatient, even though a good number of cases were tedious. He never allowed himself to check his phone, which had been vibrating with text messages every few minutes. He kept his attention on the cases before him. Some were frustrating or impossibly petty, like the woman claiming damages for emotional distress caused by visiting a haunted house at Halloween, or the man suing the school district after his son was cut from the hockey team for skipping class. Others involved ridiculous amounts of paperwork. A seventy-five-page motion was not uncommon, and Fletcher was one of those judges who read everything.

That was his job. And he knew from painful personal experience that a person's day in court might just be the worst day of his life. The least a judge could do was pay attention.

Today, Earl Mahoney left, satisfied that his sterile-bull issue would be resolved. A couple of motions were granted, a subpoena quashed. After the lunch recess, Fletcher endured a two-hour debate from opposing lawyers over a property-rights dispute. More motion hearings. A status conference. A merits hearing. In a small town, a judge had to wear many hats, dealing with whatever came through the door.

The bailiff passed a note to him. Fletcher looked at it briefly, and instantly felt a knot tighten in his gut.

"We're going to take a fifteen-minute recess," he said, punctuating the statement with his gavel. He exited through the side door and went down a short hallway to his chambers.

The door was ajar. Inside, a boy wearing Fletcher's extra robe was standing on an upended wastebasket so that the robe draped to the floor, making him look freakishly tall. He brandished a letter opener like a weapon. No, like a wizard's wand. He was working his way through the entire Harry Potter series, and dreamed of going to wizard school.

"Hey, Teddy," Fletcher said.

The kid turned in startlement, and the wastebasket tipped over.

"Whoa," said Fletcher, lunging for him. Too late. Teddy hit the floor, and the letter opener flew from his hand, skittering across the hardwood planks. Fletcher sank down next to Teddy. "Hey, are you all right?"

"That depends," Teddy said in a small voice, "on how much trouble I'm in."

"You could have broken your neck."

Teddy rolled over and sat up. "Sorry, Dad."

"Hang that robe up," Fletcher said, grabbing the letter opener and the wastebasket. "What if you'd fallen on this letter opener, huh? What if it stabbed you in the liver and you bled out before the ambulance could get here?"

"Then you would have a giant mess to clean up," Teddy said with a fake-serious expression on his face.

Fletcher watched the boy carefully putting the robe on a hanger. "What are you doing here, anyway? I thought you were going to your mom's after school."

"I am," Teddy said. "She told me to meet her here, because she's coming to talk to you."

Oh, joy. "I've got court," said Fletcher. As if she didn't know that.

"I'll be quick," said a voice from the doorway.

"Hi, Mom," Teddy said, going over to give her a brief hug.

She brushed his sandy hair out of his eyes. "Hi, baby." Then she turned to Fletcher. "I want to move."

"I don't," Teddy protested. *"Dad."*

Fletcher clenched his jaw to keep in the words he really wanted to say to Celia. "Teddy, go grab a snack in the break room."

"But—"

"We'll be done here in a few minutes," Fletcher said. "I'll see you later, okay?"

Heaving a sigh, Teddy picked up his backpack and left the room.

Fletcher turned to face Celia. She looked gorgeous and perfectly groomed, as always. Shiny yellow hair and shiny red nails, flawless veneered teeth. His trophy ex-wife. "Did you really have to say that in front of him?"

"Teddy knows I want to move."

"And you're welcome to do that. But Teddy stays with me."

"You know very well I'd never abandon my son," she said.

"Then move after he's grown." Yes, he thought. Move to Timbuktu.

"He's only ten. I don't want to wait until he's grown. There's nothing for me in this town. Everything here sucks."

"Jesus, do you hear yourself? What brought this on?" Shit, was there another boyfriend? One who didn't like the commute to a small Vermont town?

"I can't keep living like this," Celia said.

"Like what?" he asked. "Like someone who doesn't want to get a job because it interferes with all that shopping and travel?"

She sniffed. "Fletch, can't we all move to Boston? We were happy there when we first married, right? You could join a big firm with a partner track, or—"

"I'm not moving to Boston." He spoke quietly, even though he felt like yelling. "Teddy's life is here."

"What about *my* life?" she asked.

Fletcher's patience ran out. "What the hell do you want? You ended up with everything you said you wanted in the divorce, remember? The house, the Florida condo, both cars, shared custody, the retirement plan, half of all the assets—"

"Don't reduce me to a cliché. I wanted a truly meaningful life with you, Fletcher."

"You found meaning in shopping."

"Very funny. Did my happiness ever really matter to you?"

He didn't reply. He honestly didn't know the answer. What he had come to understand about Celia was that she would probably never be happy. There was always something more for her to want—a better house, a country-club membership, a vacation home in South Beach, expensive jewelry, a more prestigious social life—but attaining it never brought her joy. Her anger swirled in the atmosphere like a toxin.

She loved Teddy. That was something he'd never dispute. Everybody loved Teddy, the way everyone loved a new puppy on a sunny day. Their son was affectionate and funny and smart, the kind of kid other parents approved of and teachers complimented.

It was particularly gratifying for Fletcher, because he himself had never been that kid. He'd been the outsider, the newcomer, the motherless boy, an object of suspicion. He never wanted Teddy to feel that kind of pain, so he'd made a commitment to raise his son in the most stable, secure place he knew—right here in Switchback. Initially, Celia had agreed, but her contentment hadn't lasted. She always seemed to need something that hovered just out of reach.

He reclaimed his patience with an effort. "I need to get back to the courtroom. Can we finish this discussion another time?"

She glared at him, her beautiful sky-blue eyes turning cold. "There's nothing to discuss. I don't know why I thought you'd open your heart and your mind to me."

"My focus is Teddy. He needs us both." Fletcher softened his tone. "If you absolutely have to live somewhere else, you're free to do that. Just—please—find a way to stay in our son's life."

Her glare turned to sadness. "You know I can't live without Teddy."

"And he can't live without his mom."

She looked at him for a long moment. He could see the fight go out of her as she turned toward the door. "Tell Teddy I'll see him later, okay?"

Fletcher took a moment to get his head back into the law. The uneven wooden floor and wavy glass windowpanes of his chambers bore testament to the age of the building, which dated back to the 1880s. His framed credentials hung on the wall, and there was a plaque with engraved nameplates of all his predecessors, men and women who had walked these floors and deliberated the law for decades. These chambers had once housed Emerson Gaines, who had gone on to serve on the Supreme Court.

Fletcher had the distinction of being the youngest judge in the state. Some days, however, the youngest judge in the state didn't feel so young. A lot of life had happened to him while other people his age were still revving their engines. He hadn't planned it that way. But he hadn't been given a choice either.

Most people looked forward to Friday nights. Fridays were for decompressing, kicking back, activating weekend mode. Pizza and movies. Games at the high school—football, hockey, or basketball, depending on the season. Happy hour or dinner with friends. Fletcher was not most people. He had no particular fondness for Fridays when he had to surrender his son to his ex.

After work at court, a bunch of the guys went out for a pickup game of hoops, then pitchers of beer afterward at the Switchback Brewpub. When Teddy was with his mother, Fletcher often joined them. Then he would return home to an empty house, with the empty weekend stretching out in front of him.

This was the arrangement he had agreed to in the divorce, and he was obligated to stick to it. Life was better since he and Celia had split up. He had a house in the village, close to Teddy's school and to the courthouse. He'd dated, but nothing serious developed. Deep down, he probably didn't want anything serious. He was good at a lot of things, but making a relationship last didn't appear to be one of them.

Court business was just wrapping up at the end of the day when Gordy Jessop rushed into the courtroom, his ill-fitting suit jacket flapping, his breath coming in agitated huffs. Despite his disheveled appearance, Gordy was a good lawyer who had built a vibrant local practice over the past few years. In the days when he'd been with a rival firm, Fletcher had gone against him plenty of times. And Gordy had handled Fletcher's divorce.

"It's late, I know," said Gordy. "Sorry, Your Honor."

Fletcher glanced at the clock over the courtroom door. Shoot. He didn't want to keep his staff late on a Friday.

"What's up, Counselor?" he asked Gordy.

"I've got a petition here to revoke a power of attorney," said Gordy. He submitted the documents, which had been stamped by the clerk. The ink scarcely looked dry.

Fletcher didn't relish reading through the long sheaf of documents, but he couldn't very well make a ruling without doing that.

"Is it an emergency?"

"Um, no. Not really. But it's urgent."

"Have Mildred schedule it for Monday."

"Your Honor." Gordy shuffled from foot to foot as though he had to take a whiz. "If you could just give it a look..."

Gordy wasn't usually this insistent. Fletcher set his jaw. He glanced down at the motion, then blinked, not sure he could trust his own eyes.

The action was being taken on behalf of Annie Rush, FKA Annie Rush Harlow.

Annie Rush.

Despite the passage of time, the memories and feelings had never completely faded. Now, seeing the name on the pages of a court document, Fletcher felt weirdly self-conscious in the presence of the people lingering in the courtroom. Just the thought of her brought a flood of remembrance—dark-lashed, laughing eyes. A face that could light the world. A heart full of dreams. Joy and anger and hopelessness. And finally, surrender.

Although his heart was beating fast, Fletcher maintained his usual demeanor of professional detachment. "What happened, Counselor?"

"Her family—specifically her mother—needs the power of attorney revoked. It was assigned to her husband, a guy named..." He consulted one of the forms.

"Martin Harlow," Fletcher muttered.

"Yes. Her situation has changed radically." Gordy glanced over his shoulder at the nearly empty courtroom. The afternoon light outside the window was fading. Gordy looked back at Fletcher. Then he leaned in, lowering his voice. "Fletcher. Annie needs you."

"Thank you for expediting this," Caroline Rush said to Fletcher. "Annie doesn't need a power of attorney anymore. Especially not—" She stopped herself from saying Martin's name. "And for stopping by the house. You didn't have to do that."

"I wanted to. I'm sorry about what happened to Annie."

Caroline's hand shook as she carefully placed the legal document in its folder. She felt an overwhelming sense of relief along with sadness and apprehension. Once upon a time, she had joyfully given her daughter to Martin Harlow, believing Annie's future was secure with a husband who would love her forever. Now Caroline was taking her daughter back, and she had no idea what to believe anymore.

"Sit down," she said, gesturing at the kitchen table. "I just made a pot of coffee."

"Thanks."

She set down the French press along with a plate of salted maple shortbread cookies. "I don't have the baking skills of my mother or my daughter," she said, "but I find that if you use enough butter and maple syrup in a recipe, you don't need much skill."

He tasted one, and the expression on his face was gratifying. "Good to know."

Fletcher Wyndham hadn't been Caroline's favorite, back when he'd been Annie's boyfriend. Caroline hadn't seen the potential there. All she'd seen was an obstacle to her daughter's future. In the eyes of a mother wanting a glorious future for her child, he was merely the son of a drifter, a kid who would probably stagnate in his blue-collar job at the garage, drink beer, and play the lottery, eventually turning soft and directionless in middle age.

Looking at him now, she felt shame and regret. She wished she had looked deeper and seen an extraordinary young man. The fact was, she hadn't looked at all. Her problem with Fletcher Wyndham had nothing to do with Fletcher Wyndham. Or with Annie, for that matter. It was Caroline who was the problem.

Enough with this Fletcher kid, Caroline had said to Annie, when her daughter was teetering on the verge of changing her mind about college. Now Caroline had to admit to herself that what she was really saying was *Enough with this Ethan Lickenfelt.*

Oh, she had loved that boy in his boxy white grocery truck. She'd been naive enough to believe that loving him would be enough to create a life of blissful perfection, no matter what. At eighteen, she hadn't understood that frustration and hardship had the power to corrode even the deepest love and thwart the most yearned-for dreams.

The divide between the life Ethan wanted and the one he'd found on Rush Mountain had ruined their marriage. They were both committed to their kids and their family, but ultimately, the strain took its toll. There were only so many lies a person could tell herself before she had to let in the truth.

"Mrs. Rush?" Fletcher's voice broke into her thoughts.

She wasn't Mrs. Rush. She wasn't Mrs. anything. "Please call me Caroline."

"Caroline. I was just wondering what you thought."

"Sorry, I wasn't listening," she confessed.

"This must be really stressful for you," he said.

"Yes . . . but it's not just that. I wanted to tell you I'm sorry."

He frowned. "For what?"

She sighed and pushed the plate of cookies toward him. "It's a long-overdue apology. Really long, Fletcher, and it's awful that I haven't said anything until now. But I want you to know, I was wrong about you, back when you first moved to Switchback. A lot of people were wrong about you."

He gave a quick, slightly crooked smile. One thing Caroline had *not* been wrong about—the boy was stunningly good-looking. But that had been part of her problem with Fletcher. How could a guy that gorgeous possibly be trusted?

"Don't feel bad," he said to her. "Now that I have a kid of my own, I get how protective a parent feels."

"Thank you, but that's no excuse. I never bothered to know you, and that wasn't fair."

"I imagine you were more concerned with Annie. Besides, I was probably a little shit, anyway. The longer I work at court, the more I'm convinced that most guys are at that age."

"When I think of the role I played in keeping you apart, I feel ashamed. None of this would have happened if I'd left the two of you alone."

"Believe me, you weren't the cause of our breakup—not the first time, or the second. Annie and I managed to screw things up on our own."

"Good of you to say. But that Martin Harlow. He ought to be strung up by the balls."

"I can't help you with that," he said.

"He brought her here from L.A. via medical transport, as if she were a piece of defective merchandise, can you imagine?"

"I . . . no. I can't."

"I'm grateful she's here, though. She needs her family. Now more than ever. Her care team says it could be weeks or months before she can come home, but you know Annie. When she sets her mind to something, nothing can stop her."

He nodded. "That's the Annie I knew."

They were quiet, sipping the last of their coffee. Caroline offered a refill, but he shook his head.

"I heard about your divorce," she said. "I'm sorry."

"This might be stating the obvious, but I'll say it anyway—it happens to the best of us."

"After my divorce, people told me I should look at it as a chance to learn and grow." Have I done that? she wondered. Some days, she wasn't so sure. "It's a big change, I know. How's your little boy?"

"Teddy's fantastic. Confused about the situation, but I'm keeping things as stable as I can for him. Bought a place on Henley Street—the old Webster house. The remodel was a major project. Teddy likes being close to school."

Caroline felt another wave of regret. Fletcher seemed like a good man. Why had she never bothered to get to know him? "And what about you? Do you like it?"

He grinned. "After doing all that remodeling, I'm never moving."

8

Then

"We're moving," said Fletcher's dad, dropping a bomb into the middle of his senior year of high school.

"Again?" Fletcher set aside his civics textbook and glared up at his father. The TV was blaring the news that never seemed to cease—the whole country was trying to figure out how to wage war against a terrorist group called the Taliban. Last September 11, the world had been turned inside out by the attacks on the Pentagon and World Trade Center. A couple of Fletcher's buddies had already made commitments to enlist in the military as soon as school ended. Now, with his father's sudden announcement, Fletcher contemplated enlisting. "I'm not going with you," he stated.

"You don't have a choice. I need you, son. And you're gonna love this," Dad said, his eyes lighting the way they did when he was convinced he was onto something.

Fletcher wasn't convinced of anything. He glared at the TV, which showed soldiers being moved around the desert in lumbering transport vehicles. "When?" he demanded.

"After Christmas break."

"Shit, Dad." He looked around the little bungalow. Same shabby furniture they had schlepped from place to place, different house. He'd been okay with living in Dover, where they'd been since last summer.

School here didn't suck. He was looking at the home stretch toward graduation and thinking about what to do after. "Shit," he said again.

"Knock it off. This is a sweet deal. I bought myself a business up in Vermont—"

"Vermont?" Fletcher flashed on images of maple trees and snow. Endless acres of snow. And . . . what else? Ben & Jerry's. Cheddar and Cabot cheese. Autumn leaves. *Shit.*

Moving was the story of his life with his dad. Fletcher tried to count on his fingers the number of moves they had made. Oklahoma, Texas, Virginia, one of the Carolinas—he scarcely remembered which one—Indiana, Delaware . . . He ran out of fingers. And now this. Freaking Vermont.

His father was forever chasing after the next big thing that would put them on Easy Street. The trouble was, nothing ever panned out, because his ideas were nutty. He had once started a business turning urns of ashes into underwater reefs. He'd bought into a theme park for grown-ups featuring heavy equipment. Then there had been that herd of goats for rent to clear brush, the pizza delivery on an Italian scooter with speakers blaring Andrea Bocelli . . . If an idea was weird and doomed to fail, his dad embraced it.

"This time," Dad said, the way he always did, "things are going to be different. You'll see."

"Sure I will," said Fletcher. The idea of slogging through another move in pursuit of another nutty idea made his head hurt.

"I got a line on a car repair garage from a guy who's retiring and selling everything. The deal comes with a ready-made clientele, all the equipment and inventory we need, ready to go. This is the only garage for miles. It's a no-brainer," his dad said.

Meaning, thought Fletcher, if you had no brain, you'd think it was a good deal.

"And there's a major bonus," Dad went on. "Scooters."

"Scooters. You mean like motorbikes?" That piqued Fletcher's interest. Just a little.

"You betcha. Thanks to some obscure import-export law, Vermont is the best place to import a vintage scooter. I handle the paperwork, and we collect a nice chunk of the fee. It's a super deal. And I got this amazing espresso machine, a commercial one from Italy, too. We can set up an espresso bar right in the garage."

"Cool," Fletcher said. "Let's add a massage table. 'Sanford's Garage, Scooter Works, Espresso, and Massage.' "

"And a nail salon," Dad added. "Chicks love nail salons, right?"

"You would know."

"Quit being a smart-ass."

Fletcher knew he could argue until he ran out of words, but he also knew it would be pointless to bring up the myriad objections and pitfalls. His dad always had a ready answer for everything, even if the answer was wrong.

"If I change schools now, I might not be able to graduate on time." Holy crap. That would truly suck.

His father scratched his head. "What do you need to graduate for? You're already smart enough."

Fletcher slammed the civics book shut. "Oh, I don't know. Maybe so I have a shot at going to college? And yeah, I know the whole story of how you left home at sixteen and made a life for yourself without having to waste time in a classroom. But I'm not you, Dad."

"Agreed. You're ten times smarter than I'll ever be. That's why I need you, Fletch. Just help me get this thing off the ground, and you won't have to worry about me." He glowered at the two sets of coveralls hanging by the front door. They were from the express-oil-change place where they had both been working since the move to Dover, an outfit called Here We Go Lube-B-Lube. The place sucked ass, but it paid the rent—just barely. "That's a dead end for sure," his dad said, indicating the coveralls. "We'll be in charge of the whole show at the garage in Vermont."

Fletcher knew when an argument was lost. So with a dull sense of resignation, he simply shrugged his shoulders and said, "Cool."

The next week, they packed all their belongings into a rented trailer, hitched it up behind the pickup truck, and drove from Delaware to Vermont.

Fletcher tried not to think about what he was leaving behind—a few friends he liked to go mountain biking or to the shore with, a girlfriend named Kayla who had cried in his arms when he said good-bye, and a steady job at the oil-change place. By now, he had stopped hoping life would settle into some normal pattern. He simply went along with whatever plan his dad dreamed up, expecting nothing. Except maybe a catch. There always seemed to be a catch, some reason the plan would go awry, and they'd find themselves broke and on the road again.

The town was called Switchback, which already sounded odd to Fletcher. In order to get there, they drove along icy, snowy roads over rolling hills and up into granite mountains, winding around hairpin curves that had probably given the town its name. The higher they climbed, the colder and snowier the landscape became. The sky was a flat gray—the color of cold. Fletcher had never experienced winter quite like this—rolling acres of snow, the roadside piled high with dirty plowed snowbanks, the sky a bleak, colorless expanse of nothingness.

Finally they passed a hand-carved wooden sign that read *Switchback, Vermont. Elevation: 2207. Population: 7647.* The next sign, from the Chamber of Commerce, proclaimed, *Welcome to Switchback. Once You Switch, You'll Never Go Back.*

Har, har.

In the town center, the speed limit went down to twenty miles per hour. Fletcher had seen pictures of typical New England villages, and this place was even more . . . villagey. There was a white-steepled church and a village green with a railed gazebo, a pillared library called an atheneum, shops and small businesses that reeked of quaintness, and a grand, solid block of a high school with a notice on the marquee—*Home of the Fighting Wildcats.* The side streets were lined with slender trees and painted wooden houses, the picket-fenced yards nearly buried under thick blankets of snow.

The main feature of the town was the courthouse, a perfectly symmetrical New England classic with 1878 spelled out in the stonework in Roman numerals. The stately and majestic building sat at the entrance to a park. With the lights glowing in the windows and in the bell cupola atop the roof, the courthouse was beautiful and peaceful-looking. A handful of clerks and lawyers with briefcases were on their way home, descending the wide steps beneath the front columns.

Business looked slow at the local shops and cafés. Clearly, January was not the most popular month for tourist outings to Vermont.

Dad stopped at Sweet Maria's Coffee Shop, which smelled like heaven—coffee and baked goods and onions on the grill. They had a bite to eat, and Dad asked a guy sitting at the counter for directions to the Rookery, where they were going to stay until Dad found a place to rent. They could hardly understand the guy's speech. It sounded like a "shawt hop to Mahket Squay-ah."

The Rookery turned out to be a bed-and-breakfast inn filled with fussy-looking antiques and doilies on every surface. When they dumped their shabby duffel bags in the foyer, the hostess—Mildred Deacon—did not visibly wrinkle her nose, although Fletcher suspected she was doing it in her mind.

The day he enrolled as a new student at Switchback High School, he had one goal. He intended to turn invisible. He wanted to keep a low profile and somehow get himself to the end of the year so he could move on with his life.

He knew the drill. He had to submit his school records to the administration, meet with a counselor, and get a schedule of classes. He hoped he'd end up with enough credits to graduate.

The school counselor was a woman named Ms. Elkins, who sat on one of those big inflated fitness balls behind a cluttered desk as she went through his records. She had a gap between her two front teeth, streaks of purple in her hair, and horn-rimmed glasses with pointy corners.

"Five schools in four years," she said. "And this is number six. Wow."

Fletcher said nothing. She didn't seem to expect a reply. Through the window of the counseling office, he could see students arriving for the day. They looked like kids anywhere, moving around in social clumps, talking loudly, and shoving back and forth as they made their way to lockers and homerooms. Most were bundled up against the cold, in puffy jackets, tall boots, hats with earflaps.

"Your grades are excellent." Ms. Elkins said this with some surprise.

He nodded again, just wanting the meeting to be over.

"In order to satisfy the graduation requirements," she continued, "you're going to need to finish senior English, a science with a lab, a foreign language, and a PE credit." She drummed a pencil on the desk, then turned to her computer, studying the screen with deep concentration. "I think we can make this work. So here's the deal. I can get the schedule you need if you forfeit a study hall and take AP English. Does that sound doable?"

"Sure," he said. *Whatever.*

"Your homeroom is the industrial arts shop with Mr. Dow."

"Okay."

"What about extracurriculars?" she asked. "Sports, clubs? Theater? Band?"

God, no. "Uh, no, ma'am."

She filled out a form and hit print. "What brings you to Switchback?"

"My dad bought a garage and import business in town," he said.

"Oh—Crestfield's garage," she said in a chirpy tone. "Of course. Everybody takes all their repair jobs there. Mr. Crestfield is retiring, I hear. So your dad's a mechanic."

"That's right." Despite his lack of business sense, Sanford Wyndham had a God-given gift. He could fix anything. Through the years, he had repaired car and boat engines, small motors, huge generators, golf carts, wind machines, bulldozers, tractors—if it had moving parts, he could fix it. He'd always wanted a garage of his own, but could never afford to set himself up in business until now. Apparently a repair garage in the middle of a frozen nowhere carried a low price tag.

"Do you work on cars, too?"

"Yes," he said. "I'll be working for my dad after school and on weekends." Fletcher was good at fixing things, too. He didn't really have a choice, since he and his dad rarely had the dough to pay someone else to do the work.

"And after graduation?" she asked. "What are your plans?"

"Um." Get the hell out. Was that a plan? "I guess I'll keep helping my dad. Maybe something else."

"Have you applied to any colleges?"

Right, he thought. College. What's that? "No, ma'am."

"Well," said Ms. Elkins. "We can talk about that more later. With your grades, you're a good prospect for college. Don't hesitate to come to me if you have any questions. Anything at all."

"All right. Thanks."

The schedule page whispered from the printer. She handed it to him. "It's a challenge, being new," she said. "I'm sure you'll do all right here. This is a nice group of students, and the teachers are top-notch. You'll fit right in."

"Sure, thanks," he said. The minute he stepped outside the office, a bell rang. Some kid slammed into Fletcher's shoulder.

"Hey," said the kid. "Watch where you're going."

Nice.

The corridor was overheated and smelled like wet dog. There were flyers taped to the walls announcing a swim meet, a bake sale, a rainbow rally, a dance.

Fletcher took a deep breath and merged into the jostle and flow of students making their way to class. He found his assigned locker, then made his way to homeroom—the industrial arts shop. He stepped inside and surveyed the room. Kids were milling around, slinging backpacks and talking loudly about nothing and everything. It could have been any classroom in any high school. He found an empty spot at a table across from a girl with long yellow hair and awesome boobs. Trying to keep his eyes on her face, he gave her a nod of greeting. "I'm Fletcher," he said. "It's my first day."

She gave him a slow once-over. "Lucky you," she said. "I'm Celia. Celia Swank." She had a nice smile. She had a nice . . . everything.

The instructor was a harried-looking guy named Mr. Dow. Fletcher went to introduce himself. He stood by the door to wait his turn. At the moment, he was facing off with a small, dark-haired girl who claimed to have an urgent need for a blowtorch.

"I can't let you take that out of here, Annie," he said. "What do you need it for, anyway?"

She indicated a tray of glass custard cups. "My maple crème brûlée," she said. "I'm making it in the home ec kitchen. Please. I'll bring it right back."

He scowled at her, then glanced up at the clock. "Okay, fine. I want it returned the second you're done."

"Thanks, Mr. Dow," she said brightly, putting the torch into an overstuffed bag. "I'll save you a sample."

"It's a deal."

The girl left with her bag and her tray, a sunshiny look on her face. Her gaze flicked to Fletcher and lingered a second. Big brown eyes, inquisitive but not hostile. He held the door for her.

"Oh, thanks!" she said, and headed out into the hallway.

Dizzy chick. She was cute, though. Maybe he could . . . no. He had no intention of making friends in the small mountain town. He didn't even think that was possible. Enrolling midyear in school was pretty much a guarantee that no one would bother with him. Even so, he made a note of her name—Annie.

The morning unfolded slowly. He met his teachers, grabbed copies of course outlines, signed out textbooks, the routine familiar and slightly depressing.

Then the lunch bell rang and there was a surge toward the cafeteria. He had learned from experience that it was always possible in any high school to find a spot to sit in the lunchroom. You just had to look for a quiet, weird, disenfranchised kid no one else wanted to hang out with, and boom. He'd be glad to share his table with you, no problem.

You just couldn't afford to be picky.

Fletcher made his way through the noisy cafeteria with his tray of oniony-smelling tacos and canned corn, and a dish of mud-colored pudding that made him yearn for that girl's blowtorched crème brûlée. He spotted a kid at the end of a table by himself. He was overweight and slow-moving, with a mournful expression and pale hands. He might have faded into the background, except he seemed to favor clothes that were wack—a plaid Sherlock Holmes cap, a fake military jacket, pant cuffs tucked into combat boots. Wearing a getup like that probably made him a target, but it sure didn't make him any friends. Maybe he liked the attention.

"Mind if I sit here?" asked Fletcher.

"Not at all." The mournful expression disappeared, and Fletcher introduced himself.

"Gordy Jessop. Class of 2002." Not surprisingly, there was more to discover about Gordy if you looked past the dorkiness. Over the next few days, Fletcher learned that he had three older sisters who called themselves "lumberjills," the female version of lumberjacks. His mother was a poet who published her work in chapbooks and gave them out for free at the farmers' market in the summer, and his father was a patent lawyer. Gordy spoke French, because his mom was from Quebec, and he liked to sprinkle his conversation with French phrases, another trait that didn't exactly endear him to other kids. He didn't seem to care about that, which Fletcher thought was kind of cool. Gordy also knew a freakish amount of Latin, which was hilarious, since it was a dead language, and he had a lint trap of random information in his brain.

"Did you know 'dreamt' is the only word in the English language that ends in the letters *MT*?" he asked one day at the end of Fletcher's first week in Switchback.

"Not if you're a bad speller," said Fletcher.

"Okay, did you know there's a basketball court on the top floor of the Supreme Court building?"

"Nobody knows that," said Fletcher.

"I do. Highest court in the land."

"Ha ha."

"I kid you not. And here's something—Montpelier is the only state capital in the U.S. without a McDonald's."

"That's a relief. So, what goes on around here on the weekends?"

"Hockey and swim meets. You interested in either?"

Fletcher shrugged his shoulders. "I can swim. Never tried ice hockey before."

"I mean as a spectator."

"Swimming, then, so long as it's girls swimming," he said.

"I need to get a weekend job," said Gordy. "Do you have a job?"

"Sort of, at my dad's shop. He's just getting the place up and running, so there's not much to do yet."

"We should get jobs for the sugar season," Gordy said.

Fletcher could always use more work. "What's the sugar season?" he asked.

Gordy guffawed, his expression incredulous. "Dude. The sugar season is the raison d'être for this whole region." He explained that as soon as the weather turned, the season would begin. Everyone with more than a few sugar maples in the yard tapped their trees and collected sap. The bigger commercial ops used a network of pipelines to collect the sap, and they either sold it or boiled it in big sugarhouses. All the local places needed temporary help tapping the trees, bringing the sap to the evaporators, manning the boilers, keeping the fires stoked, transporting barrels of syrup.

On Friday after school, they drove Gordy's old Bronco up Rush Mountain. "This operation has been around the longest. I bet they need plenty of help here," Gordy said, grinding the gears as he lurched up the winding road. He was a lousy driver. Apparently he knew this, because he glanced over at Fletcher with a sheepish expression. "I don't do so hot with a stick shift."

"Takes practice." Fletcher tried not to hurl as the truck veered around a hairpin curve.

"Yeah. I'm better on the downhill."

Great.

"Rush Mountain is thirty-seven hundred feet tall," Gordy said, whipping out another random fact. "It was named for Elijah Rush, a famous abolitionist during the Civil War. Don't ask me how I know that."

"I won't," Fletcher muttered as he tried to calm his stomach.

"The Underground Railroad was a big deal in these parts. Being so close to Canada and all."

"Good to know."

They passed a rustic painted sign that read *Welcome to the Rush Family Maple Farm. Home of Sugar Rush Small-Batch Maple Syrup.*

In the distance was a big, old-fashioned farmhouse, painted white, with a railed front porch and a fence still half buried in the snow. Chimneys jutted up from each end of the house, both of them sending a twist of smoke into the sky. It was really pretty, the kind of house Fletcher used to picture when he was a little kid, living in some rented apartment and wondering what it was like to have a regular family.

The turnoff to the house had a small sign that read *Private.*

Gordy drove in the opposite direction to a small parking area paved in an unpleasant mixture of gravel, mud, and snow. A sign pointed to an old farm building designated the office, and another to a rutted track that said *To the Sugarhouse.*

A shiny black pickup with dual exhaust pipes and a gun-club bumper sticker was parked near the office building.

"Great," said Gordy, parking next to it. "That's Degan Kerry's truck."

"Who's Degan—"

Three guys came out of the office. Two of them wore high school letterman jackets. The other one had on an old Soviet army coat.

"I guess you haven't had the pleasure," said Gordy. "He's the big guy with red hair in the middle. Equal parts hockey jock and douche bag."

"Well, hello there, ladies," the guy named Degan exclaimed with a wide, phony smile.

"Hey, Degan." Gordy seemed to shrink a couple of inches. "This is Fletcher Wyndham. He's new." He introduced the other two—Carl and Ivan.

Fletcher offered a quick social nod. The other three shoved their hands in their pockets and sized him up with slow, head-to-toe glances. "Good to meet you," Fletcher said in a neutral voice. He could already tell they were amateurs as far as tough guys went. He had survived four urban high schools prior to this, so he wasn't worried about these three.

"You gonna be working the sugar season?" asked Degan.

"That's the plan." Gordy sidled toward the office. "See you around," he said.

Fletcher offered another nod. Degan planted himself in the middle of the cleared path, shoving out his jaw in an obvious challenge. Fletcher refused to take the bait. "After you," he offered, stepping aside and making a sweeping gesture with his arm.

Degan stared at him for one heartbeat too long. Studying the narrowed eyes, Fletcher could see that the kid was full of shit, because there was a faint flicker of doubt in those eyes. A garden-variety coward. Then Degan passed by, his shoulder brushing Fletcher's with more force than was necessary.

Big deal. What a tool.

As they made their way to the office, Gordy sent Fletcher a worried look. "Hey, we can go down the hill to Peychaud's if you want. I hear they're hiring, too."

"You said Kyle Rush paid the best."

"Yeah, well." Gordy sighed. "Looks like Degan and his squad will be working here."

"So?"

"So do you still want to do this?"

"Yeah," he said. "I still want to." No way would Fletcher allow himself to be run off by a couple of high school punks. He was about to explain as much to Gordy when something caught his eye.

On the slope behind and above the farm office, a girl appeared, skimming across the field of untouched snow on a pair of snowshoes. Curly dark hair escaped her knitted red cap, and he recognized her. The blowtorch girl—Annie. She was accompanied by three dogs, tossing a stick for them to chase and wrestle over.

She moved and sounded like a young kid, and her laughter carried down the mountain. Then one of the dogs noticed Gordy and Fletcher, gave a warning bark, and barreled down the hill to challenge the intruders. The other two dogs followed suit, ignoring the girl's shouted command.

A moment later, they were surrounded by dogs, barking and wagging their tails. Fletcher held out his hand to a shaggy mongrel. "Hey, buddy," he said. "Easy, now."

The dog bowed playfully, then feinted away. The girl approached them. Her big brown eyes reflected the sun, and she had a face Fletcher could look at all day long.

"Oh, hey, Gordy," she said, then eyed Fletcher with a quizzical expression on her face. She was probably trying to place him.

"Hiya, Annie," Gordy said. "This is Fletcher. We're looking for your brother."

"Kyle is in the office." The dogs swirled around her, vying for attention. One of them nudged the stick toward her. She eyed Fletcher with a slight smile. She was even prettier when she smiled. Her cheeks were pink from the cold, and she had the longest eyelashes he'd ever seen. "You're going to be on the tapping crew?"

"If he needs the help," he said.

"Oh, he needs all the help he can get," she stated. "So I guess I'll see you around." Her gaze lingered on Fletcher a bit longer. Then she whistled to the dogs and patted her leg, then headed across the snow.

Fletcher shaded his eyes and studied the girl on the hill, moving lightly on her snowshoes as she played with the dogs. On Monday, when he'd enrolled in Switchback High School, he thought it was going to be the worst thing that had ever happened to him.

Now that he'd met Annie Rush, he had a feeling that was about to change.

9

Now

"Annie? I'm Dr. King. I've been taking care of you. My team and I."

She tried to swallow. It took three tries. Her throat felt terrible, clogged with pain. She blinked until the guy's face came into focus. Dr. King. She never went to the doctor. Did she know him? He had a good face. Craggy from being outdoors. Sandy-colored hair and light blue eyes watching her with a peculiar intensity. Not the kind that made her uncomfortable, but the kind that wanted to connect.

"Oh." A single syllable, sounding like a rusty hinge. Her mouth didn't work properly. She didn't recognize her own voice at all. It was weird and thready, as if she'd been clubbing all night. She didn't do that anymore. Did she? Had she ever?

"Um . . . thank you?" She wasn't quite sure what to say to a stranger claiming he'd been taking care of her.

There was a crusty, ripping sound as soap-smelling hands opened the Velcro behind her neck. The cervical collar came away, and fresh air chilled her exposed neck. She tried to turn her head, but her neck was so stiff she could barely move it.

Questions and confusion crowded her mind. There were feelings, too, floating through her, but the only one she could name was frustration that she couldn't express the other feelings.

Someone had pushed the sitting-up icon on the keypad, and the bed raised her up. The kitten-and-stars woman had also freed her from the restraints. Annie tried to flex her fingers and toes. Something was stuck on her finger. Then she circled her feet at the ankles. All her joints felt stiff and numb. She attempted to twirl her wrists, and they didn't quite work either.

Dr. King leaned forward, looking, always looking, deep into her eyes. "You were in an accident. Do you remember that?"

She lifted her hand. Was that her hand? There was a white clothespin thing on her index finger. A heavy box in the pocket of her gown was connected to her with wires on the end of suction cups. She was wearing a hospital gown.

Because of the accident. What accident? An image flashed—a squeegee falling from a window washer's scaffold? Another flash—she was driving along a busy freeway, in a hurry to get somewhere. She was in a hurry because . . . The thought floated away.

"I nnnnn . . . need a toothbrush." Yes. Please. Her mouth was like the bottom of a cave.

Someone placed a curved tray in front of her, with a plastic-wrapped toothbrush and a sample-size tube of toothpaste. Annie reached for the toothbrush. Her fingers refused to grip it. She was too weak even to pick it up. She stared at her fingers as though they belonged to someone else.

"What h-h-happened to my manicure?" she asked in her scratchy, drunken voice, still staring at her hand.

The doctor picked up her hand, the one without the glowing white clothespin.

"I paid eighty bucks for that manicure," she explained. "It was a gel coat."

He regarded her with a look of pure male cluelessness. "I'm trying to find out if you're aware of what happened," he said. "What brought you here?"

"I drove myself," she replied. An underlying sense of foreboding flowed through her in a dark river. She felt her mind struggling to understand precisely what was going on. Maybe this was a dream, one of those dreams about an unfamiliar place, unfamiliar people coming and going.

The doctor nodded, seemingly agreeable. The kitten scrubs lady pulled a rolling laptop and screen closer to the bed. Someone else, a woman who introduced herself as Dr. Riley, came forward with a stethoscope. She listened to Annie's chest on both sides, front and back. Deep breath in. Blow it out. Then she pressed the smooth metal disk to Annie's neck, explaining that she was checking the pulse in her carotid artery.

"Do you know what day it is?" asked Dr. King.

"Unless I missed something, it's Monday." Yes. The magazine interview was scheduled for Monday. There was usually a day or two of preproduction; then the taping started on Wednesday. The show's shooting schedule usually ran like a precision clock. It was one of the many tricks she used to keep everything on budget. The quick thought flitted away, and the thread of memory unraveled.

Slight smile from the doctor as he exchanged a look with the other doctor, then turned to Annie. "There was an accident," he said. "You suffered a head injury."

She had tripped over something. *I'm fine, really*... That thought flitted away, too, on butterfly wings.

She lifted her hand again, studied the bare fingernails, clipped short. Touched her head. It didn't feel injured. But...

"Hair," she said in a reedy whisper. "What happened to my hair?"

This was confusing. When she'd left that morning, her heavy long hair had been caught in a pretty celluloid clip. Now her hair felt like... bristles. It was just...

"It's gone."

And for the first time since the waking-up time, Annie felt afraid.

"Hi, baby."

That voice. Calling her baby. The voice and the word nudged Annie awake. *Open your eyes.*

A face, hovering above like the full moon. A sweet, sad smile. And then joy. Wet joy.

The name for the face flickered and disappeared. Annie struggled to bring it back. "Mom. Don't cry, Mom." Her voice still sounded so strange. The voice of a woman who had whiskey and cigars for breakfast.

"Oh, Annie. I can't help it. I'm just so happy. I thought—we all thought . . ." Her mother looked at someone stationed at the foot of the bed. The kitten-and-stars woman again. "Can I touch her?"

A nod from the woman. A hug from Mom. Smell of the breeze in her hair. The melting sweet sensation of safety. *Mom.*

And then came Kyle. Big brother, lumberjack build, teary-eyed grin. "Look who's back," he said. Bending forward. Soft brush of lips on her forehead.

"Oh, baby. We were so scared," said Mom.

"You're going to be all right," said Dad, taking her hand and tucking a kiss inside her palm, the way he used to do when she was tiny. "For later, when I'm not here," he used to say.

Wait. Dad?

She must be dreaming. Dad left the family forever ago. And here he was—salt-and-pepper hair, white teeth, square jaw, eyes the color of sweet basil.

A pizza with sweet basil, tomato, and mozzarella was named in honor of Queen Margherita of Savoy and featured the colors of the Italian flag. The signature white cheese was made from the milk of the Italian water buffalo. Annie had no idea why this arbitrary thought occurred to her now.

"Hey," she said. Dry lips. Dry mouth.

"Here you go." Someone touched her lips with a tiny wet sponge on a stick.

The whitecoats hovered, shining a beam into each eye and giving simple commands. Follow my hand with your eyes. Touch your finger to your nose. Now close your eyes and touch your nose. Close your eyes and hold out your arms. Clap in a pattern.

She knew what they wanted, but even lifting one hand exhausted her. And lifting her arms? Forget it. They were weighted down by sandbags.

Her brain had turned to scrambled eggs. It was remarkable how few people truly understood how to prepare scrambled eggs. Fresh eggs—preferably from the henhouse in the yard—were the key to the dish. It was important to avoid beating them into a uniform, homogenous liquid; instead, they should be stirred gently with a fork in order to allow the eggs to retain their character. Add a big pinch of salt and a small pinch of pepper. Warm the butter in the pan without letting it turn brown. The moment the butter starts to foam, pour in the eggs. Count slowly to ten and then scramble them gently with a wooden spatula. While the eggs are still moist—but not wet—remove the pan from the heat. Serve on a warm plate with buttered toast. Brain food.

Food for the brain. Not *from* the brain. Annie had never been a fan of sweetbreads—a nice-sounding name for organ meat—so she couldn't exactly say what a brain looked like. Yes, she could. She had taken a class in neuroscience in college. The pictures in the textbook had caused her to quickly surmise it was not the right path.

Her thoughts were pinging every which way. Maybe her brain was not scrambled eggs, but popcorn. With the lid off the pan. A thought would form and then shoot away before she could grasp it.

Focus. Pay attention. She gave herself a stern warning.

And it was so. She swallowed a drop from the wet sponge. Icky taste of cellulose. She looked at her mother's eyes and saw the sky.

"What just happened?" she asked. Crackly voice like static on the radio.

Another whitecoat held a camera pointed at her. Was this a taping? No. His camera was not a professional model. Besides, the taping was on Wednesday, and this was only Mon—

"Whadduh . . ." The words came out malformed. She tried again. "Wad . . . What day issst?" Still malformed, running together. Her mouth was so dry. The sponge on a stick touched them again.

Dad brushed her arm, a fleeting nudge of affection. "It's good to hear your voice."

Annie had always loved her father's voice. When she was very small, he used to read her adventure stories that were supposed to be way over her head, like *Kon-Tiki, The Odyssey, Treasure Island.* They weren't over her head at all. She understood the urge to venture to far-off places, discover new things, see the wonder of the world, even if it meant facing harrowing danger. She would snuggle up into the big protective curve of her father's shoulder and let his stories carry her away to far-off lands. And then Dad himself got carried away. He wanted an adventure of his own.

Your mother and I are getting a divorce. None of this is your fault. We still love you exactly the same.

If it wasn't her fault, why was she the only one hurting?

"Your care team is calling you a miracle," said Mom. "You've always been a miracle to me, but they're talking about your recovery."

"Care team." If she concentrated on the words, they came out better. Raspy and stuttering, but comprehensible. "I have a care team? What in the w-world is that?"

"They've been taking care of you since you were brought here," Mom said.

Here. Where is here? Annie lifted her gaze to the skylight. That was where the warmth came from, the bars of sunshine she'd felt, waking up her legs, her body.

Accident. The doctor with the light blue eyes had mentioned an accident, but she couldn't figure out what he meant.

"I tripped over a cable." Yes. A memory flickered and flashed. She grasped at it, missed. She had been hurrying. Running from . . . what?

"That wasn't the accident," said Kyle. "There was a scaffold—"

Another flicker—fresh flowers, heat and smog. "The window washer's squeegee, yeah. I remember now. It didn't hit me. Came close, though."

"Just listen," said Kyle. "There was nothing about a window washer in the report. This was a workplace injury. The scaffold—some kind of platform on a lift—malfunctioned and collapsed."

Annie. A voice calling her name. *Come back.*

"Seriously?" Now she felt annoyed. She had been opposed to that lift from the start. Sure, it was less expensive, but skimping on safety was no way to economize. "Where's my phone? I'll have my assistant file a complaint." The words came from a place inside her that she didn't recognize.

"Sweetheart, don't worry about that. It's all handled," said Mom.

"What do you mean 'it's handled'?" She scowled and aimed a broody stare out the window. The apple blossoms were in full bloom, seashell pink and ivory, a graceful arch of limbs against a sunny sky.

She was allowed to climb the apple trees in the orchard on Rush Mountain. Not the maples, though. When she climbed the maple trees, she got sticky sap all over her clothes and Gran would scold her. A scolding from Gran always carried a special sting. Though she never raised her voice, her tone and the expression on her face conveyed a sense of disappointment, causing a burn of shame that cut deeper than any shrill rebuke.

Oh, Annie.

She looked back at her family. Dad. Kyle. Mom. Her family. They were far from perfect, but right now she felt only love from them. And for them.

"What is this place?" she asked. There were lab coats and doctors, yes, and warning signs and hand sanitizers on the wall, yet it lacked the tangle of equipment and high-tech feel of a hospital.

"It's the skilled nursing facility of Burlington General," said the lady in the scrubs.

Wait. What?

"Burlington as in Vermont?" Annie asked, incredulous. "How the hell did I wind up in Vermont?" Home. She was home at last. But Vermont wasn't home anymore. Was it?

"Ah, Annie." Mom inhaled unsteadily, and her eyes filled. "We're trying to explain, but there's just so much. We don't want to overwhelm you."

Worry pressed down on her chest. She yearned to sleep again, to dive deep into that pool of nothingness. She needed to sleep, but they seemed to want her to stay. *Stay with me, Annie. Stay.* The phantom voice in her head belonged to someone she thought she knew.

"You were knocked unconscious," her father said. "It was a head injury, kiddo. A bad one."

Kiddo. Why did he still call her that? She hadn't been his kiddo in decades. Head injury . . . She lifted a leaden arm, took a breath for courage, and touched her short short hair. Her head didn't feel injured.

"Is that why my hair got cut off?" She offered a slight smile. "I suppose I can handle short hair for a while." She turned to her brother, who was watching her as if she'd just pulled the pin on a hand grenade. Kyle had never been able to maintain a poker face. "What?" she demanded.

"Nothing."

"You're looking at me funny."

He glanced over at the nurse, then the cameraman. "There's nothing funny about this, squirt." That was his nickname for her. Squirt. She used to drive him crazy, spying on him and his girlfriends when he was a teenager.

He shuffled his feet. Looked at the floor. Looked back at her. "You were unconscious for a long time. Like, a really long time. It was bad. There was a chance you'd end up brain-dead. The organ procurement team wanted to—"

"Kyle." Mom bit her lip.

"They wanted my organs?" Annie couldn't get her head around that. Organ meat. Sweetbreads. Not a fan.

"No one could say whether or not you'd ever wake up," Kyle said.

Annie yawned. She wanted to sleep again. To sleep, and never wake up. Focus, she told herself. Stay here. Keep them away from your organs. "I'm awake now. So I guess, thank you for not giving away my organs."

Kyle laughed, and Mom smacked his arm.

"You said a long time," Annie whispered. "No. You said a *really* long time. What's a really long time?"

Kyle went completely sober. Everyone was silent for a few moments. Annie counted the beats of her heart. Then she said, "Mom?"

Her mother was crying again, her head bowed.

"Dad?"

"You've been gone for a year," Dad said. "That's what we're trying to explain. You lost a whole year."

"A year." The words rasped from Annie's throat.

You've been gone for a year. Those were her father's exact words.

"That's not funny," she said. She tried to grasp the idea of a year, but her mind worked with a strange lethargy. A whole year. What did a year feel like? How did a person sense the passing of time? Her thoughts formed slowly, like sugar syrup reaching the softball stage. Although water boils at 212 degrees, the sap has to heat up to 219. At that temperature, the sap is transformed into syrup.

Her father was still speaking, but Annie's mind had wandered off again. "Sorry," she said. "What?"

"No one's joking around," Dad said. "You had a lousy break, but the worst is behind you. Now we have to move forward from here."

She could scarcely move at all. Her muscles felt impossibly weak. Her limbs were gummy worms. She looked at her hands. Looked at her mother. "Is that what happened to my manicure? It's gone because I've been asleep for a year? A whole freaking year? That's impossible." It was the kind of thing people passed around on the Internet—*Woman Sleeps for a Year, Wakes Up Angry About Manicure.*

"You'll get stronger. Even though it probably doesn't feel like it, you've been exercising regularly," Mom said. "Someone on staff exercised your arms and legs to preserve muscle tone. I came at least three times a week, Annie. Sometimes more. I held your hand, massaged each finger…" Her eyes filled with tears, and she sent a desperate look at the nurse. "Darby can explain it better, I think."

The nurse at the rolling computer station ran down a list of the care routine Annie had slept through, day in and day out. There had been tracheobronchial suction, skin massage, passive exercises for range of motion. Despite all this, Annie's limbs were noodles. Her brain, popcorn. She could not even brace her arms behind her to scoot herself up in the bed. Darby adjusted a pillow behind her.

As she worked, the nurse explained that initially, there had been a breathing tube, but that had been replaced by a tracheostomy, a smaller tube in the neck, less likely to cause permanent injury, so it was better for long-term use. Now Annie was breathing humidified air.

They made a hole in my neck, thought Annie. Her hand immediately felt for it, finding a band of gauze there. I have a hole in my neck. She was about to demand a mirror, so she could see it, but then recoiled from the idea. Seeing such a thing would probably make her faint dead away.

"You'll have a sore throat for a while. Speak softly and don't strain yourself," said Darby the nurse. "Your voice will come back over time."

Mom dabbed at her cheeks with a tissue. "I read books to you," she said, "the way I used to when you were little. No one could say whether or not you heard me."

Annie's father read adventure stories. Her mother read poetry and dreamy fantasy books. *Tyger tyger, burning bright…*

"Maybe I did hear." Remembering the special, snuggly feeling of reading in bed with her mom or her dad, Annie sensed that prickle in her throat again. Would the tears come out the hole in her neck? "I don't know if I heard. I can't . . . I don't remember anything."

Her dad gave her leg an awkward pat. "You've got a lot of work to do. And a lot of people who want to help. I know you're going to get through this."

Through this. Through to where? Where did you end up when you got *through* something? What happened at the end of *through*? Was it a destination? Or another open door? An escape hatch?

She studied her father's face. It was a good face, but it belonged to a stranger. After he left the family, he had not been much of a presence in Annie's life. "What are you even doing here?" she asked him. "Don't you have a surf camp to run in Costa Rica?"

"I'm here for you," he said. "I'll stay as long as I'm needed."

"I needed you when I was ten years old," she said. "But you went away."

"Oh, yeah," said Kyle. "Issues. The case manager said we'd all be getting some family counseling. At least we'll have something to talk about."

"Show me your teeth."

"Huh?" Annie stared at the woman's badge. *Patsy Schein, Occupational Therapy.* Annie didn't know how much time had passed since her family had visited. Was it yesterday? Last week? Last year? Maybe she had dreamed them. She didn't know what was real and what was imaginary. She didn't know what time felt like.

"We're going to be doing a few simple tests," Patsy said brightly. "Come on, give us a smile with teeth."

Was *this* real? Annie gritted her teeth. She didn't feel like smiling. Then the woman had her close her eyes and raise her arms to the same level in front of her, like Frankenstein's monster on the move.

Her arms were so ridiculously weak she could barely hold them up. She needed to go to the gym more often. Supposedly they were going to take her to a gym. Someone had written it on the whiteboard opposite her bed.

Patsy instructed her to repeat a phrase—"The sun sometimes shines in Cincinnati." She was told three words—"book," "sailboat," "idea"—and asked to repeat them a few minutes later. Apparently, they wanted to see if her mind was working.

Annie knew that it was . . . and it wasn't. She couldn't stay awake. She felt groggy all the time. Thoughts shot through her head, shattered, and disappeared like fireworks. She had feelings, but couldn't always attach words to those emotions. There were things she remembered with crystal clarity, like the sound of her grandmother's voice singing show tunes, the steamy scent of summer rain on pavement, or the touch of a boy's lips the first time he kissed her. She knew the taste of the mountain air on a blue-sky day in springtime, and the silky sensation of the water in Rainbow Lake on a hot summer day.

And other things she scarcely remembered at all—the mysterious "accident" referred to by Dr. King. They said she'd been awake on and off for three days, but she didn't know what a day felt like. She wasn't even sure she knew what "awake" felt like. Was this awake, or was it a dream?

A teenage girl rolled a cart with books and magazines into the room. She was slender and pale, with some wince-inducing piercings in her lip and eyebrow, and a tiny smear of blueberry jam on her chin. She had a couple of missing teeth, but her smile had a certain sweetness that appealed to Annie. A name tag identified her as a volunteer named Raven. "Would you like something to read?" she asked.

Annie thought about this. Book, sailboat, idea. She liked to read, didn't she?

"Do you have a recommendation?" she asked the girl.

Raven shrugged. "I just finished this one." She handed over a book with an eerie cover—*The Good Neighbor.*

Annie checked it out. She opened the book. The words swam and danced before her eyes, and her hands shook from the effort of holding it. "Maybe later," she said. "Thanks." She set the book down on her rolling tray table, exhausted. "Do you like working here?"

Another shrug. "I'm a volunteer. It's okay. Better than the alternative."

"What's the alternative?"

Raven hesitated. "Judge Wyndham ordered me to do community service."

"Oh." The name tweaked some part of Annie's brain. *Wyndham.*

"It was just for being truant from school. I'm not dangerous or anything," Raven said, apparently misinterpreting Annie's expression.

"Of course not. I didn't think . . . Anyway. Thank you for the book. Stop by anytime."

"Sure." Raven backed the cart toward the door, then lingered. "Um, can I get you anything else?"

Annie took a deep breath. "Maybe . . . a mirror?"

Raven frowned. "Oh. You mean like a makeup mirror?"

"Yes, okay. That would do." What kind of bedhead did a person wake up with after a whole year? She was fairly certain she was not going to like what she saw, but she might as well have a look. "Um, I mean, if it's not too much trouble."

"Not at all. I'm supposed to be helping people here. Don't hesitate to ask for anything."

How about a year? Can I have my year back?

"I don't like to be the kind of person who worries others," Annie said.

Raven nodded. "Yeah. I get that. I'll go see if I can find you that mirror." She left for a few minutes. It might have been a few hours. Annie had trouble deciphering the passage of time. She'd lost a whole year in the blink of an eye. Maybe Raven had been gone a year.

Or not. She returned, still with the blueberry jam on her chin. Her eyes shifted furtively toward the door as she placed a small round hand mirror on the wheeled bed table. "Keep it on the down low," she said.

"What, the mirror?"

Raven nodded. "You're not supposed to have any, like, sharp objects."

"Seriously?"

The girl shrugged. "They worry about patients hurting themselves."

Annie heaved a sigh, which made her chest ache.

She picked up the small mirror. It felt heavier than an iron skillet as she lifted it and peered at her face. She knew that face, although she had trouble deciphering the emotions written on it. The skin was an unhealthy yellowish paleness. She had her grandfather's eyes—big and brown. The hair—short, zero styling. She looked like a fallen woman in an English novel, shorn by shame.

"I might want to, now that I see what they did to my hair," Annie said. Noting the expression on Raven's face, she said, "Kidding. Trust me, I am not about to stab myself with shards of glass."

Another woman showed up. Nancy, a physical therapist. Push your hand against my hand. Push your foot against my hand. Good. Swing your legs around to the side of the bed.

She put a thick woven belt around Annie's waist and helped her stand up. Annie's knees buckled, and she collapsed back onto the bed. They repeated the exercise a couple of times, and then she slept, dropping off quickly and effortlessly, as if someone had flipped a light switch.

A switch. Switchback. It was a place, right? Yes. *Her* place. She was a bird, soaring above the landscape, and she could see the painted steeple of the Congregational church, the sparkling trout streams flashing through the mountains, the outlying farms and forests, the quarry where she jumped into the clear blue water on a hot summer day. She could zoom in on the scene like a camera on a boom or quadcopter, swooping over the familiar, rambling farmhouse, noisy with her family's day-to-day life. When she drew near the scene, she felt waves of elation and joy, then disappointment and despair. Her dreams were woven of confusion and yearning.

The days flowed together, moments strung one after the other like wooden beads. Annie wanted to sleep all the time, but they kept urging her to eat. She was only allowed bland, viscous liquids. She tried to explain that this was not eating at all. Eating was a multifaceted, sensual act involving not just taste, but scent and texture, temperature and flavor. Eating was a social act among people, a way of bonding with others.

The diet she was given here was a charmless process of ingestion, consumed in isolation or with an aide sitting nearby. Annie worried about the liquid coming out the hole in her neck.

They wanted her to move, but only with the gait belt and a helper. Never on her own. The caregivers said her body was adjusting, recalibrating, and it must be done gradually and with deliberation. One of the counselors told her to imagine hitting the reset button on a computer. Rebooting. It didn't help. *Operating system not found.*

Most of the time, she didn't think or remember. Feelings were colors. The chilly blue of loneliness was a shadow on snow. The hot red filament of anger. The shifting orange haze of confusion. Yellow hope, the sun a bouncing ball on the horizon. Joy was a chimera she could never quite touch because it wasn't real.

Memories flitted and disappeared, impossible to grasp and hang on to. They told her she had to practice breathing. Breathing deeper and deeper, filling her lungs all the way to the bottom would guard against pneumonia. And so she inhaled. Exhaled. In through the nose, out through the mouth. Smell the roses, blow out the candle. Make the little blue gumball in the spirometer dance up to 750.

Everything was a revelation. The chirp of a bird in the garden. The scent of Jergens lotion. The slight weight of a pen in her hand. Was she left-handed? Right-handed? She couldn't recall. When she wrote words on paper, she used her left hand but didn't recognize the handwriting.

She was bombarded by information and advice. While in a coma, she'd had a SPECT scan, and it showed no abnormalities in her cerebral blood flow. This was good, according to the nurse on duty. Other scans were being done daily, and those results, too, were encouraging. The post-traumatic amnesia was likely to gradually subside. So long as she continued getting better, the confusion would fade away. Her crazy gaps in memory might eventually fill themselves in.

Sometimes she was wheeled in a chair around the rehab center. The place smelled like feet. Old people. Pine-scented disinfectant. She attended a group meeting with other patients in their wheelchairs. Some with walkers. A PT led them through exercises. Pass the balloon to your right. Look up, look down. For the most part, the patients were weirdly silent.

Annie learned their names easily and was told this was a sign of progress. There was Ida, recovering from a stroke. Hank, wearing what appeared to be a modified water-polo helmet on his head. Georgia had tremors all the time. And poor Lloyd, so impaired that his mother showed everyone his *before* picture so they could all see how strong and handsome he once was, totally different from the contorted figure in the wheelchair.

A social worker said Annie should practice gratitude, because most people never emerge from a prolonged coma.

Gratitude. Yes, she was grateful. For what, exactly, she couldn't be certain.

"I want to go outside," she said.

"Good idea," her caregiver said. Today's companion was Phyllis.

She was quiet and sturdy, helping Annie transfer from the bed to the wheelchair with efficient skill. The long hallway was bright and clean, lined with rolling carts and helpers with pagers and charts. A few elderly patients lolled in their wheelchairs, their blank, slack-jawed expressions igniting sympathy in Annie. Recognition, too. She was one of them.

The automatic doors parted, and in one whoosh, she was outside. The morning sun in the garden flowed over her like a healing balm. She tipped her head back and let its warmth and light play over her face. She inhaled deep breaths of air, sweet with the breeze off Lake Champlain. The air had a flavor. It was green and tender, a brightness on the tongue.

"I remember this," she said. "The feel of the sun. The smell and taste. But it's different now."

"In what way?" asked Phyllis.

Annie struggled to answer, but the words wouldn't come. "I'm hungry."

"Then you're in luck. Today's orders say you should be starting on solid food. I can take you back inside and we'll call from your room."

"I'd rather eat out here."

Phyllis hesitated, then gave a decisive nod. "You're right, it's too nice this morning to be inside. I'll get someone to bring your breakfast out."

Annie gazed up at the budding trees and the drifting clouds. Gratitude. Breathe. "I've always loved the springtime," she said.

"Me, too," said Phyllis, pushing the wheelchair to a wrought-iron table. "My kids get cabin fever at the end of winter. It's such a relief to send them outside to play."

Annie had always wanted kids. The thought jabbed into her, and she gasped from the phantom pain. Then she ran away in her head, clearing her mind until it was a vast, empty blue like the sky.

An orderly came with breakfast on a tray. He set it on the table before her and removed the domed lid with a flourish, like a waiter in a fine restaurant. "Bon appétit," he said with a grin. "Pikey—the chef—made this special for you."

Her first meal was a golden-brown pancake smothered in butter and warm syrup. It smelled so good she nearly wept with joy. She used the utensils with the squishy handles, the ones that were easier to hold, to cut a moist triangle from the edge of the pancake. The melting butter and the syrup flowed down into the void, pooling on the thick white china plate.

She took her first taste, and all of her senses filled up until she thought she might explode. It was the ultimate bite of sweet comfort. Time stopped, and there was nothing but this moment. Closing her eyes, she let a smile unfurl on her lips. "Tastes like heaven," she said.

"Vermont's finest. Your mother made us promise to use your family's syrup."

"Sugar Rush." Annie opened her eyes and kept eating. She knew with sudden certainty that when it came to awakening memory, there was nothing more evocative than delicious food. The sensual stimulation—fragrance and warmth, taste and texture—roused the slumbering past. With each bite, her memories flowed through her, powerful and vivid. Maple steam curling up to the vent from the evaporator pans. The dry crackle of wood fire.

You smell like maple syrup. That voice. She remembered it, paired it with a face. And a name—Fletcher Wyndham. He had spoken those words to her just before they made love for the first time. She heard the voice, whispering in her ear, as if it were happening to her right now. Her mind unfurled and slipped backward, seeking something that felt more real and substantial than the world she'd woken up to.

10

Then

The final days of the 2002 sugar season brought a period of calm to Rush Mountain. The flow of sap slowed naturally as the trees budded out with the lengthening days and rising temperatures. Melting snow filled the flumes with rushing water and turned the forest floor to mud.

Kyle seemed happy with the season's yield. They had made a record number of gallons of syrup, and had enough extra sap to sell raw to a big producer downstate. The crews were done, for the most part, except for pulling the spiles from the trees so the tapholes would heal.

Annie's school team had hosted a swim meet that morning. She'd competed in two races and a relay, and had placed in all three, taking first in the one-hundred breast. She'd gone from the locker room shower to a generous lunch Gran had left in the fridge at the house—Cabot cheese grated with spring onions and radishes, slathered with mayo on thick slices of bread—and a jar of spiced applesauce from last fall. Perfect after a challenging meet.

Annie let the dogs out for a run and got started on her chores. Despite the coming spring, the day was a cold one, and her hair, still damp from the shower, froze into stiff corkscrews as she hiked up to the sugarhouse. Today's boiling would be the last of the season. They stopped making syrup after the budding, because late-harvest sugar had an off flavor.

Fletcher was working alone out in the sugarbush. She saw him up the hill, using a claw hammer to pull out the spiles, dropping each sharp metal spout into a canvas bag to be cleaned and stored away until next year.

He worked the same way he did everything else, with a peculiar grace and efficiency, innately confident in his actions. Even though Annie's mom had branded him a troublemaker, he was the fastest worker they'd ever had on the mountain. Annie's mom was friends with Degan Kerry's mom, and Mrs. Kerry claimed Fletcher was a delinquent who had been expelled from his previous three schools.

And with that pronouncement, the town bad boy was created out of thin air and gossip. It only made Annie more devoted to him. He had promised to come to the sugarhouse after he finished with the last of the spiles. This made her giddy with excitement, because they would have the place all to themselves. The rest of the family had gone into town for a dedication ceremony at the school Beth ran. The Haven had moved into a historic landmark building, newly restored to provide more classrooms and housing for its residential students.

Beth was an awesome sister-in-law. She'd moved to Switchback to work as the director of a local residential school for teens. She had two little kids—Dana and Lucas—a heart of gold, and an empty bank account. After she and Kyle married, the Rush farm became a family farm again. Beth was totally smart about people. She claimed she could read a teenager like a book. Annie hoped Beth couldn't read *her,* because she totally intended to make out with Fletcher Wyndham.

Leaving her muddy boots outside, she stoked the evaporator and the boil began. The room warmed with the deep glow of the fire, and maple steam rose up through the vents in the rafters.

Fletcher showed up in the late afternoon. The mud had frozen, and his footsteps crunched on the path to the sugarhouse. Annie opened the door and flung her arms around him, loving the way the strong embrace made her feel—comforted. Cared for.

"I'm glad you're here," she said, pulling him inside and closing the door. "Can you stay?"

"I'm supposed to be helping out at the garage," he said. "Clients keep showing up. Which is good, I guess, since my dad needs the business. But still . . ." His voice trailed off, and he kissed her, then hugged her hard and lifted her feet off the floor. "I thought about you all day."

"Same here."

"I watched your first two races," he said. "I love watching you swim."

"Really?"

"You're good, Annie. Plus, you look totally hot in your swimsuit. I would have stayed for the relays, but Kyle needed my help." He picked up one of Gran's scones and dipped it in the syrup pan. "Don't tell your brother, but I'd work for syrup alone if I had to."

"You're totally insane," she said, feeling drawn to him like iron to a magnet.

"That's me—crazy," he whispered, taking both her hands and interlacing their fingers.

She stared up into his eyes, hazel green and reflecting the flames from the wood fire. She felt awkward and shy and breathless with excitement. The coals under the evaporator created a gentle glow in the sugarhouse, and as the light played over his face, she felt a flood of emotion so intense that it made her chest ache.

He leaned forward and kissed her gently. His lips held the flavor of maple, and they were soft and gentle on hers, full of promise.

"I'm nervous," she whispered.

That half smile of his. "Me, too."

She touched his cheek. "Really? I didn't think anything could make you nervous."

"You," he said, taking her hand and pressing it to his beating heart. "You make me nervous."

"I don't mean to. I don't understand. Why?"

"Because you're really beautiful, and I really like you, and I want to get this right."

Her heart melted. No one had ever spoken to her the way he did or looked at her the way he did. "News flash," she said. "I won't know if we get it right or not. I've never done this before."

"News flash," he said. "Neither have I."

"Then I suppose," she said, taking her sweater off over her head, "we shouldn't worry about getting it right."

What they lacked in experience, they made up for in enthusiasm. And tenderness. And sincerity. And frequency. As she fell into the relationship with Fletcher, the heady feelings buoyed her up and sometimes she actually felt as if she were flying. He awakened in her such passion that she felt unbalanced by it all. The feelings consumed her.

An elemental shift took place deep inside her. The world felt different in every respect. The very air on her skin felt different. The taste of things changed, colors were more vivid. She experienced the world on a whole new level, all because of the way she felt.

It was addicting, this flood of pure emotion, undiluted by anything so rational as a thought. Her heart was rearranged. She knew this was a physical impossibility, but it was exactly how she felt. She woke every day thinking of him, and fell asleep every night dreaming of him.

In between, they spent every possible moment together. She dove into loving him with a kind of reckless abandon that was utterly unlike her. She used to be a planner, cautiously plotting her course through each day. Not when it came to Fletcher.

Springtime burst over the landscape, and they went hiking together, bringing a picnic lunch to the meadow by the creek that flowed past the apple trees. They kissed as the wind blew a storm of pink and white petals down on them, and she nearly exploded from the beauty of it. He took her riding on one of his dad's imported scooters. Though she knew her mom would disapprove, she got Fletcher to teach her to operate the scooter on her own. They explored the narrow, winding roads together, and Annie brought her camera along, capturing still photos and video clips, then staying up late to edit them.

They found a quiet spot at the atheneum, in a bright corner amid the 910 section. There was a rolled-arm love seat next to a table with a hurricane lamp. "This has always been my favorite section," she whispered. "Travel and geography. When I was younger, I used to close my eyes and pick a book at random, and plan a pretend journey to that destination."

"Where would you go if you could choose anywhere in the world?" he asked, paging through a book of photos showing the salt flats of Uyuni, in Bolivia.

"Oh, no way can I answer that. I want to travel everywhere. I want to see everything in the world."

"You have to start someplace."

"I've already picked where I'm going to spend my junior year abroad in college. Aix-en-Provence. That's in the South of France." She pulled a book from the shelf, one she'd checked out numerous times. "They have these traditional farmhouses, called *mas*. They were totally self-sustaining farms, back in the day. All the buildings face south to shield them from a wind called a mistral. They raised everything they needed right there—olive oil, fruit, vegetables, livestock, dairy, even silk."

"Maple syrup?"

"Well, not that."

"I could never live anywhere that didn't have maple syrup."

"Yikes, that's pretty limiting. Look at this. It's heaven." She gazed lovingly at a spread of an eighteenth-century *mas,* surrounded by vineyards and olive orchards, all bathed in the golden glow of the sun. She glanced at him. "What about you? Where would you go if you could go anywhere?"

"I like it just fine right here." He never took his eyes off her face.

Oh, boy. "Where'd you apply to college?"

"I didn't. No way I can scrape together the dough."

"Oh." She studied the floor, sorry she'd asked. But she couldn't leave it alone. "So, um, would you ever want to go to college?"

"Sure. And yeah, I've looked into grants and loans and scholarships. It would still be out of reach for me unless I win the lottery or do something radical like join the National Guard."

"Wouldn't it make you nervous, joining the military after what happened on 9/11?" she asked.

"What happened that day makes *everybody* nervous," he said. "Ms. Elkins says I should look into night school or online classes."

"Well, okay, then," she said, sounding way too bright and chirpy. "It's a start."

Someone on the other side of the stacks shushed them.

He grinned and touched his finger to her lips. "Right. If you ask my dad—or your mom—they'd say I'll never amount to anything."

"Then you're asking the wrong people," she whispered, so only he could hear. "You should ask me."

"Okay, what do you think, Ms. Annie Rush?"

"I think," she said, winding her arms around his neck and leaning over to kiss him, "that you are going to conquer the world."

In AP English class, Annie wrote a poem in the style of Elizabeth Barrett Browning, listing the virtues of an unnamed object of her affection, and how she loved each part of him.

"Wow, you've got it bad," her best friend, Pam, said, scanning the English assignment.

"No, I've got it *good,*" Annie said, totally unapologetic. She regarded her friend with elation. She and Pam had grown up together, the kind of best friends who declared they were inseparable for life, no matter how much time and distance kept them apart. "It's so unexpected," she said. "I never knew love could feel this way."

"What way?"

"Like people are going to feel when they taste these cupcakes." She and Pam were making and decorating Lady Baltimore cupcakes, their contribution to the upcoming senior social. Working side by side, they filled each one with brandied fruit and nuts, then added a fluffy white cloud of whipped meringue icing.

Pam stepped back and regarded the tray of gorgeous cupcakes. "They did turn out awesome, didn't they?"

"Indeed. Tell your dad thanks for the bootleg brandy. It's delicious." Pam's father was a master distiller, specializing in barrel-aged small-batch whiskeys and brandies. He supplied fancy bars in New York and Boston.

"I wonder if it feels different every time it happens," Pam speculated. "Love, I mean. Not cupcakes."

"This can only come around once in a lifetime," Annie said with utter confidence. "I could never feel this way about any other person."

"How do you know?" Pam asked.

"I just do."

"My mom says I shouldn't find the love of my life until I'm at least twenty-eight."

"Why twenty-eight?"

"She says before that, people don't really know themselves."

As the school psychologist, Dr. Mitchell carried some authority. But Annie knew there had to be exceptions. She and Fletcher were exceptional. She felt it in the very core of her being. He was the one her heart had chosen, and it was nobody's fault she had found him ten years too soon, according to Dr. Mitchell's timeline.

Annie couldn't wait to show summer in Vermont to Fletcher. They went hiking and trout fishing, the dogs bounding along with them. In town, there were concerts in the park, a farmers' market every weekend, and a Sunday flea market that drew shoppers from all over. At an antique-book stall, they browsed through dusty tomes. Annie gasped aloud when she found a copy of *Lord of the Flies* in a fancy slipcase. "It's my favorite book, ever," she said. "And you're looking at me funny. Why are you looking at me funny?"

"Because it's my favorite, too. No lie, it is."

"Then we both have really good taste in books."

"That's twenty-five dollars," the bookseller said. "It's very collectible."

Annie eyed the book regretfully as she put it back. "It's a treasure," she agreed, and moved on to the next booth. She turned to say something to Fletcher, and saw that he was buying the book.

"Oh my gosh," she said when he handed it over. "I can't believe you did that."

"It's our favorite book. I want you to keep it," he said.

She nearly fainted with love for him, literally fainted. Then she took the book from him and hugged it to her chest before stashing it in her backpack. "Thank you," she said. "I'll guard it with my life."

"I've read it twice," he said.

"I've read it three times. I'm going to read this copy tonight. I have a thing for old books," she said.

"I have a thing for ice cream," he said, heading for a booth where they were filling home-baked cones with homemade ice cream.

Annie loved strolling through town with him, hand in hand, savoring their ice cream as they wandered along the shady streets.

"I like these big old houses," Fletcher said, admiring the stately homes of Henley Street.

"Me, too. If you could live in any one of these, which one would you pick?"

He looked up and down the block, then pointed. "That one, with the shutters and the porch that goes all the way around to the back."

"It's called the Webster house," Annie said. "And that's the one I'd pick, too. But not because of the back porch. I went inside once, to a 4-H meeting, so I know it has an awesome library with a fireplace."

"If it had a swimming pool, it'd be perfect," he said, finishing his ice cream. "Man, it's hot today."

"I know something better than a swimming pool," she said. "Switchback has a secret. Let's grab our suits and towels, and I'll show you."

A short time later, they drove along a rural road, bordered by deep woods, to a spot where a few parked cars hugged the grassy verge. Several kids in dripping suits emerged from a nearly hidden trail.

The trail wound through a fern-carpeted forest, lush with the fecund odor of damp earth and trees fed by a network of small, burbling springs. The forest canopy opened up around a quarry formed by smooth rock terraces, spires, and cliffs surrounding a natural pool of the clearest, bluest water in the world, illuminated by the summer sun. At one end, a series of waterfalls fed the pool with a dramatic rush. Rapid flumes created natural water slides between narrow canyon walls. There were cliffs and outcroppings for jumping, and swirling pools hiding in the shadows. The pounding of the waterfall was punctuated by shrieks of glee from the jumpers plunging into the depths.

Fletcher stopped walking and shaded his eyes. "Awesome," he murmured, taking in the scene. "What is this place?"

"It's called Moonlight Quarry. They say the pillars of the New York Public Library and the steps of the Supreme Court are made of marble quarried from right here," Annie told him. "Do heights bother you?"

He grinned. "Depends on the landing."

They dropped their towels on a smooth, sun-warmed rock ledge and climbed to a spot just below the falls. A curtain of cold, pounding water poured over them as they reached a ledge ten feet above the deepest part of the pool.

"There's only one way down," Annie shouted, her voice nearly drowned by the crashing water.

He took her hand. "Ready when you are."

They stepped to the edge and jumped, letting go of each other as they hit the water. The plunge was long and deep. No one had ever touched bottom here; it was rumored to be five hundred feet deep. She could see Fletcher's shadow nearby, flickering in a swirling stream of bubbles. Scissoring her legs, she shot up to the surface, and he joined her a second later, his face shining with delight.

"Wow," he said, treading water and grinning at her. "That was . . . *wow*."

Of all the key moments Annie had experienced, this might be the sharpest and clearest of all. In that instant, she knew a sense of happiness so powerful it was almost frightening. She wanted to hold on to the feeling forever.

The water temperature was as variable as the light—ice cold in the deep, shadowed places, and warmed by the sun in others. They found slow streams flowing over half-submerged rock, chutes with swift currents, slicked by deep green moss to form a natural water slide. The sun-heated tiers, where the water flowed down step-by-step, created small cascades that felt like a pounding back massage.

"Let's come here every day," Fletcher said.

"For the rest of our lives," Annie said.

One breezy night as she helped her mom clean up after dinner, she decided to broach the topic that had been on her mind all summer long. Kyle was down working in the farm office, and Beth was giving Lucas a bath. Their easy laughter drifted down from the upstairs bathroom. In the living room, Gran was reading Winnie-the-Pooh to Dana. Annie and Gran had made pan-fried brook trout and a salad from the garden—peas and pea shoots, mint and French breakfast radishes. Rhubarb crumble for dessert. There were no leftovers. With two kids and five adults in the house, there never were.

"I'm going to take a gap year," Annie said. She watched her mother's face drain of all color.

Annie brought the last of the dishes from the table and set them on the counter.

Her mother glared at her as she loaded the dishwasher. "I'm going to pretend I didn't hear that."

Annie realized she probably should have planned this conversation better. On the other hand, there was no good time she could have picked, and at least they had the kitchen to themselves. The kitchen had always been her favorite room in the house. The cabinets and flooring were made of taphole maple with its distinctive markings. After maples were tapped out and no longer useful for syrup production, the trees were harvested for lumber. The patterns were created by the tapping and healing of each season's holes. Each board had a story, and was a reminder of the enterprise that had sustained the family for generations.

Granddad had made the countertops from old evaporator pans, polishing the stainless steel until it gleamed like the surfaces in a high-end restaurant. When she was too small to reach the counter, Annie would stand on a step stool next to Gran and help with the cooking, caught up in the art and energy of a master in the kitchen. The adjacent alcove encompassed a round table where Gran served the most amazing meals—sweet corn fresh off the stalk, chicken roasted with lemon and rosemary, big dishes of green beans, pies bubbling with fresh Saskatoon berries. The big scrubbed table was the scene of birthday celebrations, ordinary days, serious talks, homework struggles, happy news, the ebb and flow of her family's life.

"I need you to hear me, Mom." Annie tried again. "I've already checked with the office of admissions. They'll let me keep my spot and my grant if I elect to take a gap year."

"And why on earth would you want to do that? You can't wait to leave Switchback."

Annie knew there was no point in hiding the truth from her mother. "I can't handle the idea of leaving Fletcher."

Her mother pursed her lips, but her eyes softened. "Oh, sweetie," she said. "Everybody feels that way about their first love."

Annie believed with all her heart that she and Fletcher were not everybody. Their connection was one of a kind, but she had no words to explain this to her mom. "I won't be able to focus on school if all I'm doing is missing Fletcher the whole time I'm away."

"If he truly loves you, then he'll want you to go for your dreams."

"Mom, *he* is my dream."

"I'm not going to argue with you, because believe it or not, I understand what you're saying. I might even remember what it feels like to fall in love and never want to be apart. I just want to know... What will your life look like if you stay here? How will your days go? You get up in the morning, and... do what?"

"I'll work on my projects. Reading and studying. Cooking and developing recipes. Photography and videography. That's what got me into college in the first place."

"What will happen at this time next year?" asked her mother. "Are you going to be any more willing to be apart next year?"

Annie bit her lip. Her eyes skated away from Mom's knowing look.

"I'm not trying to be mean," said her mother. "I want to make sure you've thought this through."

"I think about it all the time. Fletcher and college are not mutually exclusive."

"Then go to college. Don't let someone else—even someone you love—pull you away from that."

Annie stared at her mother, who looked almost panicked. "It's my life. My choice."

"Blowing off college is a choice you can't take back."

"I'm eighteen," Annie protested.

"Exactly. Show me an eighteen-year-old who makes good choices." Mom sighed. "Listen. When I was your age, I was in the same place you are."

"With Dad."

Mom nodded. "Don't you think I had dreams, too?"

"Sure, I guess. Like what?" Annie felt slightly guilty that she didn't really know what her mom's dreams were. She'd just assumed it was to marry Dad and raise a family on the farm.

"I was accepted to art school in New York. The Pratt Institute."

It was one of the top art schools in the country. Maybe in the world. "Seriously? You never told me that."

"Because I never pursued it."

"Why not?"

"Because I was in love. I thought I'd found something I wanted more than art school. I couldn't bear the thought of us being apart."

"You stayed in Switchback because of Dad." Annie felt a tightness in her chest.

Her mother lined up the plates in the dishwasher. "My folks wanted us to live here to help out and grow a nest egg. They had plenty of room and we were broke, so the plan seemed to make perfect sense at the time. I put off my future. Temporary arrangements have a way of growing roots when a baby comes along. I had Kyle, and don't get me wrong—I wouldn't trade being a mom for anything. But it meant that for me, school and the big-city dream just got farther and farther away. With a new baby and husband, I couldn't put my life on hold to go to school."

"So you're saying Dad held you back?"

"Yes. No. Everything held me back. I just don't want to see that happen to you."

"It doesn't have to be that way. I'm not going to get married and have a kid, like—" Annie stopped herself.

"Like I did?"

Annie felt bad for her mother. "You still did your art," she pointed out, gesturing around the kitchen. "Dad and Granddad made the loft over the garage into a studio for you. And your pictures are everywhere."

Her mom thumped the dishwasher shut and hit power scrub. "They are. But where's my husband?"

"I won't survive without you," she told Fletcher in despair as summer slid toward fall, and the start of school loomed.

He gathered her gently in his arms, his wordless affection so sweet it felt like pain.

"I don't want to go," she whispered.

"I don't want you to go," he said.

"I can't stand the idea of missing a single day with you. I'll stay. Who cares what my mom says? I'll get work, same as you, and we can both do night school and online classes."

"That sounds awesome," he said. "I think you should just turn your back on your amazing scholarship to one of the best colleges in the country, and get a crappy hourly job here in town."

"You know it wouldn't be like that."

"Shh." He touched his finger to her lips. "No way you're doing that."

"Fletcher—"

"Shut up. Don't be stupid."

Much to her mother's relief, Annie started her freshman year as planned. It was the opportunity of a lifetime and he wouldn't let her pass it up. But he was the love of a lifetime, and she didn't want to ruin it.

The owner of a busy Piaggio works in Brooklyn had offered Fletcher a room over the shop, and he was going to work on the scooters there. The place was in Brooklyn, just a bridge across from NYU.

Annie counted the days until Fletcher made his move. She fantasized about how they would walk around the city hand in hand, eat at sidewalk cafés, get takeout to share on a sunny park bench, and talk about everything in the world. The city was so busy and vibrant, its energy irresistible. She felt swept up in a storm of excitement, and the only thing missing was Fletcher.

Classes started, and Fletcher was still in Vermont. The garage was busy. He couldn't just ditch his dad. Annie tried to be patient. She tried to focus on school.

She already knew her favorite class this fall would be her photography and imaging class. One of the first assignments was to capture light and shadow in black and white. One afternoon, she went to Washington Square Park, right near campus, and took pictures of the wrought-iron railing with a tangle of locked bikes, a dog walker surrounded by his furry charges, kids playing on a climbing frame. Her best shot was of a food cart, where a guy in faded jeans and a chef's apron was making Cuban sandwiches. A bloom of steam filled the work area, and a tree branch arched over him in a natural frame, echoing the shape of his long, muscular arms. Perfect.

Annie bought a sandwich from him, even though she couldn't afford to eat outside the dining hall. He handed her the sandwich wrapped in parchment, giving her a smile so arresting that she dropped all her change in the tip jar. Then she hurried back to her dorm, a suite she shared with three other women who were impossibly messy and artistic, and called Fletcher to tell him about her day. "I can't wait for you to get here. When can you come?" she asked.

"I'm working on it."

"The when? Or the how?"

He laughed. "Both. We'll figure this out," he said.

"And once we do," she said, full of hope, "we'll get to be together forever."

Their *forever* lasted less than two weeks.

Her mobile phone rang as she was finishing a day of lectures and a photo critique. She was walking to a restaurant where she hoped to get part-time work. "Everything's so incredible," she said. "I don't even know where to start exploring. Little Italy, I suppose, would be logical. I already found a family market where they get daily deliveries from Naples. And then—"

"Annie, hey, slow down."

There was a note in his voice. Serious. Strange. She stopped walking in front of a corner fruit stand. Bees buzzed over a display of early-harvest apples.

"Something's wrong," she said, feeling a sting of worry.

"My dad had an accident. He's in the hospital. He—I'm here with him now."

"Where? What happened? Is he going to be all right?"

"He… They brought him by helicopter to the trauma center in Burlington. His leg was crushed when a power jack failed at the garage."

"My God," she whispered. The buzzing bees and the busy street with its rushing crowds fell away. She flashed on a memory of her grandfather, crushed when his tractor rolled. The expression on Gran's face that day haunted Annie. Did Fletcher have that face now? "You must be so scared."

"Yeah," he said, his voice thready with exhaustion. "I'm glad they brought him here. He's going to need… ah, shit, Annie, I can't even think straight."

"What can I do?" she asked. "How can I help? Should I come home?"

"No," he said quickly. "I mean, there's nothing to do but wait. This hospital . . . It's on the UV campus. They gave me a place to stay. You know, while he's here."

"Fletcher, I'm so sorry. How's your dad? Can you talk to him?"

"He's really out of it due to the painkillers. They have to . . . His leg isn't just broken. When the jack failed, a Jeep Wagoneer came down on him. His leg was crushed from the knee down, and he was trapped. Stuck . . . He couldn't reach the phone and he kept passing out. I was at the salvage yard when it happened, looking for a tailgate. When I got back, I heard him yelling."

"Oh, Fletcher. I want to help."

"There's nothing . . . Shit. Nobody but the doctors can help him." He paused, and she could hear him draw in a long breath. "They have to cut off his leg."

She felt ill. She leaned against the building for support. Focused on the precise pyramids of apples on display. "Oh, no."

"He was trapped in the garage for six hours. They call it prolonged ischemia. They said trying to keep his leg would mean tons more operations and stays in the hospital with no guarantee of fixing it. There could be serious complications, and he'll never be able to use it again. He won't have any sensation and won't be able to put his weight on it."

"So . . . they're cutting it off?" She brushed her hand down over her leg.

"Yeah. He has to have something called a through-the-knee guillotine amputation."

"You can't leave him," she said.

"I can't leave him," he agreed.

She felt dizzy with grief and fear. There was a lot she didn't understand. But in this moment, she knew fully and completely that nothing she and Fletcher had planned on was going to happen.

11

Now

"Tree is to acorn as sheep is to what?"

"Cheese."

The therapist marked something on her clipboard.

"The correct answer is probably wool, but sheep's-milk cheese is underrated," Annie said. "Plus it tastes better. I think about food all the time."

"Water is to ice as apple is to what?" The therapist was all business.

"Apple pie." The questions today made her feel defensive. Worried. Sometimes she had the feeling that her brain was hovering on the very edge of something big, as if it might explode at any moment.

"Can you say why you came up with that answer?" the therapist asked. She was a black woman with half-moon glasses perched on her nose, her hair done in shiny curls. Unlike a lot of the other caregivers here, she didn't wear scrubs or a lab coat, but a plum-colored skirt and sweater, and a badge with her name—Binnie Johnson, MSW, PhD.

"Because it's the correct one? And if it's not, then whoever made up this test has obviously never had my apple pie."

"So you like making pie? You're good at it?"

"I've won prizes for my pies. Seriously. Prizes."

"A sail is to a ship as a goal is to . . . ?"

"A football."

Dr. Johnson's mouth twitched a bit.

"What?" asked Annie.

"You're supposed to say to a person."

"That was actually the first thing that occurred to me, but I didn't think it was right."

"Try listening to yourself."

"What's that supposed to mean?"

"It means you know more than you think you know. Listen to your inner voice instead of someone else."

"My inner voice sounds like the announcer on *Sábado Gigante*."

"Sorry, what?"

"A Latino pop music show. Frantic and incomprehensible."

Dr. Johnson wrote something on a sticky note. She posted it on the whiteboard on the wall opposite the bed. The note said *Quiet Mind*.

After the session, Annie lay back in the bed, trying to quiet her mind. But she was bombarded with a barrage of loud, frantic voices, along with images and memories scattered like pieces of a puzzle she didn't understand. The world had shrunk to this room. Hand-sanitizer dispenser on the wall as if she were toxic. Impossible-to-open packets of lotion, which did her no good at all. Water in a cheap plastic pitcher that tasted like, well, plastic. A curved puke tray on the rolling bed table because sometimes her swallows went in the wrong direction.

She stared up at the ceiling. How could she be exhausted when all she had accomplished was a set of word-association games?

She'd been subjected to a battery of tests—physical, psychological, cognitive, neurological, and many that seemed to measure nothing but her sense of the absurd. She was considered a remarkable patient due to the duration of her coma and her level of functioning. She didn't feel remarkable. She felt weak and confused.

Thinking made her head hurt, and everything tired her out. She dozed for a few minutes or forever. An OT and an aide in scrubs showed up.

"How would you like to have a shower?" asked the OT.

Annie sighed. Until now, she'd been allowed only sponge baths. "How would you like to marry me?"

The therapist grinned. "I figured you were ready."

The room-size shower was equipped with a plastic bench and grab bars, stacks of rough-looking towels, and pump bottles of soap and shampoo. She surrendered the johnny gown without protest; all dignity had gone out the window long ago. Her weirdly pale skin bore gray, gummy outlines of old glue from IVs and monitors.

Annie pictured herself sleeping, held together by glue and medical tape. Where had she gone for that whole year? What had she lost? What was she hiding from herself?

With the aide hovering nearby, she let the water sluice down over her, and the warm stream flowing over her had made her cry.

Crying was exhausting, too, so she tried not to do it.

She tipped her face up to the shower head and wished the cleansing could go on forever. Afterward, the OT helped her dry off and put on a fresh gown. She was mortified to realize that while they'd cut off all of her hair and kept her nails trimmed, they hadn't done much about her grooming. Her armpits looked like she'd been living in a cave. Her legs—even worse. White flaccid dough covered in dark hair.

"I should have stayed asleep," she said, and they helped her back to bed.

She lay back in exhaustion and counted the ceiling tiles. Twenty-eight going one way. Forty going the other; 1,120 in all. She could do math. Her third-grade teacher was Mrs. Marge Green. She had taught the class to find the area of a rectangle by bringing in a large chocolate sheet cake and cutting it into six squares one way and five the other. The thing about sheet cake was that you had to use fresh buttermilk in both the cake and the frosting. Its tart flavor and smooth texture created a perfect balance with the bittersweet chocolate and the creamy layer of icing.

See, I do remember things, she thought. Just not everything. She wanted to have a quiet mind. She wanted to figure out who she was, not ten years ago, but right now. Or a year ago, before the long sleep. She could ask her family, but a gut-level impulse prevented this. The lost memories were hers to recover. She did not want them filtered through her mother, who tended to put her own twist on things. The staff psychologist supported this. He said the memories would return in their own time, when Annie was ready.

Dr. Johnson came back with more questions and mental tasks. "I want you to count backward from one hundred, by sevens."

"Sure," Annie said. "I'll get right on that."

"No, I really want you to do it as quickly as you can. Start with one hundred. Then go back seven—"

"Is this something non-brain-injured people can do?" Annie asked. "Hey, Raven," she called to the book-cart girl passing in the hallway, "count backward from a hundred by sevens."

The girl paused outside the door. "Huh?"

"See," Annie said to Dr. Johnson. "Nobody can do that. Let's move on."

"One hundred," said a male voice. "Ninety-three, eighty-six, seventy-nine . . ."

"Looks like you have a visitor," Dr. Johnson said. "And a smart-alecky one at that."

Annie's thumb found the sitting-up button, something she hadn't been able to do only yesterday. Progress, not perfection. One of the therapists suggested that could be her mantra. Annie had pointed out that it wasn't a mantra, but a slogan. Precision in language was the key to clarity. Specificity resulted in disambiguation.

"Wonderful," she said. "I love visitors." Sarcasm was easy, and not as exhausting as actual feeling. She pushed herself straighter on noodly arms. They didn't even feel like her arms, but like floppy appendages that belonged to someone else. Another Annie, maybe. The Annie from another time. The Annie she couldn't remember.

Her real name was Anastasia, like her grandmother. She loved having Gran's name. She missed Gran, and had no trouble remembering her. Why were her memories strongest of the people she missed the most, like Gran and—

"Seventy-two, sixty-five," said the voice from the doorway.

Annie looked over at her visitor.

She forgot to breathe. Her breath had been stolen by shock. Fletcher Wyndham had always had that effect on her.

"Mind if I come in?" he asked.

"I'll check in on you later," Dr. Johnson said, her gaze warming as she gave Fletcher the once-over before slipping out. Apparently he had that effect on lots of females.

Breathe, Annie coached herself. Smell the roses. Blow out the candle. Find your voice.

It was Fletcher, but it was some version of him that she didn't recall. Or maybe this was a Fletcher she'd never met. The boy she'd known in high school had been gangly and tough and wild. That boy had turned into a young man who was intense, compelling, driven, and impossibly sexy. This was a man in a suit and tie, though he retained a bit of his scruffy charm—longish hair and the shadow of a beard. He had filled out. Gangly had turned to strong. The scrappy attitude now read as confidence. He was different. Harder and more solid than the boy in her dreams of the past. Something that looked like pain flickered in his eyes.

But when he smiled, the smile touched a light switch in those eyes, and she saw someone who used to be her whole world.

"No, I don't mind," she said in the voice that still sounded strange to her. "Good grief, of course I don't." She gazed around the room, wondering if she should invite him to have a seat. The furniture looked ordinary, though each piece was covered with a plastic coating. Apparently, people in long-term nursing care tended to leak.

"How did you find me?" she asked him. She stared down at her legs. They were formless and pale, two long doughy unbaked loaves. Then she touched her hair. So short. Spiky. He used to run his fingers through her long hair. He used to say he loved her crazy curls.

"Your . . . I heard from your mom."

"You talked to my mother?" So weird to picture the two of them talking.

He walked over to the bed and sat in the plastic-coated visitor's chair. "I'm sorry about your accident. Your mom says you're a miracle."

"I don't feel like a miracle." Annie couldn't stop staring at him. The piercing eyes. The square jaw. He was a man made for being stared at. "But I get it. Everyone assumed I'd never wake up."

"How are you feeling, Annie?"

It wasn't the "how are you feeling?" of her care team. This morning, a social worker had given her a page of round-faced emoticons with expressions to clue her in: happy, sad, worried, angry, scared, amused.

How are you feeling? She turned the question over in her mind. "People have been asking that question a lot. Sometimes they ask *what* I'm feeling. I feel unstuck from the world. Unstuck in time."

"I don't know what that's like."

"It's like . . ." Annie bit her lip. The emotion she felt was a combination of the worry face and the sad face on her chart. *Quiet mind.* According to the staff here, she was making excellent progress. Only a short time ago, her daily activity consisted of a therapist lifting a limb and asking her to resist.

Every muscle needed strengthening, because every muscle had been asleep along with her bruised brain. She squeezed the rubber balls. Opened and closed her mouth. Shrugged her shoulders. Lifted her arms. Her knees. Her eyebrows. Everything.

She had to exercise her mind, too. The dumb analogy game was part of her routine now. In addition, she looked at cards with colors and shapes and words on them. She practiced making a peanut butter sandwich. Brushing her teeth. Writing her name, trying it with her left hand and then her right. The left hand worked better, so she felt fairly confident that she was still left-handed. She played memory games. She totally aced using the bathroom, because the alternative was unthinkable. Maybe that was what "motivation" meant.

As she explained all this to Fletcher, she stared at the floor, not wanting him to see her worry-sad face.

"That's . . . I'm sorry." He scooted the chair closer to the bed. "Annie, I'm sorry. I'm really sorry about everything that happened to you."

"You didn't cause it." She smiled briefly. "Or maybe you did, and I don't remember."

"You'll just have to trust me on that."

"Trust you." She dared to look up and study his face. That face. She used to see her whole world in his eyes. She had trusted him long ago but it hadn't been enough.

"How can I help?" he asked.

Always helpful. That was one of the reasons they'd fallen apart, years ago, wasn't it? He helped. He took care of things. Other things. Not her.

"Supposedly I'm getting all the help I need right here." She gestured at the whiteboard outlining the day's agenda—physical, occupational, and cognitive therapy. "The brain rewires itself after injury. That's why I have to relearn old habits. And it's why I can't remember certain things."

"What things?" He gave a brief laugh. "Sorry, dumb question, asking if you could remember the things you forgot."

"And yet it makes perfect sense to me." Something she recalled for certain—she loved talking to him. "It's disorienting. I'm told I have to be patient and get my bearings. People here keep telling me that my motivation is the key. I'm trying to figure out what motivation feels like."

"Shouldn't be hard for you, Annie. You've always been motivated."

Had she? The word didn't mean anything to her in this moment. She noted the perfect tailoring of his suit. Every line of it matched the trim lines of his body.

He frowned a little. "Something wrong?"

"The suit. It looks like a bespoke suit." "Bespoke" meant made to measure. She had no idea how she knew that. "I've never seen you in a suit before."

A grin flashed. Oh, that smile. Time had not dimmed its effect. "Not familiar with that term," he said. "I have to wear a suit to work most days."

"Oh. Where do you work?" Had she known this? Was it something she'd forgotten, or had she lost him so completely that she didn't know anything about him anymore?

"At the courthouse. I'm a judge. I was a lawyer, and last year I was appointed to the bench."

A lawyer, a judge.

"Wow. Just wow," she said. "That's really impressive."

"Is it?"

"You're kidding, right? Yes, it's impressive. Did I know this about you? Is it one of those things in the big black hole of all the things I forgot?"

"We didn't stay in touch, Annie." He stared down at his hands, flexing and unflexing them. "There wasn't any point."

Oh. They hadn't stayed in touch after the falling apart. Annie wondered what she knew about Fletcher, and what she'd forgotten. She didn't know exactly where he was from, but that seemed like something she'd never known. He hadn't talked about it much, even when they were young and had talked about everything. Before arriving in Switchback, he had lived in a lot of places all over the country.

"People used to say you'd never amount to anything." She pressed her hand to her mouth. "Should I not have said that? I'm blunt as a spoon, according to the doctors here. People with TBI don't always pick up on social boundaries. TBI is short for traumatic brain injury."

"Plenty of people without TBI don't always pick up on boundaries either," he said. "I see it every day in my courtroom."

"You have a courtroom. That's so cool. I always knew you'd do something important. I wish I'd been around to see it."

Judging by the expression on his face, she suspected she was blurting again. But she was also telling the truth. She knew without a doubt that he was special.

"You'll make progress. I know you, Annie. You'll get—"

"Through this," she finished for him. "Everybody says that. But nobody says what happens after getting through. And now I'm whining. I'm told the memories will come back. Maybe not all, though. Maybe some memories are lost forever, and that might be a good thing. But then I panic sometimes, worrying about all the other things I've forgotten." She studied him again, feeling a fount of emotion rising up through her chest. "There are lots of things I remember about you," she added. "I'm not sure if they're memories or dreams."

She looked down at her hands, seeing her fingers entwined. She was supposed to do ball squeezes once an hour to strengthen her hands. She picked up two balls and started squeezing. "Fletcher, why are you here?"

"I wanted to see you. But I shouldn't be here if it upsets you."

"I don't think I'm upset." She tried to figure out if she knew what upset felt like. Was there a face on her chart for *upset*? When Fletcher had walked into the room, Annie had sensed a flutter of excitement. It was not an unpleasant feeling. She was not upset.

"It's nice of you to come," she said. "You were always nice, weren't you?"

"Depends on who you ask."

She squeezed the fuzzy balls as she studied him, her hands remembering the feel of his shoulders when she gave him a hug. She would run her fingers over his sinewy arms and find his hands, and weave their fingers together. He used to smell like a combination of the outdoors and his dad's garage. When he rode one of his father's scooters, his hair held the scent of the wind for hours afterward.

"I'm staring at you, aren't I?" she said.

"I don't mind."

She felt a lifting sensation in her heart. "I remember how I felt about you," she said. "I remember *us*. We were so young, weren't we? Young and romantic. Oh my gosh, I was obsessed with you. It drove my mother crazy. She was terrified that I was going to start having your babies and get all fat and happy and never have a life of my own." She studied his face. Watched his Adam's apple move as he swallowed. The prospect of having his babies did not seem terrible. She had always wanted babies. Maybe she still did.

He rested his elbows on his knees and leaned forward. "Obsessed with me? You never told me that."

"I guess I used to have more filters. But couldn't you tell? You were the biggest thing that had ever happened to me. I couldn't imagine life without you. But it ended, didn't it?"

"It got... interrupted."

She sighed. "Memories are strange things, aren't they? You can't touch them and hold them in your hands, but they have incredible power. Because I've lost so many memories, I feel as though I've lost that power." She lifted her gaze to him. Her hands ached from squeezing the balls. "I'm whining again."

"You're not." He reached over and covered her aching hands with his. "You don't have to do this all on your own, Annie," he said, his voice low with a peculiar intensity. "I remember every single moment."

12

Then

The accident at the garage ended Fletcher's childhood as completely and abruptly as the guillotine amputation that took his father's leg. He learned a new language, like what it meant to have a high-grade open fracture with severe vascular injury and damage to the posterior tibial nerve. He learned the complicated vocabulary of the surgical wing and the round-the-clock rhythm of life in the hospital.

Something else happened, too. His eyes were opened to the fact that he was now responsible, not just for himself, but for his father, for the garage, for the day-to-day coping with living that had to be done. Even though a guy lost his leg, the world did not stop to wait for him to recover. There were decisions to be made, and Fletcher had to be the one making them.

There were questions to be answered, endless inquiries from the medical team. The hospital people said the accident had to be completely documented so his dad could make an insurance claim and apply for payments from Workers' Compensation. The paperwork, with all its attendant duties, felt overwhelming sometimes, keeping him up at all hours, on the phone, on hold, talking to people thousands of miles away, strangers who didn't give a shit about his dad's leg, who didn't hesitate to say things like "that's not a covered event." But Fletcher didn't have a choice. His father needed someone to fight for him.

It shouldn't be a fight at all. When a guy's leg got crushed in an accident, insurance was supposed to cover his medical costs. Simple. Until the insurance company made it impossible.

The day after surgery, Dad was doing okay, according to his vital signs, but he seemed dazed. He lay half sitting up in bed, studying his leg—or the empty space where his leg should have been. The nurse had explained that he was on a lot of different medicines, some of which made him drowsy and confused.

The people at the hospital said his rehab work would begin almost right away. Dad had to learn how to function with one leg and one prosthesis.

There was still more paperwork to be done. Someone from the hospital's business office had told Fletcher to fill out endless forms, and had flagged all the places that needed to be signed. Medical directives, power of attorney, financial forms, consent forms.

"You're giving me all the power," he told his father with a grin. "Better watch out."

"You do right by me," Dad said, "or I'll kick your butt."

"How'll you do that with only one leg?"

"Smart-ass."

"Actually, that booklet they left you explains that you're going to get the most high-tech titanium, badass leg ever made." He tried to sound positive, even though the insurance company said the more expensive leg was not "medically necessary." Fletcher had thought they were joking. He quickly learned that insurance companies had no sense of humor.

"A new leg. I can hardly wait." His dad's face looked gray and tired, yet his eyes were on fire with anger.

Late the night before, Fletcher had read that one of the most common issues of an amputee was rage and grief—not just for the patient, but for the family. No shit, he thought. "Dad, this sucks so bad. It makes me insane, how bad this sucks. I wish there was something we could do to make it go away. This shit happened, and it's the lousiest break in the world. Let's work through it one thing at a time."

His father gave a grim nod and signed all the necessary forms. His hand was unsteady, and the writing looked weird and spidery, which freaked Fletcher out. For the first time in his life, he looked at his father and saw an old man.

"Whatever," Dad mumbled. "Guess I won't be much use around the garage for a while." He fell silent, then snapped his fingers. "Whiskey."

"You can't have—"

"No, I mean, we could become whiskey makers. Don't need two legs for that, and it's something I've been studying. Remember that year I worked in shipping and receiving in Kentucky? There's a big demand these days for small-batch whiskey."

"Sure," Fletcher said, not wanting to get into an argument. "Sounds great." Actually, the idea of distilling whiskey didn't seem preposterous. He'd had a job at a barrel works in Kentucky sophomore year, and he'd found the alchemy of whiskey making remarkable. That a combination of branch water and grain could produce something so singular was intriguing.

Annie's friend Pam Mitchell worked at her father's distillery, and she said they needed to expand their business. But that was a discussion for another time.

Dad scowled down at a consent form to authorize the incident investigation. "It was that damn power hoist. I bought it brand new. The sales rep said it was top-of-the-line, but he lied. It's garbage, not to mention a hazard. Son, I don't want you going near that thing except to take it to the junkyard."

The comment stuck with Fletcher. A hazard.

"You get some rest, Dad," he said. "I need to go back to the garage to meet the insurance adjuster."

"Yeah, tell him to watch himself around that piece of junk."

"Will do."

As he drove up the mountain, Fletcher saw that he'd missed a call from Annie. He didn't feel like calling her back. There was nothing he could say that wouldn't hurt her. The plans they'd made seemed like a fantasy now. Still, that didn't stop him from remembering the smell of her hair and the way her lips tasted when she kissed him, and the insanely great sex they had. He had never known a person who listened the way she did. She believed in him. She *got* him. Annie lived in a place inside him that left no room for anyone else. It was hard to imagine life without her, but his entire future was different now. In one crashing instant, everything had changed.

He walked into his father's garage to find everything exactly as it had been when the rescuers had taken his father away. Fletcher felt a thrum of panic in his chest as he surveyed the damage. He was haunted by the memory of his father's voice, hoarse from calling for help for hours. Why hadn't Fletcher been there?

He'd been poking around the salvage yard on the other side of town, looking for a part, and he'd lost track of the time. Then he'd run into Celia Swank, and they'd goofed off for another hour or so, talking about how weird it was to be done with school. Their class had scattered; only a few stuck around. Celia had tried flirting with him, but he'd pretended not to notice. Her epic boobs and shiny lips didn't tempt him. But he'd shot the breeze with her, only half listening to her gossip. And the whole time, he'd had no idea his dad was pinned under a ton of metal, nearly dead. The thought made Fletcher nauseated with guilt.

The ruined garage looked like the scene of a violent crime. There were tools and rags flung every which way by his dad as he'd struggled to get someone's attention while he was trapped and bleeding, probably crazed by pain. Where his father had lain, the smear of blood resembled a dark oil stain, its peculiar odor tainting the usual familiar scent of the garage. Now it smelled more like a slaughterhouse.

Fletcher glared at the broken steel. Fucking piece of crap. So much for the top-of-the-line claims made by the tool company's sales rep. One moment of failure, and a man's life was ruined. A single event, affecting not just his dad's future and livelihood, but Fletcher's as well. All the plans he'd made crumbled into dust.

Gordy Jessop, home from the U for the weekend, came by to see if he could help. He listened with a somber expression as Fletcher told him all the gory—truly gory—details.

"Man, that blows. His leg." Gordy gave a shudder. "What a mess."

Fletcher felt like taking a sledgehammer to the monstrosity. "Dad wants me to haul it to the dump so it won't crush anybody else."

"The dump. I hear Degan Kerry works there now. Guess his reign of terror in high school came to an inglorious end."

"I'll get started as soon as the insurance guy finishes." He walked slowly around the collapsed car lift. It still had its shiny new decals, touting its features—fifteen-thousand-pound lift capacity. Powder-coated paint finish. Solid steel construction.

He bent and studied the sticker, now peeling from the twisted metal. "Solid steel, my ass," he muttered.

"What's that?" Gordy asked.

"Look at this garbage. The decal says solid steel, but it was stuck here to cover a weld. So it's bullshit." Upon further inspection, he found several more welds used instead of solid steel. A slow burn of anger started inside him. His father's life had been ruined because the shady tool company hadn't sold him the product it promised.

"Can the two of us move this out of here?" Gordy asked, bending to grasp a broken piece.

"Hang on." Fletcher felt a surge of insight.

"For what? The insurance guy?"

"Yeah. We shouldn't touch anything here. Not until it's all documented."

"What do you mean?"

"We need pictures and some kind of accident report. Not just the one from the insurance guy. We need something that's, like, totally official."

"Holy crap, you're right." Gordy quickly grasped the situation. "I bet your father could sue the pants off of Acme Automotive Lift."

Fletcher kept every single note and picture in the insurance-claim account, and he took plenty of his own, including a video he shot with a borrowed camera while the claims adjuster narrated the report. Fletcher also found a guy in town who was a safety inspector. His specialty was forestry, but he was a mechanical engineer who agreed completely with Fletcher about the defective equipment. Not only was there welding where solid steel should have been used; the lift lacked another key safety feature, something he called an armlock mechanism. The safety inspector prepared and signed an official report comparing the lift that was sold to Fletcher's dad with the manufacturer's product description and warranty.

In Burlington, Fletcher went to the university library with a special pass from the hospital, and he used the Internet for hours, until his eyes blurred and his brain ached. He buried himself in information, absorbing facts and figures like a sponge, and also making notes just in case.

The next day, he went to Courthouse Plaza and started knocking on doors of law firms. No one would let him past the receptionist desk. Before anyone would even talk to him, they wanted something called a retainer fee. The problem was, Fletcher and his dad had no money to spare. With the insurance claim taking forever and Dad in rehab for weeks, Fletcher could scarcely come up with the scratch for groceries, much less a lawyer.

He went back to the library and the Internet, reading articles and abstracts and law books. He figured out that he didn't actually need a lawyer. Any private citizen had the right to file suit if they were injured. Okay, then. His dad was a private citizen. He'd been injured. Fletcher was going to figure out how to file the suit. He worked for days, studying the steps involved in the procedure, taking piles of notes, and mapping out a strategy.

Annie called him a lot, but he didn't pick up. He had to stay focused, and she was a distraction. He sent her an e-mail saying he was busy with his dad and the garage. Since the accident, she seemed a million miles away. Then he felt guilty and called her.

"Sorry," he said. "I've got a ton of shit to do."

"I know, Fletcher." There was a waver of hurt in her voice. "I wish I could help."

"I don't need your help," he said, and it came out sounding terse. "I mean, it's just . . . ah, Christ. This is taking up all my time."

"Don't feel bad," she said. "Just know that I'm thinking about you. I miss you. I'll see you at Thanksgiving break, okay?"

"Sure. Okay." He was pissed as he hung up the phone. Not at her, at himself. At the situation. But being pissed wasn't going to get things done.

He went over the plan with his father, who told Fletcher he was out of his gourd. "Remember that old saying, you can't fight city hall?" Dad asked. "It's true. You shouldn't be wasting your time on some crazy idea. I need you to keep the garage up and running so we don't go broke."

"I'll do both," Fletcher said. "I can look after the garage and work on the case at night. You worry about getting back on your feet—"

"Don't you mean *foot*?"

"Whatever. Just let me worry about everything else."

In many ways, he'd been doing that all his life. His father had always been like a big kid—impulsive, adventurous, and irresponsible. Fletcher was often the one who remembered what they needed at the grocery store or when they were supposed to go to the dentist. At a ridiculously young age, he'd learned to forge his dad's name on school permission slips and on checks, because Dad often forgot to pay the bills. Taking on a lawsuit was just one more thing he had to do on his own.

It struck Fletcher now that he might have to take care of his father forever. *Christ.*

Dad signed more papers—grudgingly. The documents were all available on the Internet for anyone to print out and use. They were official forms to show the court that Sanford Wyndham had legal capacity to sue.

That was just the first step. Then Fletcher had to outline his case in a petition, submit his facts and findings to prove he had a case, and show that his dad was entitled to damages.

Fletcher sweated bullets over the thing. He studied the process until his eyes practically bled. He painstakingly created and filled out all the necessary court documents. From the hours of reading he'd done, he knew that every single word, every punctuation mark, was crucial.

His first seven efforts were quickly rejected on technicalities by the court clerk. Something was missing, or improperly filled out, or not relevant to the case. Each time he made the corrections and went back, the filing was rejected for a different reason. He started to feel like a contestant on a game show, getting eliminated and having to start again from scratch.

Eventually, he got every single line of every single document right, and his hearing was scheduled. Gordy's sister gave him a haircut. It wasn't a very good haircut, but she did it for free.

On his assigned court day, Fletcher dressed in his one and only suit, with a stiff-collared white shirt and a blue silk tie. He borrowed his father's good shoes, the ones Dad had bought—coincidentally—the last time he'd gone before a judge. Only that time, Dad had not been the plaintiff.

Fletcher stared down at his feet. He bent and tied the laces tight. In front of the courthouse he paced back and forth, going over and over the facts in his head. Prove you have the right to sue. Prove you have a case. Take it before the right court.

There were guys and women in suits, hurrying up and down the stairs to the columned entrance, and they all looked as though they knew exactly where they were going. A woman in a lace dress holding some flowers came out of the courthouse with a guy in a pale blue tux—a bride and groom. Fletcher speculated that another stone-faced couple trudging slowly up the stairs were at the other end of the marriage spectrum, heading for divorce.

He thought briefly of Annie. He hadn't spent five minutes talking to her in weeks. This wasn't fair to her. The decent thing would be to let her go. She was probably ready, anyway, meeting new people at college and moving into a life of her own.

Then he reined in his thoughts and checked his paperwork for at least the tenth time. This should not be so complicated. His dad had been sold a defective piece of equipment. He'd lost his leg because of it. The case seemed simple, but after preparing and filing all the documents, he knew it wouldn't be.

He wiped his sweaty palms on his trousers and headed inside to Room 4. The bench seats reminded him of church pews, and he stood uncertainly, wondering where he was supposed to sit. He picked a spot at the end of an empty bench and sat down to wait.

The judge was a woman who looked as if she ate little kids for breakfast. Ruth Abernathy wore her hair pulled back and kept her thin-lipped mouth set in a seam of disapproval. Thick, straight eyebrows met in the middle, creating a frown that appeared to be etched permanently into her brow. Dark-rimmed reading glasses were perched on the tip of her nose.

Fletcher made sure he had his mobile phone on silent. Eyes straight ahead. One of the articles he'd read claimed that judges thrived on respect and dignity.

He had to wonder about that when the first case came up. Some guy wanted to sue his neighbor whose black Lab wouldn't stop barking. The neighbor intended to countersue the first guy for spray-painting an obscenity on his black Lab. He even brought the leashed dog with the bright pink phrase on its back, eliciting snickers from the gallery. Within a couple of minutes, the neighbors were shouting at each other, until the judge smacked her gavel on the desk and told everyone to simmer down. When it turned out the dog howled only as the shift whistle blew at the gravel quarry, she ordered the spray painter to pay for the dog's bath, and sent them on their way.

Fletcher tried not to jiggle his knee in impatience through the next couple of cases. Then a cop in uniform called his case number. Fletcher took a deep breath and stood.

As he approached the long library table in front of the judge's bench, he felt like a guy walking to an execution.

Judge Abernathy consulted the packet of papers in front of her. "Mr. . . . Wyndham."

"Yes, ma'am." His palms were sweating. "Your Honor."

"And you're the plaintiff?"

"No, ma'am, er, Your Honor. That would be my father, Sanford Wyndham. He's in the hospital. Still in intensive care."

The dragon lady's nostrils flared. "I'm aware of that. I do read everything."

Then why ask if I'm the plaintiff? Fletcher wondered.

"And your father is unrepresented by counsel?"

"That's correct, Your Honor. I have his power of attorney."

"Yes, I'm aware of that, also. Who prepared this petition?" She referred to the legal document in front of her.

"I did, Your Honor."

"You're . . . a student?"

"No, Your Honor. Er, not anymore. I graduated last June."

"From?" The unibrow lifted slightly.

"Switchback High School."

The brow lifted even higher. "And you are bringing suit against"—she consulted the notes in front of her—"the Acme Automotive Lift Company."

"That's correct."

She interrogated him rapidly and thoroughly, her questions shooting at him like a barrage of machine-gun fire. He thought he did okay, because he was prepared. He had spent weeks reading and researching and studying, all the while waiting for the next round of bad news about his father.

"This is a serious claim," said Judge Abernathy. "If you sincerely want this to go forward, you're going to need representation."

"That's good advice," he agreed. "But my dad and I can't afford a lawyer."

She glared at him for so long he thought she was trying to bore a hole in him. Then she said, "Mr. Wyndham, I have good news and bad news for you. The good news is, the jurisdiction is clear and you have yourself a cause of action."

Yes. Yes. Yes. He did an invisible fist pump of triumph. "Thank you, Your—"

"I'm not finished," she snapped. "Don't you want to hear the bad news?"

Not really, no.

"Yes, Your Honor."

"It's possible that there is something here, but you are completely unprepared for the work a situation like this entails. Is this a case of product liability? Defective manufacturing? Negligence? Personal injury? Is the defendant truly at fault, or is it a parts manufacturer?"

Shit.

"This is not the domain of an untrained layman. Therefore, even though I am going to allow the suit to go forward, I have a condition. You need to find yourself a lawyer."

"But I—"

"Now, I can't force you to do that, but if you don't, this won't go well for you. Mr. Wyndham, you don't want to go it alone. Have you gone to the Legal Aid Society?"

"I have. There's a backlog. No one could say when they could get to me." The Legal Aid office had been like a developing nation, crowded and chaotic. After Fletcher had waited four hours to speak to someone, an intern told him it could be months or even longer before he could get help. Priority was given to guys stuck in jail, not suits against a big company.

The judge drew her lips into a prune shape. "Keep looking, then. And don't go calling one of those late-night eight-hundred-number lawyers you see on TV. You're obviously good at research. So do your research and find yourself a lawyer who'll work on contingency."

Shit. Shit. Shit. He'd spent nearly every waking hour just trying to get this petition in front of her.

"But—"

The gavel slammed down, and the next case was called.

Finding a lawyer was easier for the judge to say than for Fletcher to do. It seemed most attorneys had no interest in a penniless kid whose father had lost a leg. He felt like defying the judge and making his own case anyway, but he kept thinking about her tone of voice when she'd said, "You don't want to go it alone."

But the more he read about the case, the more confusing it became. He knew he needed help, and he was sick of doors being slammed in his face. Following Abernathy's advice, he made a list of lawyers who specialized in injury cases, and scheduled appointments with the top three.

This resulted in three rejections. They either didn't believe him, or didn't think he was worth their time.

Fletcher changed his strategy. He selected four graphic photos of the accident—a shot of the collapsed lift, a close-up of the "solid steel construction" decal peeled away to show a failed weld, one of Dad's mangled leg, and another of the stump on the first day postop. He printed eleven-by-fourteen glossies of the shots in vivid color. Then he made another appointment, this time with a guy named Lance Haney, who had once won a settlement for an injured worker of a lumber company. Instead of bumbling through an explanation to the law firm's receptionist or paralegal, he walked directly into Mr. Haney's office and placed the photos on his desk.

"I'm Fletcher Wyndham," he said. "That's what happened to my dad seven weeks ago. It happened because there are welds where the manufacturer claimed there was solid steel." He set down a file with the other photos, the insurance report, the OSHA affidavit, and the safety inspector's report. "I need to hire a lawyer who will work on contingency."

Lance Haney was bald on the top with a fringe of dark hair around the sides, like a monk. He wore a Mr. Rogers–style sweater over a plaid shirt, which made him look nothing like the crusading consumer advocate Fletcher was hoping for.

Haney stared down at the pictures. Unlike the woman at the copy shop who had printed them out, he didn't look as if he needed to hurl. His mild, moon-shaped face was expressionless. Then he stared up at Fletcher and said, "We're going to kick somebody's ass."

It sounded so weird coming out of Mr. Rogers that Fletcher almost laughed. Almost. He noticed a gleam in the lawyer's eye. It was cold, like a shark's.

"That's the plan," Fletcher said. "I filed a petition but Judge Abernathy said I have to hire a lawyer."

"You've been to Abernathy?" He studied a document, sucking his lips together as if he tasted something sour.

"There's a copy of the petition in the file. You'll work on contingency?"

He leaned back in his chair. "I will. I don't collect unless you collect."

"How much?"

"A case like this takes a mountain of research, investigation, discovery. Hundreds of hours, and Acme is going to have an army of lawyers at their disposal."

"But you can win this case," Fletcher said.

"I can get you a fair settlement."

"On contingency."

"That's what I said."

"How much?" Fletcher asked again.

"I'll need fifty percent."

"Half?" Fletcher reached for the photos. "Sorry, but no."

Haney leaned forward and pressed his hand down on the prints. "I'm the best you'll find in this area."

"Says who?"

He handed him a brochure. "Client testimonials. Feel free to call any one of them for a reference."

"I will. Did they all give you half the settlement?"

"Each case is different."

"So that's a no. Here's how mine is different. You get twenty percent, Dad gets eighty."

Haney pushed the photos and the file across the desk. "See you around, kid."

In a strange way, Fletcher found himself enjoying the conversation. Haney was being a dick, but he clearly wasn't stupid. Fletcher gathered up the file and put it in his messenger bag. "Have a nice day," he said.

"Sixty-forty," Haney offered.

"Dude, it's my *dad*. He's only forty-seven. Sank his life savings into the garage and has a small-business loan besides. He's got to live the rest of his life with one leg. Twenty-two."

"Thirty-five."

Fletcher's research had suggested a range of 20 to 35 percent, so at least the guy was in the ballpark now. "What's your plan?"

"I won't have one until I do more research. But my strategy in a case like this is usually to sue everybody. For everything."

Sue everybody. Fletcher liked the sound of that. "Twenty-five." He fake-looked at his fake watch. "I have to get to my next appointment."

"Twenty-eight and you've got a deal," Haney conceded. "Leave the files and come back tomorrow at nine."

Fletcher walked out onto the street into a flurry of snow. How had it turned into November already? Where had the time gone? He should be feeling a sense of relief now that the case was in the hands of a lawyer. Instead, he was consumed. He woke up each morning thinking about the case and went to bed each night still thinking about it. In between, he kept the garage going . . . and he thought about the lawsuit.

In a case like this, sue everyone. For everything. Haney explained that "everyone" meant not just the company, but the sales rep and all the parts manufacturers involved. All of them could be found liable. None of them able to give Dad his life back. But as Haney pointed out, a fair settlement could make it possible for his life to go on.

The case became an obsession with Fletcher, the way Annie had once been.

Annie went home for Thanksgiving that year, her stomach squeezing tighter and tighter with nerves as the train clacked along the route from Penn Station. Since Sanford Wyndham's accident, the phone calls, e-mails, and letters between her and Fletcher had tapered off. She tried not to take it personally. She *didn't* take it personally. He was dealing with an extraordinary circumstance, and she didn't get to be at the top of his list.

Her girlfriends in the dorm told her that was a major warning sign. A guy was supposed to make his girlfriend a priority no matter what. No matter if his grandmother was on fire, or his dog was lost, or his dad's leg had been crushed.

Annie blew off the dorm mates. They weren't any smarter than she was, and they didn't know Fletcher. Still, as the train hissed and sighed to a stop at the station, she practically jumped out of her seat. She tugged her suitcase from the rack, ducking as it crashed down into the aisle. The last thing Fletcher needed was another accident to deal with.

She dragged her case to the exit of the train car and stepped out onto the platform of the old-fashioned redbrick station. The station dated back to 1875, and in the snowfall, it looked misty and detached from time.

A shock of cold air greeted her; Vermont winters were usually well under way by Thanksgiving. A trickle of passengers moved down the platform. She spotted Fletcher near the exit, recognizing his lanky form, limned in the glow of a wrought-iron gaslight. She called his name and waved, and ran the rest of the way to greet him.

Dropping the handle of her suitcase, she leaped up, hugging him, clinging with her arms and legs. "Oh my gosh," she said, her voice muffled by the collar of his jacket. "I missed you so much."

He set her down gently and held her close for a few seconds. And somehow, in those few seconds, she knew. She just knew. This was nothing like the blissful reunion that had played out in her head during the journey home. They did not meld together seamlessly, their hearts beating in tandem, their conversation effortless, the way things had been last summer.

Taking a deep breath, she pulled back and gripped his arms, taking a moment to study him. He was different in ways she hadn't anticipated. He looked thinner and harder, the handsome angles and planes of his face honed by worry and work. He even smelled different, wearing the sweet oily scent of the garage on his skin and hair. He seemed distracted, when all she wanted was for him to swing her up into his arms. He didn't, though.

"Thanks for picking me up," she said.

"Sure. Of course." He leaned down and pulled the suitcase through the lobby to the parking lot.

Her mother had wanted to pick her up, but Annie had dug in her heels. She wanted all the alone time with Fletcher she could get. Even a forty-five-minute drive up to Switchback counted as alone time.

As he put her suitcase in the trunk and drove away from the station, she wondered if it was going to be forty-five minutes of awkward silence. She tried not to let it happen. First things first.

"Catch me up on your dad," she said. "How's he doing now that he's back at home?"

"Better, now that he's out of rehab. That rehab place was grim. Now he gets around on crutches, and we have a wheelchair for the longer hauls."

"Will he . . . is he going to get an artificial leg?"

"Sure—a prosthesis. But that'll take time. He has to do tons more rehab—physical and occupational therapy. Then he'll get a temporary leg while a custom one is being made."

"I feel so bad for him." She turned sideways on the seat and studied his profile. He kept his eyes on the road, the wipers batting away the blowing snow. "How are you doing, Fletcher?"

"Okay. Busy. I know more about stump care than you want to hear."

"I do want to hear. Tell me all about your typical day." She hoped there wasn't a note of desperation in her voice.

"Seriously?"

"I want to know what this is like for you."

"No, you don't." He turned up the volume on the radio. Usher was singing "U Don't Have to Call."

She spun the radio knob to off. "I said I did."

He shot her a glance. "Every morning, I help him get up and take a piss. Sometimes he makes a mess, so I put him in the shower on a stool. Sometimes he falls and cusses me out. Then I haul him onto the bed so he can dress himself. While he's doing that, I make breakfast and hope like hell I can convince him to eat."

Annie winced, picturing the two of them struggling over everyday matters. "Is something wrong with his appetite?" She was aghast. People who didn't love to eat were a mystery to her.

"Something's wrong with his attitude," Fletcher said. "I can't blame the guy," he quickly added. "Anybody who's been through that is bound to have problems." Fletcher's hands flexed on the steering wheel. The headlamps of an oncoming car briefly lit his face, which looked as if it had been carved in marble. "He doesn't want to eat, doesn't want to shower, doesn't want to exercise, doesn't want to do anything but drink beer and watch TV."

That didn't sound one bit like the Mr. Wyndham she'd gotten to know over the summer. The guy she knew was positive and easygoing, more like a buddy than a dad. "Poor guy," she said softly. "It must be really hard for him. And for you."

"I don't mind that it's hard. I'd do anything for my dad. But it sucks when nothing changes. Every day I have to nag him constantly, and sometimes it works, but sometimes I just throw in the towel and go to work. And after work, I nag him some more to eat, and eventually help him get to bed. And then I get busy on the lawsuit."

"I don't understand. Isn't that lawyer you found taking charge of the lawsuit?"

"Sure, but there's a lot more to it than that. Dad and I have to do research and attend depositions, write statements, submit tons of paperwork. It's a big, stupid mess, and it's taking forever."

She sat quietly, digesting this. She knew Fletcher. He was the sort of person who didn't do things by half measures. He jumped in with both feet. He probably went over every single step and every document with the lawyer. "You're both coming to Thanksgiving dinner tomorrow, right?" she asked.

"Annie." He stopped the car at the bottom of the driveway and put it in park. "It's really nice of you and your family to offer, but Dad and I aren't coming."

Her heart sank. On the train, she had pictured everyone gathered around Gran's table, extended with the extra leaves, about to dig into the best meal of the year. There was nothing like a shared feast to bring people together.

She swallowed hard, finding her voice. "What, do you have something better to do?"

"Hell no. There is nothing better than eating at your place, are you kidding? It's just that my dad's in a lousy mood all the time, and it's a major chore just to get him out of the house. He'd be a real downer at your Thanksgiving feast."

"He'd be welcome, and so would you be." Right. Her mom had resisted when Annie had broached the topic, but ultimately, Mom had opened her heart to Fletcher and Sanford. No one in the Rush family could tolerate the idea of someone missing out on Thanksgiving dinner. "It's what families do, right?" she added. "Just because someone's in a rotten mood doesn't mean he should be shut out."

"We're not family." His voice was quiet and tight.

She could feel the discomfort emanating from him, and although she yearned to reach out and take his hand, she sensed her touch would not be welcome. "Yes, you are. Or, you will be, once you're sitting at the table with everyone else. Fletcher—"

"Listen, I realize you and I made plans," he said.

Annie knew then that he wasn't talking about Thanksgiving dinner. "We did," she said. "This is just a temporary setback. A bump in the road."

"I can't go running off to New York. Not now. Not next month or even next year. It's nuts to believe we have a future together. Our lives are too different now. I know you know that, Annie. Don't pretend you don't."

The icy note in his voice chilled her to the bone. To the heart. "Don't give up on us. I can take a leave from school. I'll come back, help you with your dad."

"You don't want to do that."

"Yes, I do."

"Then *I* don't want that. Jesus. Don't you get it? I don't want your help, I don't want you leaving school, and I don't want you coming home to Switchback."

On Thanksgiving Day, Fletcher spent the morning rereading a lengthy motion to dismiss from the opposing team of lawyers. He now knew this was a delaying tactic. It was meant to mess with the plaintiff's head, characterizing the suit as a ploy to squeeze money from a big company. It was also designed to create more hours of work for Lance Haney, perhaps causing him to make a mistake, like a small technicality of some sort so the case would be thrown out.

He looked up the precedent cases cited in the motion, and a couple of them did exactly what the Acme lawyers intended—they made him worry that the case would be dismissed.

He sent Haney a detailed e-mail reminding him about the deadline to respond, and asked to see the response before it was filed. Fletcher knew all his micromanaging was annoying to Haney, because the lawyer told him so, often and loudly. Fletcher didn't care. He didn't want to make friends with the guy. He wanted justice for his dad.

Haney—and his dad, come to think of it—told him he was getting too wrapped up in the case. He should leave things to the lawyers and justice system. Fletcher ignored them both. Attorneys and judges didn't care the way he cared. To them, it was just another day's work. To Fletcher, it was his father's future.

He felt shitty about the way he'd left things with Annie last night. She'd done nothing wrong. *He'd* done nothing wrong either. But since the accident, things had shifted and he couldn't put them back the way they were. One moment, the best part of life had lain in front of him like a vast, undiscovered country. The next moment, his options had narrowed down to one—sticking by his father.

No matter how much he wanted to be with Annie, he knew it was best for both of them to move on. Well, best for her, anyway. As for Fletcher, he had to pretend he didn't care, when in reality, his chest ached as if he'd been shot. Yesterday when he'd seen her getting off the train, his heart had nearly exploded, and it had taken all his strength not to hold her close and never let go. He hadn't told her that part, though. There was no point, and it would only make both of them feel worse than they already did.

So when he heard a car door slam and saw Annie marching up the front walk with a wicker basket in her arms and a shopping bag over her shoulder, he was confused. What part of "good-bye" did she not understand?

"Don't look at me like that," she said as he opened the door. "I didn't come here to beg and grovel." She walked past him and moved into the living room. The basket exuded a savory aroma so delicious that Fletcher nearly fainted. "I'm here to see your father."

"He's not—" Shit. Fletcher glanced around the house, self-conscious about the way it looked. He kept everything picked up—but not in a neat, good-housekeeping way. The floors were bare and most of the furniture had been shoved against the walls to give his dad plenty of room to maneuver.

Dad was dressed—sort of. He wore his usual getup of track pants that zipped up the side, an old gray sweatshirt, one tennis shoe, and two days' worth of whiskers. At least he hadn't started drinking yet.

He was stretched out on the sofa, staring glassy-eyed at the TV. The pregame chatter was just getting started, an announcer predicting a big upset in some football rivalry or other.

"Hiya, Mr. Wyndham," Annie said in a friendly voice. She set her things on the kitchen counter. Delicious smells filled the room. Fletcher had an urge to fall face-first into the basket.

"Hey, Annie girl. Good to see you." Dad attempted a smile. "I'd get up to give you a proper greeting, but as you can see, I'm indisposed."

She went over to the couch and perched on the seat next to him, like a tentative little bird. She was so pretty, with her shiny hair and bright eyes, her face open and eager. Fletcher had heard that people all have their dark places, but he'd never observed that in Annie. She was as bright as the sun, all the time.

"I'm sorry about your accident," she said to his dad. "And about all the hard times you've been having."

Dad muted the TV, then folded his hands behind his head. "Yeah, it's been a laugh a minute."

She leaned down and picked up last night's beer bottles—four of them. "Looks like you had a party and I wasn't invited."

"That's what I do. I party. I might take up smoking again, like I did when I was in high school."

"Oh, that would be just swell," she said, completely deadpan. "Then you would be a one-legged, alcoholic cancer victim. That's like a trifecta of woe."

Fletcher pressed his lips together, resisting the urge to laugh at the expression on Dad's face.

"You're cheeky," Dad said with a scowl. "You've always been that way."

"Nobody says cheeky anymore. I don't even know what it means. But if it means I'm bringing you a Thanksgiving feast and the pleasure of my company, then yeah. I'm cheeky."

"You brought dinner."

"I brought dinner. Fletcher said you weren't coming to the farm, so I decided to bring it here."

Dad scowled at the TV, which showed a montage of thick-necked football players in training. They were running rapidly through a course of tires, their thick legs pumping like pistons. "Your heart's in the right place, but I'm not hungry."

"Yes, you are." She carried the bottles to the kitchen and put them in the recycling bin. Then she regarded the stacks of files and banker's boxes on the dining table. It was all stuff to do with the lawsuit. Statements and motions and documentation. Mr. Haney called it "work product."

"This has to be cleared away," Annie declared. "Give me a hand, will you?"

Fletcher had everything organized. "But—"

"Fine, I'll move it myself," she said.

He decided not to resist. *She* was impossible to resist, and he knew the meal she'd brought would be epic. She and her grandmother cooked like pros. He and Dad hadn't had a normal meal together since before the accident. "I'll take care of it," he said to Annie. He moved everything to the mud room while she wiped off the table.

"Paperwork has no business on the dining table. Gran always says you shouldn't work where you eat."

"Who says we eat at the table?"

"Today, *I* say. We need plates and glasses and cutlery. I brought everything else." She turned into a whirlwind, bringing out colorful place mats and cloth napkins, candles in holders, and covered dishes of food. She finished setting the table, lit the candles, then went over to his dad and picked up the crutches leaning against the armrest of the sofa. "Dinner is served. And if you dare say you're not hungry, I'm taking it all away."

Fletcher felt mesmerized by the incredible aromas wafting from the table. "He's hungry," he told Annie. "We're both starving."

"Speak for yourself," said Dad. "I don't feel like eating."

"At least be sociable," Annie said. "You can do that, can't you?"

"My leg fucking hurts," Dad exploded. "I don't feel like getting up."

Fletcher crossed the room in two strides. "I know your damned leg hurts. But you don't get to talk to her that way. Ever. I once had a dad who told me cussing at a woman is not okay. What happened to that guy, huh? Now get your ass up and let's eat."

Dad's eyebrows lifted, and he gave Fletcher a glimmer of respect. Then he hoisted himself up on the crutches and transferred himself to the wheelchair. Gripping the wheel handles, he made his way to the table.

Annie seemed completely unruffled by the whole exchange. She started a pot of fresh coffee, then uncovered the dishes one by one. "Today, for your dining pleasure, we have turkey that was brined overnight in salt water flavored with maple syrup." Like a skilled waiter, she made a flourishing motion with her hand over the platter, which included two glistening drumsticks. "The turkey comes from Earl Mahoney's farm. His meat is free range and organic. We roasted it in sage butter. And we have homemade sweet potato hush puppies with sriracha ketchup, dressing with wild mushrooms and walnuts—" She caught a look from Fletcher's dad. "Don't judge until you taste it. I know everybody has strong opinions about dressing, but this will change your mind. Where was I? Garlic mashed potatoes and gravy, brandied cranberry compote, and pumpkin pie in a maple pecan shell."

"Uncle," Dad said, grabbing his stomach as he positioned himself at the table. "I surrender. This is manna from heaven. And just so you know, I'm not letting you leave. Ever." He was grinning with more happiness than Fletcher had seen from him in weeks.

She sat down, motioning for Fletcher to do the same. In a gesture as natural as it was charming, she took each of their hands. "In my family, we don't give silent thanks," she stated.

"Of course you don't," Fletcher murmured. He loved her so much in that moment he couldn't see straight.

"Don't be cheeky." She winked at Dad and then lowered her gaze. "We give thanks for this delicious meal, for football on TV, and for each other." She gave their hands a squeeze and let go. "How's that?"

"Perfect," Fletcher said. "Hey, listen—"

"Then let's eat." She served them each an enormous plate of food. It was without a doubt the best meal Fletcher had ever had. He found himself wishing he had a spare stomach so he could eat this all day. His dad dug in and gave a soft moan of pleasure. He didn't stop eating until he'd finished seconds of everything.

Annie had a small taste of each dish. "You're not hungry?" Fletcher asked.

"I don't want to ruin my appetite," she explained, dabbing her lips with a napkin. "I have another feast to attend." With that, she stood and reached for her parka. "Mr. Wyndham, it's really good to see you."

"You betcha, sweetheart. Thank you. Really." Dad gave her a satisfied smile and patted his belly. "And I'm sorry I was such a bast—a grumpy old man."

"I'll forgive you if you eat up all the leftovers."

Fletcher walked her to her car. "That was incredible. Totally unexpected. I don't know what to say."

" 'Thank you' works." She smiled, though he caught a glint of sadness in her eyes.

"That was really nice of you. I wish . . ." The cold wind cut through his shirt. "I feel bad about being stuck here." He gestured toward the house. "You see how it is with my dad."

She nodded, not smiling anymore. "Yes."

"And then there's all the legal stuff—"

"Isn't that what the lawyer's supposed to do? Handle the legal stuff?"

"Sure, but there's a ton of research to be done. I was up half the night finding a case to cite to support our motion to compel the equipment company's executives to answer questions even when their lawyers instruct them not to . . ." He could see her eyes glazing over. "Anyway. It's complicated."

She crossed her arms in front of her and regarded him thoughtfully. "You like this. Don't deny it. There's a part of you that's totally into this."

So she knew, then. She knew his deep-down secret, the thing that had taken him by surprise, the thing that was so powerful he couldn't ignore it. He *did* like this process. He liked the research, the logic, the dives into case studies and precedents. He liked the way a case was built, brick by brick. And even though Haney complained and told him to quit micromanaging, Fletcher refused to take a step back.

"I need to do everything I can to help," he said. The wind plucked at his thin shirt. "Anyway, thank you. You're awesome." He pressed his hands to his sides to keep from grabbing her and holding on to her forever.

Her smile expanded. So did her sadness. So did his. "That's me. Awesome. See you around, Fletcher. Good luck with your dad." She got into the car and slammed the door, fast and hard.

Shivering in the brittle November cold, he watched her drive away, the car lights glimmering in the gloomy afternoon snow flurries. Then he turned and went back inside. His dad was savoring another piece of pumpkin pie with a dollop of maple-sweetened whipped cream. He took a sip from a steaming mug of coffee. "Son, is that the girl you dumped last night?"

"Yep, she's the one."

"You're an idiot. You know that, right?"

"Yeah, Dad. I know."

Annie drove up Rush Mountain in tears. She couldn't call it a breakup. Yet she felt broken, because she and Fletcher were losing each other.

He'd said as much last night, although she truly hadn't grasped the situation until the moment she'd walked into his house. Then it had hit her like a knock on the head. His life revolved around his dad, the garage, and the lawsuit. There was no room in their world for her.

When she walked into the kitchen at the farm, she cried some more in her mother's arms.

"I know it hurts," Mom said. "I'm sorry, baby."

"No, you're not," Annie said. "You wanted us to split up."

"I never wanted you to get hurt. My goodness, no mother would wish that on her child. All I want is for you to figure out your own life before you try to make a life with someone else."

"It doesn't matter now. Everything worked out exactly the way you wanted it to. He has to stay in Switchback, and I have to go."

"You'll be all right," Mom said. "It'll take time, but I promise, you'll move ahead and you'll be fine."

Annie and Fletcher never spoke again of putting their lives together. It was simply impossible. He stayed with his father, of course. There really was no other choice. And Annie stayed in college.

Initially, missing him felt like a raw ache that wouldn't heal. But time did its part. The mournful passing of weeks and then months dulled the pain. The physical distance felt like an enormous gulf, and the bond that had once seemed invincible thinned to a fragile thread.

Their paths diverged like a train track splitting off at a one-way junction. Annie was swept into the world she had wanted to inhabit long before Fletcher came along. She lost herself in classes on storytelling strategies and the language of film. She learned to operate all kinds of cameras, lighting and lenses, honing her knowledge of digital frame and sequence by venturing out on shoots and tapping into the energy of the city. She aimed her camera at subjects that excited her, like the food carts and playgrounds near Washington Square, or the fish market up at Hunts Point.

She found part-time work at a buzzy new restaurant called Glow. She went to live concerts all over the city and acquired a fake ID so she could go to bars with upperclassmen.

Eventually, she figured out how to think of Fletcher without letting her eyes fill up with tears. And finally, she figured out how to avoid thinking of him at all.

13

Now

Kyle and his wife, Beth, were there the moment Annie managed to stand on her own. She used to require two helpers and a gait belt around the waist. Every movement called for intense concentration, and after only a few minutes, she felt as if she'd run a marathon—short of breath, shaking muscles, sweat running down her temples. The care team didn't let up. She had to practice and practice, and now she was supposed to get up and stand on her own two feet, all by herself.

Her brother and sister-in-law tried to act nonchalant as they sat together on the sofa in her room, holding hands while they watched her. The PT specialist waited next to the bed, ready to grab the waist belt if her legs melted, which they sometimes did.

"This might take a while," she warned them, fiddling with her wristbands. The ID band had a bar code that was scanned every time she took a pill. There was another band that said *Fall Risk* in bold letters.

"Take all the time you need," Beth said.

"I've never understood that phrase—'take all the time you need.' What if I take less than the time I need? Or more? Will I get in trouble?"

"It's just an expression," Beth explained. "I suppose it means don't rush yourself. But don't dawdle either."

Annie could tell she was making the two of them nervous. "You're not yourself," her mom had said yesterday. Was she not acting like herself? Who was she acting like?

She glanced at Nancy, the physical therapist du jour. Nancy simply gave her a firm nod, a you-can-do-it nod.

I can, thought Annie. I can do it. She had come a long way since an organ procurement team had started hovering, waiting to hear if she would be declared brain-dead. Everyone kept saying how lucky she was; most people never recovered from a coma. She was young and healthy and the injury was not as bad as it could have been, primarily a bruised frontal lobe with no broken bone. She didn't feel lucky, though. She felt... lost.

As she regarded her brother and Beth, Annie's heart filled. These two. Kyle had been such a big part of her world when she was growing up. Eight years her senior, he had been a combination of playmate and coach, striking a balance between teasing and teaching. With Kyle urging her on, she had learned to be fearless on the mountain, whether on a toboggan, snowboard, or skis. He'd shown her the best place for catching pollywogs in the springtime, how to play mumblety-peg, how to shoot a layup and do a racing dive off the starting block.

He had shown her that not all men were like their dad, walking away from their families.

And Beth. She and her two kids, Lucas and Dana, had joined the family on a wave of noisy joy. She and Kyle had two more, Hazel and Knox. Mom liked to call them Icing and Cake. The icing on the cake. It was important that the two balance and complement each other. You didn't want the cake to be overpowered by strong flavors or textures in the icing. This was why browned butter was a key ingredient in icing. It was smooth and rich without adding sweetness.

"I'm not ready to stand up yet," Annie said to Nancy.

"It says on your assessment from yesterday that you are," Nancy replied.

"I need a nap," Annie said. When she slept, she dreamed of long ago. Yet in her dreams, it didn't feel like long ago. The drifting images of the past seemed as if they'd happened only moments before. When she slept, her mind filled with colorful autumn days, raking leaves in the yard. Ice-skating on Eden Mill Pond. Riding her bike, working in the garden with her grandmother, going to the harvest fair. Frying sage leaves for the dressing at Thanksgiving. Everything seemed so real until she woke up to the fluorescent-lit reality of the rehab center.

"Caroline's worried you'll have trouble waking up again," said Beth.

"And miss all this awesome action?" Annie looked around the room. On the wall opposite the bed was a corkboard decorated with handmade cards from her nieces and nephews, and the paintings her mother had done. Her brother and sister-in-law had brought another Caroline Rush original today. It was a touching, elegiac landscape of the view from the front porch of the farmhouse. The apple orchard was blooming, and the whole mountainside glowed with the spring green of budding sugar maples. Her mother had a special talent with light and shadow. Annie wondered what Mom's life would have been like if she'd gone to art school. Would she have stayed married to Dad? Or would she have set herself up in a loft in SoHo, joining the New York art scene?

"How about you give it a shot," Nancy suggested. "I'll be right beside you. Show us you can get yourself out of bed."

Stated in those terms, it didn't seem like standing up should be such a big hurdle. She went through the drill they'd taught her. First push yourself up to sitting. Bring your legs over and down. She glared at her scrawny legs, encased in yoga pants. Over and down. And there she was. Scoot to the edge of the bed. Feet shoulder width apart. She wore garish yellow tube socks with nonskid rubber dots on the bottom. Lean forward, nose over toes. Use your core strength, and straighten up.

After a few false starts, she stood with the bed behind her, only slightly winded.

Nancy set the old-lady walker in front of her. "Way to go," she said. "Hang on and steady yourself. How do you feel? Any dizziness?"

"Total dizziness," Annie said, placing the palms of her hands on the walker handles. "But it's all right. It's fine."

"Good job," said Beth. She got up and gave Annie a hug, leaning across the walker. "You're amazing. We're so proud of you."

"For getting out of bed? The bar is set low, then."

She practiced walking up and down the hall, flanked by Kyle and Beth as they passed the wide doorways of the other rooms, with neatly lettered name cards and warnings posted—*Oxygen in Use. Cardiac Diet. Fall Risk.* Raven, the book girl, wheeled her cart by.

Left foot, right foot, stay in the box of the walker. Don't push it in front of you like a lawn mower or a shopping cart. It was strange, having to tell herself how to walk. Still, she preferred moving around to lying in bed.

Kyle and Beth listened intently to Nancy as she reiterated the importance of regular daily exercise. "We're part of your discharge plan," Kyle said. "They want to make sure we can help you when you get home."

Home. The picture that popped into her head when she thought of home was an old one, like a vintage postcard propped on the desk at the office, a reminder of the reason a person worked so hard. She could see the place like an image from one of her dreams of long ago. One of her dreams that felt like yesterday. She could perfectly envision the country road winding up the hill. The hundred-year-old farmhouse where she had spent her childhood, on a mountain named after her mom's great-grandfather, was painted white with a wraparound porch, the garden surrounded by a white picket fence. Orchards, flowers, a trout stream, a pond, sledding hills . . . paradise. The expansive Rush sugarbush covered the hills all around the farm, and tucked away in the woods was the sugarhouse, where the magic happened every winter.

"Keep going," Nancy urged her, and Annie realized she had stalled out in the middle of the hallway, unable to think and move simultaneously. "When you get to the lounge room, you can sit and visit for a little while."

She felt breathless and shaky by the time they reached the seating area in the lounge. Its decor was as bland as the rest of the facility, but there was a nice rock fireplace and a wall of shelves crammed with all kinds of books.

"Fletcher Wyndham came to see me," she told Kyle and Beth.

Kyle whipped around to face her. "What did he say to you?"

"Um, just . . . You know, he heard I was here. I suppose he decided to come for a visit. That's what people do sometimes, visit a sick friend or relative. He once told me that after his dad's accident, no one came, so he probably figured that people in the hospital need visitors, even if they say they don't."

"Oh," said Kyle. "I guess that's okay."

She didn't want to tell her brother about the wild tangle of emotions Fletcher had stirred in her. She wasn't ready to speak of the memories, good and bad. "You seem really tense, Kyle. Was he not supposed to visit?" She paused, considering this. "I'm not really his friend or his relative, am I?"

"It's fine," Beth said softly, touching Kyle's arm. "Annie, would you like to have other visitors? Your old friend Pam Mitchell would love to come. So would Professor Rosen, your mentor at NYU. And Coach Malco—she's still in charge of the swim team, and you were one of her stars, remember?"

Swimmers, take your marks.

"It's your call," said Beth. "We don't want to overwhelm you with everything at once."

"People keep saying that," Annie said. "Do I seem overwhelmed? Or just plain whelmed? Is that even a word?"

"The goal is to get you well enough to come home," Beth said.

"When?" Suddenly Annie wanted that with all her heart. She yearned for it so hard she wanted to hit something.

After her brother and sister-in-law left, Annie slept for a long time. When she woke up, she went to the dining room for lunch service instead of eating in bed. Eating a solitary meal from a rolling tray made her feel lame, so she resolved to get moving and sit at a table. The other patients were silent and uncommunicative, wrapped up in their own injuries and illnesses.

Annie didn't like the dining room. Everyone sat at separate tables, eating alone, except those who couldn't feed themselves and had an aide spooning food into their mouths. It was preternaturally quiet and depressing. No wonder most people took their meals in their rooms.

Eating was supposed to be a communal activity. Performed alone, it was merely a body function.

"Can I join you?" she asked the old woman at the next table.

"Uh," said the woman.

Annie took it as a yes, and moved to the large square table. "I'm Annie."

"Mavis." The woman sat a bit straighter in her chair. She was ancient, with wispy white hair and glasses on a beaded chain.

Annie saw a guy watching them and gestured at the empty chair next to her. His name was Jax. She remembered him from group. "Would you like to sit here?"

And then several other patients were staring at them. "We need more room at the table," said Mavis.

"Good luck with that," murmured Jax. "Iggy's on the floor today."

Iggy was everyone's least favorite orderly, a rule Nazi with a clipboard and an attitude. Someone said she was a former corrections officer.

Annie motioned to her. "Can you help us move some of these tables together?"

"I'll have to check."

"Check what?"

"With my supervisor."

Annie offered a sweet smile. "Good idea. We'll just wait while you go do that."

Iggy clutched the clipboard to her chest, did a crisp about-face, and marched from the room, probably hoping to find a supervisor who would quote policy stating the tables couldn't be moved.

"Okay, go!" Annie said in a loud whisper.

Those who were able got up and moved the separate tables together into a long banquet arrangement.

When the Nazi returned, her eyes blazed as she took in the rearranged dining room. "The furniture is not to be moved without a work order."

"Okay," said Annie. "We'll keep everything right here, just like this."

The nostrils flared. The hands gripped the clipboard tighter. She did another about-face and strode to her post by the bus cart.

Annie and the other patients formed a tribe of broken people. Yes, they were broken but they were still human. Sitting family style reinforced this. There was Wendell the logging accident victim. Jax the daredevil, once a motorcycle gang member, was now a stone-faced cyborg whose chest was surrounded by a metal cage, his head crowned with a spiky apparatus that made him look like a character in *Game of Thrones.* Ida was beautiful in profile on the right side, but the whole left side of her face looked as though it was melting. Stroke victim. There were others at the far end of the table, and Annie resolved to get to know them next time.

She remembered the power of food to bring people together. To heal.

"This food sucks," someone said.

"We're on a special diet," answered Luanna, a heart patient.

"What's it called? The disgusting-food-weight-loss program?"

"It's not disgusting. Bland, though."

"I used to eat fire-roasted chipotle peppers on crackers," said Jax.

"I used to make my own huckleberry jam," said Ida.

"We can do better," Annie said softly.

"What's that?"

"Better. We can do better. Let's do better." Annie knew she had extremely high standards. She could tell, just from the taste and texture, that the kitchen used institutional ingredients and methods. She looked down at her plate of overcooked vegetables and starchy potatoes. "Did you know that the average fruit or vegetable travels around fifteen hundred miles before it's sold to a consumer?"

"Nope," Mavis said, poking a fork at her ham steak. "Never heard that."

"Forty percent of fruit and twelve percent of vegetables come from other countries," Annie continued, plucking facts from some corner of her awakening brain. "So to keep food from spoiling during shipping, the produce has to be picked before it has a chance to fully ripen. Most people don't understand how important ripening is. When produce is allowed to ripen naturally, it absorbs nutrients from its surroundings—the sun and rain and soil. So fruits and vegetables that ripen during shipping are lacking in essential nutrients."

"Good to know," Ida said, taking a sip from her water glass. "Back home, I try to get all my fruit and veggies from the farmers' market."

"That's great. If everyone would do that, we'd all have healthier diets."

"It's pricey stuff, though."

"But so much better for your health. Think of it as saving money by keeping you in better health." Annie rolled her chair back from the table and wheeled herself over to where Iggy was standing—and sulking. "I'd like to meet the chef."

"The chef." The woman frowned. "Oh, you mean the kitchen manager."

"Could I do that?"

She pursed her lips. Then the frown eased. Perhaps she'd made her peace with the furniture moving. "Lunch service is over, so I suppose Pikey wouldn't mind. You want a push?"

A few minutes later, Annie was in the big commercial kitchen, surrounded by stainless-steel shelving and countertops, prep and cleanup areas. Pikey was a tall black guy in a white chef's coat, checked pants, and black clogs. Annie perked up immediately. There was something quite irresistible about a guy in chef's clothes.

"Hey, Sleeping Beauty." He wiped his hands on a tea towel and shook her hand in greeting. "That's the staff's nickname for you," he added.

"I've been called worse," Annie said.

"Haven't we all? What can I do for you today? The floor staff's been telling me you haven't been eating much. No appetite?"

"I do have an appetite, but unfortunately, it turns out I'm picky."

He nodded and stroked his chin. "Sounds like something my first wife would say."

"Food is my life," Annie blurted. The blurt came out of nowhere but it felt true.

"Honey, food is everyone's life. Some of us just understand it better than others."

She eyed the glass-front cold box filled with produce in bins from a Chicago warehouse. The shelves were lined with gallon cans of ingredients and giant plastic tubs of oil and other condiments. "You like working here?"

"Oh, yeah. It's kind of a trade-off. I used to work for a high-end resort over on Saranac Lake. Fiddlehead ferns in butter and thyme, brook trout meunière, fancy stuff."

"Do you miss it?"

"The cooking, yeah."

"Then why did you leave?"

"At the resort, my schedule had me working when everybody else was off. Now I got my nights and weekends back. Working here gives me time with my family."

Family again. It was important to everyone. Like food. Like breathing.

"Do you enjoy the work itself? The cooking?"

"It's just okay. The menus are set by a staff dietician, and the supplies come from a big distributor, so a lot of it is pretty basic." He gave her a quick tour of the facility, and Annie felt excited, talking about food with someone who knew his way around a kitchen. She was itching to get her hands on some food prep.

"What about getting ingredients locally instead of from a big distributor?"

"I'm not in charge of purchasing. I could suggest it at our monthly meeting."

"This place is surrounded by acres of garden space," Annie said. "It's on the activity calendar every day—we're supposed to go outside and help with the gardening. It's therapeutic. Suppose the gardens were filled with vegetables and fruits and herbs instead of flowers."

"Hey, the whole kitchen staff would be all over that. Girl, I like the way you think."

"Really? I have no idea how I think," she said. "Ever since I woke up, I have to think about everything until something makes sense."

"You're making plenty of sense now. A creative thinker. I like that. Are you a chef?"

"No. I . . ." Annie let her voice trail off. She felt her shoulders tense, and her mind raced away from a dark, gaping hole of indistinct images.

Pikey must have sensed the shift. "I'll tell the activities director."

"Activities director. This is like being on a cruise," said Annie. She didn't know whether she had ever been on a cruise.

Inspired by the garden project, she didn't bother falling asleep after lunch. Sleep was for people who had nothing better to do. She went to her room, found her writing practice book and a soft lead pencil and eraser. She spent a long time lost in thought, diligently sketching a garden plan. The grid-ruled paper made it easy to draw the beds and arrange things according to plant height and irrigation needs. It was a good plan. She had grown up on a farm, and making a garden plan was an annual ritual in her family. Each year after the sugar season, they'd all sit down with the seed catalogs and decide what they wanted to grow in the summer garden. Remembering those times, she rolled up her sleeves and got to work. When she finished, she regarded her sketches with satisfaction. It was an excellent start.

She still wasn't sleepy, so she decided to do some organizing. The OT people wanted her to create her own system of organizing belongings—clothes, books, writing supplies. She didn't have much—a few changes of clothes, hospital-issued toiletries, things to read, puzzles and games, her feelings chart and gear used in therapy. In the bottom drawer of the nightstand, she found a stack of forms and papers bound into file folders. Medical and insurance forms. A lot of the notes were written in shorthand with numerical codes, but she was able to decipher bits of information about a subdural hematoma and her brain hemorrhaging inside her skull. Since it was a closed head injury, a drain had been put into her skull to relieve the pressure until the swelling and bleeding subsided. She touched her head, trying to picture the drain. Was it like a tiny spigot, the sort used to draw off samples from a barrel of whiskey or wine? The secondary diagnoses were harder to translate, and she lost patience and put the medical information away.

In a bag marked *Patient Belongings,* she came across a long skinny clasp envelope. She upended it on the bed, and a thick file folder slid out, followed by a gold ring. A wedding band.

Annie recoiled briefly, as if the ring were a spider. A flicker of pain started in her temples. She carefully picked it up and slipped it on her left ring finger. It was far too loose and looked strange on her hand, so she took it off. Maybe it belonged to someone else. Maybe it had been left behind by another patient.

She put the ring back in the envelope and opened the folder. There was a legal document with official-looking seals, bound at the top with a big clip. *Decree of Divorce. In Re: The Marriage of Martin Harlow (petitioner).*

A sting of fear shot through her. Martin Harlow. Who was that?

The petitioner.

Her name was on the document as well. She was the respondent—Anastasia Rush.

She stared at the page for a long time. Tried to figure out which face on her feelings chart showed the way this document made her feel. ☺ ? ☹ ? ✌ ?

Decree of divorce. I'm divorced.

She knew what divorce was. It had happened to her parents. It had happened to her family. To her childhood. To her entire conception of what her family was.

And now she, too, was divorced.

She had been married to a person but she didn't remember it. She was divorced from him, and she didn't remember that either.

Her first impulse was to grab the phone and call her mother. She had memorized the number and knew how to get an outside line. She reached for the receiver, then hesitated. The psychiatrist had encouraged her to let the past return on its own. Annie needed to think this over before quizzing her mother about everything. The memories had to be *hers.*

She lay back on the bed and closed her eyes. She did this for the rest of the day. And the day after that, interrupting herself only when the schedule called for yet another therapy session.

She searched her thoughts, but the memories weren't there. Every once in a while, something fluttered like a shadow at the edge of her vision. A flicker. A feeling, a fleeting image. But the moment she tried to focus on it, the shadow dissolved like the impossibly friable remnants of a dream upon waking.

She was practicing independent walking in the rehab gym when things began to change.

With Nancy coaching, Annie braced herself between two parallel bars, putting one foot in front of the other while concentrating on her balance. A melody came from the big-screen TV in the corner of the large, mirrored room. There was a flash in the dark, a split-second vision of a half-naked man in cowboy boots.

She froze, clutching the bars, and stared at the screen. The tune coming through the speakers was nondescript, but mildly engaging in a twangy, neo-country-western way. It had been chosen for its brevity and simplicity and because it was available royalty-free at a low cost. And it stuck; the simple tones of the slide guitar became a powerful branding mechanism for the show.

Nancy was saying her name, asking her some question or other, but Annie stayed focused on the screen as the opening credits flashed over images of a ridiculously handsome, laughing chef in work-worn blue jeans, an apron over his broad chest, his muscular arms on display. Close-ups flashed—the flare of a fire, the flourish of a beautifully plated meal. As the brief ditty closed, the frame froze on the chef while his perky cohort hovered at his side, a glowing satellite to his shining sun. Then the still shot came to life.

"I'm Martin Harlow," he said, offering the camera a look that was filled with a warm welcome, as if he wanted to reach out and hug the viewer.

"And I'm Melissa Judd," said the blond cohost with the cheerleader smile.

"And this," they said together, "is *The Key Ingredient.*"

"Yo, Annie," said Nancy. "You need to take a break?"

She felt dazed. All the blood had dropped from her face, leaving her lips and cheeks ice cold. She tried to speak, but the words seemed to float inaudibly out through the hole in her neck. She tried again, and managed to whisper, "I don't need a break. I have to stop, and watch this show."

"Watch what? Oh, that program? I think it's a rerun." Nancy gamely helped her into a wheelchair and positioned her to face the TV.

Yes, it was a rerun. The key ingredient for that episode had been smelt. Filming the sequence had been crazy and fun. They had all gone smelt dipping at night in a cold Canadian river. Scooping up nets full of the small, silvery fish by the light of lanterns had provided plenty of entertaining footage. The resulting dish was a triumph. Flash-fried in a simple coating of crumbs and smothered in aromatics and butter, the smelt was mild and sweet, fresh with the elemental taste of the outdoors.

"That's my show," Annie whispered, flooded by memories so intense and swift that her head pounded. She felt as if she'd swallowed a chunk of ice, and her brain was freezing. "That's my show."

"It's everybody's show these days," Nancy said. "Everyone I know watches it."

"No, I mean it's—" Annie broke off. They already thought she was loopy, and she didn't want to miss a moment. "I just really want to watch this."

"Sounds like you could use a break." Nancy picked up her wrist and checked her pulse. "It's a cool show," she added. "I watch it all the time."

Annie didn't move a muscle as the episode progressed. Maybe she didn't even blink. Even the commercials held her captive. The sponsors of *The Key Ingredient* were treated like royalty. Their advertising dollars made the entire production possible. She had sat through endless meetings with producers and media planners. She and the staff had worked fourteen-hour days, creating demo reels and hosting events for sponsors. Martin rocked the meet-and-greet process, turning on the charm in order to sell spots. The courtship of sponsors had never been Annie's favorite aspect of the job, but she knew its value. It was all in a day's work.

For the rest of the afternoon, Annie binge-watched the show on the computer in the lounge room. The trickles of memory coalesced like a gathering wave, then crescendoed to a deluge. She felt herself plunging back into the lost days of her life like a swimmer taking the first dive off the racing block, breaking the surface and shooting smoothly into the middle of the lane. She dove into the forgotten times, when she'd had a career, a home, a husband. *Martin.*

Martin Harlow. The Petitioner. He'd encouraged her to keep her name when they married. Adopting the husband's name was outmoded, especially when the wife was incredibly talented in her own right. Oh, he was a charmer, wasn't he? She had tailored the show just for him. She'd worked for years to ensure its success. *The Key Ingredient* had been her idea. Her best and brightest, a passion she had pursued since college.

Finding the key ingredient, acknowledging its source, and building a story around the dish was a simple enough concept, but the execution was complicated. Annie's role was to make everything run seamlessly. She was good at her job. She'd won awards, even. She remembered the surreal feeling of holding an Emmy trophy in both hands, smiling for the camera, thanking her amazing and talented husband, her dear friend Melissa …

When her mother showed up later that day, Annie was still staring at the computer screen. She was parsing through memories and recovering them in fits and starts, in splintered pieces, still trying to see the whole picture.

Her mom was with one of the social workers, which probably meant someone had called her to say Annie was behaving strangely. Maybe they were worried that Annie couldn't handle so much information at once, that her head would explode.

She took off the headphones and set them on the table next to the computer. "I saw the divorce papers. I heard the theme song from the show."

Mom sat down next to her and gave her shoulder a squeeze. "Are you all right?"

"I can't even begin to answer that. Why didn't you tell me about my life?" Her voice cracked with pain.

"There's just so much. We didn't know where to start." Her mother sent an uncomfortable look at the social worker. "The doctors warned us not to inundate you with everything at once, especially the painful things that happened. We don't want to traumatize you further when you've been making such amazing progress."

"Good call," Annie muttered.

The woman offered a calm smile. "You can take all the time you need," she assured Annie. "In my experience, memories come back when the person is ready."

Annie bristled at the condescension in the social worker's voice. "What do you mean, *ready*? It's my life. My past." She clutched the arms of her wheelchair in frustration. She had wanted to remember on her own, not be told by someone else what her life had been like. But she also needed to know. *Now.* "There are too many gaps. Why can't I just remember? Why can't you help me do that?"

Mom reached over and gently pried her grip loose from the chair arms. "Of course we can. Tell us what you remember, and we'll help with the rest."

14

Then

In the autumn of her senior year at NYU, Annie walked through her favorite sections of Washington Square Park, looking to shoot something. She had signed out a state-of-the-art cinema camera from the film school lab in order to film a documentary. The assignment was to incorporate video and still photography, voice-over narration, and an interview. It would be her most important project to date—the senior thesis.

She wanted to nail it. But she lacked one glaring, critical factor—a topic. She had been racking her brain for weeks. Her classmates and the members of her study group all seemed totally inspired and driven. They were working on global warming. The vaccination controversy. Returning veterans. Ground Zero, so eerily close to campus.

"Don't pay attention to the others," Professor Rosen told her. "Pay attention to you. What's the big thing that you want?"

Everything. But of course, that wasn't helpful. She was going to have to narrow it down.

Professor Rosen, who happened to be her senior thesis adviser, was known to be exacting, demanding, critical, and fiercely intelligent. He had a Pulitzer, a Peabody, an Oscar, and a temper. He was also honest and, unlike a lot of his colleagues, unafraid of sentiment in film. His essay arguing that *It's a Wonderful Life* was a better film than *Citizen Kane* was one of the most controversial and inspiring pieces he had published.

"Tell me your five favorite films, and I'll tell you who you are." Those were his first words to the students in the first class Annie had taken from him. Most students cited the titles they thought he wanted to hear—*Birth of a Nation, Rules of the Game, Tokyo Story, Battleship Potemkin, Das Boot*—the kind of films that made Annie's eyes glaze over.

To her surprise, Rosen had challenged those choices. "Don't tell me what's important or influential or groundbreaking. I want to know what you love. What moves you. What makes you want this path."

After hearing that, Annie had not hesitated. *The Wizard of Oz. Last of the Mohicans. The Shawshank Redemption. Ratatouille. Chocolat.*

"I applaud your candor, if not your taste," he had said, looking up at her from the pit of the lecture hall. "You're a hopeless romantic who loves food, and believes in striving, and who doesn't listen closely enough to the one voice that matters."

"What voice is that?" she'd asked. "Yours?"

"Very funny," he said. "Yours."

That exchange had garnered chuckles from the gallery and ignited a blush in her cheeks. Ever since that moment, Professor Rosen had been her mentor. He was cranky, for sure, but under his guidance, she brought out work so good she surprised even herself.

Today, however, the magic wasn't happening. She kept trying to figure out what she wanted to say with her senior project. Too often she couldn't hear her own voice. Maybe she should go home, have a chat with Gran. Like Professor Rosen, Gran brought out the best in Annie, only she was a lot nicer about it.

Going home was problematic, though, because visiting Switchback meant seeing Fletcher. Three years after the breakup, she still thought about him when she was lonely. Or when she was with her friends—those who were so earnest all the time. Or so intimidatingly brilliant. Or so boring in their obsession with partying. She thought of Fletcher when she was out with a guy whose kisses failed to set her on fire, or when she grew homesick for mountains and forests and fresh streams and open roads.

She and Fletcher were done, the two of them. He had devoted himself to running his father's shop and carrying on with his legal claim. The settlement negotiations had been going on for three years. There was always another petition to be filed, another motion, another conference with lawyers. There seemed to be no end to the process.

Leaving Fletcher behind did have a hidden benefit. She pursued her studies like a girl possessed. Not just at school, but at Glow, the Michelin-starred restaurant where she worked on the weekends, absorbing knowledge like a sponge, practicing her knife skills and sauté techniques, shadowing the fascinating Claire Saint Michael, a rising star in the culinary world. If Annie had had a boyfriend, she would have been too distracted to focus on work and studying.

She was supposed to be finding inspiration for her project, but Annie caught herself thinking of the past and of Fletcher as she walked through the park that day. What was he doing? Was he happy? Did he think of her, or had he moved on?

She shook off the questions and pulled her mind back to the present. Her best ideas seemed to happen when she looked outward at the world. And she loved the world she'd inhabited during her college years. She loved letting her mind wander and speculate about all the disparate lives that intersected here in this park, a vibrant green place amid the bustling city.

Washington Square Park had a figured concrete arch, a couple of statues, and a central fountain. The shaded walkways, lined with park benches, were a haven for workers on their lunch break, nannies pushing strollers, tourists snapping pictures. There were people eating takeout at picnic tables and students lying in the sun, shading their faces with open textbooks. The playground and dog runs were busy with kids and dogs. Retirees sat thoughtfully over their games in the chess- and Scrabble-playing area.

She thought about approaching the two old men at their chess game, possibly asking to interview them on camera. And then a distinctive aroma wafted past her—an amazing smell that stopped Annie in her tracks. She lifted her nose like a hound on the scent, turning in the direction of the wind. In one corner of the park was a collection of food carts surrounded by milling pedestrians. Most had the standard offerings—hot dogs, falafel, soft pretzels, meatball subs.

There was one cart, manned by a lone cook hard at work over a flat grill, that emitted the most glorious aroma she'd ever smelled. It was a perfect mixture of caramelized onions and crisp-skinned meat, mingling with the yeasty sweetness of fresh, eggy bread. Brioche, perhaps. She had mastered the creation of brioche in the interdisciplinary class she had done while studying in Provence. Following her nose, she jostled her way to the cart.

It was marked by a hand-lettered tent sign on the ground that said simply *Martin M. Harlow, Chef Proprietor,* along with a Web address and a phone number.

Annie craned her neck to see over the group of people lining up for his wares. And what she saw there was even more compelling than the delicious aromas. Martin was amazing to behold. He wore jeans that were faded in all the right places. His shoulders and arms were gorgeously sculpted, gleaming in the afternoon sun. His blond, wavy hair was caught back in a casual ponytail, and his face had the perfect texture of a five o'clock shadow. He worked with intense focus and competence. He reminded Annie of Vulcan laboring over his forge, only instead of the forge, he worked at a perfectly seasoned grill set into the cart.

She skirted the edge of the crowd, studying him with rapt fascination. The simple menu was posted on a chalkboard affixed to the front of the cart. He offered duck confit with a choice of Stilton or smoked cheddar, served in a soft brioche on a bed of caramelized red onions, grilled goat cheese, crunchy duck scratchings, sweet rocket, Dijon, and truffle honey. A confit was a slow-roasting method, braising the meat slowly in fat until it was meltingly tender. It seemed sophisticated for a food cart, but judging by the crowd, the guy had a following.

"How's the food here?" she asked the guy next to her. "Have you tried it yet?"

"Oh, yeah," he said. "I'm a regular."

"And?"

"It's duck on a bun," he said matter-of-factly. "What's not to like?"

Annie smiled and waited her turn. The chef offered her a bright, open grin when she stepped up to the cart and placed her order. She watched him prepare the dish, his technique crisp and precise but not fussy. He was a dynamic figure, his movements swift and sure as he kept up a stream of banter with his hungry patrons. He had an easy, charming manner, and he was easy on the eye, too.

He served his creation wrapped in parchment, with a crumbling of coarse sea salt on the top of the bun. It tasted every bit as delicious as she'd anticipated, and she savored each bite slowly. His suggested beverage pairing was an ice-cold Orangina soda. Its tingly sweetness was perfect with the food.

Who was this guy, and how had he come up with the world's best sandwich? She hung back and observed him through the lunch rush. Then, during a lull in the action, she waved her hand to get his attention.

"Hey, mind if I film you?" she asked.

It was the perfect thing to say. His face lit up like a scoreboard. The broad, engaging grin had an aw-shucks quality to it that made her smile, too. His eyes were the blue of a forget-me-not blossom.

"For you, anything," he declared.

"I'm Annie," she said, powering up the camera. "Just pretend I'm not here."

"Nice to meet you, Annie. I'll try to pretend, but I'm not in the habit of ignoring pretty girls."

She liked the flirty gleam in his eye. "Ignore the camera, then," she suggested.

A couple strolling hand in hand approached the cart. They were the kind of dreamy New York couple Annie often saw in the city's parks and boulevards—unhurried, well dressed without being flashy, romantic in a subtle way. Annie used to think she and Fletcher would be like that one day. She captured their gestures and expressions as they scanned the menu and placed their order.

Martin adjusted the flame under the grill and started on their order. A few more customers stepped up, and he seemed to have no problem tracking each request. He was like an orchestra conductor as he single-handedly filled the orders. He stayed in constant motion, a one-man show as he grilled the red onions on the perfectly seasoned surface and assembled the sandwiches. The simple presentation, with an Orangina in its frosted bulb-shaped glass bottle, made Annie's mouth water all over again.

While he worked, he chatted up the customers as if he were giving a cooking demo. Annie kept the camera steady. He gestured at the buns steaming under a glass cloche to one side of the grill. "I get the brioche from the master baker at Le Rossignol, a guy I know from culinary school."

"Where'd you go to culinary school?" a woman asked.

"Texas," he said. "It's got a fancy name—Le Cordon Bleu College of Culinary Arts." His French pronunciation was more than respectable.

"Is that where you learned this dish?"

He grinned. "No, ma'am. I came up with it on my own in my apartment a couple of blocks from here. I confit the duck in my kitchen and then crisp it up on my grill here."

"So what's your secret? Is there, like, a special ingredient?" asked another woman. She was probably a student, and she looked as if she was half in love with him.

"There's no secret. I just use the best ingredients I can get my hands on. Favorite source is a farm up the Hudson Valley a ways."

Annie was in heaven. She'd found the perfect subject—a photogenic guy, using local ingredients and creativity, totally in his element. He didn't seem at all awkward, and the backdrop was great. She captured the scene from the widest of shots, panning around the children's play area, the dog run, and the shady walkways, then homed in on the smallest of details—the chef's strong hands, the gleam of the sun through a strand of truffle honey, a customer's shuffling feet on the pavement. Eventually, the crowd dwindled. Martin covered his tent sign with a *See You Tomorrow* message.

"Shutting down is only the start of my day," he said.

Annie kept the camera rolling. "What's your favorite part of the day?"

"How about when a girl offers to take my picture?" He grinned. "Okay, seriously? Favorite part of my day is when the cart is all set. My ingredients are ready, and I'm firing up the grill, and folks are just circling through the park, thinking about grabbing a bite to eat. Getting started. It's kind of a high for me. Is that weird?"

"Not at all. And thanks for letting me film. I'm a student at NYU, and I'm supposed to be working on my senior project."

"Tisch Film School?"

"That's right." She was impressed that he knew it.

"So what's your topic?"

"That's the problem. I don't have one yet."

He took off the apron, giving her a glimpse of rippled abs and cut chest. Then he put on a Keep Austin Weird T-shirt.

"But I think I know what I'd like the topic to be," she added.

"Yeah?" He was breaking down his booth, putting ingredients away and cleaning the equipment. "I'd make an awesome topic."

No false modesty there. But he was right. Annie described the project and what it would entail. "You'd have to get used to me being your shadow," she said.

"You make an extremely attractive shadow. I'd love to do it," he added. "I'd be honored to be your senior thesis."

"Really?"

"Hell yes. But I have a condition."

Great. A condition. Since starting college, she had met her share of tools and douche bags. Please don't be one of them, she thought. "What's that?" she asked. "What's your condition?"

"Let me make you dinner."

She grinned. She was going to rock this assignment. "I think I can handle that."

"It's not a date," Annie told Vivian, one of her suite mates, as she got ready to visit Martin Harlow on a breezy Saturday night. She had shown her roommates some of the raw footage from the other day. All three of them had practically fainted when they saw Martin.

"Are you going to sleep with him tonight?" asked Shauna.

"Yes, she is," said Vivian.

"Am not," Annie protested. "This is work. It's—"

"Those are date undies," Vivian pointed out, eyeing Annie's lace-trimmed bikini. "Way too pretty for every day."

"They are not date undies, and I won't apologize for liking pretty ones. They are going to stay totally concealed."

"Why wouldn't you want to date him? Those pictures you just showed us are going to haunt my dreams for a long time."

"I don't even know him. I just think he's going to be a great topic for my documentary." She took a pair of dark wash jeans and a colorful A-line skirt from her crammed closet. "Thoughts?"

"The jeans. They're super tight, and they look hot on you."

"Fine, I'm wearing the skirt, then."

"It looks like something you'd wear to the farmers' market."

"You have a good eye. I actually bought it at the Fulton Street Market a couple of weeks ago. It's made from recycled saris."

"It really isn't a date after all," Vivian conceded, her expression tragic.

"Told you so." She paired the skirt with a tank top and a cropped sweater, and resisted the urge to put on makeup. Maybe just some lip gloss.

But despite her protests, she felt as though she was going on a date. Dinner with a guy who wanted to cook for her. That seemed . . . datelike. Except she had an ulterior motive, and a heavy backpack crammed with photography gear. She wanted him to be the subject of her documentary, nothing more. Getting personal could ruin everything, and this was too good to ruin. The very first time she filmed him, she had felt it—the hum of a tuning fork deep in her core, resonating through her. That was her voice, speaking to her clearly. Sure, he was eye candy. But there was something more to this man. He had a passion for his craft, and he had a kind of driven, sexy energy that translated beautifully on camera.

She walked to Martin's place in Greenwich Village. It was a walk-up to a loft with brick walls, exposed beams, and high ceilings.

"My humble abode," he said, offering a mock-formal bow and a sweep of his arm as he opened the door for her. He was casually dressed in jeans and a white T-shirt, his feet bare and his hair slightly damp.

It wasn't humble. It was incredible. How could a street vendor afford this? Family money?

"Thanks for having me," she said. "And for doing this. You're being a really good sport about it."

"I'm a born performer." He took her backpack from her, raising his eyebrows at the weight of it. "Want to start filming right away?"

Good Lord. The guy was a dream come true. "Sure. I just need a couple of minutes to set up." While she worked she checked out his place. It was all one big, airy room, with a low sofa and one of those expensive new flat-screen TVs anchored to one wall, a desk area, and a big platform bed, neatly made up. The main feature was the kitchen. It had a commercial gas range with an industrial-quality stainless-steel vent hood, an array of knives and utensils that made her itch to work alongside him. Maybe that was his X-factor, that he invited collaboration. She'd studied it in her classes, the way a viewer got involved in a story by identifying with the subject and wanting to be part of it. Audience investment, it was called.

She set the tripod next to the bar-height counter and started rolling. He served her a handcrafted rye old-fashioned with a dense Luxardo cherry. She sipped the delicious, bittersweet drink, feeling absurdly sophisticated. The camera captured the action as he put together dinner.

"I took a chance that you don't have any food allergies or aversions."

"Good guess. I have an aversion to food that doesn't taste good, but something tells me that isn't likely to happen in your kitchen."

"I've had my share of failures." He cooked with supreme confidence, frying feathery hen-of-the-woods mushrooms in olive oil and serving them over hummus seasoned with coriander. Then he offered her a delicate tomato tart with caramelized onions and shavings of fennel, pouring a dry rosé. Dessert was a pear-and-apple compote drizzled in butterscotch sauce made with coconut milk.

She felt blissed out by the wonderful food. "I might never leave," she said. "Can I move in tonight?"

He laughed. "Good food will do that to a person."

"And yet you're single. Why aren't women hanging around here like stray cats?"

"Right now I'm giving everything to my cooking. I mean, I'd love to find someone, but this is taking all my focus."

She leaned back in her chair with a sigh of contentment. "That meal was fantastic."

"Thanks."

"Every single dish was vegan, wasn't it?" she said, smiling at him.

"Yep." His eyebrows lifted in surprise. "Some people don't notice that at all."

"Best meal I've had in ages."

"I like to show my range," he said. He wouldn't let her help him wash up. Instead, she filmed him while he worked and told her about himself. He was born and raised in Texas. The Harlows were a longtime restaurant family who had three hugely popular barbecue places in Houston. After culinary school, he came to New York to make it on his own, doing something completely different with his food. He didn't have the kind of backing he needed for a restaurant, so he'd launched the food cart.

He poured them each two fingers of grappa as a digestif. She adjusted the camera on the tripod as he carried the drinks to the seating area. "How did you come up with the perfect formula for your cart?"

"By trying—and failing. A lot," he said with a self-deprecating grin. "I started out with Cuban sandwiches. Then I tried grilled cheese, Spanish tapas, even egg custards I learned to make in Macau."

"You studied in China?"

"Spent a year in Asia. Loved every minute of it. But it was the year in France that gave me the winning formula—the confit method. I finally came up with a dish that sets me apart and keeps people coming to the stall."

"Judging by the crowd I saw, it's a big hit."

"It wasn't always. Business was slow at first, and then I had a lucky break. There was a write-up in *Time Out New York* by Guy Bellwether. He's a foodie with a huge following, and he gave me raves. By the next week, my till had quadrupled." Martin sipped his drink. He showed her a collection of tear sheets from various publications. She perused some of the headlines. *A New Standard in Street Food. The Must-Have Sandwich. Martin Harlow's Secret Sauce.*

She laughed. "Secret Sauce? Really?"

"Hey, I don't write that stuff."

"The reviewer makes a good point. The sauce is key."

"I think so, too."

"Your truffle honey is lovely. The flavor is completely subtle, but without it, the dish is just another yummy sandwich."

"Exactly. You get it. I love that you get it. How does a film student know so much about cooking?"

"My first love," Annie said. "My grandmother is the greatest cook I know, and she believes every recipe has a key ingredient. The one that defines it. In fact, I was thinking I would call my project *The Key Ingredient*."

"I like it," he said. "I like the way your mind works."

Annie's mind was not working. It was playing. *Back to work, Annie.*

"What else can I tell you about?" he asked, turning to face her on the sofa.

"Whatever you like," she said. "I want to know what drives you, what excites and inspires you."

He took the small glass of grappa from her and set it on the coffee table. He leaned in toward her and held her face between his hands. "You," he said quietly, gazing into her face. "You excite me. You inspire me."

"Martin." Her heart sank. She didn't want to flirt with him. She wanted to film him.

He shifted back, palms out, all innocence. "You can't blame a guy for trying."

"Actually, I can. Seriously, if this is going to work, we need to act as colleagues. Professionals. When a filmmaker gets too involved with the subject, the film is doomed."

"Did they teach you that in school?"

"Yes, and I learned from experience. Freshman year, I did a short piece on a bike messenger who got injured on the job, and I felt really sorry for him. My film turned out maudlin and terrible. So I need to stay detached."

He picked up his glass and saluted her. "Right. Good luck with that."

"Martin."

He offered his aw-shucks grin. "Okay, back to work. I know what you're asking. I'm inspired when someone gets me, the way you do. When someone understands that I'm not just making sandwiches in the park. I'm excited when someone makes me feel right about what I'm doing."

"Oh." She was flustered by his sincerity. "In that case, I'm glad to help."

She could tell Martin was looking at her lips. She could tell he wanted to kiss her. It was flattering, and she kind of wanted him to. It was rare for her to feel this kind of attraction.

Yet she had to pull back, reminding herself that kissing would only complicate matters. Martin Harlow was supposed to be her senior project, not her boyfriend.

And yet for the first time in forever, she started to think there could be life after Fletcher Wyndham.

15

Now

I'm ready to go home." Annie addressed the care team assembled at the conference table. Her parents were present as well, sitting side by side as they eyed her anxiously. She wished they would relax and quit looking at her as if she had a bomb duct-taped to her chest.

"You've all helped me enormously," she said, and a lump rose in her throat. "Far more than I'll ever know, since I slept through most of it."

Smiles and nods all around.

"Now it's time to be on my own." She sounded like an inmate trying to convince the parole board to let her out. Her fate was up to a committee of people who purported to know what was best for her.

The doctor, social worker, various therapists and nurses regarded her with kindness. Yet she could tell they were skeptical. She could read their expressions now without referring to the feelings chart with the round faces on it. Wasn't that a sign of progress?

"I like your confidence," Dr. King said. He was awesome. No one had expected her to emerge from the coma. Most patients in her situation existed in a frightening twilight state, never fully returning to themselves. But Dr. King had not given up on her. Annie had defied the odds, and she gave credit to this team.

"I want to get better. I *am* better." She looked around the table.

"'Better' isn't the same as going back to exactly the person I was. I can't swear I was all that great in the first place."

"You were you. And now it's time to let go of the person you were. Try to recognize the new person emerging from all this, and welcome her. It's a process. A grieving process. Not a literal death, but a loss."

The comment hit Annie in a way she was completely unprepared for. The former Annie was gone. Who was she now? Who did she want to be?

Life anew. What a concept. She felt excitement and then fear. And then many more fears. This was her new normal, they said. The trouble was, "normal" simply felt strange. Unfamiliar. Beginnings were like that, weren't they?

"It's the start of a journey," said Dr. King. "It's filled with opportunities you might not have envisioned before."

"I don't know what I envisioned. There's still so much I don't remember."

"You don't have to worry about remembering every little thing. The past you is gone. You're born again, but with a superpower—you have the benefit of prior knowledge. You don't have to reinvent the wheel every time you want to make a move."

She let out a long, slow breath, then faced her parents. "So. What do you think of the new me?"

"We've always thought you were amazing. The new you is even more amazing," said her mother.

Mrs. Rowe, the social worker, spoke up, reporting that Annie had a safe and supportive environment to return to—her childhood home in Switchback, where her parents and brother would look after her.

"Parent," Annie corrected her, aiming a pointed look at her father. "My mom is single."

"I'm here for you, too, Annie," said her father, his eyes softening as he seemed to absorb the wound.

"Your father will be a part of this as well." Mrs. Rowe put on a pair of reading glasses and checked one of her papers. "Ethan Lickenfelt, isn't that correct?"

Annie's father nodded. "Yes, ma'am."

"Your role is described here as emotional and financial support, companionship, and strength-training support."

"That's correct," he said. A light sheen of sweat formed on his forehead.

"So in other words, all the stuff he didn't do when I was a kid," Annie said.

Her father winced. "I thought you had memory problems."

"The family will continue with regular counseling appointments," Mrs. Rowe told the group, aiming a pointed look at Annie.

"My favorite," she said.

"Humor and sarcasm are excellent coping mechanisms," the staff psychologist said to Annie. "Don't let them mask your struggle."

"I want to help," her father said quietly. "I'm sorry I wasn't around when you needed me, but I'm here now. I'm staying with my folks in Milton. They're getting on in years, so I'll be taking over their business."

Annie paused, absorbing this. The idea of his living and working close by was simply . . . confusing. She looked at her mother. "Did you know about this plan?"

Her mom clutched her purse in her lap in a death grip. "He told me this morning."

"And you're okay with it?"

"I—yes. We want you to have as much support as we can give you."

Her father sent Mom a grateful look. "We're all committed to giving Annie everything she needs."

"Wow," said Annie. "It's like some cheesy movie where the estranged parents come back together for the sake of their dying child, and discover they love each other once again."

"That's not funny," said her mother. But surprisingly, color bloomed in her cheeks.

At the end of the meeting, they all agreed that Annie was ready to be discharged, provided her family delivered on their promise to continue her therapy at home. She felt a jumble of emotions—gratitude, trepidation, and a low-grade grief she didn't understand. She thanked everyone, doled out hugs, accepted their good wishes, posed for pictures.

"Your life is going to be amazing," Dr. King said. "The next move is up to you."

"I have no idea what move I want to make."

"You don't have to recognize what is in front of you, not yet. In time, everything will come into focus. How long this takes is different for everyone. Be patient with yourself. Reach out to the ones who love you. I'm excited to see you build the life you want."

Tears stung her eyes. "I'll work on it," she said softly. Now that she remembered her career in California, she knew she had to go back to it, but it seemed impossible at this point. She needed to get stronger. She needed her family.

After everyone left, Annie and her parents went back to her room. She stood in the middle of the floor and turned around slowly. The walls had been stripped of the artwork and cards, the daily notices and schedule. The bed was stripped down to its waterproof mattress. Her life was stripped down to this moment.

Her stomach gave a little flip of panic as she thought about how long she had been here in this cocoon, walled off from the world like Aurora, dead asleep in her enchanted tower. The difference being, Aurora had woken up to Prince Charming. Annie had woken up to divorce papers.

She took a deep breath, squared her shoulders, lifted her chin, and followed her parents down the hall to the parking lot.

"All righty, then," Mom chirped, her brightness failing to mask a shadow of concern. "Let's get going."

"You want to ride shotgun?" asked Dad, holding open the front passenger door. "You always wanted to ride shotgun when you were a kid."

I'm not a kid, she thought. But she said, "Sure, if that's okay with you, Mom."

"Of course."

Dad turned on the radio, probably to chase away the silence. The drive to Switchback bombarded her with memories. Having both parents in the car triggered a slew of long-forgotten images. End-of-summer trips to and from the city to buy school clothes. Class outings to the Robert Frost farm and the Calvin Coolidge homestead. Holiday trips to Burlington or Montpelier at Christmas for performances of *The Nutcracker Suite* and Handel's *Messiah*. Joyous drives to the hospital to see Kyle and Beth's babies. The past flashed by Annie like the scenery through the car window. Home. She was going home. It wasn't just a place.

And the town wasn't just a town. The covered bridge spanning the river bore a fresh coat of barn-red paint, its passageway opening in welcome. This town, with its tree-lined streets and old brick and wooden buildings, had been the backdrop of her childhood. She was flooded by nostalgia at the sight of the library and schools, the shops and riverside park with its arched footbridge, the bandstand in the park where she'd sat with her friends on a blanket and listened to summer concerts, the sports fields and stadium where she'd spent every Friday night in autumn, cheering on the Wildcats.

Her nerves eased as they made their way up the mountain. She instantly connected with the painted house where she had grown up. It was surrounded by gardens and orchards and the sugarbush as far as the eye could see. The beauty of it made her chest ache. Why had she left this place?

She'd followed a dream—to New York. And then to L.A., each part of her journey taking her farther away—to another place. Another life. Another home.

Which place was home? The town house in Laurel Canyon? It was bright and sleek and modern, with a gourmet kitchen and a deck extending from the master bedroom with a view of the city in the distance. When they were just getting settled in L.A., she and Martin practically had to sell a kidney in order to get the place.

They'd been happy there, hadn't they? She recalled having friends over for happy hour, hanging one of her mother's paintings, shower sex, picking out furniture. She'd made a life with a man who'd given up on her and shipped her back to her mother. Should she contact him? See if he'd changed his mind now that she'd woken up?

Something inside her shrank from that idea. *Not yet.*

But where was home? The place in L.A. or here in Switchback?

She walked into the farmhouse kitchen on her own two feet, hearing the familiar creak and snap of the screen door behind her. With one great inhaled breath, she knew what home was.

Just the sight of the large, scrubbed table brought back echoes of the past, moments of joy and tragedy and everything in between: We're getting a divorce. Your brother's getting married. Your grandfather died. You won a blue ribbon at the state fair. You've been accepted to NYU.

This was where her deepest memories resided.

She remembered loving Gran and losing her. She remembered losing Fletcher, winning him back, and then losing him for good. But of course, that hadn't lasted. Gran had gone, and Annie and Fletcher had fallen apart, and she had moved on.

To Martin. She had trusted Martin. She had given him her dream. But while she was sleeping, she had lost him, too.

16

Then

Annie was soaring when she realized her documentary was nearly done. She had shot hours and hours of raw footage of Martin, had taken hundreds of still shots of him, his craft, his world. When it came to Martin Harlow talking about himself and his work, there was no dearth of material. Yet he managed to be compelling, whether talking about foraging for ramps and morels in the springtime, or finding the perfect presentation for a simple dish. He was as generous with his time as he was with his cooking.

She disappeared into the project, editing late into the night, culling through the hours of footage and splicing together the story with his words, ambient noise, music, street scenes, clips from their drive up the Hudson Valley, touring organic farms. The making of this film became more than simply an assignment. While working on the final cut, she hit a creative zone she'd never found before. Going for hours without stopping, she was fevered, almost high. She had no sense of time passing, and when her mobile phone rang at five in the morning one day, she realized she had been up all night. She found her phone too late and missed the call, but there was a message from her mother: "Gran is sick. You need to come home."

Annie slept in her grandmother's bed that night, the way she had as a little girl when she was lonely in her own bed. The room was down the hall from the one she'd occupied as a child. And just like when she was young, she would lie amid the downy comforters and pillows while she and Gran talked about life and food, and family and dreams.

This time, there was a special poignancy to their conversation. Gran's illness had come suddenly and she was in hospice care, refusing categorically to try invasive and risky treatments. She was determined to exit her life the same way she had lived it—on her own terms, in her own time. She was extremely frail, but the lively light in her eyes still glimmered when she gazed into Annie's face. "You're very special to me," Gran said. "I know you're aware of that, but I still want to make sure you hear those words."

"Aw, Gran." Annie had been fighting tears from the moment she'd boarded the train from New York. "Please don't leave me."

"I won't," she said with a gentle smile. "Keep me in your heart, and you'll always know where to find me." With a trembling, paper-light hand, she stroked Annie's hair. "And yes, I know it's not the same. Nothing stays the same, ever."

"I hate that."

"No, you don't. Big changes are what keep us moving forward."

"Aw, Gran," she said again. "I don't even have the words for how sad I am."

"Then think of the wonderful times. What a beautiful life I've had. So full of everything important. It's still beautiful today."

"I'm glad you can say that," Annie said. "I'm glad I'm part of it."

Another smile, sweet and tired. "It's lovely to see you going for your dreams."

"Is that what I'm doing? Going for my dreams?" Annie's voice wavered. She was losing the one person who truly understood her. The idea frightened her so much. "This is the only place in the world that feels like home to me. But when I think about what I want for myself, it takes me far away from here."

"Ah," said Gran with a slow, sage nod. "These choices aren't always easy, but the answers will come. Be patient with yourself. Listen to yourself."

Annie offered a wobbly smile. The advice sounded remarkably similar to what Professor Rosen had told her. "I would, but I keep contradicting myself."

"I was very unsure of myself when I married your grandfather and moved up from Boston. In those days, it was like going to a foreign land. I didn't know if I would fit in here in the northern woods. I had no idea whether or not I would love living on a farm and making sugar, or if I would find friends. As it turned out, I found my whole life here, all I ever wanted, and many things I didn't know I wanted."

"How did you know Grandpa was the one? I mean, you had your whole life in Boston. Your family and friends. And then you met a farmer from Vermont . . . He must have seemed so different from everyone you knew."

"He was. Making a life with him seemed so unlikely for a city girl. And then I had a key moment. Do you know what that is?"

"A key moment. Tell me."

"That's the moment when everything changes. There's before, and then after. And once a key moment occurs, there's no going back to before. You make a choice, and it's like ringing a bell. You can't unring it. A key moment is a feeling. Your heart tells you. The point is, you have to pay attention."

"Do I not do that?" Annie sighed. "A key moment. I will have to look for one."

"Then I have no doubt you will find it."

"I'm not even sure I am going to like the things I want," Annie confessed. "I've loved everything about my studies. I've learned so much. I have big ideas and ambitions." She smoothed the quilt over Gran's shoulder, feeling the delicate, birdlike bones underneath. "Things like that keep me busy. But sometimes I get so lonely I ache all the way to my bones. I have friends, it's true. So many of them are pairing off now that we're through school. Three of my roommates are already engaged."

"Do you want to be engaged?"

"No." Annie's reply came swiftly. "I mean, not anytime soon. It would be amazing to be in love again, though."

"And you will be."

"When?"

"You and your burning youth. You don't get to choose when. You just have to stay open to the possibility."

Annie thought about the guys she'd met in school. She went on dates. She let them get close. And then she let them go. Every time she met someone, her thoughts always circled back to Fletcher Wyndham, and the firestorm of emotions he stirred in her. No one she'd known since then measured up.

She turned on her side and tucked her hand under her cheek. "I don't want to have to be in the world without you, Gran."

"You don't have a choice, my love. I know you're going to be all right."

"I won't. I'll fall apart."

"If you do, then we both lose. Because it means I failed to teach you anything."

"You've taught me everything."

"No. You're just getting started. Everything you need to know is right here." Gran touched Annie's forehead. "You simply have to know yourself and know what you need. And what you want. And how to get there."

"Simple," Annie whispered. "Gran?"

"I'm here."

"Is there anything you regret? Anything you wished you'd done?"

"Not that I know of. If there was something I wanted, I did it. With your grandfather, in the kitchen, with the family. I have no regrets. That's quite a blessing, isn't it? To have no regrets."

Gran smiled, but it was a tired smile. Mom said she slept a lot. Last night after Annie's arrival, the hospice nurse had met with the family, helping them prepare for the road ahead. Saskia Jensen was a wise, incredibly kind woman who listened more than she talked. One piece of advice she'd offered occurred to Annie now.

"Saskia told us we shouldn't leave anything unsaid," she told her grandmother. "Have we said everything? How can that be possible?"

"We're very lucky, you and I, Annie. I know you love me," Gran whispered. "I've felt that from you every day of your life. I know you've given me so much to be happy about, and so much to be proud of."

Annie shut her eyes, containing the tears. Then she opened them to gaze into her grandmother's face. It was the most beautiful face in the world, her eyes the color of dark amber syrup, her lips bowed in a slight smile. The lines of her face were a road map of a life well lived.

"Have I ever said thank you?" Annie whispered. "Maybe that's what was unsaid. Thank you, Gran, for every little thing. When I think of you, I think of everything good in the world. And I can't believe I never said thank you."

"Oh, sweet Annie. You just did."

Annie fixed food, all of Gran's favorites, but Gran could barely eat. She tasted tiny samples of homemade butterhorn and crème brûlée, and she admired Annie's creations, but Gran was content with her Pedialyte and the occasional soda cracker. Annie made smoothies for her to sip on—a sinful chocolate concoction made with real malt powder Annie had bought from a gourmet shop in New York, and another with maple syrup and nutmeg.

They moved Gran's bed downstairs to the keeping room, a small fireplace area adjacent to the kitchen. When the house was first built, Gran said, it was where people stayed when they were ill, or about to give birth. Or dying. The room had a picture window facing the back garden.

A last blast of winter suddenly blanketed the yard with dreary snow, threatening the delicate buds on the apple trees. Thick, untimely snowflakes drifted down steadily through the night, erasing all traces of yesterday.

Unfazed by the spring storm, the kids bundled up and played outside. Gran watched the fun through the window. Annie helped them build a snowman. They dressed him in Grandpa's old plaid hunting cap with the earflaps, and he held a sign lettered with the lyrics to Gran's most favorite song—*You Are My Sunshine.*

Gran wouldn't hear of Annie putting off the end of school. She had to finish the work she had started, Gran said, and could come for visits on the weekends. As the weeks rolled by, Annie watched her grandmother fading away, bit by bit.

One Saturday in May, Annie took the utility vehicle into town, just to get out of the house and to meet her friend Pam Mitchell, to catch up. Pam had become, of all things, a master distiller of whiskey, following in the footsteps of her father. She worked for her family's operation, a small-batch distillery, which shipped its specialty spirits to high-end bars downstate and in Boston.

"Show me around," Annie insisted. "And can I film your operation?"

"Of course. You're going to love it."

"You know me well."

Pam showed her the container with the secret family recipe—corn, malted barley, and toasted flake rye. "Looks like birdseed now, but after we add the well water and whiskey yeast, we'll strain out the solids and pipe the liquid into the still. The neighbor's pigs get the leftover solids, and he claims the livestock have never been happier."

The shiny copper still was located in an old converted horse barn, now redolent of fermented mash. Annie inhaled the heady aroma while Pam drew off a sample of the clear liquid and gave her a taste. "This is the white dog whiskey—that's the term for unaged spirits that used to be called moonshine."

Annie took a small taste and made a face. "Yikes, that's lighter fluid."

"It's awful until we age it."

The former horse stalls were crammed with white oak barrels, each toasted on the inside with a hard char to give the whiskey its flavor. There were fifty-five-gallon drums filled with the wash—grains and corn boiled to produce alcohol. "We're only producing about twenty gallons a week. Then it goes into the barrels for wood aging," Pam continued. "Here's a shot of the same spirits, seven months later." She gave Annie a snifter. The whiskey was the color of grade-A maple syrup. It tasted of smoke, sweet vanilla, and toasted pecans.

"Wow," Annie said. "It's fantastic."

"Thanks. It's an art, for sure. I've been working on the balance of flavors. I call this one our secret recipe—it tastes like bourbon, but smoother and more delicate."

"I'll say." Annie filmed and took still photos. She was inspired by her friend's operation, and the alchemy of water and grain being transformed by the process.

The bottling operation occupied another part of the building.

"I like the mason jars," Annie said.

"Thanks. I'd love to create a fancier bottle, but we're stretched too thin right now.

"We get fifty bucks a bottle these days," said Pam. "Sounds like a lot, but the overhead is steep. Dad's hoping to find a silent partner. Each barrel alone costs eighty bucks." She indicated a collection of worn oak barrels stacked by the loading dock. "Most of those are at least twenty years old.

After a while, we don't reuse them. I hope to give them a second life with folks who want to turn them into something else—furniture, carving, maybe even barrel aging something else. It's kind of a thing these days."

An idea leaped, fully formed, into Annie's mind. "Such as maple syrup."

Pam grinned. "I like the way you think."

"Let's not think. I know it's madness, but let's do it. Suppose I send you a couple of drums of syrup. Would you barrel-age it for me?"

"Sugar Rush? Absolutely. It's a plan." Pam poured them each another taste. "How cool are we? All grown up and doing something mad together."

"To being all grown up," Annie said. "Even though it's not all it's cracked up to be."

"Well, we can drink," Pam said with a twinkle in her eye. "That's something." They clinked glasses.

They talked of their high school days and traced the journey their lives had taken them in the past three years.

"We should play a drinking game," Pam said. "Every time one of us says 'Do you remember . . .' we have to take a drink."

"In that case, we wouldn't last five minutes. And drinking your fifty-bucks-a-bottle hooch would probably tick off your dad. Fill me in on the gossip," Annie begged. "I've been a million miles away."

"I got nothing," Pam said. "I work all the time."

"Come on, give me something."

"Well, I'm seeing a guy. Not just seeing him. I'm falling in love with him."

"Pammy!" Annie's heart soared for her friend.

Pam blushed. "His name is Klaus and he's a sommelier. He works in Boston. It's hard, being apart. We've already talked about moving in together, though."

"Good for you. I hope it works out."

"Me, too. The trouble is, I can't leave the distillery. We're so small,

I have to be here all the time. And much as I love Switchback, I'm not seeing a lot of opportunities for a sommelier here in town."

"Gran would tell you the heart will find a way."

"Ah, that's nice. How's she doing? I mean, is she comfortable?"

"I think so." Annie drank the rest of her whiskey, the liquor trickling through the thickness of tears in her throat. "She drifts in and out. It's terrible, losing her, but she seems to be at peace. We've had lots of good talks." Annie took a deep breath. "And she wouldn't want me mooning about her. More gossip, please."

"Let's see. The health department shut down Sly's Burgers and Fries for code violations."

"Oh my gosh, I love their burgers and fries."

"Sly promises to clean up his act and reopen. His new slant will be local ingredients, grass-fed beef, organic produce."

"Good for him. It's good for all of us."

"Ginnie Watson caught her husband cheating on her with a woman from his twelve-step group. I think it's known as the thirteenth step."

"Whoa." Annie remembered Ginnie from high school—quiet, well behaved, devoted to her boyfriend, whom she'd married the week after graduation. "I feel bad for her."

"She'll be all right after she gets over the shock. There ought to be a rule that no one gets married until they're at least old enough to drink."

"Hear, hear."

"Oh, and Celia Swank was engaged to this rich guy—he's a partner from the resort at Stowe—and then he dumped her."

"I bet she didn't take that well." Celia had never been quiet or well behaved, just wildly beautiful and obsessed with money and shopping. Her notorious moment in high school came about senior year, when she made out with a student teacher from the U, thus ending his career before it began.

"My guess is, she misses the money more than the guy," Pam said.

Everyone had a friend like that, Annie reflected. Even in this day and age, there were women who didn't trust themselves to be their own support. They looked to a man to take care of them. Annie was glad she came from a long line of strong women who knew how to navigate the world on their own.

"We always hear money doesn't buy happiness, but we keep thinking that it will," she observed. "The richest guy in town, old Mr. Baron, is one of the most miserable people I've ever known."

The kids in Switchback had all been scared of him, she recalled. The lumber millionaire was angry and stingy, waving people off his porch when they came to raise money for 4-H or the school band. He lived in a historic mansion filled with art and treasures, but his wife had left him long ago and his kids never went to see him.

Annie thought now of the steady stream of family and friends who came to see Gran, and she knew one thing for sure. Money was *never* the key ingredient.

"I agree," Pam said. "If money was important to me, I wouldn't be making artisanal whiskey. And by the way," she added, "just so you know, Mr. Baron is not the richest man in town."

"No? Who is it, then?"

"Sanford Wyndham—your old flame's father."

Annie's gut lurched. Just the name roused a flurry of emotion. "How's that?"

"That lawsuit, remember? Over that horrible accident? Apparently, it's finally been settled, and he was awarded a fortune. Still runs his garage, though."

"Wow. No kidding." She thought of how driven and obsessed Fletcher had been about the case. For a long time, she had assumed that was the reason they'd parted ways. Now she knew better. Like poor Ginnie and her cheating twelve-stepper, they'd simply been too young.

"You should look Fletcher up," Pam said.

Annie smiled. "Sure. I'll tell him now that he's from a rich family, I want him for my boyfriend again."

When Annie got home, a car she didn't recognize was parked in the driveway. She headed inside, where Kyle was helping the kids with homework.

"Dad's here," Kyle said, looking up from the kitchen table. "He's in with Gran."

Annie felt a buzz of nervousness in her gut. The whiskey samples she'd had with Pam had worn off, and she wished they hadn't. Dad was here. She slipped into the room. It was dim and quiet, with music softly playing on the radio. "Hey," she said.

"Hey, yourself." He looked tan and fit in khaki trousers and a white shirt with the sleeves rolled back. He stood up and held out his arms.

She leaned briefly in for a hug. No matter how much time had passed, he still had the dad-smell, the one she'd snuggled up to when she was little and he read her stories in bed. "I didn't know you were coming."

"I wanted to see her."

Annie took a seat on the opposite side of the bed. Gran seemed to be deeply asleep.

"I'm so sorry, sweetheart," Dad said. "You and your gran have such a special bond."

Annie nodded, at a loss for words.

"I'm staying with my folks," he said. "They sent their love, and this." He produced a wicker gift basket overflowing with gourmet food.

"That's nice," said Annie. "I'll give them a call tomorrow."

They sat in silence, one on one side of the bed, one on the other, Gran in between, eyes closed, scarcely breathing. Annie studied the beloved face, now pale and gaunt. She wondered what Gran was dreaming about.

The past and the people she'd loved? Or had she moved on to some other place, the next place you didn't get to see until it was your time?

"I loved your grandmother," Dad told Annie. "I like to think she loved me, too."

"She never said," Annie bluntly replied.

"I hope it means she held me in her regard." He smoothed the blanket over Gran's shoulder. "I don't blame you for being hard on me. I wish we were closer."

She watched his hand, stroking so gently over the soft blanket. "I wish that, too."

Annie didn't say anything more. She was thinking about the fact that men left. She knew it wasn't a hard-and-fast rule, but that was what happened in Annie's world. Her grandfather had left one day, had an accident in the woods, and never came back. Her father had left, and he returned twice a year to see his kids. People asked Annie's mother why she almost never went out with guys, but Annie knew the reason. Mom didn't want to get tangled up with a man only to watch him leave. It seemed like a good enough plan to Annie. She didn't plan on getting involved, or if she did because she couldn't help it, she intended to leave before the guy left.

She stood up, feeling oppressed by the atmosphere in the room and by her own dark thoughts. "I'll see you later, okay? Send me a text if you want to go for coffee or something while you're here."

"Sure. See you around."

She left, leaving the door slightly ajar and feeling awkward.

Turning back, she saw her father bow his head and let loose with great, gusting sobs that racked his tall, slim body. Annie froze, trying to decide whether to go back into the room and comfort him, or to give him his privacy. Maybe if she knew him better, she'd know what to do.

But she didn't. She didn't know him. And she didn't know what to do.

The next day, Annie went to see her father and his parents in a town twenty miles away. The visit was predictably stiff, with long gaps of silence broken by the smallest of small talk. That was what happened, she realized, when you lost touch with someone.

Afterward, she decided to stop in Switchback for a bite to eat before heading back up the mountain. She parked near the Starlight Café and stepped out of the car, catching her breath at the sudden drop in the temperature. It was early evening by then, the cold a brutal sluice of air from the north. As the wind skirled down from the heights, she felt a light stinging sensation on her face. Tilting back her head, she glared at the purple sky. "Oh, no way," she said aloud. "No freaking way."

But this was Vermont, and the weather didn't care that it was May. The snow flurries quickly turned to flakes, blanketing the emerging crocuses and tulips in the flower beds of the courthouse park.

She shoved her hands in her pockets and walked on, thinking about what Gran had said. No regrets.

Annie suddenly forgot she was hungry. The GreenTree Garage was two blocks away. As she passed the town's familiar shops and businesses and restaurants, she tried to figure out whether this was a good idea, or an ill-considered impulse, the kind that seemed brilliant until she thought it through.

No regrets, she reminded herself. If she didn't look Fletcher up, she would never know.

Know what?

She spotted him in the main bay of the shop, working next to his father on a car with its hood propped open. Watching the two of them working in tandem reminded her of how close they had always been. Two against the world, Fletcher had once said. Even doing mundane tasks, they were a team, passing tools back and forth, chatting together. The intimacy of their bond was a palpable thing. Fletcher had seen his father through one of life's most horrific ordeals, and Annie suspected they had grown even closer than ever because of it.

Her filmmaker's eye framed the shot of the two men silhouetted against the glowing shop light. It gave them the look of an Edward Hopper painting, an ordinary moment, frozen in time. Fletcher and Sanford would have made an interesting topic for her documentary. Maybe she should have . . . no. Just no.

She took a deep breath and rummaged in her bag for a lipstick. The best she could do was lip balm. Piña colada–flavored. Who thought that flavor was a good idea? She put the lip balm away and hastily chewed on a breath mint. Then she approached the open door of the garage bay, steadying herself on the slippery pavement.

A flutter of nerves erupted in her stomach, but she forced herself to keep going. "Hi, guys," she said, stepping into the garage. A filament heater on the wall provided a welcome blast of warmth.

"Annie! Long time no see." Fletcher turned to her with a grin of surprise and delight. He looked incredible, even in his coveralls and safety boots. The long rebel hair of his high school days was gone. Yet somehow, the haircut made him even better-looking.

Fletcher appeared . . . the same, but different. He was bigger. More solid than the boy she had known in high school, or the driven young man who had sent her away because he had no time for her. As he hung up a tool, then said something and grinned at his father, she felt a twist of yearning deep inside. That smile. It was the same one that had regularly set her heart on fire. The memory had never quite left her.

"Hey there, stranger." Sanford stepped forward with a slight swagger. "Get on in here where it's warm. Now, we'd both like to give you a proper bear hug, but that'd ruin your pretty outfit."

"I'll take a rain check." She went into the cluttered office area to wait while they peeled off their coveralls and washed the grease from their hands at a big utility sink. She took in the smell of lubricant and new tires, the calendar and posters on the walls of girls in bikinis, modeling tires and tools.

"I just turned off the coffeemaker," Sanford said. "It's still hot. I can fix you a cup."

"Oh! Thanks, I'll help myself." She poured the sludgelike substance into a mug at the coffee station. Living in the city and working at a high-end restaurant had turned her into a coffee snob, but she gamely took a sip. "I wanted to stop by and see how you're doing."

"Absolutely fine," Sanford said, wiping his hands on a towel. "And I'd love to stay and chat, but I'm off to meet a lady friend."

"Really? That's nice." She noticed a flush of color in his face.

He put on a parka and gloves, and turned the sign on the door to read *Closed*.

"Yep," he agreed. "It sure is. Fletch, don't forget to set the alarm when you lock up."

"Will do."

She watched Sanford go, unable to avoid focusing on the way he walked. His gait was smooth and sure, and when he got into his car, she realized she couldn't tell the difference in his legs.

"Is he as good as he looks?" she asked Fletcher.

"Yep. The prosthesis is state-of-the-art. Microprocessor in his knee. He's doing great. Spends more time at his girlfriend's than he does at home these days."

"Well, I'm glad. I mean, I'm happy for him." She leaned back against a counter stacked with paperwork. The feeling inside her tightened and intensified. "How are *you* doing?"

He hung his coveralls on a hook behind the door. "I'm good. You?"

"I'm . . . not so okay." She felt a tingle of tears in her throat. "My grandmother is sick."

"Oh, no." He turned and sent her a soft look. "I'm sorry to hear that."

She shivered. Hugged herself. "She's home, but in hospice care now. I'm . . . We're all just trying not to be sad all the time."

"She wouldn't want you to be sad."

"I know. It's so damned hard. When Gran leaves us, the world will be totally different. I just love her so much, Fletcher."

He flipped some switches on the wall, activating the alarm. "Let's go get a real drink."

She poured the coffee down the drain and rinsed the cup and carafe. The idea of drinking with Fletcher was irresistible. "Good plan."

The snow was coming down hard as they walked the two blocks to the town center. The Switchback Brewpub was warm and cozy, with a nice fire going in the potbellied stove, a few guys shooting pool. They ordered two pints on tap and sat in a booth, both on the same side of the table. His thigh brushed against hers, and she shifted, feeling a curious warmth. A familiar warmth. Being next to Fletcher was like putting on her softest, most comfortable sweater.

He took a sip of beer and turned to face her. "How's school?"

"Nearly done. Graduation's only a couple of weeks down the road."

He lifted his glass. "That's great, Annie. You did it. You're a college graduate."

They sat together in silence for a few minutes. A peculiar melancholy settled over Annie, and she started talking with him as if they were mere acquaintances. He used to know everything about her. She used to revel in the touch of his hands and his lips on her body and wonder at the ease with which she gave him her trust, her heart. She thought about the plans they'd once made together. She thought about the dreams they'd shared and imagined where the two of them would be if they had seen them through. Would he really have come to New York, made a life with her there? Or had that just been a teenage fantasy? More likely, they would have ended up like Ginnie and what's-his-name.

"Pam said you settled your lawsuit," she said.

"Yeah, finally."

"That must be a relief."

"It is."

"I don't know what you went through, but the fact that it took three years... wow. I'm glad it's behind you. Pam says your dad's a gazillionaire now."

Fletcher laughed. "Let's just say he won't have to worry about money ever again. He'd still rather have his leg back, but he's made his peace with that. I think settling the suit gave him a sense of justice, too. The cause of the accident was pretty clear-cut right from the start."

"Good. Justice was served. Now what?" There was a tiny flame of hope within her: Could we try this again? Please?

His grin flashed. "Funny you should bring up justice. I've decided to go to law school."

"No. Seriously?"

He nodded. "I learned a hell of a lot with the suit. Got a bachelor's degree in prelaw, mostly through online classes. The judge in our case was really encouraging, told me to go for it. I scored high on the LSAT, and I'll be starting classes in the fall."

"Fletcher, that's so cool."

"It's been a long, crazy road. My dad had his struggles, but he's in a good place now. He'll be fine without me."

"Does he know how lucky he is to have you?" she asked. "Honestly, Fletcher, you've been amazing through all of this."

He shook his head. "I did what I had to do. And I'm not going to lie. It was no picnic. But I learned a lot, and I found something I want."

He had plans, then. He was moving forward. "To us both, then," she said, tapping the rim of her glass to his. The old ache of yearning pressed hard against her heart.

He smiled. "To us both. Question."

"What?"

"Do you have a boyfriend?"

She flushed. "No. What about you?"

"No boyfriend. That's not the way I roll."

"Ha ha. Are you seeing anyone?"

He shook his head. "Nope." Then he pressed his leg against hers. "I've been too busy."

"You mean, with the lawsuit?" She felt a warm shiver.

"Busy missing you."

Oh, boy.

She stared at his eyes. His lips. "I've missed you, too."

Annie pictured their love like the embers in an almost dead fire, buried deep in powdery ashes. Then with a gust of fresh emotion, they burst to life again. The weekend turned into a rampant sex fest. She was starving for him, literally starving. She had no idea if it was born of her sadness over Gran, his relief at the end of his father's ordeal, or the scintillating chemistry that had bound them together from the moment they'd first met. She only knew that the feel of his arms around her, the press of his lips on hers, and the joining of their bodies felt completely right.

They had the house all to themselves. She didn't ask why, didn't ask if Fletcher had told his father to stay away, or if Sanford had other plans. All she knew was that being in his arms was like coming home again. Everything in the world took on a special glow.

"What's that smile?" he asked, looking down into her face as they lay together in the late morning, drowsy with pleasure from their wake-up sex.

She ducked her head, nestling into his muscular shoulder. "Just . . . fantasizing. Imagining."

"Imagining what?" He traced the curve of her thigh with his hand.

Annie hesitated. Everything about this moment was magic. She didn't want to ruin it. "It's silly. I was picturing the house we'd live in one day."

"That house on Henley Street?" He didn't seem at all surprised by her comment.

"I can't believe you remembered," she said. "Yes, the Webster house. But it's going to need some work. We have to make sure it has a gourmet kitchen." She stretched and wound herself around him. "Bookcases in every room. I love books."

"I know," he said. "I know what you love."

"Lots of windows and skylights, because, well, Vermont. A garden full of tomatoes and herbs. And the back porch needs a wooden swing. One of those rustic ones of peeled logs, with soft cushions long enough to stretch out on for a nap."

"I like porch swings," he said.

"I like *you,*" she said, and planted a row of kisses across his chest. The house she imagined faded into another kind of fantasy, and they made love again. She felt caught up in the wonder of being with him again. But she wasn't a teenager anymore, and she had questions.

"We fell apart before," she said. So that wasn't a question.

"We did."

"What if that happens again?"

"I suppose it's up to us."

"All I know is that I want to be with you. All the time."

"That's going to be hard. You're down in the city. I'm up here until school starts."

"We'll find a way," she said.

"Okay. Yes," he said, pulling her into his arms. "Let's do that. Let's find a way."

Annie's cohorts in study group organized a screening night for their senior projects. She had trouble focusing, because her mind was filled with Fletcher and what they'd started. With an effort, she reminded herself that final presentations and evaluations were a week away.

Everyone's nerves were growing taut. The group had been together since sophomore year, holing up to prepare for projects and exams, propping each other up through romantic breakups, failed tests, family troubles. Over the past few weeks, Annie had been leaning on them hard as she braced herself for Gran's passing.

There were five of them in the group, and the screening would take hours, because although the films were short, the discussions and critiques were likely to carry on long into the evening. It was necessary work, of course. This was a make-or-break project for film students. The evaluation committee was headed by the notorious Professor Joel Rosen.

Annie had taken her first film class from Rosen, so it seemed fitting that he would be evaluating her last. When she thought about how far she had come, she prayed it would be far enough.

The group screening was both awe-inspiring and intimidating. When she viewed her friend Padma's piece on a public lying-in hospital in Bengal, Annie could not find a single flaw. Shirley's film showing the daily life of an assisted-living memory-care facility was unexpectedly funny in all the right places. Moe's study of prison tattoos was visceral and important. Royston, whom they'd nicknamed Richie Rich, had put his father's money to good use. He'd flown to Greenland to show in heartbreaking detail how global warming was destroying the Inuit way of life.

It was the dinner hour by the time Annie's screening came up. After she'd viewed the others, her confidence was threadbare. Her cadre had all done such wonderful, important films. She only hoped her passion for the topic would elevate it from being just another piece on food. But come on, really? Duck on a bun. What had she been thinking?

"Let's not break for dinner," she told the group.

The moaning was loud, the cussing even louder.

"Knock it off," she said with a laugh. "You know I'd never let you starve. You know I have a plan."

"True. Your study snacks are so legit, Annie. Please say you brought something." Moe clutched at his stomach.

"You're all totally spoiled," she said. "I've been spoiling you since sophomore year." And she'd delighted in doing so. She had treated her study group to samples from her culinary classes or leftovers from work at Glow. Sometimes she made things from scratch, using the humble hot plate and toaster oven in her dorm room. Her iced maple bars were legendary.

"I did better than that," she stated. "I brought some*one*."

"This should be good."

She checked her BlackBerry. Yes, everything was happening right on schedule. "Follow me," she said, then turned to the room monitor. "We'll be right back. And don't worry, we'll bring something for you."

They went down to the street level. A billow of fragrant steam plumed from the food cart in the parking lot adjacent to the media building.

"Oh my God," said Shirley. "What in the world is that wonderful aroma?"

"You're going to love it. Trust me on this." Annie led the way to the cart.

"I should be on my knees, like a pilgrim going to Lourdes," said Royston.

"Please don't," said Padma.

"I'm drooling. I'm dying," said Moe.

Martin was doing his signature Martin thing, creating his duck confit on brioche for the study group. Or, in the case of Padma, who was vegetarian, a duckless confit with wild mushrooms. Annie had splurged on two good bottles of Madiran, a red wine from Gascony in the southwest of France. The refreshing astringency of the wine worked perfectly with the hot, smoky confit. Her group went nuts for the salty, falling-apart flavor of the duck.

"I don't even know you," said Shirley to Martin, "but I want to marry you."

Martin offered his affable, lopsided grin. "Too late. I'm going to marry Annie."

She stuck out her tongue at him. "Very funny."

"Just you wait."

"Way to butter us up for your film," Padma said with a teasing grin. "I could watch *The Gong Show* for the next hour and still be happy."

"Are you hating on *The Gong Show*?" Royston asked. "It's a classic."

"Don't start," Shirley warned them. "We've got to finish upstairs. We only have the screening room until nine o'clock."

Once they had devoured the mouthwatering sandwiches and finished the wine, they helped Martin close up his cart and invited him up for the final screening. "Cool," he said. "But don't look for any help from me. When it comes to filmmaking, I'm green as a Granny Smith apple."

Annie's stomach was in knots by the time the room darkened and the blank screen glowed. She might be making a horrible mistake, assuming her film was good because she loved it. But wasn't that what Gran had always taught her, that if she loved something enough, then she would be good at it? She loved making films. She had to be confident that she was good at it.

Martin surprised everyone with buttery-smooth homemade chocolate truffles to eat with the last of the wine. "Okay," said Royston, "you can't marry Annie. You have to marry me."

Martin laughed easily, taking in their admiration with his usual aplomb. He loved food and cooking, and knew he was good at it. Annie wondered if he ever questioned himself the way she did.

"Okay, let's start," she said, taking a final sip of wine. The lights went down, and the screen came to life.

The opening was unscored, beginning with one sound alone—a sizzle. Then there was a clatter of utensils. Crowd noises faded in, each element layering on more texture. Sounds were added like instruments coming into the overture of an urban symphony, quietly building to a crescendo—the ambient street noise around Washington Square Park. Dogs barking, children laughing, car horns and sirens, a street performer tapping a marimba. Then the shot peeled back to reveal the topic—Martin Harlow and his food cart.

"Oh my God," Shirley declared, smacking Annie's arm. "This is genius."

"Shh." Padma shushed her.

The shot lingered on Martin working at his grill. Then the score rolled as the credits began. Annie felt a shiver of pride as the title scrolled: *The Key Ingredient. A film by Annie Rush.*

The narrative plunged right in. She had made the choice to let the story tell itself as opposed to a back-and-forth interview. Martin was a natural raconteur who spoke as he worked. She had edited each scene so that the motions of his hands and utensils coordinated perfectly with his words. His banter with customers was unforced, particularly with the good-looking female customers. Their trip to the farms upstate formed a backdrop for Martin's story. He talked about the family barbecue restaurants in Texas, his travels, his ups and downs as he tried to launch an enterprise of his own in New York.

The piece concluded with a montage of faces, accompanied by a great song Annie had found—a fusion of French music and country guitar. The credits rolled to a slow, thoughtful end. Then she held her breath, waiting to hear what the others thought.

"Before we start, let's hear what the subject of the film has to say," Padma suggested.

Martin sat forward in his chair, resting his wrists on his knees and blinking as the lights went up. "Wow," he said. "I'm blown away."

"In a good way?" Annie asked.

"Oh, hell, yes. I've never watched myself working. It's kind of surreal. In a good way," he added with a grin.

The critique was mostly complimentary, and Annie breathed a huge sigh of relief. They liked it.

"It's nine. We need to clear the room," Royston announced. "Good work, everybody. We'll all sail through finals."

"Your lips to God's ear," Moe said.

Martin walked out with her. "I want to buy you a drink."

"Just one," she said. "I need to prepare my notes for the evaluation committee."

"You've got nothing to worry about. It looked perfect to me." He took her to a dim, divey place not far from her dorm and ordered her a rye old-fashioned, which was her go-to cocktail since he'd introduced her to it. When the drinks came, he raised his glass. "You rocked it, Annie. I knew you would, but that was even better than I thought it would be."

"I'm glad you liked it."

He leaned toward her. "I could kiss you."

Oh. She took a quick sip of her drink, the sweet sting of the rye warming her throat. "I'd rather you didn't."

"I'm real good at it," he said with a charming smile.

Yes, she thought, he probably was. "I'm sort of… I started… I'm seeing somebody. I mean, a guy—"

"Someone new?"

She felt shy, protective of what had started to bloom between her and Fletcher. She couldn't stop thinking about him. They had a history together, but it was a broken one. "Yes, and no. A guy I used to know. Back home."

He sighed. "Is it serious?"

"Serious enough for me to say I'm not going to be kissing you tonight."

"Shit. That's serious for sure."

"We'll see." To change the subject, she handed him a USB stick with the final cut on it. "All yours," she said.

"Great. After seeing this, my family will finally quit worrying that I'm panhandling in the streets of New York. Another question. Can I show this to my agent?"

"An agent. You have an agent?"

"Sure. He's a talent agent. I took some acting classes when I first came here."

"You wanted to act?"

"Naw. But I wanted to learn some tricks of the trade. I signed with a guy who reps several TV chefs. They were my idols, growing up. I'd like to show your film to Al."

"Well, of course." Annie was surprised and pleased. An industry professional was going to look at her work. "You can use the film any way you like. There are a couple of trailers and previews, and a short demo reel with some highlights. I gave you a lot of still photos, too. You could put them on your website."

"Sweet," he said. "You are so damn sweet, Annie Rush. Whoever that guy back home is, I hope he appreciates you."

The inevitable phone call came. Gran was gone. She had passed quietly one night in springtime, and Annie's world shifted on its axis. The pain of this grief was like nothing she had ever felt before. There was nothing to compare it to, though she tried, because she wanted to convince herself that she would survive. She'd been devastated at the loss of her grandfather; she had raged and struggled through her parents' divorce, but this ran so much deeper. A piece of her had been lost, leaving a gaping, unhealed void. There were some moments when the sadness sat like an actual weight upon her chest, so heavy she could scarcely breathe.

The only time she felt normal was when she was in Fletcher's arms. He was her soft place to fall, the one she could turn to and pour out her heart. "It's impossible," she confessed to him on the day of the memorial service, attended by at least a hundred friends and neighbors. "I had no idea it would be impossible to say good-bye to the love and joy and hope we had. I can't do it. I just can't."

"Maybe dying is awesome," he whispered. "Maybe it's like Club Med."

She laughed through her tears. "Stop it."

"Club Dead."

"You're awful."

"I know I am. I know." He didn't tell her to be strong, that she could cope and carry on, but he held her gently, helped her breathe, and showed her that it was possible to move from one moment to the next without completely falling apart. Everyone else offered sympathy, but Fletcher offered his heart.

Although it seemed impossible to find joy in the depths of her grief, Annie sensed that this was what Gran had been trying to tell her all along. She finally understood. This hurt she felt was the price of loving with her whole heart. But having Gran in her life had been worth every moment of pain.

And something happened as she sobbed in Fletcher's arms. She felt an unexpected, piercing joy.

This, then, was Gran's parting gift to Annie. To find happiness even in the deepest sorrow. This wrenching sadness showed her how important Fletcher was, how vital.

In time, the grief turned into a dull ache with occasional flares of agony. It was like a fading bruise Annie forgot about until she bumped into a memory. *Gran.* It was the little moments that pierced most sharply, the remembrance of a smile, a gesture, a soft-voiced phrase.

Despite the pain, Annie did what Gran would have wanted for her. She pulled herself together and looked forward. She knew the best way to honor her grandmother was to create an amazing life. That was what Gran had wanted for her all along.

There was one problem with this. What did that life look like?

The week before commencement, Annie's phone rang. "It's Joel Rosen," said the caller.

"Oh, Professor Rosen. Hi."

"Annie, I need to set up a meeting with you. It's about your senior thesis."

She felt a thrum of nervousness in her chest. Was the evaluation a bad one? Had she screwed up? Violated some principle or other? Chosen a topic no one would take seriously?

"Of course," she said, and braced herself. Rosen was never effusive. His praise tended to be measured, his criticism pointed and sometimes harsh. She prided herself on having a tough skin, but this project was meant to be her crowning achievement. She had poured everything she had into it, all she'd learned and the things she believed would show the art and craft she'd learned over the past four years.

She arrived at Rosen's office five minutes early, and walked in to a surprise. Professor Rosen wasn't alone. The three men stood as she paused in the doorway.

"Martin," she said, catching her breath. "What are—" She cut herself off, remembering her manners. She wiped her palms on the sides of her jeans. "Professor Rosen," she said, then turned to the stranger next to Martin. "I'm Annie Rush."

The man smiled and shook her hand. "Alvin Danziger. Pleasure to meet you."

"I told you about Al," said Martin. "My agent." Martin was nicely dressed in dark jeans and a crisply pressed shirt under a sport coat. His hair was styled, and he was looking very Matthew McConaughey. His agent was chubby and sharp-eyed, dressed in somewhat shabby trousers and a striped shirt. He hardly resembled the titan of industry she had pictured when Martin had told her about him.

Mr. Danziger set up a laptop on a low table in the office.

"Pleased to meet you," she said, flustered. Then she turned to Joel Rosen. "What's going on?"

"Let's have a seat." Rosen gestured at the sofa-and-wing-back-chair grouping by the desk. "This type of meeting usually features nicer beverages, but we wanted to set this up right away."

"About . . . ?"

"Your film, of course," said Alvin. "I love it," he quickly added. "And that's not an exaggeration. If anything, it's an understatement."

"Well," she said, unable to keep herself from smiling. "I'm flattered."

"Get used to it."

"No, don't," Professor Rosen quickly chimed in. He'd always told his students to worry when the flattery started.

She grinned at them both, and gave them both the same answer. "Okay."

"Here's what's going on," Alvin told her. "Your film—along with the clips and stills you gave Marty—has been online for less than a week."

"Online," she echoed. "What do you mean?"

"We put it on Martin's website, with links to Facebook, and that new site called YouTube, and some other networking channels."

She had taken classes on media and the ever-expanding social network. It was a vast, unexplored territory, a new medium, but no one had a clear understanding of its power.

"I see," she said. "I told Martin he could use the material any way he wants."

"So check it out. Here's what I did." Alvin clicked the keyboard. "Or rather, I hired an expert to do it. This chart shows the progression of unique page views."

She leaned forward and scanned the chart. "Wow, a thousand views. That's so cool."

Rosen shook his head while Martin sat back on the sofa and grinned with delight. "Look again," said Rosen. "It's not a thousand."

She leaned closer, studied the chart, and gasped in shock. "Holy smokes. Each *unit* stands for a thousand views. So are you saying my film has had a million views? That's incredible."

"It's awesome," Martin stated. "By now, the number has probably doubled. It's going up exponentially."

She tried to picture strangers sitting in front of their computers, watching her documentary. Looking at the photos she'd taken. A million strangers.

"Well," she said slowly, "this is good, right?"

"This is great," Al said. "Your film is a hit."

"My e-mail is exploding," Martin added. "I've had everything from job offers to marriage proposals. And some other crazy proposals, too."

She felt dazed. Her chest nearly burst with pride. "That's fantastic. All these people looking at my film. It's unbelievable." She laughed. "Martin, you are never going to keep up with the demand for your confit."

"It's gone way beyond that," he said.

"What do you mean?"

For the first time since she'd known him, Professor Rosen broke into an ear-to-ear grin. "Brace yourself, Ms. Rush. The ride is about to begin."

"What do you mean? Sorry, this is all pretty new to me."

"What he means is, there's been interest from a production company," said Mr. Danziger. "Serious interest. A production company called Atlantis is partnering with a new network focused on food and lifestyles. They're looking for fresh talent and shows aimed at a young demographic. After seeing your short—and particularly after seeing the number of views online—the company executives want a meeting. In L.A. As soon as possible."

"A meeting." Annie felt goose bumps. "What does that mean?"

"Just that. They want to meet with you and Marty to talk about creating a show."

"A show?" Annie realized she was echoing him, probably sounding like the rank amateur she was. "Like, a television show?"

Martin laughed aloud. "You got it, babe."

Annie was beside herself. She couldn't keep from throwing her arms around Joel Rosen and giving him a hug. "This is a dream come true," she said. "It can't be this easy."

He laughed and patted her on the back. "Trust me. It's not."

The moment she left Rosen's office, Annie called Fletcher with her news.

"I'm amazed but not surprised," he said. "And totally proud of you. Way to go, Annie."

"Thanks. My head is spinning. Spinning! Professor Rosen said it would be quite a ride. I didn't realize it would be like a Tilt-A-Whirl."

He laughed. "You always liked a wild ride. Remember the carnival in Stowe, the summer after high school?"

"I was the only one who didn't get sick on the Looping Madhouse." She sighed. "I wish you were coming to California with us."

"Me, too," he said. "Feels like it's been raining up here since 1968."

"I miss you," she said.

"Ditto."

"I'm coming home after this trip."

"I can't wait to see you," he told her. "But I'll wait. You're gonna knock them dead out there."

Annie arrived in Switchback late at night, dragging her luggage into the house, buoyed by excitement. It was too late to call Fletcher, but her mother was still up, eager to hear the news.

"I don't know where to start," Annie said. "It feels as if I just hopped on a speeding train. Everything is happening so fast."

Her mother beamed at her. "I'm thrilled for you," she said. "And so impressed. I want to hear everything." They curled up on the sofa together, nursing mugs of tea in front of a roaring fire. It was hard to believe she'd left the hot glare of Southern California only this morning. The long journey home had taken her from L.A. to New York to Burlington, and the production company had hired a car to drive her up to Switchback. A production company. A hired car. It was a whole new world for Annie.

Exhausted and elated, she described the dizzying rounds of meetings in California. The network was a start-up, but it was funded by a giant media company. Atlantis Productions wanted to work with her and Martin to develop a new, fresh take on the ever-popular cooking show. No more chatty chefs in kitchens putting together premeasured ingredients out of prep bowls. They wanted to expand on her idea of taking the production to the streets. They wanted a pilot with an option for more episodes.

A few days before, she was a newly minted graduate. She now had an agent and an entertainment attorney. She even had a job title—producer.

"I can't even believe I'm saying it, Mom. It's barely real to me."

"Believe it, Annie. You've worked so hard for this. You deserve it." Mom reached over and brushed her forehead with a gentle touch. "Gran would be proud of you. But she wouldn't be surprised. She always believed in you, a hundred percent." Her eyes misted. "God, I miss her."

Annie took her mother's hand. "So do I. It must be even harder for you."

"I'm an orphan. What a strange, awful feeling."

"Oh, Mommy. I'm so sorry." It wrenched Annie's heart to see her mother looking so lost. "How can I help?"

Mom squeezed her hand. "You're helping. You have no idea how much. We'll be all right. She'd want us to be all right."

As Professor Rosen had warned her, plunging into a television production wasn't going to be easy. For Annie, the hardest part was the conversation with Fletcher.

GreenTree Garage and Scooter Works had undergone dramatic changes since Sanford's settlement. She found Fletcher there, not working in his coveralls, but wearing jeans and a crisp white button-down shirt. In the garage area, four young guys were working on scooters while a man with an Italian accent talked to them. To Annie's surprise, Fletcher was talking with her sister-in-law, Beth.

When he saw Annie, he offered a smile that made her heart skip a beat. "She's back," he said, pulling her into a hug and burying his nose in her hair. "Damn, girl, I missed you."

"Same here," she whispered, then stepped back and greeted Beth. "Let me guess," she said. "Your students are combining Italian with auto mechanics."

"Good guess," said Beth, then laughed at Annie's expression. "Fletcher and his dad were kind enough to sponsor the program. The school and the garage put together a voc ed initiative. We've started a training program for kids wanting to learn mechanics. Speaking of which, I'd better go supervise." She excused herself and went into the garage.

"You're sponsoring a program?" Annie asked Fletcher.

"Dad and I are. Seems like a good way to help out the community."

"Beth must be so grateful. She's always scrambling for funding and looking for options for her students."

Fletcher took her hand and walked over to a shiny dark blue roadster. "Let's go for a drive. I want to hear all about your trip."

She didn't know much about cars, but the power of the engine was palpable as he drove away from town. She gave a little squeal as he opened it up on the highway.

"You like?" he asked, sending a grin her way.

"I do. You're living large, Fletcher Wyndham."

"It's my dad's. The settlement is for him, not me." He downshifted and took a curve with smooth expertise. "Yeah. I am. It still feels strange to me sometimes."

"I'm happy for you and your dad. What happened was terrible, and I'm proud of you for turning it all around."

"Wait until you see the house he bought."

A few minutes later, he turned up a long driveway flanked by blooming meadows. The house was ultramodern, built of glass and stone, set into the brow of a hill overlooking a valley to the west. There was a multicar garage, a trout stream and pond, and an enclosed pool and hot tub. "This is amazing," Annie said, getting out of the car.

"It was built by a Turkish guy who made a fortune in yogurt," said Fletcher.

"I'd heard about that, but I've never been up here."

"Dad bought it already furnished, seeing how we've never really owned furniture before. Never owned a home, for that matter."

She sent him a sharp glance. "It's great," she said. "Wow, life has changed so much for your dad. Mostly for the better, I hope."

"He's making the most of the settlement. I might end up with a stepmother who's a tire model with a Russian accent, but I can't complain."

"A tire model?"

"You know, the bikini blondes on the tire posters they send out to garages."

She laughed.

"You think I'm kidding? Wait until you meet Olga."

"I'm sure she's very nice," Annie said. "Is your dad here?"

He checked his watch. "Hope not." He slipped one arm around her waist and pulled her against him. "I want you all to myself."

She caught her breath, and her skin started to tingle. "Yeah?"

"Yeah. Let's go inside."

There was a ravenous quality to their lovemaking. It was a little scary, how much she craved his touch. It was like needing the next breath of air—elemental, vital, sustaining. There were things he knew about her and places he found that no one else had ever come close to. They made love three times, the first frenzied encounter in the foyer against the door, in a moment so urgent they barely made it inside. Afterward, he took her to his bedroom and made slow, sweet love to her on a ridiculously large, comfy bed. A bit later, they watched her film in the media room and he made love to her again.

She slumped back on the sofa, feeling dazed. "That was . . ." Her voice trailed off when she couldn't find the words.

"Yeah," he said, tugging his jeans back on with a lazy, contented smile. "I know."

She pulled her dress on over her head. She'd bought it at the hotel boutique in L.A., but the only thing he'd seemed to notice about the dress was how easily it came off over her head. Then she tucked herself against his shoulder and gazed at the large screen on the opposite wall. He replayed the end credits, which rolled to a song they both loved, "Everybody's Got to Learn Sometime" by Beck.

"Tell me about L.A.," Fletcher said.

"I was going to, but I got distracted." She tried to smooth her wild curls. "So many meetings. So many people I had to get to know. It's a little scary." She told him about the concept for the show the production company had in mind.

"Unbelievable. You're going to be working on your own TV show."

She laughed, but at the same time, excitement fluttered in her chest. "It's early days. Actually making it happen is still a very big maybe."

"After watching your film, I'd call it a sure thing. Seriously. You're really talented."

She planted a long, hard kiss on his mouth. "What I learned at all those meetings is how much more than talent I need in order to make it in TV." She talked about the agent and attorney, the whirlwind of creativity that had exploded in her meeting with a group called the writers' room. "There was this incredible energy in that room. I really think they expect this to work out."

He absently rubbed her arm. "Sounds amazing. What's next?"

She paused, took a breath. "They want me to work with their writing and production team. Then we'll shoot a pilot." She felt light-headed just talking about it. "I'm freaking out, Fletcher. I'm trying to be realistic. Most projects fail in development and never see the light of day, so I don't want to get my hopes up."

"Are you kidding? You deserve to have your hopes as high as you want."

She climbed into his lap and straddled him on her knees. "You are the sweetest guy. How did I get so lucky?"

He kissed her. "By being you. When do you go?"

And there it was. The hard part of this. "I leave week after next. And..." She moved her hands on his shoulders. "They're giving me a stipend to move out there, and setting me up with a furnished apartment. I'll be living in Century City."

"For how long?" he asked, and she could feel his muscles tensing. Then he answered his own question. "Indefinitely." His voice was very quiet.

Annie heard what he wasn't saying even more clearly than his words. She climbed out of his lap and settled next to him. "This chance—in L.A. It's everything I've ever wanted. Everything I've been working for all through school."

"And what you want is in California."

"Yes." Her stomach tightened with nerves. "What about us? Will there still be an *us*?"

He was quiet, staring at the frozen screen at the end of her film. Then he said, "You've made a lot of plans before asking those questions."

She felt a terrible sense of foreboding. "I don't want to lose you again."

"Then we'd better figure out how to stay together."

"You could come to California," she said.

"Law school, remember?"

"Of course I remember. I think it's wonderful. And . . . when I was on the plane, I kept thinking about how this could work. California has law schools. Good ones. Like UCLA or USC. Pepperdine."

"No doubt. But I have other plans," he said. "California's not in those plans."

"At least be open to the possibility." She hoped she didn't sound desperate or whiny. "I know it's a long way from here, but your father seems to be doing great, and those schools—"

"Are fine, like you said," he agreed.

"So what's the problem?"

"I'm not interested in those schools."

"But we could—"

"I've been accepted at Harvard."

She stared at him, shocked. "Harvard Law School." Suddenly the West Coast schools lost their sheen. "Holy cow, you never told me that."

"You never asked."

He was right. She hadn't. Why hadn't she asked? Was she so focused on her own plans that there was no room for his? Please, no, she thought. Please don't let me be that person.

"Listen," he said, gently taking her face between his hands. "There are TV productions on the East Coast. In Boston, even."

"Not like this. Nobody in Boston is offering me a shot."

"Your film got a million views. Any production company would be impressed by that."

"But only one offered me my own show."

"Right. So let's just say I tell Harvard no thanks, follow you to California. You said yourself most shows don't make it. The whole thing could be over in a couple of months. I blew off Harvard for what?"

"I'm not asking you to blow off Harvard."

"You just did."

She had invested so much in NYU, far too much to ignore this opportunity. "And you asked me to blow off *The Key Ingredient*. I'm going after a dream I've had all my life."

"And you've only known me for a few years," he snapped.

"You said it. Not me. And that's not what I meant. It feels as if we've known each other forever."

"Annie." He looked deeply into her eyes. "You know what you need to do. And so do I."

"Yes." The reply came swiftly, but so did a crushing regret. "Fletcher—"

"I wouldn't ask you to choose. And you wouldn't ask me." Leaning forward, he gave her the gentlest of kisses.

That kiss. It was too gentle. It felt like sadness and regret. It was the kind of kiss that meant good-bye.

"So we just . . . what? Call it quits, just like that?"

"I'm not following you to California. And I won't ask you to blow off this opportunity." His eyes narrowed.

"You're being intractable." So am I, Annie realized. Because he was right. She was not about to walk away from a chance like this.

"I'm being realistic."

She was angry, too, simmering with frustration. They weren't starry-eyed teenagers anymore. She and Fletcher were adults now, putting their lives in order. Their plans put up a roadblock, and neither could see a way around it. Her chest hurt. Her throat hurt. Everything hurt.

She looked steadily into his face, and it was far too easy to understand what was happening. They were both starting something brand new, something that would take their entire focus. They were falling apart—again.

"Don't call me," she said. "Don't write or e-mail or send me a text message. Let's just . . . leave it."

"Is that what you want?"

Men left. That was what they did. The only way to keep that from happening was to leave first. Before he bailed on her. Before he had a chance to break her heart again.

"Yes," she said, hoping he didn't hear the waver in her voice. "It is."

17

Now

It's the circle of life," said Annie's mom, bringing a basket of dirty clothes to the laundry room just as Annie was transferring clothes from the washer to the dryer.

"What?" asked Annie. "Laundry?"

"With four kids in the house, yes."

"Does it bother you, doing the family's laundry day in and day out?"

"It's a chore like any other. A labor of love. Beth works so hard at the school, and your brother is out working from dawn to dusk." Annie's mom sighed. "I wish he'd gone to college."

"He always hated school," Annie reminded her. More memories poured into her from some invisible cloud: Kyle walking to school each day like a condemned man to the gallows. Their mother's lectures about grades. Arguments about his conduct while Annie poked her nose in a book and pretended not to hear.

If you don't do better in school, you'll end up just like your father.

So? At least he's happy.

"College isn't for everybody," Annie said. "Especially Kyle. Remember how he could never sit still? He's still that way, always doing something with his hands. He has a great family and he takes good care of them."

"I suppose."

"What do you mean, you suppose? Doesn't he take care of them?"

"He loves them all, and he's a good man. A good family man. A family man who plans to grow marijuana."

"I think it's cool," Annie said. "Once the law changes, he won't be doing anything different from what the Mitchells are doing with their whiskey making."

"I know, Annie. And I'm not worried about the pot."

"Then what, Mom? What are you worried about?"

"Money. When it comes to finances..." Mom's voice trailed off.

"Not so good?" She caught a flash of panic in her mother's eyes. "What's going on?"

"Oh, Annie. I don't want to burden you or make you worry."

"Too late. I'm burdened. I'm worried. Come on, Mom. Spill. How bad is it?"

"Let's go up to my studio. I've got it all on my computer." She smiled at Annie's expression. "Don't look so surprised. I put the ledger books away a long time ago. We've gone all digital."

Annie followed her mother up to the loft above the garage. The office cubby was separated from the art space by a tall shoji screen, because Mom didn't like distractions when she painted.

Her mother had kept the books for the farm all her life. She was good at it, and she didn't make mistakes. It turned out Annie was good at it, too. She realized this when Mom showed her the latest digital spreadsheets. As a producer on her show, Annie could look at financials with a practiced eye.

The Rush financials were bleak. The maple syrup operation made a small profit. The logging and cider brought in their fair share, but after all the bills, expenses, and taxes were paid, there wasn't much left over.

"Oh, boy," she said.

"The farm has always run close to the edge," Mom said. "We never would have made it this far if..." She stopped, darted a glance at Annie.

"If what? Come on, Mom."

"If your dad hadn't been supporting us."

"The child support, you mean." Annie had always had a love-hate relationship with the concept. She was the child. The check had been her support. But what she had really needed couldn't be delivered by check.

"He sent more than that. He still does, to this day. It's kept us afloat. Small producers have never gotten rich off of maple syrup."

"Is that what you want?" Annie asked. "To be rich?"

Mom burst out with a hearty laugh. "I'd better not want that. Because then it would make me a big fat failure." She shook her head. "All I've ever wanted is for our family to be comfortable and secure. And we have been."

Annie touched her hand briefly. "Thanks to you. I'll probably never know how hard you worked to keep things together after Dad left and Gramps died."

"I didn't ever want you to worry. I don't want you worrying now."

Annie moved the screen aside and stepped into the main part of the studio. Skylights flooded the space with light, and the entire place was filled with her mother's paintings, on the walls, leaning stacks on the floor, propped on easels of different sizes. Annie was used to her mother's landscapes and beautifully rendered still lifes, portraying the bucolic charm of farm life. The paintings on display now were totally different.

"What's all this?" she asked, looking around the room. She breathed in the oily scent of paint as she studied the work. The big canvases were alive and hectic with wild abstractions on fire with color and feeling. They were alive in the way Mom's precise renderings of country life had never been. The work had a peculiar energy that excited Annie.

"I've been working on some different pieces," her mother said. There was a nervous flash in her smile.

"Why haven't I ever seen these?"

"Most of them came to me while you were sleeping. I was imagining what might be going through your head."

"And you think it was that?" Annie was fascinated.

"That's probably what was going through *my* head."

"Well, I think it's fantastic."

"You like?" Her mother's face lit up. "I have others. I did a series of abstract pieces when Gran died. It was such an emotional time for me." The older paintings were stored on a rolling rack. The newer pictures expressed exaggerated emotions with lyrical sweeps of intense color that were both mesmerizing and hard to look at.

"I've always known you're talented," Annie said. "These are extra special."

"Thanks. That's really nice to hear."

"Have you ever thought about having an exhibit? Or a show or something?"

"Honestly? I think about it all the time."

"And?"

"And . . . what? It's just a fantasy. I'm self-taught, Annie. My only fine-arts training comes from art lessons on PBS, and lately, YouTube videos."

"With your talent, you don't need more education."

"Suppose I *want* more education?" Mom said.

"You should go to Pratt," Annie suggested. "You were accepted there once and you didn't go. Maybe now's the time."

Mom laughed again. "I just finished telling you how broke we are. And now you want me to go to the Pratt Institute."

Annie browsed through the other paintings. They were carefully cataloged in chronological order, showing how her mother's work had changed over the years. The early work was beautifully crafted and exuded charm, depicting an idealized world. There were hints of her inner fire in her renderings of sky and cloud and water, and it was fascinating to see the progression toward abstraction. She was looking at her mother through new eyes, not just as her mom, but as an artist with talent and vision and something to say.

"It doesn't matter what I want" she said. "What matters is what *you* want. Looking at these . . ." An unexpected welling of tears caused the colors to meld and waver in front of Annie's eyes. "You're amazing, Mom. You've had this incredible gift all your life, but you've spent your time devoted to us—Kyle and me, your parents, the farm, now the grandkids. We never really noticed, because you've been so quiet about it."

"Was I? That's probably because I don't have anything to complain about."

"You were so young when Dad left."

"I'm glad you think thirty-nine is young."

"You never dated. Most women remarry after a divorce."

Mom looked wistful. "Some of us find love only once."

Annie wanted to help. She was good at helping, wasn't she? The farm, the family—had she abandoned them, heading off to L.A.? She mulled it over as she carefully drove into town to go to the market. The shopping list was a mile long. With eight people in the house, they always needed supplies.

The local shop was familiar, and full of faces from the past. Annie smiled and told people she was feeling fine and happy to be home. She wondered what they were really thinking. Did they pity her, the woman whose husband had divorced her while she was in a coma and woke up with nothing?

She nearly collided with another cart in the cereal aisle, and looked up to see Celia Swank. "Oh, hey," she said. "Hi there."

"Annie." Celia offered a tense smile. She had been the most beautiful girl in high school, and she was still beautiful, her silky hair expertly done with blond highlights, her nails shell pink to match her lipstick, her teeth preternaturally white. She was wearing skinny jeans and an expensive-looking silk top, carrying a designer bag. "It's good to see you."

"Yeah, I'm . . . It's good to see you, too." Was it? She was still relearning social cues.

"I heard you were injured. I'm sorry to hear about your cooking show. That must be such a loss for you."

"Yes, it is," Annie admitted. *The Key Ingredient* was her show. *Her show.* Was she just going to surrender? Suppose she wanted to reclaim her show? What would that look like?

"We should get together," Celia said. "Catch up."

Ten years before, Celia Swank had been no one to Annie, just a girl she knew from high school. Celia had the life Annie would have had with Fletcher, but she'd thrown it away. It made Annie mental.

"To be honest," Annie said, "I'm not sure we'd have much to talk about."

Celia's eyes narrowed. "We could always talk about Fletcher."

"Why on earth would we do that?"

"Both of us are his exes," Celia pointed out. "Both of us failed."

18

Then

"For a guy who got himself into Harvard, you sure are a dumb-ass," Fletcher's father said. He took two cold beers from the fridge and handed him one. Three years after the accident, Sanford had turned into a different person. He was still that big kid with his big ideas, but something about the trauma and recovery had changed him. He acted more like a father now than he ever had when Fletcher was growing up.

"What am I supposed to do?" Fletcher asked. "Follow Annie to California and . . . what? Carry her purse around for her? Drive her places? Get a job as a grease monkey?"

"Fine," his father said, taking a swig of beer. "Be that way. Wallow in misery, and then when you're my age, you'll look back and wonder what happened to your life."

"Is that what you do, Dad?"

His father roared with laughter. "Me? Dude. Honestly, I look at you and I feel nothing but gratitude. Look at our life. We did good. We're doing good. I'm not miserable. I'm the opposite of miserable."

"That's great, Dad. I'm not miserable either."

"So you're okay with letting that girl run off to California."

"I'm sure as hell not going to beg her not to."

His father sighed. "If staying together is important, you'll make it work."

Fletcher kept trying to picture what it would be like to move to California. He'd have to say no thanks to Harvard Law and start the application process all over again for a West Coast school, putting off his plans for yet another year. Even if he did that, nothing was certain. If Annie's project didn't work out, then what? Would she move on? Go back to New York? Go somewhere else?

Fletcher had spent his life moving from place to place. He was done with all that. He wanted to stay put. He wanted to make a life for himself that made sense. A place to call home.

Neither he nor Annie would compromise. They'd parted ways—again. It was the right thing to do, even though it felt all wrong. He handled the situation like any red-blooded guy might. He got roaring drunk and banged Celia Swank. She was hot, and she wanted him.

And—he couldn't dismiss the reality—he had money now and he wasn't naive enough to believe that didn't matter to Celia. After a few drinks, her motivation didn't matter to Fletcher. She was good in bed. Damned good. Almost good enough to distract him from memories of Annie.

With Annie, the sex was something more than sex. It was a kind of closeness he could only ever feel for her. He tried not to miss it too much.

Celia was a welcome distraction, because he didn't have to think too much when he was with her. He took her sailing on Lake Champlain in his father's new boat. They had a weekend at Château Frontenac in Quebec City, went mountain biking, and even tried skydiving. It was all mindless fun, diverting in a way he needed just then. Only as summer started to fade and he was getting ready to move down to Cambridge for law school did he figure out what she really wanted.

"I'm pregnant," she said.

Of course she was.

Is it mine? He bit his tongue to keep from asking. Celia was a lot of things, but stupid wasn't one of them. She would not trap him like this unless she was confident of whose DNA she was carrying around.

Had she trapped him? Or had he wanted this on some level?

It was the oldest trick in the book, and he'd gone for it hook, line, and sinker. Yes, he'd been careful. Super careful. Yet still, Celia had managed to engineer a condom fail.

A kid. This woman was going to have his kid. And so he made a decision, the kind of decision that couldn't be taken back.

With contracts signed and Martin in place as the resident chef and host of the show, they were getting ready to start on the pilot episode. Annie and Martin showed their latest demo reel to Leon and his team. It was good, maybe their best yet, but they rejected it. Again.

The casting director finally said it aloud, the thing she knew no one wanted to tell her. "You're not right for this role."

"Neither is anyone else we've tested," Leon pointed out.

Martin fiddled with his phone. "Can I make a suggestion?"

"Please," Leon said. "Time's running out."

Martin typed something on the laptop that was attached to the big screen. "I met someone in my yoga class . . ."

He hadn't told Annie about this. She frowned as a not-very-good audition reel played across the screen. The talent—Melissa Judd—was lovely, but her delivery was rough and wooden, her personality overly brassy.

"That's the look we're going for," the casting director said.

"It is?" asked Annie, but no one was paying attention.

"She's the one," Leon said. "I mean, she's going to need some serious training, but Annie can help with that."

"I can?" Annie stared at the frame frozen on the screen of the darkened room. "You're kidding, right?"

Martin grinned and patted her shoulder. "Annie Rush, meet your new best friend."

Annie drove herself to her apartment, feeling dejected. Her show had turned into a runaway train, and she was barely hanging on to it. The endless meetings and planning sessions, which had been so exciting at first, now left her exhausted.

"Snap out of it," she muttered, poking her key into the lock of her apartment door. An "executive efficiency," it was called, a euphemism for a drab rental that had seen better days. She set down her things and poured a glass of wine, settling in to spend yet another evening working. Her computer was like an appendage; she spent more time with it than she did with actual people.

This is what it takes to launch a show, she reminded herself. If it was easy, everyone would have a show. But it wasn't easy. The kind of program she'd dreamed about—a cooking show that celebrated the ideas closest to her heart—was going to take a lot of hard work.

She reminded herself that the production company was in her corner. They, too, wanted a young, hip program about good food, well prepared, locally sourced, the dishes accessible to any viewer. They had even used her title—*The Key Ingredient*—and made her a producer.

This was supposed to be a moment of triumph, the culmination of a long-held dream. And yet, when she glanced at the time on her computer and saw that it was just before midnight, she felt a wave of exhaustion and frustration. Tears squeezed from her eyes. Then the flood began, and she broke down in sobs—great, dragging, ugly-cry, what-the-hell-am-I-doing sobs.

Life was happening at warp speed all around her. It was unfolding like the pages of a flip-book of little animated stick figures. But at the end of each day, she found herself alone in this crappy apartment, hunched over her workstation with no one to talk to unless she wanted to talk about the production. The beach was only a few miles away, and she'd been there exactly once to film a fish market in Venice. The people playing volleyball, riding bikes, and Rollerblading through the park looked foreign to her.

She missed Gran. She missed Fletcher. She needed him with a yearning so powerful that she shook with it. The two of them had been so close, so intimate, so insanely happy together. How could they have simply given up on their love and parted ways?

At the time, it had seemed like a mature, rational decision. She and Fletcher had both acknowledged that there were too many complications to sustain a relationship. What kind of life would it be, living on opposite sides of the country? She thought her life would be so full she wouldn't notice the ragged, gaping hole where her heart used to be.

He was keeping his end of the bargain by not calling, sending e-mails or text messages. They had made a clean break.

She finished off the bottle of wine and looked around the bland apartment. Listened to the blare and grind of traffic that never ceased. Heard the silence of her own loneliness. Being away from Fletcher created such emotional pain that she couldn't eat or sleep. Sometimes she thought she couldn't even breathe.

"This is insane," she muttered, speaking the truth aloud for the first time since moving out here. "The way I'm living is insane."

And with that, Annie jumped up and burst into action. Twenty minutes later, she was in a taxi, headed to the airport. She spilled her guts to the driver, who barely spoke English. "I have to do something," she said. "There's one more red-eye flight to Boston that's leaving in an hour. I have to do this. I don't want to second-guess myself or lose my nerve or let anyone talk me out of it."

She was traveling light—ID, phone, wallet. There was a moment of temptation—"Maybe I should call Fletcher," she murmured, watching the amber streaks of sodium-vapor freeway lights out the window. "No. He'd only bring up all the usual objections, and I don't want to hear them."

The taxi veered onto the airport exit and delivered her to her departure terminal. "What we had—we *have*—is worth saving. If I have to contort my life like a pretzel in order to make this work, I will." She forked over the fare along with a big tip.

"Good luck with that," said the driver in a thick accent.

The damp, blustery weather swirled around Annie as she exited the taxi in front of Hastings Hall, a couple of blocks from Harvard Law School. She had only managed to doze on the red-eye, so she didn't mind the slap of chilly air.

Cambridge was quiet in the early morning—a few earnest-looking joggers with earbuds and leggings, a knot of students clutching their morning coffee and pastry as they made their way back to the residence. She slipped through the entrance in their wake, and found Fletcher's apartment number posted on a mail slot.

Her heart skipped a beat as she stood in front of his door. Her hair was a halo of damp frizz, and she probably had circles under her eyes, but she hoped he would look past that. She hoped he would understand when she explained that she didn't just want him. She wanted a life with him. She wanted forever with him.

Here we go, thought Annie, knocking firmly at the door.

Fletcher opened it, and she stepped inside. It was a spare, furnished apartment, not so different from her place in L.A. Small, smelling faintly of soapy steam from the shower.

The surprise on his face was something more than surprise. It was...

shock? Concern? "Annie. Hey, I didn't know you were coming here. Is something wrong?"

"It is, but not in the way you think." She spoke without preamble, not wanting to lose her nerve. "*No.* That's my answer."

"Your answer." He furrowed his hand through his hair. Looked around as though seeking an emergency exit. "Uh, to what?"

"When you asked me if the show in California was what I'd been dreaming of, I said yes. Turns out I was wrong. The correct answer is no."

"Oh. So that didn't pan out?" He rubbed the back of his neck with his hand.

"On the contrary, the show seems to be working out great. But here's the thing. It's a job, but it's not my dream. I discovered that there's a difference." She took his hands in both of hers, welcoming the familiar warmth of his fingers. It felt so good to touch him. The thing about living alone was that, other than the occasional social handshake, you never touched anyone.

"Annie—"

"I hate the way we left things between us," she said, breathing a sigh of relief at getting the confession out at last. "I hate not being with you. I miss you every minute of every day. Nothing is right without you."

"Annie, hold on a second."

"No, let me finish." She stepped toward him and touched two fingers to his lips. Those soft lips she couldn't stop thinking about. "What I came to say is that I made a mistake, leaving you. I'm in love with you, Fletcher. I have been for a long time. Forever. And it's not going to go away and I can't live my life without you. Do you hear me? I love you. I *love* you. Nothing makes sense without you. So I flew all night long to tell you that. And to ask you—can we figure out a way to put our lives together? Please?" The words came out in a stream of emotion. She felt vulnerable and hopeful, a bit scared, but also filled with certainty.

Maybe he didn't feel the same way, but she was going to be brave. She was not going to let fear or false pride stop her from saying what was in her heart. No regrets.

"So that's it," she said, holding his gaze with hers. "I love you, Fletcher. I don't want this to end. I don't want *us* to end."

"Annie," he said. "Stop talking. Just stop." He stepped away from her, rubbed the back of his neck again. "Aw, Christ. It's too… There's something I need to tell you."

The stiff set of his mouth touched off a tingle of apprehension. She'd been sure he loved her. She'd been certain he would want to make a plan with her. "What is it?"

"I can't… I still feel…" He seemed to be fumbling for words. Then his gaze hardened. "We can't be together."

"No, don't say that. I've been thinking about it nonstop, and I know it's going to be complicated, but we've always been complicated, haven't we? Still, don't you think what we have is worth saving? We could—"

"I'm getting married to Celia Swank." He bit off the name as if it tasted bitter.

For a few seconds, she couldn't process the information. I'm getting married to Celia Swank. It sounded like the start of a bad limerick.

She stood in stunned silence for several long seconds. At some point, she realized the shower had been running since she'd arrived. It stopped suddenly. Then there was the creak of a door, and in walked Celia, wrapped in a towel. "Hey, Fletch, do you think we could—" Celia turned to stone when she saw Annie. "Oh. I didn't realize we had company."

As all the blood in her body seemed to drain to the floor, Annie took a step back. Then another. A feeling of mortification swept over her in a wave of wildfire. "Wow," she whispered, winding her arms across her middle as if to hold herself together. "Just… Wow."

Celia's eyes narrowed. "I'm going to get dressed. It's going to take a few minutes. That should be long enough for you to say whatever it is you came to say." She whirled around and slammed the door behind her.

Celia Swank. Celia? Really? Annie felt a burn of resentment toward the woman. Then she realized her resentment was for Fletcher.

"How long did you wait after I left?" she demanded. "Did you start nailing her as soon as I headed for the airport, or did you at least wait until my plane left the ground?"

"Annie, I'm sorry. I—"

"Sorry? Sorry? For what? You must be thrilled. You found someone who wants to follow you to Harvard. Good for you, Fletcher." As she spoke, she backed toward the door, suddenly needing to flee. She groped behind her for the door handle and found it, stepping back into the hallway and nearly colliding with a guy carrying a tray of hot coffee.

"Watch where you're going," the guy said.

Fletcher looked as if he wanted to say something more. Annie realized that it didn't matter what else he told her, what explanation he could offer. He was going to marry Celia Swank. End of story. It was the end of *their* story.

"All right, then." The world felt different to her now—alien, inhospitable, cold. The way it had felt when her father had left. So much for the romantic, transcontinental journey to bare her heart. "There's nothing more to be said. Except, I guess, good luck with that."

"Hang on, Annie, listen—"

"To what?" she demanded, scorched by humiliation. "You've told me everything I need to know. Good-bye, Fletcher."

19

Now

Annie was awakened by the uncanny sense that she was being watched. She opened one eye, and then the other. The blur next to her bed resolved into a chubby, earnest face.

"Knox," she said, gazing at her small nephew. His head was just about level with the height of her bed. "I didn't hear you come in."

"Mom said I have to be quiet," he told her.

"Well." She pushed herself up on one elbow. "You were very quiet." She scooted over and patted the spot next to her. "Climb on in."

He gave a fleeting smile and hoisted himself into the bed next to her. "Can Dug come?"

"Okay."

Knox leaned over and said, "Dug, up!"

In a flash, the shiny brown dachshund bounded onto the bed, greeting them with ecstatic swipes of his whiplike tail. Annie smiled and twirled the dog's silky ears. "I like Dug. He's cute and gentle."

"Yep." Knox peered into her face. He was solemn, his skin impossibly soft, his eyes unabashedly searching.

"Hey, do you remember me?" she asked him. "You were really little last time I visited. You were still in diapers."

"I'm a big boy now," he said, showing her his undies, printed with some superhero she didn't recognize.

"Yes, you are. And you're very nice to visit me in the morning." She sat all the way up, looping her arms around her drawn-up knees. The room had the same lace curtains that had hung in the same two gabled windows all her life. The bookcases and study nook brought back memories of novels she'd read, homework she'd struggled over, friends who had come for sleepovers.

"When I was little, this was my bedroom," she told her nephew. "It's the guest room now."

"Am I a guest, or do I live here?" Annie wondered aloud.

He looked at her blankly. His chubby hand absently patted the dog's head.

"This room has a secret hiding place," Annie said. "Want me to show you?"

He nodded eagerly. She swung her legs over the side of the bed and planted her feet on the floor. It was a relief not to have to think about every single movement these days. Her legs felt strong at last as she crossed to the built-in bookcase against the wall.

"Over here," she said, releasing the hidden latches. The bookcase swung outward on hinges to reveal a space behind, now draped in cobwebs and dust bunnies.

Dug skittered into the nook, sniffing madly. A spider ran for cover.

"Spiders are yuck," Knox said, taking Annie's hand.

Her heart melted a little at the moist softness of his fingers. "I think so, too, but they don't want to hurt us." She found a flashlight in the drawer of the nightstand. "Hold that for me, will you?"

Knox eagerly complied, crouching down next to Annie. She showed him a little corner cubby where she'd stashed an old Hush Puppies shoe box. She blew away the dust and opened the lid. "See? Treasures."

Knox eagerly inspected her trinkets, a collection of odds and ends left over from her childhood. Looking at the random objects, Annie was flooded with memories. Each item was attached to a specific moment she could recall with perfect clarity. Her collection of honor beads from Campfire Girls were in an old blue Crown Royal pouch, reminding her of the clubby after-school meetings she'd attended with her friends. The engraved metal dog tags worn by her childhood pet, a loyal Lab named Bunky, brought on a sweet-sad stab of affection. She and her little nephew sifted through the box, examining the carnival prizes, key chains, a mood ring, a Mariah Carey CD, a love note from a boy in her sixth-grade homeroom. There was a book of matches and a packet of rolling papers, half gone. She paged through a packet of snapshots, feeling an ache of nostalgia. "This is what I looked like when I was about your age," she said, showing Knox a Christmas-morning shot of her at the age of three or four, hugging both her new doll and her old dog. There was a shot of Annie driving the tractor when she was so small she had to stand up to reach the pedals. Another showed her and Gran in matching aprons, making something wonderful in the kitchen. The most recent, probably just before they got a digital camera, was a picture of Annie with Fletcher Wyndham on prom night. Ancient history.

"Look at us," she said to Knox, remembering how handsome and grown-up Fletcher had looked. His rented tux wasn't a perfect fit, and it had a faint odor of benzine and mothballs, but he had shown up with a corsage and his heart in his eyes, and they'd danced the night away. The beaming young woman in the photo had no idea what the future held. "We were so happy. So clueless."

Her nephew gave a solemn nod, but was more drawn to a cluster of Mardi Gras beads. There had been an early sap flow one year, and her dad had celebrated by throwing a Mardi Gras celebration for all the workers and friends.

"I'm hungry," Knox said, draping the beads over his head.

"Me, too. Let's go make breakfast."

He took her hand and they went down to the kitchen together, with Dug skittering along behind them. Holding on to his tiny fingers, she decided that there was more healing power in a little kid's touch than in all the hours of therapy she'd had. Knox had an open mind and an open heart. He didn't judge, but simply observed, and he said exactly what was on his mind the moment he thought it.

They were the first ones up. Light from the rising sun flooded the room, touching the countertops and utensils with gold. Annie had always loved the way the kitchen looked in the morning, before anything had been touched. The copper utensils gleamed over the stainless-steel countertops. The glassware and baking pans were lined up in the cabinets. The empty table seemed to be waiting just for her. She stopped and took it all in, her senses filling not just with memories, but with a feeling of possibility. The daily nausea of fear was gone, just like that.

She touched her nephew's shoulder. "What's the best thing for breakfast?"

"Blueberry muffins," he said without hesitation.

"I think we can handle that." She fired up the gas oven.

Most of the ingredients and utensils were stored where they had always been. The big pantry still held the dry scent of flour and spices. The iron Griswold muffin pan, Gran's favorite, was in the baking drawer. Gran would never use any cast iron but Griswold, which was challenging, since the line had been discontinued decades ago.

Annie set her nephew on a barstool at the counter, and they got to work. She narrated the recipe to the little boy as she put together the ingredients—eggs and buttermilk, a dab of melted butter and the dry ingredients, the frozen berries. "I sound like Gran," she said softly, "talking to me." She smiled at Knox. "She was my grandmother, and my very best friend, all my life. Do you have a best friend?"

He nodded at Dug, who sat eagerly nearby, hoping for a morsel.

"That's nice," she said. "Dug is a great friend to have. Let's see if he likes blueberries." She tossed one to the dog and he sniffed it with suspicion. Then he lapped it right up.

She got back to work on the muffins, her mind settling quietly to the task. The work was restorative, giving her a sense that she was reclaiming herself. Knox happily helped her stir and fill the pans, and she let him steal a few more blueberries. While the muffins baked, she made a pot of pour-over coffee and set out the cream and sugar, the butter and jam. As the smell of the baking muffins filled the kitchen, Knox put his sticky hands on her cheeks.

"Why are you crying?" he asked, his eyes wide with apprehension. "Does your head hurt again?"

She took his hands, placed a kiss on each one, and summoned a smile. "I'm not hurt. I'm the opposite of hurt. This morning, you made me very happy. Being in this kitchen makes me happy. We took what we had and we made something, and it's going to be delicious."

"When?"

She indicated the windup timer. "As soon as you hear the ding."

The aroma of coffee and breakfast brought the rest of the household to the table. Annie dried her tears, but they nearly flowed again when she watched her family gathering around the counter. The sight of her mom pouring coffee, Beth loading up her tote bag for work, the other three kids digging in, Kyle reading some kind of farming journal, filled her heart. She was home with her family. A lovely sense of rightness enveloped her.

The older kids doled out hugs and hiked down the steep driveway to the school-bus stop, and Beth headed off to the academy. Knox declared that he was going to make a fort for his trolls, and got to work under the dining room table with a cardboard box and some Lincoln Logs. Annie, Kyle, and their mother lingered over second cups of coffee at the kitchen table.

"What are you reading?" Annie asked her brother.

He held up the journal.

"*Cannabis Selection Guide*? So you really are planning to grow pot."

"That's right," he said. "I'm going to plant a sunny acre on the south slope."

"Seriously? Was it legalized in this state while I was asleep?" Annie asked.

Her mom shook her head. "No, and I keep trying to tell him it's a waste of time. If you put all that thought and energy into the sugarbush, we could probably turn things around."

"I'm laying the groundwork," Kyle declared. "The legislature's going to approve legalization for recreational use—there's a bill before them now—and when it does, I'll be ready. There's a fortune to be made, and I've got four kids to feed and educate."

"Cool," said Annie. She remembered smoking pot. She had gotten high just enough times to decide it wasn't for her. All it did was make her muzzy-headed and lazy. "Is Beth on board with this?"

"It's . . . a negotiation."

"Ah." Their mother scowled at him. "I suppose it could be problematic if the director of a school for wayward teens was a pot farmer."

"Not after it's legalized," Kyle said. "She'll come around."

"And if she doesn't?" Mom asked, sipping her coffee.

Kyle went back to his reading.

Before her parents' divorce, Annie remembered tense conversations between them, sotto voce—as if she couldn't hear. The disconnect between Dad wanting to head to the tropics on an adventure and Mom wanting to stay at the farm had never been resolved. His yearning for something different had been like water in the cracks of solid stone, freezing and ultimately breaking the whole thing apart.

"Half of all marriages end in divorce," Annie pointed out, peering at her brother over the top of the journal. "So, statistically, my divorce is good for you and Beth, right?"

"Beth and I are fine," he said, getting up from the table. He cleaned up the breakfast dishes and went to work. He was logging today, taking some of the spent maples to a mill over in Greensboro to be peeled, milled, and cured for lumber. The bark would be used to mulch the garden and orchard.

Annie felt a wave of affection for her older brother. He was devoted to his family. He never seemed to be looking beyond the life he had at something else, like a surf camp in the tropics . . . or a TV career in L.A. Annie envied Kyle his clarity in knowing what he wanted.

Yet based on the financials her mom had shared, she worried about the old place. What if it had to be sold? What if a developer bought it, or a big sugar operation?

After Kyle left for the day, Mom sorted through some mail, making a face as she showed Annie a mailing from a retirement organization, touting effortless senior living. "How did I get on this list? Oh, that's right. I'm old. When did that happen? When did I get old, and how did I forget to have a life?"

"Don't say you're old, Mom. You're not. You look fantastic. And just look around this room. You *do* have a life."

The kitchen and breakfast nook were filled with family pictures, keepsakes, and artifacts from eight generations of Rushes. The walls were ice blue, hung with her mother's original paintings in frames that coordinated with the leaded glass of the bay window.

"Yes," she agreed. "I do. Of course I do. Is it the life I want? I have no idea."

"Now you're whining. Go paint something. You're always happy when you're painting. I'll watch Knox."

"Maybe later. There's something I need to show you. Two things, actually, and I know you're going to have questions."

"Okay." Annie was curious as she followed her mother to the den. They turned on *Sesame Street* for Knox and then sat together on the sofa. Her mother handed her a thick, ivory-covered photo album with *Our Wedding* embossed in gold letters into the cover.

"Only if you feel up to it," Mom said gently.

"I made blueberry muffins this morning. I'm ready for anything." Annie's hands felt cold, though, as she laid the book in her lap. The photographer's name was printed on the inner cover under *Annie+Martin*.

Turning the pages slowly, she felt herself tensing as she took in the shining expressions of the people in the photos, assembled on the beach on a golden evening in September.

"We were all so happy for you that day," Mom said.

"Everything seemed just right, didn't it?" Annie and Martin had planned the beachside ceremony together, focusing on good food, live music, and nonstop dancing. The barbecue meal had been hosted by Martin's family. Though the Vermonters and the Texans had little in common, they bonded over pulled-pork sliders, Texas sheet cake, and wine from the Santa Ynez valley. Annie perused a montage of the Rushes and the Harlows. "Even our families got along great, as far as I could tell."

"We did," Mom agreed. "The Harlows seemed like lovely people, and I could tell they adored you. Martin's mother told me how excited she was about the show, and how grateful she was that it had all started with you."

Annie gazed down at a group shot of herself with Martin and his parents and siblings. It was like looking at a picture of a stranger. A stranger in a beautiful dress with a beautiful smile.

She didn't know what was going through her head at that moment. She could see, just vaguely, the diamond ring on her finger—a conflict-free, princess-cut solitaire in rose gold. He'd sold his motorcycle in order to buy it.

Had she loved him? Yes, she had.

The way she'd loved Fletcher? Not even close. It was like the difference between a lightning bug and a lightning bolt.

But Annie hadn't known that back then. She and Martin had a dynamic, exciting partnership. They were utterly compatible. They worked as a team, challenged each other, talked about plans for the future, made each other laugh, gave each other lovely orgasms on a regular basis. It was love. A kind of love. Now she realized it wasn't enough. She hadn't loved him *enough.*

Where was that ring now? Annie wondered. She'd found it in her Patient Belongings bag. What should she do with it? Hock it?

She lingered over a picture of Melissa wearing a Céline sheath, her slender arm raising a glass of sparkling water as she gave a toast. Annie could still remember the music and the laughter that day. She remembered Melissa asking her if it was the happiest day of her life. They had been friends, she and Melissa. Annie had handed the woman a role on the show. Now she couldn't recall how she'd answered Melissa's question.

"Well," she said, closing the album with a thud. "I have no idea what to do with this. I mean, what do you do with pictures of people you're done with?"

Mom hesitated. "You don't have to decide now. Here's something else." She handed Annie another thick, leather-bound book. "I've always meant to organize this into a scrapbook. I thought that one day I would surprise you with it, but..." She hesitated again. "It's never finished."

Annie looked at the cover. "*My Brilliant Career.* I guess it's finished now, eh?"

Mom gave her a gentle shove. "Stop it. This is a new chapter, and it's going to be even more brilliant. In fact, that's what I'll call the next part—*My Even More Brilliant Career.*"

"Right."

"I've always been so proud of your accomplishments, Annie. And you *are* brilliant, and you've done so much in a short time."

Annie was touched. "Well, then. I feel the same way about your career. And I don't think I ever told you that, and I should have."

"What? My career? I have no career."

"You have something better. Your family and your art. When you showed me your abstract paintings, I nearly fainted. I love how talented you are, and I'm going to nag you until you do something besides collect your paintings in the studio."

"Do something," Mom said. "Like what?"

"You tell me. Have a show. Pursue your studies. Do more with your art."

"That's pretty far-fetched."

"About as far-fetched as me producing a TV show straight out of college?"

Her mother opened her mouth, closed it, then gave a short laugh. "When did you get so wise? Was it that bump on the head?"

"Maybe." Annie opened the album, which seemed to be filled with photos and clippings about her dating back to the toddler years. "Wow. I can't believe you did this."

"It's a work in progress. I always meant to embellish the pages, or something, but I never got around to it. Oh my gosh, look how cute you were."

There were pictures of Annie in the kitchen, sometimes with Gran, sometimes solo. She always looked utterly serious when she cooked and baked. The photos showed that this had never been a form of play for her. It had been more of a calling. A passion.

Judging by her deep satisfaction with this morning's baking, it still was.

There were clippings citing her performance in high school swimming, her appearances on the dean's list in college and write-ups of Glow, the restaurant where she'd worked. After the college years, the collection expanded to include articles from glossy national magazines—*Variety, Entertainment Weekly, Food & Wine, Good Housekeeping, People.*

The headlines shouted out the growing popularity of her show: *Upstart Network Rolls Out Fall Schedule. Atlantis Productions Launches Innova-*

tive Cooking Show. Rising Star Martin Harlow Takes Cooking to the Streets. The Key Ingredient *Is Key to Success for Cooking Show.* Key Ingredient *Wins Third Straight Emmy.*

"I won an Emmy for single-camera editing," Annie said. "Oh, my Lord, that was amazing."

"I know. We all got dressed up in red-carpet outfits and watched the webcast," said her mother.

Annie studied the accompanying photo of herself holding the trophy and thought about what a big moment that had been for her. She wore a victor's smile, and a dress that had cost her more than she'd spent on her first film. Since it was a technical award, it was a Web-only broadcast. All the big food journals had covered the event.

"I burst into tears when your name was announced," her mom said. "Such a moment. And it all started with your senior project in college."

"I never could have predicted the impact that one video would have."

"No one could have. But I always knew you'd make it, Annie. All that talent."

Annie found an article from a day she remembered well. "This was my first dual interview with Martin. *TV Guide,* 2007."

The photograph showed them beaming at each other and toasting with champagne flutes. The flutes were by Lalique, the premier sponsor of the show's website.

"Look how happy we were," Annie murmured. She and Martin were newly engaged and flushed with excitement over the series premiere. The maple syrup episode—which she was sure would be a disaster ending in cancellation—had been a ratings triumph. Landing the interview had only enhanced their sense that they were on the right path.

The interview started out with their oft-told "meet-cute" story—an eager film student, a penniless but gifted chef, combining their talent to create a new kind of show. The interviewer's questions were not exactly hard-hitting, but now Annie remembered a moment that had surprised her. The journalist asked Martin how he had come up with the show's title—*The Key Ingredient.*

"It grew organically out of the content" was his unhesitating reply, which had been printed right there in black and white. "Each dish has that one key ingredient that defines or elevates it. The story focuses on that."

Annie recalled being totally taken aback by his response. She hadn't contradicted him during the interview. Afterward, she felt mystified rather than hurt. She had no idea why he hadn't told the truth. When they were alone, she'd asked, "Why didn't you give me credit for coming up with *The Key Ingredient*?"

"We came up with it together," Martin had replied with a breezy wave of the hand. "That's how I remember it."

She had let the moment pass. In all the whirlwind of the show's success, it seemed a minor point. Maybe she should have called him on it. As time went on, other seemingly minor things cropped up—he would appropriate a twist on an idea, a turn of phrase, and each time, she'd let it pass rather than make a fuss over it. They were a team, after all, she rationalized. It was their job to work together.

In light of what she had discovered later, she had to wonder if his manipulation had been deliberate. Had he meant to eclipse her, positioning himself as the driving force behind the show?

"He took things from me," she said to her mother now. "Little pieces, here and there. Ideas. Inspiration. Credit. Nothing major, nothing I could really call him on. He simply helped himself. And I let him."

"You were a couple," her mother said. "You seemed happy."

"I was. But . . ." She felt a niggling discomfort, and quickly turned the page: *Culinary Duo Makes a Splash.* The article focused on the relationship between Martin and his cohost, Melissa. "I wanted to host the show with him," Annie said quietly. "But I was voted down."

"I always thought it was a terrible decision."

"And I always thought it was Leon's decision and I had to stick with it, because he was the executive producer. Now I wonder if Martin might have planted the seed." She thought about the many screen tests they'd created together. She and Martin had rhythm, certainly a strong enough rapport to get a green light for a pilot episode. They were both knowledgeable and quick-witted. Had he worried about competing with her?

"What did they call you?" Mom asked. "Too ethnic? Too alternative?"

"Something like that."

"They should have kept you in front of the camera. Instead, they picked that bland girl no one can remember. She wasn't bad, but she wasn't great."

"Martin found Melissa himself. Did I ever tell you that?"

"What do you mean, he found her?"

"They met in yoga class. The casting director didn't want to give her a second look, much less a screen test. She was just another shrill, talking head on a late-night shopping show. But Martin was her advocate." Annie's blood suddenly chilled. She had a swift, indelible image of Martin and Melissa, naked in his trailer. This was not an imagined memory. It was as real as the heavy photo albums sitting in front of her.

"What?" her mother asked, worriedly studying Annie's face.

"Martin and Melissa. They were having an affair."

"Oh, Annie. No."

Annie winced as a black fog filled her mind. Pain shimmered through her, and she felt a sick sense of shock and anger. "It was . . . oh God, Mom. I saw them together."

"I didn't know," Mom said, casting a worried look at her. "Sweetheart, I'm so sorry. That must have been horrible."

"I walked in on them in Martin's trailer," Annie said, the memory unfurling in her mind like a tawdry reel. "Then I walked out. And that's when the sky fell."

"The accident, you mean."

"It's my last memory before my big nap."

Mom took the collection of articles from her. "Let's put this away for now." Annie sensed something furtive in her manner.

"What?" she asked. "I think after what I just figured out, I can take it."

Mom sighed, pulling out an issue of *People* and handing it to her. "This was published after the accident. I saved it because you look so gorgeous in the photos, and the journalist was obviously impressed by you. Then the accident happened, and she did a follow-up with Martin, heretofore known as that sneaky bastard."

"What's it about?"

"He gives his rationale for divorcing you."

"Because Martin would surely have a rationale for shipping his comatose wife to Vermont and divorcing her," Annie said, more incredulous than offended. "Let me see that."

Martin had always been a master of spin, and when he worked with a media coach—a wizard named, no kidding, Jim Dandy—the message was honed to a work of fine art. The follow-up to CJ's piece was headlined *In the Aftermath of Tragedy, a Wrenching Farewell.* Martin was portrayed as a young husband in the prime of life, cruelly robbed of his wife—and his future—unless he could bring himself to let go and move on. He declared that asking a judge to appoint a guardian ad litem for Annie, then filing for divorce, was the most difficult thing he'd ever done, but he couldn't exist in the twilight zone of a man whose wife was gone "in every way that mattered," he explained. "She's still so beautiful, but she's not my Annie. I need to let her go and leave her in peace."

"Ah, that poor, poor man," Annie murmured.

"He's a rat bastard," her mother said, "but I'm not sorry he brought you home. The idea of you trapped in L.A. was horrifying to me. If he hadn't offered, I would have insisted. Lucky for him, he volunteered to bring you home."

"Bring me? You mean he came here? To Vermont?"

Mom nodded. "I hugged him and we cried together. I truly believed he was as devastated as I was."

Annie nodded and stood up, holding the back of the sofa to steady herself. The morning she'd spent with CJ came back to her in dagger-sharp images. A physical ache started in her chest, so powerful that she touched her breastbone and wondered if this was what a heart attack felt like.

"Let's go check on Knox," she said, needing a distraction.

The little boy was fast asleep in front of the TV. There was a PBS art show on, a rerun of the guy with frizzy hair painting happy little trees. She switched it off and pulled an afghan over Knox. His sweet little face was slack and smooth, his moist lips pursed. He stirred, tucking his fist under one cheek. Gazing at him, Annie felt a fresh wave of emotion. He was so beautiful. So innocent.

"Love this little guy," her mom said, brushing her fingers over his brow. "I love them all, but he's something special, I suppose because we spend so much time alone together. Your brother might have some cockeyed ideas, but he makes pretty babies, doesn't he?"

Annie nodded. She bent down to pick up the trolls and trinkets strewn around Knox's dump truck. She came across an old key attached to a Sugar Rush key chain, the one in the shape of a maple leaf. Her hand tightened around the key chain, the edges of the maple leaf biting into her flesh.

An icy chill took her over, and she stood, staring down at the key chain. She was inundated by jumbled images and sounds. The scent of lilies. *Delivery for Annie Rush.*

"Oh my God," she whispered, dropping the key and pressing her hands to her stomach. "Oh my God."

"What's the matter?"

"I was pregnant."

"What? No." Her mother stared at her, aghast.

The entire morning came flooding back—the quarrel about the buffalo. A flower delivery. *People* magazine. Two pink lines. *I'm pregnant.*

Slowly and carefully, she walked away from Knox and sank down on a love seat across the room. Her mother sat next to her, arms circling Annie. She poured the story out in broken phrases. "Did you know?" she asked her mother.

"No. Oh my gosh, no." Her mother's voice shook.

Annie finally had all the puzzle pieces in place and could see the events of the day rolling through her mind like frames of a film. She relived her elation the moment the pregnancy test turned up positive. As if it had happened only yesterday, she experienced her soaring hopes as she drove to the studio to give Martin the news, already fantasizing about the baby with a sense of joy so big she'd nearly burst with it.

How quickly that joy had been shattered. The dim trailer, the shocked faces of two people she had trusted. Her hasty, stumbling exit. Martin had come after her, calling her name, looking absurd in his shin-high cowboy boots and boxer shorts. That was the last image in her mind before she heard a metallic clanking sound and felt a whoosh of air. She did not recall feeling fear, only a hangover of shock and horror at what she had seen in the trailer.

And then there was nothing. Utter blackness. A whole lost year of nothing, until *Open your eyes.*

She and her mother sorted through the reports and claim forms that had been filed about the incident. After the collapse, everyone within shouting distance had come running. By the time the ambulance arrived, a swarm of workers, along with Martin, had extracted her from the equipment. She was rushed to a level-one trauma center.

"It's here," Annie said, staring at a densely printed hospital form.

"There's a numerical code, but if you look at the fine print at the bottom . . ." She showed her mother the form. *Loss of the products of conception from the uterus before the fetus is viable.*

Annie wondered what had gone through Martin's mind when he found out she'd been pregnant. Guilt? Sorrow? Relief?

"It's horrible." Her mother held her close. "I'm sorry I didn't see that before. There was so much to take in. When Martin called and told us to come, the doctors said it was to say good-bye to you."

Annie winced, imagining her family's pain as the organ-harvesting team circled like buzzards over a fresh carcass. Then her brain scans offered a glimmer of hope. She defied the prognosis and didn't die. She didn't wake up either.

"It's so strange," she said, "when I imagine lying there with life going on all around me, decisions being made, my future being planned, and I was just oblivious."

"You're not oblivious now."

"I'm hungry now." Knox rubbed his eyes and yawned. Then he climbed into Annie's lap, curling up like a bird in a nest. "Can you fix something?"

"Aw, buddy," she whispered into his sweet-smelling hair. "I can fix anything."

20

Annie went into a frenzy of cooking and baking. She made pasta with fresh eggs from the henhouse and created a sublime lasagna with creamy béchamel sauce. She baked bread with snips of rosemary and a salt crust on top. Tarte tatin with a perfectly burned amber crust came out of her broiler. She made salads sprinkled with sweet woodruff flowers and nasturtium, and drinks sweetened with homemade simple syrups flavored with berry extracts. She treated her mother to a strawberry-rhubarb cordial.

She was almost manic in her pursuit of the perfect scone, or the most velvety hollandaise, or the lightest chiffon cake. If she focused on the art and craft of cuisine, she felt safe and in control. The kitchen was the one place where she felt most like herself.

With each dish she created, she reclaimed bits and pieces of her identity, her memories and dreams. There were moments when she could almost feel Gran holding her hand, pressing it into the soft dough, and rolling it gently into a smooth, pale loaf. "Don't let the things you have to do take over the things you love to do," Gran used to tell her.

Annie didn't *have* to do anything. She was in limbo. But she loved the kitchen. It seemed like the only place that kept her insulated from her nightmares. Now she was left to knead bread or stir a risotto as she tallied up her losses—her marriage and her trust in a man she had loved.

Her career and the program she'd created—*The Key Ingredient.* And, worst of all, the dreamed-of, longed-for possibility of having a child.

I never got the chance to love you, she silently said to the baby she'd lost.

To keep herself from collapsing in rage and grief, she filled each day with cooking. Her family gratefully consumed all of her creations, though she could tell they worried. She didn't blame them. But working in the kitchen was the only way she could remember who she was. While in the middle of making saffron cauliflower, Annie finally grasped the choice she was facing. She could either let this thing destroy her, or she could reclaim herself. There was no middle ground.

She finished the dish with a sprinkle of parsley, then sent a text message: CAN WE TALK?

"He's beautiful."

Fletcher turned to the speaker behind him. He'd been expecting Annie since she'd sent him a message—CAN WE TALK?—but he wasn't prepared for the quick flash of happiness he felt when he saw her.

Her smile widened as she tracked Teddy's progress. The kid was swinging hand over hand from the monkey bars in the city park near the courthouse. He hoisted himself up to the timber fort, waved to a couple of kids, and climbed down to join them.

"Your boy is really beautiful," Annie said. "I bet you get that a lot."

"A fair bit." His son was yellow-haired and blue-eyed like his mom. People said he looked like his dad, but Fletcher couldn't really see that. Teddy was lithe and athletic, happy to embrace anything that involved running and climbing.

Annie looked good. Really good. Her short, curly hair was as shiny as her smile. She was wearing shorts and a sleeveless cotton blouse. Her scuffed canvas sneakers made her appear impossibly young, hardly different from the girl he'd known in high school. She'd filled out a little, and no longer resembled the wan, sickly woman he'd visited at the rehab place. This was the Annie he remembered, whose curves he had once mapped with his hands and lips and body.

"Thanks for meeting me," Annie said. "I know you must be busy."

"Not too busy for you. I usually try to coordinate a court recess so I can hang out with my kid for a few minutes."

"You must also be an awesome lawyer to be appointed to the bench at such a young age."

"That's me," Fletcher said with a twist of irony. "Awesome. How are you?" he asked.

"Baking," she said. "Cooking and baking, that's how I am."

"Okay. So is that a good thing?"

"It's a thing. Mom thinks I'm hiding out in the kitchen. Not facing up to my issues."

"What do you think?"

"Hmm. What do I think?" She touched her chin with her index finger. "I think most people can't tell the difference between fancy ketchup and regular ketchup. I think the NBA three-point line is the work of a genius. I think spending two hours at a hair salon does more for a woman than two hours of psychotherapy." She patted her shiny hair. "I just came from Sunny's."

"Your hair looks nice."

"Thanks." She set a bakery box on the bench beside him. "Raspberry-almond butterhorns. I thought you and Teddy might like a snack."

Fletcher lifted the lid of the box and was hit with the sugary, buttery scent of homemade pastries. He couldn't resist taking a bite of one. "Teddy and I might want you to move in with us," he said.

"I'm divorced," she said. "I guess you knew that."

"So am I."

"I didn't have a choice. I got conked on the head and woke up divorced." She sighed and walked over to a bench in the shade, motioning for him to join her.

"That's not how my divorce went," he said, taking a seat. "Sometimes it felt like I got conked on the head, though." Or maybe not, he thought. There had been times when the divorce had been more like ripping the veins out of his arms while conscious. Celia had been a nightmare throughout the entire process. She'd contested him on every point, from Teddy's visitation schedule to his inheritance of his dad's estate. She had tried to turn the division of assets into World War III, but she had overestimated Fletcher's attachment to their stuff. He really didn't care if she took the furniture, the wedding crystal, and the artwork. He was completely fine with her walking away with Waterford lamps and Persian carpets, designer furniture and two pricey cars, jewelry and all the stuff she'd acquired in a buying frenzy shortly after the wedding.

All Fletcher had truly wanted was time with Teddy. For the boy's sake, he stayed focused on avoiding the constant drama that swirled around his troubled and angry wife. He kept reminding himself that she was the mother of his child, and he was stuck with her. At the end of everything, Fletcher had been awarded equal time with Teddy. He'd settled for a house on Henley Street, near the school and courthouse, and ended up with a life that looked nothing like the life he'd once imagined for himself.

"Well, I'm sorry it happened to you," Annie said. "I'm sure it was painful. And difficult."

"The pain's gone. It's more like a low-grade disappointment that we didn't make it." It occurred to Fletcher that this was one of the most honest conversations he'd had about his divorce. It was strange, talking to Annie about personal things, the way they used to long ago. "And now it's over. We're all better off, Teddy included."

She shot him a glance. "What would Teddy say?"

"That he's better off. Although sometimes I wonder if he says so because he's trying to spare my feelings. I feel bad, shuttling him between his mom and me, week in and week out."

"I was about Teddy's age when my folks split up. And I absolutely did not think we were better off. Sorry, but I didn't. Just talking from the kid's perspective."

"Does that mean he's going to turn out all twisted?"

"Like me?"

"That's not what I meant. Geez—"

"I'm giving you a hard time. And now that I look back on the situation, I remember arguments that struck like lightning. I would hide out in my room, feeling sick to my stomach. But it was my family, and I wanted it to stay intact." She briefly touched his arm. "This isn't helpful, is it? I wish I could tell you we all came through unscathed. But I felt . . . scathed. Is that a word? Anyway, we got ourselves sorted out."

Teddy and his two buddies were playing some rough-and-tumble chase game now, wielding sticks like broadswords. They were engaged in some kind of fake combat, treating the large climbing gym like enemy territory. Celia tended to gripe about boisterous play, warning Fletcher that it would make their son aggressive. Fletcher disagreed. Teddy knew—and had always known—the difference between playing rough and bullying.

Annie was studying Teddy and his friends, with a soft-eyed thoughtfulness.

"What's that smile?" she asked.

"I'm waiting for you to tell me the boys are getting too rough."

"They'll let you know—loudly—when it stops being fun." She laughed at their clumsy jousting.

His smile lingered. It was damn nice, talking to someone who didn't sit on edge all the time, ready to jump in and start managing Teddy. He was amazed at how comfortable he felt with her. How drawn he was to her. A powerful urge to touch her overtook him. Maybe just take her hand. He didn't, though. This was new. He didn't actually know what *this* was. A feeling. A memory. He only knew it was fragile and tenuous.

"We're gonna go shoot some hoops," Teddy yelled. Without waiting for an answer, he and his friends raced for the basketball court.

"*Now* what are you thinking?" he asked her, because suddenly her gaze had drifted far away at something he couldn't see.

"I was pregnant," she said very quietly, staring straight ahead.

Damn. He'd been expecting some other quirky piece of trivia to come out of her, like how the heart of a shrimp was in its head. "Oh," he said. What the hell else did a guy say to that?

"I lost it due to the accident." She spoke even more softly, still keeping her gaze distant and unwavering.

"Aw, Annie. I'm sorry to hear that."

"I had just found out. I went to tell my husband the news, and that's how I discovered he was cheating."

Ouch.

"It was the mother of all bad days," she said. "Newly pregnant, find out he's banging his cohost, get hit by half a ton of falling metal, lose the baby."

"I don't know what to say. Damn, Annie."

She turned slightly to face him, and her expression was so sad that he felt it, too. "I slept through it. I didn't feel the baby go. It was there, and then it wasn't, and I didn't even feel the loss."

Oh, man. He felt his heart unravel in his chest. And then Fletcher did the only thing that made sense to him. He took her in his arms and pulled her into a gentle hug. "You can do that now," he said. "You can cry now."

And boy, did she ever. The waterworks came like a storm. He felt totally useless. He didn't even have a Kleenex to give her, so she groped in her purse and found one, and cried some more. He looked around the park, feeling self-conscious. Teddy was caught up in his basketball game and not paying attention, which was good, because if he saw his dad embracing a weeping stranger, he'd probably think it was freaky.

Yet Fletcher didn't want to move a muscle. She fit against him like the missing piece to a puzzle he'd been trying for years to complete. She smelled like a hair salon and like the Annie he'd known so long ago, her skin soft with its own subtle, unique essence. She had been given up for brain-dead and gone a whole year. She'd awakened to find herself divorced. She'd lost a baby in the accident. Now she had to figure out how to put her life back together and move on from here.

There were eerie similarities between her accident and his dad's. Yet hers seemed a lot worse than the trauma his father had suffered, because at least Dad had kept control of his life. To have everything ripped away while you were sleeping had to be overwhelming.

After a few more minutes, she grew quiet and still. Very slowly, she moved away from him on the bench and pressed the Kleenex to her cheeks. "And to think," she said, "you were going to spend your break kicking back and hanging out with your kid in the park."

"Yeah, how did I get so lucky?"

She tucked away the Kleenex. "Meltdown over," she said. "For the time being."

He tried not to seem too relieved. Was this why she'd wanted to meet with him? Did she need a friend? What did she need from him? "When I got your text . . ." he prompted.

"I need a lawyer. There was a settlement with the hydraulic lift company. I know you're familiar with this kind of thing." She opened a document on her phone and showed him. "I'm worth a lot more asleep than awake."

He was impressed by the figure, but not overly impressed. Her medical bills, personal losses, pain and suffering were undoubtedly sky-high.

"The thing is," she said, "Martin controls the settlement funds. Now that I'm awake, that doesn't seem right. The accident happened to me, not to him."

"You're right," Fletcher said. "You do need a lawyer. Gordy Jessop can help you."

"That's what I thought you'd say. So he's the best?"

"Absolutely. I've gone against him in court, and I've presided over his cases. He's the one you need."

"All right. I'll call him." Her gaze tracked to the basketball court, where Teddy was trying to do a layup. "I'd like to meet your son."

"Teddy? Sure."

"I won't tell him to his face that he's beautiful," she said.

"That's probably best. He's at that age."

"Ten years and two months." She glanced up at him. "Yes. I did the math a long time ago."

"You did?"

"I was obsessed with you, Fletcher. Embarrassingly so. Of course I did the math. Celia was pregnant when I showed up and asked you to come back to me."

He nodded, remembering that day in fine detail. It had wrecked his heart to hear the words from her at last. *I love you. I want to be with you.* By then, it was too late to give her the answer she'd wanted to hear.

He often wondered how their lives would have unfolded if he'd been free that day. If he'd waited a little longer before plunging into rebound sex with Celia... but he couldn't look back. He had sent Annie away with hardly an explanation. What else could he do? Celia had just broken the news to him about her pregnancy. If he wanted any part in the child's life, he was going to have to step up.

His initial offer to Celia was to provide child support and share custody of the child. She'd rejected the idea out of hand. She wanted to be married. She claimed to love him, but Fletcher wasn't that stupid. He knew what she loved, and it wasn't him. He also knew Celia held the trump card—a clear understanding that Fletcher would do whatever it took to be a dad. There was no way a child of his would come into the world and go through life without a father.

"I did what I did," he said to Annie. "Now I have Teddy, so I can't say I regret a single moment. I'm sorry I hurt you."

"And I'm sorry I—" She broke off. "We should stop apologizing to each other. Life happened, and here we are."

"Timing was never our strong suit," Fletcher said.

She nodded. "Your father's accident. Then I moved to California. And then Teddy. Could be the universe was trying to tell us something."

"Like what?"

"That we weren't . . . meant to be."

He studied her profile—delicate, thoughtful, haunting. "You don't really think that."

"No. I don't."

"Here's a thought. What if we quit worrying about the timing and made this moment our time?"

She turned and gazed at him with her heart in her eyes. "And suppose we didn't worry about what happens when the moment is over?"

"What if we decide it doesn't have to be over?"

She smiled, soft and sad. "That's too big a 'what if.'"

No, he thought. It wasn't too big. "Would you like to go out with me?"

"Out . . . where?"

"I don't know. Somewhere nice. Dinner and a movie. On a date."

"A date. Oh my gosh, that sounds fun."

"Now you're being sarcastic."

"Look, I can't . . . I shouldn't. No, Fletcher. This isn't about timing. I can't go on a date with you. I can't be romantic with anyone until I figure myself out."

Damn. "So you'll just . . . what? Hide in the kitchen and bake?"

"Yes. Maybe I will." She stood up, moving slowly, and blotted her face one more time. "It feels terrible to say this, but I have a long way to go before I'm recovered enough to be myself again. In fact, Dr. King says I'll be someone new. I might turn out to be somebody you don't even like."

He grinned. "Sure."

"Don't you need to be somewhere? Judging something, or whatever you do?"

He nodded. "Come on. I'll introduce you to my son." The other kids had left, and Teddy was dribbling the ball by himself. Fletcher motioned the boy over. "This is Annie," he said. "She's a friend of mine."

Teddy offered a quick smile. "Hi. I'm Teddy." He stuck out his hand with a little awkward flutter. But he looked her in the eye and shook hands with a firm grip, the way Fletcher had been coaching him since he was a tyke.

Annie looked delighted. "I was watching you play basketball. You're pretty good."

He grinned. "Thanks."

"Is Ms. Malco still the PE teacher at school?"

"Yes, ma'am."

"I'm not a ma'am," she said. "Ma'ams are old ladies. I'm just Annie. Malco was my PE teacher when I was your age. I grew up here. Did she teach you the game of horse?"

"Um, don't think so."

"It's a basketball game for two. Want me to show you?"

Teddy's eyes lit up. "Sure."

Fletcher checked the tower clock again. "I have to go. I'll be done at the usual time, Ted."

"Okay, Dad. See you later."

He left them to their game, feeling ridiculously happy that they seemed at ease with one another.

"I have to warn you," Annie said to Teddy as Fletcher walked away. "I'm kind of uncoordinated."

"I'll go easy on you."

"No way. The first rule of any game is that you always play to win."

21

Annie thought long and hard about her conversation in the park with Fletcher. *What if we quit worrying about the timing and made this moment our time?*

No. She couldn't start something with him. But she wanted to. Now? No. Her life was a mess. She had too many things to figure out. She lived at the farm with her family, but was it her home? She didn't know. She wasn't sure she wanted it to be. All she knew at the moment was that she was safe and happy in the kitchen.

"Hello, gorgeous." The kitchen door clapped shut.

"Hey, Dad." She smiled, though a flashback haunted her. How many times had he come through the back door with a grin and a "hello, gorgeous"? It had been his standard greeting at the end of each workday. After he'd left, she used to feel a little jump in her heart each time the back door slammed, followed by a sinking disappointment when she realized he was gone for good.

"I just made a batch of jam tarts," she said. "Help yourself."

He grabbed one from the tray, took a bite, and rolled his eyes. "Fantastic. Tastes just like the ones your grandmother made."

"Her recipe, of course. There's really no improving on perfection."

He looked around the kitchen. "Where is everybody?"

"Let's see—Kyle took a load of lumber down to Darrington Mills. Beth's at work and the big kids are at school. Knox has preschool today, and Mom is painting." She grinned. "Only a month ago, I couldn't say my own name, and now I'm keeping tabs on everyone."

"You've always been sharp as a tack. It's good to see you getting back to your old self."

"How would you know?" She couldn't stop herself from asking the obvious question. Her voice flat but crisp. There was no trace of raspiness now. The tracheostomy scar had all but disappeared. "It's been twenty years."

He winced. "I screwed up, and it hurt you, and I can't change that. I'm here now, Annie. And I know you better than you think. I know your smile lights up the world. I know you're sweeter than this jam tart, and smarter than anyone has a right to be. That hard edge is new, though."

She nodded. "I don't like being hard. But being sweet stopped working for me. I was so sweet that my husband cheated on me and stole my life."

"He's a tool. I wish I'd seen that in him. How can I help?"

Annie gave a bark of laughter. "Break his kneecaps?"

"I'd like to, but it wouldn't do any good."

She sobered. "I know, Dad. I appreciate your wanting to help."

"Have you contacted him? Does he even know you're back?"

"I don't know. Gordy—the lawyer who's helping me—is going to handle Martin." She shuddered. "How weird is that? I was married to the guy and I was in a coma and I can't even call him now that I've woken up."

"Do you want to?"

"No," she said quickly. "Let's not talk about Martin, okay?"

He finished his tart and washed up at the sink. "What would you like to talk about?"

"How are Nana and Pops doing?" she asked.

"They're all right. They'd love to see you."

"I'd love that, too." She wasn't close to her father's parents. After he took off for Costa Rica, she didn't see much of them.

"They need a lot of help these days," he said.

"Is that why you moved back?"

"Part of the reason."

"And the other part?"

"Annie, don't tell me you're baking again—oh." Mom came in, her painting coveralls spattered like a Jackson Pollock original. She stopped cold when she saw Annie's dad. "Ethan. Hey. I didn't know you were coming over today."

They studied each other for a tense moment. It was strange seeing them together, as strange as it had once been to see them apart. Mom looked flustered, touching the kerchief she wore on her head when she painted.

"I wanted to see our girl."

"Oh. All right." Mom checked out the baking tray. "If you keep feeding me like this, I'm going to get fat."

Her mom wasn't fat. She was still young and pretty. And at the moment, she was blushing like the face on the feelings chart with pink-tinged cheeks.

Annie felt an unexpected tingle in the air. All through her rehab, her parents had spent more time together than they had since the divorce. At first, she thought they got along for her sake. Sometimes, though, she sensed a wistfulness in them. Nostalgia, maybe.

"I'll tell you what," she said, making a quick decision. "I'll take away the temptation." As she spoke, she boxed up some of the jam tarts. "I promised these to Pam. Can I use the car?"

"She's driving?" her father said, his posture stiffening.

"The doctor said it's all right," Mom told him.

"The doc said I could," Annie said at the same time.

"That's great, Annie."

Was it? she wondered. How was it great that a thirty-three-year-old woman was able to drive a car? In L.A., she'd driven like a pro, navigating traffic with confidence. No one had questioned her fitness or judgment.

As part of her rehab, she had to undergo tests of her reaction time, perception, sequencing skills, and judgment. She'd repeated each test several times before they gave her the green light.

Annie grabbed her keys and purse and headed out the door. She wondered what her parents would talk about in her absence. Did they worry aloud about their daughter? Reminisce about the past? Argue in sharp voices, the way they had before the divorce?

In one of the family therapy sessions, they'd been told to avoid adopting problems that didn't belong to them. Good advice, but sometimes it was hard to figure out who owned what problem.

Holding the pastry box flat, Annie got into the car. She narrated the steps to herself—another technique from rehab. Say it while you do it. Yes, that made sense, but it felt tedious. Sometimes she talked to herself in a fake English accent or a Minnie Mouse voice. But nothing changed the fact that tasks she used to do without thinking now had to be relearned, step-by-step.

Focus, she told herself. You get to drive now. Don't blow it.

She stayed focused during the drive to town, and then along the farm road leading to the distillery. She hadn't been back to the place in years, and she was eager to see how the local whiskey-making operation was coming along.

She recalled pitching an idea about the Mitchells' whiskey in the writers' room back in Century City, but she'd been shot down. People remembered the previous taping they'd done in Switchback and how it had nearly ended in disaster, and no one was eager to return. They had compromised, doing a special on Casa Dragones tequila. Annie had never been happy with the episode. San Miguel de Allende was a lovely town in the mountains of Mexico, but the product was so expensive that most viewers could only dream of tasting it.

Melissa had fallen ill during the trip. Martin had gone to her suite in the night, bringing her crackers and ginger ale.

"If it isn't my favorite head case," Pam said, coming out to the parking lot to greet her. "You look fantastic. I'm liking the short hair."

"Thanks." Annie held out the box. "Strawberry jam tarts."

"You're wicked. I'm trying to watch my weight. Still haven't lost my extra baby pounds."

Pam had a baby, a little boy. She and Klaus, the sommelier from Boston, had married. He had moved to Switchback and they'd started a family. Annie felt a small flutter of envy. *A baby.*

They went inside, and Pam showed her the latest improvements around the place—another shiny brass distilling kettle, rows upon rows of casks and barrels stamped with the distillery logo, an expanded bottling operation. The place smelled of the angel's share—the invisible vapors that escaped as the liquor aged. Their brand name was Switchback Sugarbush, and judging by the expansion, it was catching on.

"This place has grown since my last visit," Annie said.

"We've come a long way since the horse barn."

"So business is good?"

"Business is hard. We've been able to expand thanks to a silent partner." She kicked off her boots and slipped on a pair of clogs. "Sanford and Fletcher Wyndham."

Annie lifted her eyebrows. "Oh, boy."

"They rescued us from drowning. I'm grateful for the infusion of funds, but now the challenge is to keep up with demand. My dad's whiskey won a big award, and the latest batch was sold out within a day." She poured a taste from a numbered and signed bottle and handed it to Annie.

The amber liquid sparkled in the light. Annie tasted it. "Lovely. Pam, this is so great. And this bottle. It looks like a collector's item." It was in the same mason jar they'd always used at the distillery, but now there was a beautiful label depicting a stylized tree with leaves of gold foil. All the key words were present—"small batch," "artisanal," "handcrafted."

"Packaging is everything. People like that homemade feel," Pam said. "In your case, all the words are true. Everything is distilled and bottled right here, right?"

"Yes. We're committed to that. We don't want to be the kind of 'small-batch' whiskey that's actually mass produced in Indiana and sent out to bottlers. We're hoping consumers will read the fine print. We've opened our place up for tours." At the far end of the shelves of aging barrels, she showed Annie a marked keg. "Here's why I wanted you to come over. I've been saving something for you. Remember this?"

Annie bent down and read the hand-lettered label—*Sugar Rush*. With bittersweet clarity, she remembered the day they'd filled the barrel with maple syrup. "Wow, I had forgotten all about our experiment."

"It's just been sitting here ever since."

"Sugar Rush aged in a whiskey barrel." Annie stood back and regarded the old oaken cask. "Barrel aging is a thing these days."

"I know. I've got all kinds of requests to buy my used barrels—for vinegar, hot sauce, fish sauce, bitters, any form of alcohol, you name it." Pam put her hand on the rough-hewn cask. "Do you think it's spoiled?"

"There's one way to find out."

"My thoughts exactly. I hope this one aged gracefully. How cool would it be if it turned out?" Pam went to the tasting room and returned with a tap and two crystal snifters. "Here goes. Moment of truth." She tapped the barrel, and a thin, dark amber stream of syrup flowed from the spigot into each glass.

Annie held the snifter up to the light. "I like the color. Oh my gosh. The smell." It was a gorgeous commingling of maple and bourbon. She tapped the rim of her glass to Pam's. "To aging gracefully."

They each tried a tiny sip, just a wetting of the lips with the smooth, viscous liquid. Their eyes met, and they sipped again.

"Well?" Pam asked, eyebrows lifted.

Annie nearly swooned from the flavor of the barrel-aged syrup. A smoky, boozy essence shimmered through it, giving the liquid a complex depth. "Incredible."

Pam offered a dazzling smile. "This definitely has the wow factor."

Annie savored another sip or two. The flavor was multilayered and intense with the rustic taste of maple. She carefully set down her snifter. "I think we might be onto something."

"My thoughts exactly." Pam beamed at her. "Can we barrel-age some more?"

"Of course. We've got plenty put by on the farm that hasn't been bottled yet. It's good to have a project."

"Totally. Hey, we could try cold-smoking it, too. Or how about this? We could create a craft cocktail with this syrup that would knock your socks off. What about an old-fashioned made with Sugar Rush instead of simple syrup?"

"Good idea."

Pam took another taste of the Sugar Rush. "This is amazing. I love it so much I would marry it."

"How is married life going for you, anyway?" Annie asked.

"Ups and downs, mostly ups. Hudson and Klaus are my whole world now. Having a baby changed me in ways I never expected. Not just my dress size. It's like he rearranged my heart."

The old yearning tugged hard at Annie and the void of sadness gaped wider. Some days, she couldn't stop thinking about her lost baby. "Ah, Pam. That just sounds so lovely. I'm really happy for you."

"Thanks. You know what I'm happy about right now? This amazing syrup. Let's bottle and sell it."

"Just like that."

"We can, you know. The bottling operation has been upgraded. Let's get Olga to come up with some label designs. She does beautiful work. She's the one who redesigned our whiskey label."

"Olga, the model with a Russian accent?"

"Oh! You know her?"

"No. Fletcher said his dad was dating someone named Olga."

"He married her a few years ago. She's great. Her specialty is woodcut prints, and she's a graphic designer as well. Come and meet her."

The office area occupied a new building constructed of peeled logs and glass picture windows with a deck overlooking the neighboring hills. Olga was at a workstation in front of a computer and a bulletin board covered with clippings. She was probably in her forties, but she still had her voluptuous bikini-model looks and smoky Russian accent.

"It tastes brilliant," she said when they gave her a sample of the syrup. "We must give it a special label." Then she turned to Annie. "So. You are Annie Rush of Rush Mountain. Sanford and Fletcher have always had the nicest things to say about you."

"Really?" Annie wasn't sure what to make of that. "What sort of things?"

"You were very kind to them after Sanford's accident. And you became famous for your television program."

"*The Key Ingredient,*" Pam said. "Everyone in town watches that show. Annie gave the commencement speech at the high school after she won an Emmy Award, and my mom says half the kids wanted to work in television after hearing her."

"Are you here for a visit?" asked Olga. "Do we get to meet Martin Harlow? You are married to him, yes?"

"I'm married to him, no. I mean, we're divorced."

"You are?" Pam gaped at her. "You never told me."

"Nobody told me either. I just recently found out myself. In the rehab place. Discovered the divorce before I even remembered the marriage."

"Wait a minute," Pam said. "He divorced you while you were in a coma?"

Olga said something in Russian that needed no translation.

"My thoughts exactly," Pam said. "Wow, that's a dick move." She lined up some whiskey shots, and they each had one.

Annie gave them a quick summary of events. It felt good talking to women friends, knowing they were entirely on her side.

"Podonok," Olga spat, *"gavnoyed."*

"When she's mad, only Russian will do," Pam said.

"Well. I appreciate the outrage on my behalf," Annie said. "I'm handing the situation over to Gordy—my lawyer."

"Oh, he is good, that one," Olga said. "He created my *prenubzhy*."

"Prenup," Pam translated as she refilled their tasting snifters. "Annie, I hate that you're going through this along with everything else. Tell us, how we can help?"

"You're helping," Annie said, indicating the whiskey. "Whatever Olga said—that helped, too."

"I can't believe Martin did that. How did he get past the PR nightmare? Didn't the tabloids call him out?" Pam asked.

"Nope, just the opposite. Martin and his handlers are experts at spin," Annie replied. "The articles that came out played up the tragedy of his loss, and how awful it was for him to be married to a turnip while he was in the prime of life. He deserved to move on and blah, blah, blah. What they neglected to say was that he moved on even *before* I became a turnip."

"What a cheater," Pam said. "What a waste of air."

Olga volunteered to drive Annie home from the distillery. Annie was only mildly buzzed from the whiskey shots, but she didn't want to chance driving. Olga drove a luxurious SUV with eighties classics cranked up loud. After a while, she turned the volume down. "You were Fletcher's lover."

Annie stared out the window as they passed the granite hills and the river valley. "It was a long time ago. We were just kids."

"Fletcher is a good man. He would never cheat. Perhaps there is still something between you."

"I'm not ready to explore that."

"You will be. The heart will heal, and then it will open up again."

"I hope you're right." Annie wondered if Fletcher would still be interested when she reached that point. She certainly didn't expect him to wait. As they'd both admitted, they had a knack for bad timing.

Olga parked in the driveway at the farm. "Your home is beautiful. Fletcher told me about this place."

He did? Annie couldn't suppress a smile. "Would you like to come in?"

"No, thank you." She studied the house and gardens. "I would like to get started on your label."

When Annie walked into the kitchen, her mother and brother were fixing dinner. The kitchen smelled of simmering pomodoro sauce and baking rolls, two of Mom's specialties. She spotted her father in the backyard with Knox and Hazel, pushing little Knox on a swing. Had her dad spent the whole day here? That was different.

"Stop what you're doing and get over here, you two," she said, setting her parcels on the table.

Something in her tone caught their attention.

"You're tipsy," her mother said.

"In a good way. I need to show you something." She paused and regarded her mother. "Do you mind if Dad joins us?" She had realized that if they were going to pursue this idea, they'd need his help.

"No, of course not." Mom touched her hair, then took off her apron and went to the back door. "Ethan, can you come in for a minute? Annie wants to show us something."

Her father came right away, his face somber as he checked Annie out. "Everything all right?"

"Absolutely." Annie took out the bottles of wheat whiskey and bourbon Pam had sent home with her.

"No wonder you're tipsy," her mother said.

"She's been drinking?" her father asked.

"Oh, for heaven's sake, I'm not in high school anymore. Just listen, okay?" She hesitated, trying to remember the last time the four of them had been together as a family. Her wedding to Martin, she supposed. Dad had not given her away in the traditional sense. Under the circumstances, that had seemed disingenuous. She had held her head high and walked alone into the arms of her bridegroom.

Annie shook herself free of the memory as she removed the small sample jar of syrup she and Pam had prepared.

"What's that?" asked Kyle.

"Our new project. I think we might have hit on a new product to launch. A moneymaker."

He eyed the jar of amber liquid. "Yeah?"

"Four words," Annie said, opening the top. "Listen carefully."

"We're listening." Their mother sat down and folded her arms on the table. Dad sat next to her. The image of the two of them took Annie back to her childhood, when she'd eagerly shown her parents a good report card, a baby bird she'd rescued, or a plate of cookies she'd made all by herself. Now their expressions were much the same—indulgent pride.

"Barrel-aged maple syrup." She helped herself to a warm roll, fresh from the oven. Dipping the bread in the syrup, she gave them each a sample and watched them taste it.

"Wow," said Kyle. "Man, that's good stuff."

"I've missed your rolls, Caroline," Dad said to their mother.

"You're supposed to be tasting the syrup," said Mom. "Delicious. Does it contain alcohol?"

"No, just the flavor. It's amazing, right? Sugar Rush, but with an extra kick. We aged it in a whiskey barrel." She told them about the drum of syrup she'd given Pam years ago. "I forgot all about it. Now we have fifty-five gallons of this stuff." She explained the plan of bottling and labeling it as a high-end gourmet product.

Dad leaned back in his chair and crossed his legs. "When can you get it to me? I mean, I assume I'm here because I can take care of the approvals and distribution. That's how I met your mom. Did we ever tell you that?"

"Ethan," their mother said. "It's ancient history—"

"You never told me how you met," Annie said, then touched her forehead. "Or maybe you did, and it got erased from my hard drive."

"I was driving the produce truck for my folks, and I came up the mountain for a load of apples. Went back down the mountain with ten bushels of McIntoshes, a few cases of syrup, and the phone number of the prettiest girl I'd ever met."

"And now we're supposed to all go 'aww,'" said Kyle.

"Whatever," said their father. "We fell in love, we raised a family, and things changed." He was looking right at Mom when he said the words. She stared back at him, her expression soft and immeasurably sad.

That was how love worked sometimes, Annie reflected. It filled every nook and cranny of your heart, and then one day you realized it had gone away. She wondered where those feelings went. Maybe they trickled into the atmosphere to be inhaled by someone else, a stranger who suddenly saw someone across the room and instantly fell in love. That would be totally cool, right?

Annie wondered if she had lost Martin's love in a moment, or if it had been a slow leak, invisible to her until the end. She was trying to remember what it felt like to love Martin, and oddly, she could not.

"... help in any way I can," Dad was saying to her.

Annie blinked, backing away from the thoughts swirling through her head. "With the syrup?"

"Sure," he said. "If you're willing. If we're all willing." He looked around the table. "Want to team up?"

In that moment, Annie remembered what it felt like to be a family again. There wasn't a picture for it on her feelings chart, but it was a tangible thing, warm and soft as fresh rolls from the oven, a cocoon of safety surrounding them all.

Now she realized that this was the feeling she'd been seeking when she told Martin she wanted a baby. She hadn't found it with Martin, though. She'd had to come all the way home to recapture the feeling.

And then the moment passed, and Kyle said, "This product is awesome. It's the kind of thing you want everyone in the world to taste. I say we do it."

"I'm in," Annie said. "Mom?"

Her mother's hands pressed down on the tabletop as if she was trying to hold it down. Then she noticed what she was doing and eased up. "Dinner's ready. Ethan, would you get the little ones inside and washed up? And open a bottle of wine?"

"Are you asking me to stay?" His grin failed to mask the nervous flicker in his eyes.

"For dinner," she said, tying on her apron.

22

Caroline Rush finally had an inkling of what Annie must have experienced, waking up to a world turned upside down. She felt that way now, as twilight settled over Rush Mountain and she took her youngest grandson upstairs for his bath. The older kids were cleaning up after dinner while Annie, Beth, Kyle, and Ethan lingered over the last of the wine, talking about Annie's idea for the maple syrup. Caroline could hear the deep murmur of Ethan's strange-yet-familiar voice gliding into laughter now and then as he visited with their adult children.

Holding Knox's tiny hand to help him into the tub, she caught a glimpse of herself in the bathroom mirror. She looked . . . flustered. That was probably the word for it. Her ex-husband had just eaten dinner with the family. His presence in the home they'd once shared was unsettling.

"This is from Grampa," said Knox, plunking down in the warm water and pulling a little action figure on a surfboard from his bin of toys.

"Yes, it is. He sent it last Christmas."

"What's that say?" Knox pointed to the words on the board.

" 'Pacific Rush Surf Camp.' It's the name of Grampa's place in Costa Rica."

Knox made a shushing sound as he glided the surfer over the water. Caroline gently shampooed his hair and soaped his little bony shoulders. She and Ethan had named the camp together, back when they thought they would be partners forever. Back when Caroline had truly believed that buying a beach compound in Costa Rica had been pure fantasy, something to talk about in bed after the kids were asleep and they were too tired for sex.

"I'm gonna go to Grampa's beach," said Knox. "I'm gonna see the ocean."

She scooped water over him to rinse, and wiped the cookie crumbs from his face. "That sounds fun."

Caroline hadn't been prepared for the sucker punch of hearing he had met someone in Costa Rica. He had left her for a dream, not a woman. She should have been prepared, though. Ethan was incredibly handsome, with the kind of affable charm that drew people to him.

She'd taken secret delight in Annie's description of Imelda—the snare-drum voice, the sweat running down between her boobs, the onion breath—and then Caroline had felt evil for taking delight. She'd wanted to get past the hurt, the anger, the disappointment.

She lifted Knox out of the tub and wrapped him in a towel, loving the soft, dewy feel of a freshly washed toddler. "You smell minty fresh," she said, planting a kiss on his damp head.

"So do you," he said politely.

She supervised the brushing of his teeth. He got ready for bed all by himself, pulling on undies and jammies like a pro. He wasn't a baby anymore. The transition always happened so fast, and it made her wistful. Grandbabies were life's sweetest reward, and she craved them with all her heart. When she'd learned of Annie's lost baby, Caroline had wept until she couldn't see straight.

Knox must have sensed the dip in her mood, because he gave her a nice hug and a kiss.

And just like that, her mood lifted. "I don't need dessert tonight," she said. "You are sweeter than maple sugar. Let's go tell everyone good night."

"Okay."

She looked again at the woman in the mirror. Still flustered. She needed a swipe of lipstick. Just gloss; she didn't want to be too obvious. Didn't want him to think she was primping.

She took Knox downstairs and he made the rounds of hugs and kisses, including the two dogs, Hootie and Dug. When Caroline watched Ethan swing the little boy up to the rafters, then down for a kiss, she flashed on a younger Ethan with Kyle, both of them chortling with glee. They'd been a happy family, hadn't they? What had happened to them?

Two words, she thought—communications breakdown. She had never told Ethan of her high-flown dreams of art school and a career as a painter. She'd meant to, but once Kyle came along, she hadn't seen the point. Why bother getting misty over something that was never going to happen?

And Ethan had never told her that he hated working for the Forest Service and the family business. Out of loyalty to Caroline and her parents, who gave them a home in the big, rambling farmhouse, he had tried to like the logging and the sugaring, being tied to acres of land that had sustained the Rush family for two hundred years. At the time, she hadn't sensed his discontent, just as he hadn't sensed her yearning to pursue art school.

Would things have turned out differently if they'd been honest with one another? She didn't know. What she did know was that it was impossible to hide from a dream. Unfulfilled yearning had a way of eking out somehow, causing invisible cracks in the foundation.

Knox extended the tucking-in privilege to Annie. "I want to read *two* books," he said.

"I think I can handle that. How about you pick one, and I'll pick one."

"Go, Dog. Go!" he said immediately, heading for the stairs.

Ethan bagged up the trash. "Are the garbage cans in the same place?" he asked.

"No," she said. "I'll show you." Caroline held open the back door. "Over here. We had some trouble with bears, so it's different now."

Darkness had descended, and a few early stars pierced the sky. Caroline used her phone to light the way around the side of the house to the bin. Once a week, Kyle hauled the recyclables and trash down to the transfer station.

"Pretty slick," said Ethan, checking out the bear-proof mechanism. "I could use something like that in Dominical. Not for bears, though. For monkeys."

Caroline didn't know what to say to that. The name alone reminded her of the slashing arguments they'd had over it. When Kyle was a senior in high school, he'd been eager to take over the maple business—almost as eager as Ethan had been to hand it off to their son.

Ethan had shown her pictures of a Costa Rica surf camp, reminding her of the conversations they'd had before the kids came along. He'd found a property. He wanted to buy and develop it.

Caroline assumed he was kidding. It sounded so far-fetched that she'd actually gone along with the fantasy for a while, describing the breezy open veranda she'd like to design, swagged with colorful woven hammocks. There would be a special corner for her easel and paints, where she could see the ocean and listen to the waves while she worked.

When it became clear that Ethan was serious about developing the property, her objections failed to stop him. "I've lived this life with you for nineteen years," he'd said, his voice sounding tired with regret. "I've tried to like it. The truth is, Caroline, I can't do this anymore. Come with me. Let's all go together."

She refused to consider it. There was the farm, and her parents. They couldn't just dump it all in Kyle's lap for the sake of Ethan's daydream.

He claimed he had to leave her—leave their family—in order to save them from himself, and the angry, frustrated person he'd become. He craved a more exciting and varied life, and if she wouldn't join him on the adventure, he swore he'd go it alone.

Caroline had not been blindsided by his discontent. She'd seen it coming. A part of her was relieved to say good-bye to the tension and darkness of living with someone who yearned for another life. Even so, the abject terror she'd felt at the prospect of raising the kids without him, the worry over sharing custody with someone who lived half a world away, had overtaken her. What she could never admit, even to herself, was that the Rush family maple farm had never been her dream either. She did love it, but this was not the life she'd pictured for herself. Still, it was a safe, familiar home for her children, and with Kyle coming along so quickly after they married, it had made sense to stay.

Ethan had never really found a moment of contentment in their life here. The idea that he was just sticking it out until Kyle was old enough to take over made Caroline wonder if he'd ever loved her at all.

Now, years later, a hot spike of anger broke through. "Maybe Imelda could scare the monkeys away," she said to Ethan.

He laughed, unfazed by the remark. "I'm not with Imelda anymore. Haven't been for a while." Then he grew serious. "You've always had my heart, Caroline."

The statement hit her in a soft spot, but she held on to the anger. "You have a funny way of showing that. You couldn't wait to get out of here."

"I did wait. And I tried. Christ, I waited nineteen years, and I tried like hell to make it work. Then when I wanted to go to Costa Rica, you balked."

"Did I? Did you even ask me? Maybe there were things I wanted, too."

"Like what? And how was I supposed to know to ask?"

"I wanted to study art," she admitted. "I wanted to go to the Pratt Institute."

"In New York? I thought you loved the farm," Ethan said.

"I loved *you,*" Caroline shot back, then gasped, wishing she could reel in the words she'd just blurted out. "But you took off."

"Then why did you stay after I left? You could have gone anywhere."

"I needed a place to raise our kids. I needed help from my parents, and when they got older, they needed *my* help. God knows, you never gave it a thought."

"That's not fair."

"Oh? And what's fair, Ethan? Answer me that. Was it fair for you to leave?"

"I left so I wouldn't self-destruct. But I never stopped loving you. I never stopped missing you." He raked a hand through his hair—that abundant ash-blond hair, as sexy now as it had been in his youth.

"Why should I believe you? Those are empty words."

"You're right. They're empty unless I do something about it."

"So you're going back to Costa Rica in order to . . . what? To love me some more?"

He grew quiet, and in the darkness, she couldn't read his expression. "I'm not going back."

"That's news to me."

"If you'd talk to me about something other than Annie, you might have learned that I sold the surf camp."

"You're lying."

"The paperwork is being processed as we speak."

She felt a dull sense of shock. "You abandoned your family to build that place. Was it all for nothing?"

"No—God, no."

"Then why would you do something like that? Why would you sell your dream?"

"Because ultimately, it was empty, as empty as me saying mere words. The place is paradise. I wish you could have seen it. But even after all this time, it doesn't mean a thing without you."

"And you're just telling me this now?" She stared at him, incredulous.

He took a step toward her. "I'm ready to move on to the next big adventure."

"Oh, really? And what is that?"

"What if I said the next big adventure was you?"

23

Swimmers, take your marks."

Annie sat on the top bleacher of the aquatic center, high and dry. She wore her old, woven wool letterman's jacket over a new swimsuit. At her feet was her lettered team duffel bag with a towel and change of clothes.

The buzzer sounded, and Annie tensed briefly, conditioned by years of training right here at this pool. It was twenty-five meters long and L-shaped, with the diving area at the far end. The lanes were demarcated with floating ropes.

The young swimmers dove off the blocks, torpedoing through the water with all their strength. Coach Malco walked along the deck with her stopwatch and clipboard, exactly as she had done when she was Annie's coach. The race—a fifty free sprint—ended within about thirty seconds.

Annie turned to Pam and Olga, who had accompanied her to the pool. "I competed in a triathlon a couple of years ago. And I finished."

"No surprise there," Pam said, and told Olga, "She was always the best athlete on the team."

Annie sighed. "Now I'm challenged by walking from the locker room to the rec pool."

"You don't have to do this today," Pam said.

"Yes, she does." It was Coach Malco, seemingly unchanged from years past. Same iron-gray hair, marble-hard expression, steely glint in her eyes above the reading glasses. "Get over there in the rec pool and start your workout, Rush."

"You have no mercy." Annie levered herself up.

The coach grabbed her hand, helped her down the bleachers, and pointed her in the direction of the rec pool. "Welcome back, Rush," she said, and offered a quick smile.

"Thanks. I'm sick and tired of being sick and tired."

She managed one lap. It was a start. It felt good to be in the water, though she was ridiculously weak. Pam and Olga swam with her, urging her on. She dragged herself out, panting but triumphant. Then she spied Fletcher, Sanford, and Teddy coming toward her.

"That's three generations of handsome right there," Pam murmured.

"Olga, look!" Teddy ran up to her, brandishing a cloth badge. "I'm a flying fish." He turned to show Annie. "I made flying fish."

"Cool," Annie said. "Congratulations." She tried not to check out Fletcher in his swim trunks, but failed. It was impossible not to check out Fletcher in his swim trunks. She felt an intense burn of lust, and suddenly it hit her. She had gone more than a year without sex. Her cheeks flared with heat as she looked up at him. "Hey," she said.

"Hey, Annie. Back in training?"

She felt her cheeks turn redder. There was a time when she had shot effortlessly through the water. "Just getting started."

"Help me out with my leg, will you, buddy?" Sanford said to Teddy, heading over to a bench.

"You didn't call me back," Fletcher said.

He'd left her a voice mail and a text. "I didn't call you back," she said. "That was totally rude of me. I'm sorry."

"Don't be sorry. Just say yes. As in, yes, I'd love to go out to dinner with you."

"Fletcher—"

"Dad," called Teddy. "Dad, let's go!"

Fletcher stared at her intently. "Call me back," he said.

Annie caught up with Olga, who was walking toward the locker room. "You told them we'd be here?"

Olga offered an elaborate shrug. "Pam and I think you need a man."

"I need a life first," Annie said. In the locker room, she caught a glimpse of herself in the mirror. "Ick," she said. "I'm pasty. And hairy."

"Yes," Olga said bluntly. "You need a lot of help."

"Not the kind you got in rehab," Pam said.

And without further discussion, they took her to the Maple Grove Day Spa for a facial and waxing, manicure and pedicure, followed by a trip to the Peek-a-Boutique for a new outfit and makeup.

Annie studied her image in the shop mirror. The coral sheath dress fit perfectly. The strappy wedge sandals showed off the pedicure. She still wasn't used to having short hair. She tried to tell herself that it was a good thing, starting her life over with new hair. But lately, she wasn't so good at lying to herself. "These curls are awful," she said.

"Oh, come on," said Pam. "They're adorable."

"I look like Betty Boop."

"*She's* adorable."

"She's a cartoon."

Olga combed her fingers through Annie's hair, expertly styling it with a few pins. "Better," she said. "You need more lipstick and blush."

Annie knew it was useless to argue with Olga. She submitted to the finishing touches, then checked the mirror again.

"Look at that," she said, unable to keep from smiling. "I've rejoined the living."

"It's good news," said Lorna Lasher, the brand consultant Annie's father had hired. She had convened a meeting one Friday morning at her office in Burlington to go over the plan to launch the barrel-aged Sugar Rush. Everyone around the table—Annie, her brother, her parents—leaned forward, tensing.

"We like good news," said Annie. Since the pool workouts, she looked and felt strong.

"Don't we all? You're approved for distribution, which was a no-brainer, thanks to your track record. The labeling is finished, so you're good to go."

"Nice," said Kyle. "Everything's bottled and ready for shipping."

Annie's father kept watching Lorna. "That's not the good news," he said.

She grinned. "You're right. That's the *expected* news. The good news is, I got you placement in the media." She passed out a list of broadcasts, websites, and magazines that were going to feature the new product.

Mom gasped. "*Oprah Magazine.* The holy grail." Her mother looked especially pretty today, Annie observed. She'd had her hair done and wore a dress that showed off her figure. Annie wondered if it was for the meeting—or for Dad.

"The *Today* show," Annie said. "Even better."

They went over a plan for the product launch. Everything about the meeting felt familiar to Annie—the jargon, the rapid-fire discussion, the charts and spreadsheets. Everything—except her father. It was strange, seeing him in this context.

There were things she noticed now that she had not realized as a child. He was a good businessman. He kept control of the meeting and created a plan with Lorna that made perfect sense.

And he had some news of his own. He had finalized an order for a hundred cases of syrup from upscale gourmet shops all over New England and upper New York, with his family firm as the sole distributor.

Afterward, they went to lunch at an old restaurant on the shore of Lake Champlain. The building used to be an icehouse, but for as long as Annie could remember, it had housed a restaurant famous for family celebrations—graduations, bar mitzvahs, weddings, and anniversaries.

Walking through the door was like stepping back in time to the day of Kyle's high school graduation. She was ten years old, dressed in her favorite pin-tucked summer dress and sandals. Back then, they'd been a party of six, her grandfather seated at the head of the table, Gran at his side. Annie remembered standing at the deck railing to watch the Lake Champlain ferryboat. She'd ordered a Shirley Temple and lobster claws with pappardelle pasta, feeling entirely fancy when the dish arrived. In that moment she knew nothing but happiness and security, never imagining it would be the last time the family celebrated anything together.

A couple of days later, Dad had announced that he was leaving. And just like that, the sky fell down.

Now, twenty years after, Annie realized her father's leaving was key to the way she thought about men.

"Everything all right?" asked her dad, leaning across the table toward her.

"Oh, fine," she said, waving away his concern. "Just . . . thinking."

"About what?" He offered her the dad smile, the one that used to make her proud to have the handsomest father in all of Switchback. She had idolized him, put all her admiration and trust in him—and then he'd left.

"Thinking about the last time we were all together at this restaurant," she said, shrinking from telling him—or anyone—what was truly on her mind. "Gran and Gramps were with us."

"Kyle's graduation," her mother said, darting a glance at her father.

Annie studied her parents now, sensing . . . something. She caught Kyle's eye and tried to convey a what's-going-on question, but he was Kyle and he was a guy and he was clueless.

The sommelier came with a bottle of Billecart-Salmon, and she knew for sure something was happening. "Pink champagne," she murmured. "And so early in the day. What's the occasion?"

"Let's have a toast," her father said, once all their glasses were filled.

"To barrel-aged Sugar Rush," Kyle said. "And to our other new product, Head Rush."

"Wait," said Annie. "Head Rush?"

Her parents exchanged another look, both seeming as mystified as she was.

"I qualified for a growing permit to supply a licensed dispensary."

"Oh my God. You're going to grow pot," said Mom.

"Awesome," Dad said under his breath.

"For medical use only," Kyle told her, "until it's legalized, which is likely to happen in a year or two."

"And Beth's on board with this?"

"Mom. Quit worrying. Beth is fine with the plan."

Their father took a sip of champagne. "You'll figure it out on your own. The syrup, the farm, the weed—everything."

"That's been the idea all along, Dad," said Kyle. To Annie's knowledge, her brother had never directly confronted their father about leaving, but there was an edge to his comment.

"What your father is trying to say is that he—I—*we* won't be directly involved from here on out," said Mom. "We've got plans."

Annie's skin prickled. We? *Plans?*

"What kind of plans?" asked Kyle.

Their parents looked at one another again. They reminded her of nervous teenagers trying to figure out how to admit to a fender bender. There was something about them, something new and awkward, that made them *look* like teenagers.

"Your father and I . . . We're moving in together," Mom said in a rush.

"What?" Annie exploded.

"Jesus," Kyle said at the same time.

Dad took Mom's hand. "Since I've been back, we've been ... talking."

Annie had a sneaking suspicion that "talking" was code for ... She wouldn't let her mind go there.

"We're getting a place in New York," Dad said. "We found an apartment in Chelsea."

"What the heck are you going to do in the city?" asked Annie.

"I'm going to start continuing ed classes at Pratt, and your dad's expanding the fine-food division of his distributorship to Manhattan."

"You're serious," said Kyle.

"We are," said Mom. "It probably sounds rash or sudden, but we're serious. And happy. And we want you to be happy for us. Happy *with* us."

She was glowing. *Glowing.* Annie had not seen her mother glow since she was a young mom, being waltzed around the kitchen when Dad came in from work.

This was her shot, Annie realized. Her mother's shot at art school, the one she hadn't taken all those years ago. Annie felt nothing but pleased about that. But getting back together with Dad? With a guy who had walked away from her twenty years before?

"I do want you to be happy," Annie said.

"But," her mother prompted.

"I'm skeptical," Annie said. "How do I know this is going to work out better than it did the last time?"

"You don't know," Dad admitted. "You have to trust. I can promise you, we're in this to make it work. And we will."

"Do you hear that?" Annie asked her brother. "Does any of this make sense to you?"

He was in the middle of chewing on a dinner roll. "No," he said. "The one it has to make sense to is Mom."

"And it does," their mother assured them. "You'll see."

Annie took a gulp of her champagne. Dear Lord, it was delicious.

She took another sip and stared across the table at her parents. Her reaction was a jumble of feelings that were going to take a long time to sort through. She was completely taken in by the sweet fantasy of a mended family, by how young and fresh this renewal made them seem. At the same time, she felt a dark rumbling of resentment. Why couldn't they have figured themselves out years ago, back when she was a kid who needed both her parents?

Love comes in its own time, Gran used to say. You don't get to declare when or how.

It's never too late to have the life you want.

"When?" Annie asked.

"When you're better," Mom said.

"Oh, come on. Do you mean to say you're waiting for me to give you the green light? Don't you dare put that on me."

"Seems like we're all full of new plans," Dad said, wisely changing the subject. "What about you, Annie? What do you want your role in this to be? Besides goddess of barrel aging?"

"You have a clean slate," Mom added. "Life anew, like Dr. King said. You can go anywhere. Do anything."

Her brother polished off the last of the champagne. "If you could do anything you want right now, what would it be?"

She felt a wave of love as she looked at them—her family. They had pulled her out of the dark, rescuing her from a twilight existence. She owed them everything, yet all they seemed to expect from her was to begin again.

Fletcher was just stepping out of the shower when his mobile phone and the doorbell rang, almost at the same moment. Out on the back porch, Titus gave a woof of warning. Great timing. He slung a towel around his waist and went to find the phone, leaving a trail of wet behind him. He found the phone on his bedroom bureau—missed call from Annie Rush.

Annie was calling him. She'd finally decided to return his messages.

The doorbell rang again, so he tugged on a pair of jeans and hurried to the door.

Annie.

"Hey," he said, holding open the door. "Come on in."

She slipped inside and stood in the foyer, her hands gripping a recycled shopping bag with undue tension. Her gaze felt like a butterfly unsure of where to alight as it moved over his damp bare chest.

It didn't suck to have her checking him out. She looked beautiful tonight. Different…

"I was in the shower," he said, taking his time as he did up the top button of his jeans. "Just got in from mountain biking."

"I tried calling first, but you didn't answer." She offered a shy grin. "Okay, I called you from the driveway."

"Fair enough," he said. "I don't mind you dropping in. Not one bit."

"You're sure? I mean, Friday night—"

"You're not interrupting a hot date."

"Maybe I *am* the hot date," she said. His reaction must have been transparent, because she quickly added, "Don't panic. I'm kidding."

He wished she wasn't. "Come on in." He led the way to the big living room, which connected to the open kitchen.

"You bought the old Webster place," she said, looking around at the fireplace, the bookcases, the leaded-glass windows and skylight over the kitchen, the French doors leading to the back deck. "It's really beautiful, Fletcher."

"We picked it out together, remember?"

"Of course I remember, even though it was forever ago."

"Olga did the decorating." He ducked into the laundry room and found a T-shirt in the dryer. He didn't want her thinking he was some tool who walked around the house with no shirt on.

"Olga's great."

"She says the same about you. Ever since she heard you created her favorite show, the woman hasn't stopped talking about you. She's obsessed with *The Key Ingredient*."

"It's not my show anymore," she said.

"Olga says it's gone downhill lately."

Annie winced, and he was sorry he'd said anything. "It's Friday night," he said. "Let me get you something to drink."

"Thanks," she said. "I brought something."

"Yeah? Now, that's service."

"It is not," she said. "I just didn't want to drink alone. Is Teddy here?"

Fletcher shook his head. "With his mom."

"Okay." She paused, bit her lip in a way that made him want to grab her and kiss her. She set out a bottle of bitters and an orange. "I need ice and a shaker. And a muddler, if you have one."

"Pretty sure I don't have a muddler."

"A wooden spoon, then." She instantly made herself at home in the kitchen, reminding him of the Annie he used to know—smart and a little bit bossy, sure of herself. She found a cutting board and knife, and helped herself to a pair of glasses, the fancy lowball ones a client had given him back when he had the law office.

"We're having old-fashioneds," she said. "Pam and I came up with a special recipe to highlight our barrel-aged maple syrup." She took a bottle from the shopping bag. "Here, open this. And have a taste while you're at it. We just finalized a deal to distribute it."

On impulse, he touched the tip of her finger into the syrup and licked it off.

Annie gasped and snatched her finger away. "Hey."

"Wow," he said with an unapologetic grin. "I didn't think you could improve on maple syrup, but this is out of this world."

"Sugar Rush has gone gourmet," she said. "We already have standing orders for the new batch."

We. Did that mean she was back to the family business?

Working with complete focus, she mixed the drinks, finishing with a brandied cherry and a twist of orange peel. The drink was amazing. He was usually a beer-and-pool kind of guy, but this one seduced him totally—the bite of Pam's whiskey, the remnant of syrup coating the bottom of the glass, and most of all, the way his eyes met Annie's as she tapped the rim of her glass to his.

"To . . . new beginnings."

"Are you getting the help you need from Gordy?"

"I think so. It can't be fun for him, dealing with a piece of work like Martin Harlow," she said.

"I'm sorry you're going through this," he said. "I don't know what else to say."

"That's okay. It's been strangely easy to get over him."

"Because he cheated?" Fletcher would have cheerfully flattened her ex if the coward would show his face.

"Yes. Also because . . ." She set down her glass and folded her arms in front of her. "Because I didn't love him enough. And this is going to sound crazy, but I feel guilty about that. We were a good team, working together. The marriage part . . . it was a little stale. It happened gradually and I didn't realize there were problems, or maybe I was in denial."

Oh, man. Fletcher knew what that was like. He had been determined to make his marriage to Celia work. They both wanted the best for Teddy. He had cultivated their family like a master gardener, planting roots in this town, encouraging Celia to surround herself with the things that made her happy. In the end, he came to the same realization about the marriage as Annie had—there was love, but not enough.

"Don't beat yourself up over it."

She offered a fleeting smile. "Do I look like I'm beating myself up?"

"You look like you're enjoying a delicious cocktail." He took her hand. "Let's go out back, enjoy this weather. And there's someone out here you should meet. His name is Titus."

Titus, the Bernese mountain dog Fletcher had adopted soon after the divorce, greeted them with snuffles and sneezes of joy.

"He's beautiful." Annie handed Fletcher her drink, then sank down on one knee and cradled the dog's big head.

Celia had deemed dogs messy and smelly—which they were—and refused to have one. The moment Fletcher was on his own, he'd acquired the messiest, smelliest dog he could find. Titus had a broken tail and a crooked smile, and he'd been abandoned at the edge of town. Fletcher and Teddy loved him like crazy.

Annie stood and brushed the dog hair from her dress. She stopped abruptly as a soft gasp escaped her. "You have a swing."

"I have a swing."

"It looks exactly like . . ." Her voice trailed away. She slipped off her sandals and sat down on the swing, causing the chain to quietly click.

"It's no coincidence." He sat beside her, not close enough to touch.

She tucked one leg up under and dangled the other on the porch floor, turning to face him. "You remembered."

"I did."

"The other things, too," she said softly. "Bookcases in every room. Windows and skylights and a fireplace. A garden full of tomatoes and herbs. You remembered everything."

"I did."

She swirled her drink in the glass, then set it on a side table in a nervous gesture. "My brother's going to start growing pot on our property."

"That's awesome."

"How can you say that? You're a judge. You're supposed to frown on things like that."

"Not if he's operating lawfully. Kyle is doing it lawfully."

"And you know this . . . how?"

"Because I know Beth Rush and her crusade to transform the lives of every kid who comes through the doors of her school. No way she would jeopardize her mission."

"Good point." Annie surveyed the yard. It was surrounded by a tall fence and a taller hawthorn hedge to contain Teddy and Titus.

Annie settled deeper into the cushions of the swing. "My parents are getting back together."

"Hey, that's great," he said. "Isn't it?"

"I don't know. They're moving to New York City. They took the train down from Burlington after lunch today to check out warehouse space, or so they said. Something tells me they just wanted to get away together. So I'm . . . I guess I want to be happy for them. Still processing it."

He was full of questions. He wanted to know why she was here. He didn't ask, because he didn't want to scare her off. So he waited. Listened. It was something he'd learned on the judge's bench. Get quiet and listen, and the story would come out.

"They're going to do what they're going to do, and I'm okay with that. But then I asked them when this grand plan was going to unfold, and they said after I'm better. That's passive-aggressive, right? I'm already better. I can drive. And drink—not irresponsibly. I can think. What are they really waiting for?"

She set the swing in motion with a nudge of her foot. "My world has changed many times since the accident. I'm finally coming out of the fog, and I don't need anyone hovering around, worrying that my head is going to explode. My head is fine. *Fine.*"

"I'm glad to hear it," Fletcher said. "I'm glad you're better." He got up and lit a few citronella candles to stave off the bugs as the twilight deepened.

"I need to make a plan," she said. "That's the part that scares me. Every time I make a plan, something happens to screw it up."

"Come on," he said. "Look at everything you've accomplished. College, then your own show right out of school, now this new syrup—"

"That's one way of looking at it. But remember, I made a plan to be with you, the summer after high school, and it turned out your dad needed you more. And then we tried again, and it seemed like it was really going to work, and I went to California, and by the time I came to my senses, you were having a baby with Celia. So I don't see the point of planning anything."

"Then don't make a plan," he suggested.

"Thus proving you don't know me at all," she said.

"I know you too well," he pointed out.

"Oh, I'm sure."

He carefully set down his drink, turned to her, and took her face between his hands. "I know you," he said, looking into her eyes. "I know you like porch swings and bookcases and fireplaces. I know you can make sugar cookies without looking at a recipe. I know you had a secret hiding place in your bedroom where you stored your keepsakes, and some of those keepsakes have amazing stories. I know what you see when you point your camera at a subject. I know that when you smile, it makes your lips look even softer. And by the way, I know exactly what those lips feel like. And taste like, and how they feel when they kiss me anywhere on my body..."

"Fletcher. Are you coming on to me?"

"Absolutely. I thought about you when I hung this swing," he said.

"Thought of me. How?"

"Well," he explained in a low voice, "kind of like this."

"Fletcher!"

"Shh. I've got neighbors."

She laughed softly. "A reputation to uphold. Maybe we should go inside."

"Or not." He turned her just so, and the swing became a slow carnival ride, and she made a gasping sound that was probably audible next door, but he didn't care.

24

Spending the weekend with Fletcher had not been Annie's plan when she'd knocked on his door. But she was beginning to think the best things that happened weren't part of any plan. They just happened. She disappeared into the experience as though diving into a stream, following the current wherever it took her.

He was different, all these years later. She was different. But the deep, powerful connection that had always existed between them was still there.

Now that her marriage had ended, intimacy took on a special significance. After being with one partner all this time, she found herself wondering, Am I still good enough? Desirable enough? Can I still please someone new?

But Fletcher wasn't new, was he? There were things about him that she'd never forgotten. There were things he knew about her that no one else had ever known, from the smallest of secrets to the grandest of truths.

After the old-fashioneds and the porch swing, she'd raided the mostly unfortunate supplies in his kitchen—boxed mac and cheese, white wine, a handful of cherry tomatoes and basil from his garden—and put together a dinner from his humble ingredients. Afterward, they curled up in bed together with bowls of maple-walnut ice cream and listened to Serge Gainsbourg songs drifting from a hidden speaker. Then they made love again, and later they half woke in the night and went at it yet again, and in the morning, they greeted the dawn with fresh ardor. It was marathon sex, unflagging and voracious, as if they had been flung back to their teen years, just discovering each other.

On Saturday, they walked to the farmers' market, loaded up on fresh food, then brought it back to Fletcher's. Annie fixed fresh mint martinis, a tomato tart with Cabot cheese, buttery lady peas with charred onions, and for dessert, huckleberries drowning in crème fraîche flavored with nutty Frangelico liqueur.

"I'm never letting you leave here," Fletcher said, bringing a second helping of berries into the bedroom after dinner.

The berries and cream sweetened their lovemaking, and they lay together deep into the night, listening to the peepers singing in the garden. Miles from sleep, Annie got up and made a batch of salted maple popcorn, then climbed back in bed with him, bringing along her laptop.

"I want to show you something. These are the very earliest tapings I did with Martin, back when *The Key Ingredient* was in its formative phase. The segments never aired because they cast someone else."

She felt as though she was looking at a different person. Yet despite the rough quality of the reel, the Annie in those pieces was eager and bright, bursting with passion for the topic. It felt strange, seeing Martin by her side. She was able to regard him with dispassion. There was no ache of loss, just a sense that he was someone she used to know. She wondered why losing him didn't hurt more.

Because she'd never loved him the way she'd loved Fletcher.

"Is it just me, or are you stealing the show here?" Fletcher asked, touching the pause button.

"I'm stealing the show," she said in a quiet voice. "I didn't realize it at the time. That's why they didn't want me on camera with Martin. It might be why *Martin* didn't want me with him. I'm a scene stealer."

"That's you," he said with a chuckle. "The camera loves you, and you're a thief. You steal things. TV shows. Hearts..."

"Knock it off," she said, secretly delighted. "I showed you that for a reason. I want you to see what I was doing when I first got started."

"You miss doing that show in L.A."

"Yes." She could not lie to him. "I try not to look at the trades too much," she said, "but it's hard to resist. That was my life not so long ago."

They spent a lazy Sunday morning eating cereal from oversize bowls and browsing through the *New York Times.* She wanted to lie on his Chesterfield sofa and watch old movies and forget the whole world. Probably not the best idea. He had work in the morning, and she had . . . what?

"I know that face," Fletcher said, placing a soft kiss on her temple. "What are you worrying about?"

Annie bit her lip, trying to force herself to think things through. She wanted to explore what was restarting between them, but the stakes were high. She knew what would happen if she stepped through this door.

She wasn't sure she wanted to go there. She'd left Fletcher—not once, but twice. Why? Because her father had left? Because she never wanted to experience the devastation and loneliness she'd felt after her father took off?

"Come to dinner at the farm," she said, surrendering to impulse. "I'll make a fantastic Sunday supper."

"Say no more. I'm there. What can I bring?"

"Just your good self." She jumped up and began pulling on her clothes, and she laughed as his eyes devoured her. "Maybe a flak jacket. It's my family, after all."

Annie's parents had just returned from the city when she burst through the back door, toting bags from the market. "I'm making Sunday supper," she told them.

"Yay," said her mother. "How can I help?" Mom looked preternaturally young. She was wearing well-fitting dark wash jeans and a crisp white shirt, with cork-bottom sandals, a colorful scarf that resembled a Kandinsky watercolor, and dramatic hoop earrings. She also wore a dewy flush, and Annie tried not to let her mind go there, but she couldn't help observing that her mom had the look of a woman who had just gotten laid. Then she worried that she had that same look.

"You could set the table," Annie suggested. "I'll get the roast in and then I need to jump in the shower."

"I'm going to put the leaf in the table," Mom said. "Now that we're nine for dinner . . ."

"Make that ten," Annie said, hastily unloading the groceries.

"Who's the tenth?"

"I invited Fletcher."

Mom's head snapped around to face Annie. "You did?"

"Be nice, okay?"

"Of course I'll—" Her mother broke off. "You were wearing that on Friday."

Annie looked down at the coral-colored shift dress she'd worn to the meeting. It was slightly wrinkled from having been slung over a chair at Fletcher's house all weekend. "I'll change after my shower" was all she said.

As Annie fell into the as-yet-undefined affair with Fletcher, she remembered something she used to believe with all her heart—life had grace notes. These were moments so sweet that they could be tucked like the smallest of keepsakes, never to be forgotten. She discovered many such moments with Fletcher. She felt a glow of warmth just looking at him. She was so smitten. She almost didn't trust how happy she felt.

She grew stronger every day, and floated through fresh summer days that held sweet echoes of her own childhood, when her family was still whole and the world felt completely safe. They took Teddy on picnics and got drenched in peach juice running down their chins. They even got him to jump into Moonlight Quarry from a dizzying ten-foot-high granite outcropping.

They went creek hiking and lay in the grass, looking at clouds. They brought produce home from the farmers' market and had elaborate cookouts, listened for the tinkling bells of the ice cream truck trolling through the village. They stayed out late, running around after dark barefoot on the damp, dewy grass, catching fireflies.

She and Fletcher visited all their old favorite places, but this time they didn't worry about curfews or future plans or anything but being together. From time to time, Annie would catch a piercing sentiment when she saw Teddy's delight at finding a bird's nest, his pride at catching a trout, his gentle affection for the dogs when he came up to the farm, or his unadulterated glee with the water slides at the quarry. She couldn't help thinking about the baby she'd lost in the accident. She grieved for all that potential that would never be reached, the sweet little body she would never hug, the eyes that had never glimpsed the wonder of the world.

Then the wave would recede, and she would count herself lucky to be alive, to have this unexpected time with Fletcher, to have her family and the farm and everything exactly as it should be.

There were moments when she felt a happiness so complete it didn't even seem real to her.

At the same time, the idyllic summer joy felt fragile, as if the least little shift could cause it to disintegrate.

To guard herself against those worries, she nurtured a fantasy of staying holed up right here in Switchback, falling back in love with Fletcher, getting to know his boy, one day having a baby with him. Yes, she dared to think it. To imagine it. To *want* it.

Her parents made their move to the city. Kyle and Annie worked long hours, launching the barrel-aged syrup with more success than they'd ever imagined. "Consumers are a mystery to me," Kyle said, more than once. "They squawk at paying ten bucks a quart for regular syrup, but they're happy to throw down fifteen for a fancy pint bottle of barrel-aged." The rate at which they had to step up production gave new meaning to the name Sugar Rush.

"This is fantastic," said Beth, joining Annie and Fletcher in the newly installed teaching kitchen at the school. "The students are going to go crazy when they see this place."

"The good kind of crazy, I hope," Annie said. She felt a surge of accomplishment as she looked around the finished space. Funded by Sanford's foundation, the kitchen was designed to prepare students with both life and job skills. Annie had set it up so that lessons could easily be filmed, with a big console in the middle of the room and mirrors angled to show the action.

"Seriously," Beth said, "this is beautiful. Fletcher, let me know when you and your father can come for the dedication after school starts."

"Will do," he said. "Glad you like it. Who knew my dad—a high school dropout—would end up funding education?"

"I have a feeling he got a nudge from the judge," Beth said. That was how she referred to Fletcher's work in juvenile court. When dealing with at-risk kids, he tended to nudge them toward better alternatives instead of having them sent up to the juvenile facility at Woodside.

"Speaking of which—the judge has an early meeting tomorrow," he said. "I need to go prepare." He brushed a swift kiss on Annie's forehead. "See you tonight?"

She smiled and nodded, turning to watch him go.

Beth gave her shoulder a gentle shove. "So. You and Fletcher . . . ?"

Annie nodded. "Me and Fletcher."

"I'm glad, Annie. He's great, as I'm sure you know."

She did know. Fletcher was amazing. He could go anywhere, do anything, but he stayed here in this town, where he'd set down roots after a peripatetic childhood he rarely spoke of. He had come here with his father, and now he stayed for Teddy. And probably because he'd never had that in his life, a permanent home, a community. His son was happy here. He felt safe.

"The foundation has been so generous with the school," Beth added. "He is such a good guy."

"I hear that all the time, from everyone."

"The main point is, do *you* believe it?"

"With every cell in my body."

"But . . . ? I can hear the 'but' in your voice."

"You have sharp ears, then." Annie turned and looked at the setup they'd created for the school. She could so easily picture a video production here, and the thought of working again excited her. Yet another part of her wanted to devote all her energy to Fletcher. "I'm falling in love with him. Again. Hard."

"And this is a problem?"

"It's awesome. I can't even believe it's happening."

"Let it happen, Annie. Let yourself be happy."

"I want to. I do. But my life imploded, and I don't even know if I can trust my own judgment. The show . . . I had a whole life in California. It was taken from me."

"Do you want it back?"

"I don't know what I want."

"Are you trying to talk yourself out of it? Are you trying to get me to talk you out of it? Because if you are, you're barking up the wrong tree."

"It's not that. I want this to happen. But maybe . . . not so fast. I need to sort myself out before I get tangled up in a relationship. I want to be independent again. I have to start all over from scratch. Is it possible to do that while I'm in a free fall?"

Summer ended in Switchback the way it had for generations. The whole town gathered at the lake for a Labor Day picnic. It was the last chance for kids to swim in the cold clear water, the last chance to sit around drinking beer, relaxing and soaking up the sunshine before autumn descended, the last chance for watermelon and corn on the cob and thick slices of Brandywine tomatoes fresh from the garden.

"They say if the tomatoes don't ripen by Labor Day, you'd better get out the chutney recipe," Annie told her eldest niece, Dana, who was helping her make blackberry crisp for the picnic. More accurately, Dana was looking at Annie's laptop, which sat open on the counter, while Annie made the dish. At seventeen, Dana was awkward and adorable, far more interested in boys and makeup than in cooking. She was also a smart cookie, even more interested in traveling the world than in boys and makeup.

"What's chutney?" asked Dana.

"It's a kind of relish," Annie explained. "Originated in India and Nepal."

"Have you been to India and Nepal?"

"Both." Annie went back to chopping. "We filmed there for the show—India, Nepal, and Bhutan. If you click the tab for my remote server files, you can see pictures."

Beth always said Dana was her wanderlust child. "Where would you go if you could go anywhere in the world?" Annie asked.

"Everywhere," Dana said. She leaned into the computer screen. "Starting with Bhutan. It looks amazing."

"You sound like me at your age. I hope you do get to go everywhere.

We made Ema Datshi in Bhutan—hot peppers and yak's-milk cheese over red rice." The shoot had gone well, even though Melissa had complained nonstop about the muddy mountain roads, the lumbering bus rides, and the bathroom facilities. Annie remembered feeling nothing but enchantment, which emanated from the snowy peaks and shadowed gorges, the lush forests cloaked in every shade of green and flickering with the unreal colors of exotic birds. The air had a clarity she'd never before sensed, and the villages were redolent of woodsmoke and frying chilies.

"What's the best place you've ever been?" Dana asked.

"Right here." Annie laughed at the girl's expression. "I know it sounds lame to you now, but it's actually a good feeling, to realize your favorite place is the place where you are. Although in order to find that out, you have to go away to lots of other places."

"What's this folder, the one called 'Annie in the Kitchen'?" Dana asked, clicking on a file storage link.

"Wow, I haven't looked at those in years. They're digitized versions of some old VHS tapes I recorded when I was little. Do you know what VHS tapes are?"

"Yeah, old videotapes."

Annie nodded. "I used a video recorder to produce cooking shows of me and Gran in the kitchen."

"Cool. Can I watch one?"

"Sure. It should play if you click on it."

"Okay—here's one called 'The Secret to Perfect Pasta.'"

Annie grinned as she set the first batch of crisp on a cooling rack. "I don't even remember that, but judging by the title, I was very confident."

Knox, Lucas, and Hazel wandered in, probably lured by the scent of baking blackberry crisp. Annie's recipe featured ground almonds in a streusel topping, and a touch of almond extract and lemon with the berries, creating a perfect balance of flavors. Anticipating her hungry nieces and nephews, she'd made a small one for home, and a few larger ones for the picnic.

"You must be the taste-testing squad," she said. "Just in time." She fixed each of them a small serving with a sidecar of vanilla ice cream, and they looked at the treat as if they'd discovered El Dorado. Annie's special bond with her brother's family felt particularly strong in that moment. The kids reminded her of the richness of her own childhood.

"You're the best," said Knox.

"I don't know about that, but I bet my blackberry crisp is the best."

Hazel nodded. "No wonder Teddy Wyndham said his dad is gonna marry you."

Annie stared at her. "Teddy said what?"

"That his dad's gonna marry you." Hazel dug in. "And he should, if it means he gets to eat like this."

"When did Teddy say that?" Annie's stomach churned.

Hazel shrugged her shoulders. "Recess, I think."

"Okay, let's watch," Dana said, angling the laptop so everyone could see. "It's Aunt Annie doing a cooking show when she was little."

The first reel featured Gran. "Look at her," Annie said, her heart blooming with love for the woman on the screen. "That's Gran. My gran." She wanted to fall into the picture, wanted to feel her grandmother's hand and inhale the floury scent of her apron.

Gramps stepped into the picture and gave her a kiss, stole a cookie, and left with a grin on his face. "He likes my cookies," Gran said with a twinkle in her eye. "I've never seen a man who couldn't be made happier by eating an iced raisin bar."

Annie felt a phantom squeeze of warmth. They're not gone, she thought. They're still here. Still with me.

"I remember her," Dana murmured.

"Me, too," said Lucas.

"I wish the whole world had known her," Annie said.

"We do now," Dana pointed out. "Not the way you did, but she seems so alive here."

And that, Annie realized, was the value in what she did. Her art and craft kept things alive.

The next file featured Annie. She took a seat on a kitchen stool and hoisted Knox into her lap. He was utterly silent, his mouth full of warm blackberries and melting ice cream. The opening shot showed a little girl of about nine, with her hair in pigtails tied with polka-dotted bows, and a chef's apron her mother had made her, with her name embroidered in the middle.

"I'm Annie Rush," the girl said directly into the camera. "Welcome to my kitchen."

Annie was amazed. Her voice sounded like Minnie Mouse's. She didn't remember producing this specific episode, but she did recall wanting to achieve the same look as her favorite cooking shows. She had created carefully lettered cards with the opening credits: *Starring Annie Rush. Written by Annie Rush. Recorded by Annie Rush. Special Thanks to Anastasia Carnaby (aka Gran).* She had labored mightily over the lettering.

The nieces and nephews were mesmerized as Annie demonstrated the pasta lesson. "It's all about the dough," she said. "Starting from scratch is the only way to go. The best flour to use is called semolina." She paused and held up the bag. "After that, all you need is an egg, salt, and two tablespoons of water. The most important thing is, you have to knead the dough until it's smooth. Work in all the crumbly bits. And whatever you do, don't let the dough dry out. You'll know when it's ready . . ." Here she stumbled a bit, though she never stopped the kneading rhythm with the heel of her hand. "You just know. Your hands—they know."

Annie watched the girl on the screen. The joy on her face was infectious. As a child, she had always believed she could do anything if she loved it enough, and she loved cooking that much. Her childlike wonder and passion came through as confidence and knowledge.

And she had star power. By now, Annie had worked in the business long enough to recognize it. She had a way of engaging with the audience and with the subject matter that held people's attention. It was written all over the faces of her brother's kids. Yes, she had star power.

Now she went back into the skin of her nine-year-old self, and began to remember what it was *she* loved. There was a time when she had fervently believed she could do something simply because she loved it. This was it, she realized. This was how to begin anew. She had to start from scratch.

25

Annie finally found a way to reconnect with her past and her old dreams. The key, after all, was simple. Go back to the original dream.

Paging through her grandmother's cookbook, she felt Gran come alive again in the deepest corners of her heart, where the small blessings of life were only hiding.

Getting out the old camera gear and renting better equipment from a place in Burlington, she started filming again. She laughed and played in the kitchen, recording herself, her nieces and nephews, friends who came over to hang out, leaning against the counter, eager for samples and gossip.

She filmed herself making cookies with Knox, whose cuteness nearly broke the camera. She created a happy hour segment with Pam and Klaus, featuring the Sugar Rush old-fashioned and a clover club cocktail—"Shake that shaker like you're mad at it." She did a homemade ricotta demo for a local book club whose members were all divorced—"Squeeze that cheesecloth like it's your ex-husband's . . . wallet." For the staff of the local library, she created snacks and drinks inspired by literature—catcher in the rye bread, green eggs and ham, madeleines of maximum remembrance.

She dove into the work, capturing the laughter, the mistakes, the banging pans and spilled ingredients. She stayed up late to find the perfect sound tracks as she self-produced, filmed, and edited her own pieces. The old work flow that used to take her over kicked in again. She spent hours creating reel after reel, honing them sometimes one frame at a time.

This was what she loved—the preproduction, recipe testing, shooting, animating, and editing, darting back and forth in front of the camera and behind during filming. Like the nine-year-old Annie of long ago, she became her own writer, producer, and star, reveling in unfiltered creative freedom.

The new reels were a celebration of the deeper pleasures of home cooking for friends and family, though they were not entirely focused on cooking. She mused aloud about the nature of family, the bonds that held people together, the meaning of home. This was *her* key ingredient, and it had nothing to do with fatty duck livers, water-buffalo milk, or venomous fish. The key ingredient to life lay beyond the kitchen.

Regaining confidence along with her deepest, most authentic voice, Annie was ready to take the next step.

She went to see Fletcher, because on the nights he didn't have Teddy, she couldn't keep herself away. But more than that, he was becoming her best friend again. "I want you to see what I'm doing now."

She linked up her computer to the big screen and ran a short piece she'd labored over for hours. The simple opening credits lasted mere seconds, twelve beats of a great song and the title *Starting from Scratch*.

Fletcher didn't move a muscle as he watched. When it ended with the credit screen, he turned to her. "This is what you've been working on?"

"Yes. I love doing this. I miss it. And it bugs the hell out of me to see that I'm nothing but a footnote buried in old production details."

He indicated the screen. "This is not the work of a footnote."

Now she felt a flutter of nerves. "I have a dozen segments ready to go."

"To go where?"

She took a deep breath. "Live. On the Web."

"Another cooking show?"

'Yes. And no. I won't be doing anything like the material that's al-
ly out there. I'm far from the perfect host, but I know what I'm good
think people will connect to that, maybe even find inspiration. No
e stunt cooking. No more crazy episodes about catching frogs in a
mp or insects in Asia. I just want to share with people who love food
want to learn." She showed him a bit she'd done at the rehab center, making pizza with Pikey and a patient who had lost an arm, and another with the guys at the fire station.

She regarded the town of Switchback with a filmmaker's eye. The independent shops and restaurants, the painted church steeples, library, and courthouse, the brick-paved streets lined by clapboard houses and picket fences would be the backdrop for future productions. As her online channel expanded, day by day, she reveled in the feedback—even the criticism—from her viewers, feeling a sense of connection that had been missing from the network production. She could take her webcast out among the old barns and trout streams, the farms tucked in among the mountains. She wanted to highlight a genuine farm-to-table connection, sharing the things that had once inspired her, but had been slowly buried by her busy lifestyle.

"What do you think?" she asked him.

"I think you're magic," he said, turning off the screen and taking her in his arms. "I always have."

She woke up the next morning drowsy from lovemaking. Fletcher was already up and freshly showered, wearing a crisply pressed shirt, a blue necktie hanging unknotted around his neck. He brought coffee in a French press on a tray with two mugs. "Check your computer."

"Um, good morning?"

"Oh, yeah. Good morning. Check your computer."

She scrambled to sit up and grabbed for the coffee. Her channel had gone live for the first time last night. She opened the page and studied the analytics. "I have views," she said. "I have followers."

"I wanted to be first," he told her, "but there were already four thousand subscribers when I woke up."

She set aside her coffee and scooted up on her knees to help with his tie, looping the ends in a loose knot. "Ten years ago, I got my start with an online video. Is it pathetic that I'm back here again?"

"It's cool. The world is different. You're different. More talented, more sure of yourself. Your channel is going to be huge."

"From your lips," she said, kissing his coffee-warm lips, "to God's ear." She kissed his ear.

He slid his hands down her torso. "Do you know how easy it would be to blow off the world and stay right here with you all day?"

"Maybe we should do that."

"I have to go perform civic duties."

"Fine." She neatened the knot of his tie, then let him go. "I've been dreaming up an episode on pumpkin soup with fried sage-butter croutons." She reached for her laptop just as an e-mail popped up. She must have made some audible sound, because Fletcher leaned over and brushed his lips against her shoulder.

"Everything okay?" he asked.

She nodded, although every cell in her body turned to ice. "It's a note from my ex."

She deleted the note without reading it, and tried to shake off the feeling of violation. It wasn't terribly hard, because she suddenly had a lot of work to do. In order to keep the momentum going online, she had to produce material regularly, and the quality had to be impeccable.

In the next few weeks, subscribers signed on in droves. Major publications wrote about her and sent referral links. With the sort of hyperbole found only on the Web, she was dubbed tomorrow's brightest food star. Her well-crafted reels appealed to everyone, the articles touted, not just foodies and professionals. Her authentic, smart segments resonated with anyone needing a fresh approach to life.

She should not have been surprised when Alvin Danziger called, but she was. Her agent was part of a past she hadn't dealt with yet, and the phone felt cold in her hand as she listened.

Alvin said, "Empire wants a meeting."

She didn't move, except to tighten her grip on the phone. The production company was one of the biggest in the business, working with major networks, not just in the niche markets. By comparison, Atlantis was a small player. Finally, she found her voice. "I'm listening."

The first person she wanted to share the news with was the last person who wanted to hear it—Fletcher. Because once again, Annie was being pulled in a different direction.

They met at one of their favorite places on a Sunday afternoon—Moonlight Quarry—to hike with Titus.

The season hovered on the edge of fall and winter. The last of the confetti-colored leaves clung to the tree branches, the sky was a clear sharp blue, and the air held a bite of cold. Annie had always liked this time of year. To her, it meant getting out her favorite sweaters, jeans and boots, the crackle of leaves underfoot, football games, cinnamon donuts, and apple cider.

When Fletcher saw her, he swept her up into his arms and swung her around, looking so happy it nearly broke her heart. Not so long ago, she just wanted to hole up and be with him and forget the rest of the world.

But no. She couldn't belong to him. How could she belong to anyone until she belonged to herself?

They hiked around the periphery of the quarry. Titus went crazy, bounding around and sniffing out the wildlife. He flushed a quail, and the bird made a rattling noise as it sped skyward.

Annie tucked her hand around his arm. "Something came up."

"I'm not going to like it," Fletcher said, correctly reading her tone.

They sat on a rock ledge overlooking the pool. Annie looped her arms around her drawn-up knees and stared at the still blue water. "I'm going to L.A."

Nothing. No movement. Not a sound.

She didn't want to insult him by making excuses or rationalizing her decision. "I'll be getting an offer to take *Starting from Scratch* to a major network. I'm not saying I'll agree to it, but I want to hear what they have to say. If I don't, I'll always wonder."

They sat quietly for a while. "You'll always wonder about us," he said.

She braced one hand behind her and turned to face him. "I won't wonder," she said. "I already know."

"You're leaving."

"I need to face up to what happened to me. Reclaim what's mine."

He touched her cheek, then leaned forward and softly kissed her lips. "This is the third time we've said good-bye," he told her. "I'm not doing it anymore, Annie. I'm not."

"Neither am I. Fletcher—"

"So we both agree. Because last time, you changed your mind and came running back—"

"You knocked up Celia before my landing gear was down in L.A. That didn't work out so well for us, did it?"

"Okay, I deserved that, but we're different people now. And there's Teddy. I'm not going to budge an inch because of him."

"I wouldn't ask you to."

"Then . . ."

"Then you'll just have to trust me."

"Trust you. To do what?"

"To make this work. Place has nothing to do with it. What matters most is what two people want together."

"I know. Annie—"

"I have ambitions. You have your judgeship and your unswerving sense of obligation to Teddy. That doesn't make us bad people."

"It makes us people who can't seem to coexist in the same space for more than a few months."

26

It was remarkable how quickly Alvin Danziger, the talent agent, flipped his loyalty from Martin to Annie. Equally remarkable was how seamlessly she rejoined that world. The culture was familiar—endless traffic and small talk, catered events and schmoozing, New Age cafés full of whispering vegans and sitar music, the brash nightlife of trolling paparazzi and loud, close-talking hopefuls. At the end of the whirlwind of meetings, the offer appeared before her in a hand-delivered parcel, like an invitation to a formal ball.

Annie found herself at a crossroads. Finally, her own show, reflecting her own vision. Everything would be exactly as she wanted it, right down to the last detail.

She promised an answer and then went to find the hired driver furnished by Empire. Before she could consider the next step, she had to take care of something on her own. There was no way to move on until she revisited the past.

She found Martin and Melissa doing a gig in Pasadena, one of those episodes so larded with sponsors and product placements that the whole thing seemed like an infomercial. Annie had never liked those episodes, although they were necessary to stay on budget.

The shoot was taking place at a rather lovely old-California mansion, probably to garner publicity for the place as a wedding venue.

Melissa was by herself, fishing a mike wire out of her blouse. She was pregnant and glowing. Annie nearly threw up when she saw the graceful, distinctive belly.

Setting her jaw, she walked over to Melissa. "I'm looking for Martin."

Melissa looked from side to side as if seeking an escape route. Then she set down the mike wire and battery pack. "Annie, I'm so glad you're better."

"Thanks. Where's Martin?"

"I think he went to the terraced garden in back for a photo shoot."

Fighting a wave of nausea, Annie went toward a wide outdoor staircase.

"Hey, wait. Please." Melissa came after her, slightly breathless from exertion. "There's something I want to talk about."

Annie eyed her belly. "It's pretty self-explanatory."

"I feel so bad about everything that happened." Melissa spoke in a desperate rush. "I know there's no excuse and I don't expect forgiveness. But I have to tell you, I made a terrible mistake—not just sleeping with Martin, but *choosing* Martin. He's not in love with me. He's in love with himself. I'm afraid . . . oh God. We're not going to make it. I just know I'll end up going it alone."

"Your point?"

"When I got the note that you wanted to meet with us today, I couldn't help wondering about things. I woke up this morning thinking, What if neither of us teamed up with Martin? What if the team was you and I?"

"Me," Annie said automatically.

"What?"

"You and *me,* not you and *I.* It's an indirect object." She realized Melissa was not getting it.

"I'm trying to say I'd like to partner with you on something entirely new. Just the two of us. Just us girls."

Oh. Goody. "Sure, Melissa. Have your people call my people."

"I'm serious. We could come up with something fantastic, I know we could. We don't need Martin. You and I have a history. A bond of trust."

Annie felt no anger. She simply felt . . . depleted. "Melissa, see if you can understand this. The person I mistrust the most is the one who tries to steal from me behind everyone's back."

"That's not what I'm suggesting."

"Have you run your idea by Leon? By Martin? By anyone?"

Melissa's silence was the answer. Annie wasn't the least bit surprised. "And speaking of Martin . . ." She turned her back and hurried away.

Annie walked down to the garden of California autumn splendor—asters and mums, Chinese lanterns and colorful grasses whispering against a terra-cotta wall. Her ex-husband was yukking it up with a couple of ridiculously attractive girls in neoprene sheath dresses and expensive shoes. He was the picture of studied elegance in skinny jeans and a navy jacket over a black T-shirt. He'd been freshly made up for the shoot, and his skin looked strangely smooth.

When he saw Annie, he didn't miss a beat. "You'll have to excuse us," he said to the two beauties, and they drifted away.

"Let's get one thing straight," Annie said to Martin. "I'm not here because you summoned me."

"I take it Alvin already called you."

Annie wasn't about to say anything to Martin about that.

"I had to see you. Annie, I need to level with you."

"How exciting."

"I don't blame you for anything you're thinking right now," he said. "Nothing's been the same since the accident. I lost something so special that day."

It was all about him, she observed. Always.

"I'd do anything to turn back the clock and start again," he continued.

"Anything?"

"I want us to be *us* again. The team we've always been." He offered his sweetest, blue-eyed sincerity.

The old Annie might have been tempted. That Annie had honed self-deception to a fine art. She could encounter any problem and convince herself that it didn't matter. The new Annie had lost that technique. She simply couldn't lie to herself anymore. She couldn't lie and pretend she could be happy with her life in L.A., with Martin and the show.

"And what part of 'team' was it that had you making a grab for my share in the production and my accident settlement on the grounds of common property?" The look on his face told her Gordy had been on the right track. "Oh," she said, "you weren't expecting that, were you? I was so much easier to deal with when I was on life support, wasn't I?"

"That's not fair. I was destroyed, Annie. Every expert I consulted told me you'd never recover."

"And how inconvenient for you that I did."

"Please. Can we start again? I know you don't want me to be your husband anymore, but let's partner again on the show. Together, we won't just turn it around. We'll reinvent it and make it bigger and better than ever."

"Are you serious?"

"Completely. I need you again, Annie. Without you, the show veered off track. The production budget is bleeding us dry, sponsors are pulling out. Somebody said the C-word."

"Cancellation."

"Don't let them take you down, Annie. You built this show. Together, we can keep it from failing. I need you. I made a stupid mistake, and I'll do whatever you want me to do in order to make it right."

Martin. Begging. It was a wonderful thing. Annie recognized the opportunity for gloating or even retribution. Then she surprised him—and herself—by simply saying, "Good luck with that." She turned away.

He hurried after her, planting himself in her path. "I didn't want to have to bring this up, but we signed a multiyear contract for the show. You're in breach of that." He handed her a copy. "But let's not get into a legal battle."

"Good idea. Let's not."

"Work with me, Annie. We're the dynamic duo, remember? We can make it." He offered a smile she knew all too well—the persuasive, charm-your-socks-off Martin smile.

It was amazing to Annie that he still thought it would work on her. "Martin," she said. "On the very first day I met you that day in Washington Square Park, you showed me exactly who you are. A user, an opportunist, a narcissist. I just didn't see it. You stole from me, not only in the material sense, but you appropriated ideas, anything that would advance your career."

"Whoa. That knock on the head rattled your brains. I have no idea what you're talking about."

"You wouldn't. You don't even recognize what you're doing, what you've always done."

He clenched his hands into fists. "After the accident, I was a wreck. I felt sorry for you. I grieved so hard. Now you've woken up and you're bitchier than ever."

"Bitchier than ever. Was I ever bitchy? I don't remember that."

"Why do you think we grew apart?"

"Oh, good. You're blaming me."

"Come on, Annie. Work with me here."

"I'm done with this conversation."

"So that's a no."

"That's a hell no. I won't make a deal with you."

"I wanted to do this cooperatively," he said. "I don't have to. When was the last time you went over your contract? There's a noncompete clause—remember that? The only way around it is if I release you from it. You can't do your show without me."

Ah. So he knew about the Empire offer. There were no secrets in this business.

"I can, and I will." She tried not to show fear. He was up to something. She just knew it.

"Then you'll regret it."

"Ah, regrets. I think I get it. Is that Martin-speak for 'See you in court'?"

The confrontation left Annie shaken. Why did she let him have power over her, even now?

Because he did. All the things he'd taken from her had left her empty. Creating a new production was not going to fill her up.

She asked the driver to pull off the highway at the Colorado Boulevard Bridge viewpoint in Pasadena. Still agitated from the meeting, she got out of the car and looked up the contract on her phone. What Martin had said appeared to be true. How ironic that after all that had happened, he still wielded his power over her.

And how ironic to find herself standing here at this bridge. The hundred-year-old structure had a grim nickname—Suicide Bridge. Generations of troubled people had flung themselves to their deaths from the graceful steel-and-concrete arches, making one final plunge into the arroyo below.

Why here? Annie wondered. There were plenty of high places in the area—skyscrapers, scaffolds. But jumpers were drawn to the bridge. There was something mesmerizing about it, she realized, wandering along the figured stone railing. Barriers had been put in place, but if you jumped wide enough, you could clear them.

Swimmers, take your marks.

It would be so easy.

But that was for cowards. Annie knew what she had to do. She resolved to find a way to make this work.

27

The fly rod made its familiar whip-snap in the clear evening air. Then the blue-winged olive fly popped onto the surface of the water in the ring of the rise, precisely where the wily trout had surfaced to feed.

"Nothing," Fletcher muttered. "That was a perfect cast, and I got nothing."

"Try being imperfect for once in your life," Gordy said, casting a few feet downstream from him. His fly tangled briefly in some weeds, then popped free. There was a flash of movement as a big trout latched on. Gordy tried to reel it in, but the line went taut and then slack as the fish got away.

"What's that supposed to mean?" Fletcher knew he could have hooked that fish, no problem.

"Just psychoanalyzing you," Gordy said cheerfully. "And reminding you that there's much more to life than being Teddy's dad and being good at your job."

"Thanks, Gord. I had no idea."

"Why'd you let her go?"

"Because she doesn't need my permission." He sent out another cast, aiming for a calm meander in the stream. For the third time, Annie had left, heading off to L.A. in search of a dream. He finally got it. He just needed to make his peace with it.

"That's not what I mean, and you know it," said Gordy.

"What I know is that she's left me three times."

"There's where you're wrong. See, she left. That doesn't mean she left *you.*"

"What difference does it make?"

"Damn, if you don't know that, I can't help you."

"Who says I need your help?"

"Maybe it's Annie who needs your help. And since I'm speaking as her lawyer, that's all I can say at this point, although—holy shit!" Gordy's line went taut. The trout leaped, its underbelly flashing in the twilight. It was a big one, a fighter, but Gordy was determined. He struggled and slipped on a rock, letting out a yelp as the frigid water filled his waders. He kept fighting, refusing to let go of the rod.

Fletcher set down his gear and hurried over. "Hey, don't float away on me," he said.

"I got this... Jesus, it's cold."

Fletcher tossed him the net. Gordy flailed, then managed to net the fish and slog ashore. His lips were blue, though he was grinning from ear to ear as he inspected his fat, shiny catch. "Now, that's a fish," he declared, shivering as Fletcher took a picture with his phone.

Fletcher noticed an incoming message—from Annie's brother. "Good timing on the fish," he said. "We have to go—now."

Annie landed with both feet on the ground. She had left L.A. with her dignity intact and a sense of what lay ahead. She wanted to get back to a place where food was real. And love was real. Yet when Fletcher showed up in the chill of early evening, her stomach pounded with apprehension.

"My brother shouldn't have called you," she said, meeting him on the porch. She resisted the urge to throw her arms around him.

"You should have called me."

"I was going to. You're freezing," she added.

"Gordy and I were fishing." He hung his coat and left his boots by the door.

"Come on in. I made coffee." She went into the kitchen and filled two mugs.

"So, your meeting in L.A. . . ." he prompted. His expression hardened as though he was bracing himself.

She had asked him to trust her to make this work out, and he hadn't done that. "I'd have carte blanche to write, produce, and host my own show."

"Wow." His smile was forced. "Congratulations, Annie. I'm happy for you."

"You are not. You want me barefoot and pregnant in Switchback."

"I'd be lying if I said I didn't fantasize about that." He wrapped his hands around the coffee mug. She loved his hands—the shape and strength of them, the way they touched her.

Focus, she told herself. "I'm staying here."

His eyes lit up. "That's great."

"I don't have a choice. There's a legal entanglement with my ex that would force me to share the production with him. It's complicated."

"I'm a lawyer. I can do complicated."

"I'd have to take him to court. I'm not up for that. Just the thought of having to deal with him on any level makes me ill."

"Hand everything over to lawyers. A good one will protect you."

"I wish. If it was anyone other than my ex, I'd be up for a fight. But Martin . . . I just can't. He's toxic to me. He helped himself to my life's work, and then he cheated on me. Oh, and did I mention he and Melissa are having a baby together? God, Fletcher. I hope you never have to deal with a betrayal like that."

"I'm sorry, Annie." He studied her for a long moment. "Suppose he wasn't standing in your way. Would that mean you could go ahead with your show?"

"I imagine it would, yes."

"And what would that look like? Doing your own show?"

"I could finally create the program I always wanted."

"In L.A."

"Well, yes."

"You miss it, then. You miss L.A."

"I miss the energy. The creativity. The excitement of making a show. But—"

"You should have what you want, Annie. You should have everything you want."

After only a few days amid the congested freeways of L.A., Annie felt soothed by the slow pace of Switchback as she went to pick up the champagne for tonight's celebration. They had probably ordered too much, but champagne would keep. It was always better to have too much than to run out.

Even though it was good to be back, Annie worried about the question Fletcher had planted in her mind. What would her life here look like? Would she languish, unfulfilled, as her mother had for so long? Or would she flourish like the maples in the sugarbush, coming into her own the way Gran had as a young bride? If she was honest with herself, if she went back to her reasons for leaving Vermont in the first place, were they about fulfilling someone else's dreams, or her own?

"Annie! Hey, Annie!" Teddy Wyndham waved and ran over to her as she wheeled the flatbed cart of champagne from the liquor store out to the truck.

"Hey yourself." The sight of Teddy always made her smile. He was as bright and cheerful as a song. Over the summer, she'd fallen in love with him, too, coming to care about him in ways she hadn't expected.

"Let us help you with that." Fletcher lifted a case and Teddy quickly grabbed the other side. Annie knew Fletcher could have hoisted the box by himself, but he was the kind of dad who gave his kid every chance, big and small, to succeed.

"Do me a favor and take the cart back."

"You got it," Teddy said.

"He's so great," Annie told him. "He seems completely happy and secure."

"Thanks."

"I understand why you want his life to be here, Fletcher."

"Sometimes I wonder how much this place has to do with it."

"It's a factor. But there are other things. I mean, Degan Kerry grew up here..."

"Then again, so did the inventor of roll-on butter and bacon spray."

He shut the tailgate of her truck. "I like running into you on a Saturday morning. I'm glad you're back."

Flustered, she dug for her keys.

"All set, Dad." Teddy joined them again. He looked at Annie. "We're going skating at the ice rink, and then there's a game after. Wanna come?"

The feeling of almost-tears persisted, but Annie forced a smile. "Thanks, but I need to get going. I have a wedding to attend."

"Yeah?" Fletcher eyed the cases of champagne in the truck. "Who's getting married?"

"My parents."

Snow flurries danced through the sky as Annie loaded up the empty bottles, along with flattened boxes and packing material to take to the transfer station. The sun was just coming up, so Fletcher's arrival startled her.

"I'm busy," she said without pausing in her work.

"I can see that." He lifted the second blue bin into the truck, then climbed into the cab next to her and buckled up. "That was a lot of champagne for a small wedding."

"It was. We had quite a celebration." Clearly he had something on his mind, so she put the truck in gear and drove down the mountain.

"That's good. Your folks deserve to be happy." He flopped a thick envelope onto the console between them.

She glanced at it. "What's that?"

"A draft of the new settlement with your ex. All you need to do is sign, and you can go ahead with your new production. He won't stand in your way."

Annie nearly choked with surprise. She had just made her peace with the missed opportunity. "Are you serious?"

"I'm a judge. I'm always serious. Haven't you heard the expression 'sober as a judge'?"

She turned on the wipers to bat away the flurries. "What made him change his mind?"

"He didn't. He would have kept his hooks in you any way he could, if that was possible. But it wasn't, because he made a stupid move after the accident."

"I don't get it. I mean, Martin made a lot of stupid moves. Which one are you referring to?"

"He divorced you in the state of Vermont."

Annie didn't think that was so stupid. "He won a more favorable settlement than he would have in California," she said. It was old news.

"Yes, but it also means Vermont statute applies to the settlement, and he'd never win in Vermont. You'll want to go over it with Gordy, of course. You have to authorize everything, but that's just a formality. Once you sign off on this, Martin Harlow will be out of your life, and you can do whatever you want with your show."

The bottles in the back clinked together as she drove over the gravel road to the transfer station. She didn't say anything for a long time. She was trying to figure this out. After conceding that the new deal wasn't an option, she had been prepared to stay in Switchback. Now that it was back on the table, the decision was in front of her once more.

They were the first ones at the dump. The attendant was Degan Kerry, sitting in the gate kiosk with his morning coffee and cigarette. Since high school, he had grown soft and surly. He scrutinized her load, raised his eyebrows when he saw her passenger, then waved them through.

She backed up to the deep steel-walled container, and they both got out. Grabbing a big green glass bottle, she hurled it into the container. It bounced, but didn't break.

"I don't get it," she said to Fletcher. "You wanted me to stay here, but now you're fixing it so I can go to L.A. after all."

"I want you to have a choice. You shouldn't be here by default, but because you choose to be here." He helped himself to a bottle and shot it into the container, where it shattered.

Annie threw her next one harder, and was rewarded by a satisfying shower of splintering glass.

"Good shot," he said. "You smashed it to smithereens."

"Smithereens. Where does that word come from, anyway?" She hurled three more bottles in quick succession. "I told you to trust me and you didn't."

"I told you I loved you and you didn't listen."

"When?" What a stupid question. In one way or another, Fletcher Wyndham had been telling her he loved her since they were in high school. Yes, things had happened.

"I'm telling you now. And what you need to know is that I never really stopped. I know what I want from life and from you. From us. And you should have what *you* want. But I understand your caution."

"You think I'm being cautious?"

"It's a lot, I know. Teddy and I . . . we're a lot." He broke another bottle. Snow flurries swirled around him.

"Yes. You are."

They hurled the last of the bottles, one by one, until the truck bed was empty. The flurries thickened into flakes. Annie grabbed his cold hands in hers. "Listen. Everything that's happened to me has led me back home. Back to you. Back to the big dream I had a long time ago, the one that got lost along the way."

"*The Key Ingredient,*" he said.

"The key ingredient before it was a TV show. The key ingredient when I knew exactly what it was." She pressed herself against him, and his warm lips touched her forehead, the sweetest of benedictions. "I'm starting from scratch, Fletcher. I want to start from scratch with you. With *us.* And Teddy. Forget what we did in the past. Forget that I ran and that I didn't listen to myself and I was afraid. Start from scratch with me."

EPILOGUE

After

"I can't believe we're arguing about this," Annie said, tying on her apron. The teaching kitchen at Beth's school now doubled as her studio for *Starting from Scratch.* The webcast had become so popular that broadcasting from home was no longer feasible.

"Because it matters," Fletcher said simply. Her camera-shy husband made only rare appearances on her show. When there was a Fletcher sighting, her fans went nuts on social media. Today, he'd agreed to a small role, but she was starting to regret inviting him. Camera 1 was already rolling, because she never knew when a moment would emerge from the chatter.

"Gran used to say all arguments are about power," she said.

"Gran was probably right." Fletcher snatched a bite-size homemade cream puff from a tray.

She smacked his hand with the back of a wooden spoon.

"Hey!"

"Gran also used to say that the spoon speaks when words alone are not enough."

"I don't think that's what she meant," Fletcher said, savoring the purloined bite.

Annie moved the tray of cream-filled *pâte à choux* away from him.

Since I'm the one who's the size of a water buffalo, I have final say on the name."

"Come on," Fletcher said. "Panisse? What kind of a name is that for a poor, innocent baby?"

"It's a lovely name, that's what kind it is. Lovely and unique, just like our little girl will be." She smoothed a gentle hand over the mound of her thirty-six-weeks-and-counting belly.

"I looked it up. *Panisse* means chickpea fritters."

"Nobody knows that."

"I know it. Anybody with a search engine knows it. Let's move on, Annie. What about Julia, like the late, great—"

"I'm bored already," Annie declared with an elaborate yawn. Her viewers had been cheering her on through her pregnancy, sending name suggestions from around the world. "Taste," she said, dipping a spoon into the caramel sauce that was warming on the stove.

The slowly melded blend of cream, sugar, butter—and a touch of maple—brought a smile to his face. "Makes me want to marry you all over again." He slipped an arm around her waist and bent down to whisper, "Bring some of that home tonight, and I'll—"

Teddy came in from school, dropping his backpack on a chair with a thud. "Hey," he said. "Something smells amazing." At thirteen, he was tall and gangly and hungry all the time.

"Ted, buddy, help me out here," Fletcher said. "She's trying to call my daughter Panisse."

"That's awesome."

"See?" Annie gave him a cream puff dipped in caramel sauce, and Teddy's face lit up. "Your son has excellent taste in names."

"Come on," Fletcher said. "Give me something I can work with."

"I like creative names," she said, arranging the puffs on Gran's favorite Salem china platter. "Aquaria—that's the name of this china pattern. And since she'll be born in late January..."

"No," Fletcher said. "Just no."

"Keegan's mom called her new baby Maple," Teddy said.

"Not helping," Fletcher said.

"Tree names. That could work," Annie said. "How about Liquidambar?"

"Also awesome," Teddy said, earning another sample.

Fletcher cuffed him on the head. "You're just saying that so you can keep eating."

"Both of you, wash your hands and you can help me put together the croquembouche," Annie suggested.

"Croak and what?" Teddy and Fletcher went to the sink.

"It's a French pastry," Annie said. "It means something that crunches in the mouth. You make a tower of all these little filled cream puffs and drizzle it with caramel."

"And then die of happiness," Fletcher said.

"It's a lot fancier than our usual demo, but since it's my last before little Ganache makes her appearance, I wanted to go all out." She was stockpiling episodes in order to savor a long, sweet welcome for the baby.

"Ganache." Fletcher looked directly at the camera. "You see what I'm up against?"

It was such a singular feeling, knowing her broadcast reached every corner of the earth. And as it turned out, people the world over had the same joys and struggles, the same devotion to life and love, food and family. And second chances. And starting from scratch. There was value in beginning anew, putting something together from carefully chosen ingredients and making it wholly your own.

She never once regretted turning down the network offer. All the creative control in the world, the most artfully lit sound stage, could never replicate what she was able to do right here in this close-knit community, surrounded by family and friends.

In the past two years, she'd completed the journey that brought her ome. She'd revised and republished her grandmother's cookbook, and was working on one of her own. She'd launched the barrel-aged Sugar Rush.

And in a flurry of autumn leaves in the maple grove on Rush Mountain, she'd married the love of her life. Now she was expecting a baby. Fletcher was her heart's home. Sometimes when she thought about how much she loved him, she forgot to breathe. And then she would remember again, the way she'd had to relearn after the accident—smell the roses, blow out the candle.

ACKNOWLEDGMENTS

This book started with a storm—and a celebration. I wrote the first words of the novel during a snowstorm that brought all of New York City to a standstill one January week. Being snowed in at a midtown hotel turns out to be a fine way to launch a work of fiction, particularly this one.

A celebration occurred that week, too. I was welcomed by William Morrow/HarperCollins with a feast of home-baked treats inspired by my previous novels and prepared by Jennifer Hart, Jennifer Brehl, Helen Moore, and Tavia Kowalchuk, whose lavender scones, morning glory muffins, apple strudel, and pignoli cookies made for a delightful meeting.

All novels should have such an auspicious beginning. I must thank my literary agents, Meg Ruley and Annelise Robey of the Jane Rotrosen Agency, and my publishing team: Dan Mallory, Liate Stehlik, Lynn Grady, Brian Murray, Tavia Kowalchuk, Pamela Jaffee, Carrie Bloxson, and their associates at HarperCollins. Then there's the home team—Willa Cline and Cindy Peters, keeping me alive online. And as ever, the brain trust—my fellow writers Elsa Watson, Sheila Roberts, Lois Faye Dyer, Kate Breslin, and Anjali Banerjee—whose generosity knows no bounds. Special thanks to Marilyn Rowe and her eagle-eyed proofreading skill.

And finally, I end where I began—with a sweet, cherished memory of my father, me tucked in his lap, surrounded by his comfortable smell of old wool and pipe smoke, reading *Go, Dog. Go!*

